Praise for the novel

Men in Kilts

"With its wickedly witty writing, wonderfully snappy dialogue, and uniquely amusing characters, MacAlister's latest is perfect for any reader seeking a deliciously sexy yet also subtly sweet contemporary romance."
—*Booklist*

"A fun, fast-paced, and witty adventure. . . . *Men in Kilts* is so utterly delightful, I read this book nearly all in one sitting." —Roundtable Reviews

"Katie MacAlister sparkles, intrigues, and is one of the freshest voices to hit romance. . . . So buckle up, for Katie gives you romance, love, and the whole damn thing—sheep included." —The Best Reviews

"*Men in Kilts* is filled with warm, intriguing characters and situations, and the atmosphere is fiery as Katie and her silent Ian irresistibly draw you into their story." —*Rendezvous*

"Wonderfully witty, funny and romantic, *Men in Kilts* had me laughing out loud from the first page. . . . A definite winner."
—Romance Reviews Today

"This book hooked me from the first paragraph and kept me smiling—and sometimes laughing out loud—to the last page. . . . I thoroughly enjoyed *Men in Kilts* and recommend it highly."
—*Affair de Coeur*

continued . . .

Noble Intentions

"Sexy, sassy fun!"   —Karen Hawkins

"If there is such a thing as a Screwball Regency, Katie MacAlister has penned it in this tale of Noble, Gillian, and their oh-so-bumpy path to love. Readers are in for a wonderful ride!"
—The Romance Reader

"This is without a doubt one of the funniest historicals I've read . . . [an] outstanding book."
—The Best Reviews

"[MacAlister has a] captivating voice and charming storytelling skills [and] impeccable style."
—Inscriptions Magazine

"Delightful and charming! A wonderful romp through Regency England."   —Lynsay Sands

The Corset Diaries

KATIE MacALISTER

AN ONYX BOOK

ONYX
Published by New American Library, a division of
Penguin Group (USA) Inc., 375 Hudson Street,
New York, New York 10014, USA
Penguin Group (Canada), 10 Alcorn Avenue, Toronto,
Ontario M4V 3B2, Canada (a division of Pearson Penguin Canada Inc.)
Penguin Books Ltd., 80 Strand, London WC2R 0RL, England
Penguin Ireland, 25 St. Stephen's Green, Dublin 2,
Ireland (a division of Penguin Books Ltd.)
Penguin Group (Australia), 250 Camberwell Road, Camberwell, Victoria 3124,
Australia (a division of Pearson Australia Group Pty. Ltd.)
Penguin Books India Pvt. Ltd., 11 Community Centre, Panchsheel Park,
New Delhi - 110 017, India
Penguin Group (NZ), cnr Airborne and Rosedale Roads, Albany,
Auckland 1310, New Zealand (a division of Pearson New Zealand Ltd.)
Penguin Books (South Africa) (Pty.) Ltd., 24 Sturdee Avenue,
Rosebank, Johannesburg 2196, South Africa

Penguin Books Ltd., Registered Offices:
80 Strand, London WC2R 0RL, England

First published by Onyx, an imprint of New American Library,
a division of Penguin Group (USA) Inc.

First Printing, May 2004
10 9 8 7

PUBLISHER'S NOTE
This is a work of fiction. Names, characters, places, and incidents either are
the product of the author's imagination or are used fictitiously, and any resem-
blance to actual persons, living or dead, business establishments, events, or
locales is entirely coincidental.

ACKNOWLEDGMENTS

Writing is such a solitary endeavor, I'm always grateful for my online friends who keep me sane while I'm writing a book. For years the ladies at RBL Romantica (www.rblromantica.com) have done a magnificent job of supporting romance books and their writers, and I am truly grateful to be considered one of "their" authors. RBLs, I salute you.

Sunday
August 29
Early morning-ish
Seattle

"Hello?"

"Do you still have long hair? You haven't cut it since I last saw you?"

That's how it started: with an inquiry into the status of my hair. I hope that doesn't say something about how the whole thing is going to proceed. Hair is just so trivial. In the grand scale of things, that is—it's certainly important when it looks awful and you have to run to the store to pick up a fifth of whiskey and a bottle of Pamprin.

"Yes, I do still have long hair. Why?"

"Oh, good, you'd hate the wig. I heard it smells. You have a valid passport too, right? Didn't you go to Mazatlán last year?"

I twined a strand of the aforementioned hair around my finger and glared at the phone. Why on earth had Pierce called me up to inquire about my hair and Mazatlán?

"Yes, I do and I did. What wig? Why are you asking me all these questions? And when did you get back? I thought you were in London working for the BBC."

"Oh, I left them. They had no scope, no scope at all. I'm still in London, but I'm working for an independent channel now. Excellent! I knew you'd be perfect for this. I'm overnighting a package to you. You can read the notes and the rule book on the plane, 'K?"

I blinked a couple of times hoping it would aid my thought processes in straightening out the tangled mess of his conversation. It didn't help. "What package? What plane? Pierce, what are you talking about?"

He sighed noisily in my ear, then muttered something about never understanding women. "It's all very fabu and you're going to love it, and you won't believe the strings I had to pull to get this for you, but the job pays *ten thousand dollars,* and since I owe you big time, I moved heaven and hell and got the job for you. You can thank me later; right now you have to pack. But not much, because they'll take your measurements on Tuesday and should have the basic necessities done by Wednesday, Thursday at the latest. You're still an eighteen, right? I can tell them that, and they'll get started."

"Job? You got me a research job that pays ten grand?" My head swam at the thought of all that money. Bills, I could pay off the remainder of Peter's medical bills. And get the roof repaired. Maybe there would even be some left over so I wouldn't have to drive around on bald tires. The money would certainly come in . . . hey! "What measurements? What basic necessities? Don't you *dare* tell anyone I wear a size eighteen! I'll hang you by your balls if you do!"

He sighed again, then spoke very deliberately, enunciating carefully as if I was the one who wasn't making sense. "The measurements are for the wardrobe, honey. I have to tell them your size, so they know what sort of costumes to find—Cynthia was much smaller and her wardrobe wouldn't fit you. Of course, she had to wear the wig and you won't, so there are compensations. There's no research other than reading the rule book, no genealogy other than you being a duke's wife. Now that we have that settled, are there any other questions? I'm on a very tight schedule, and I have to get back to Roger and tell him you're go, and then there's a million other things to take care of. You just have no idea how busy I am."

I breathed heavily through my nose for a moment, then said, just as carefully and slowly, "Pierce, you're quite, quite mad, aren't you? Or drunk. Whichever it is, I don't have time for this game."

"Don't be ridiculous." This was said in his usual sharp, quick manner. "You can't tell me that the genealogical research business is so brisk that you can't take a month off to film a television show, especially not when there's ten big ones for you at the end of it. Get hopping, Tessa. Your plane leaves tomorrow night at . . ." There was a faint sound of paper rustling over his muted mumblings. ". . . I know that lovely little bit of crumpet wrote it down here somewhere—such a scrumptious boy, but no brains whatsoever . . . Ah, here it is. Yes, as I thought, your plane leaves at six tomorrow night. Gives you all the time in the world to pack and tie up loose ends. But don't pack too much, you won't need any clothing unless you want to stay after the show's over."

"Pierce, I haven't the slightest idea—"

"I've told you and told you! It's a TV show!"

I blinked a half dozen more times, then rallied my wits. "You got me a job on a TV show? An English TV show?"

"Yes, yes, a thousand times yes! All you have to do is be the duke's wife. It's very simple; even a child could understand it. Honestly, honey, you need to make a little more effort to pay attention. I don't want Roger thinking you're not fit to be a duchess."

I slumped down into a nearby chair, staring sightlessly out the window at the cows wandering through the tall yellow flowers in the pasture across the street from me. Violet-green swallows swooped and dove, tracing an intricate aerobatic roller coaster pattern in the early morning air, but their loops and twirls and midair twists had nothing on Pierce's conversational manner. A few deep, calming breaths later, I was able to start figuring out what he was trying to tell me. "Pierce, dear heart, you are aware that I'm not an actress, yes?"

"They don't want actresses, silly! They want real people, and you're perfect for the part because of your ancestors."

I rubbed my forehead. Undergoing a conversation with Pierce was never something I took lightly. "OK, so you got me a job involving no genealogical research despite the fact that that's the only thing I know how to do, a job that pays a lot of money for a month's work. Exactly what am I supposed to do for a month on a TV show if not act?"

"Did you clean your ears this morning? I TOLD YOU! You're a duke's wife. Your job is to give him an heir in exchange for his title."

I fell out of the chair. "WHAT? Pierce, I'm thirty-nine years old! I'm too old to have children! And I don't even know this guy!"

"Tessa, now you're being obtuse—"

"I'm sorry for being so picky, but I'd like to know a man before I go about trying to give him an heir!"

"It's the TV show! You're an American heiress who's marrying the duke for his title. Just like that one you told me about . . . what's her name . . . Constance Vanderbilt?"

"Consuelo Vanderbilt," I said slowly, the fragments of what he was saying starting to coalesce in my mind. I crawled back into the chair. "You mean the TV show is about a duke with an American wife?"

"Yes, yes, that's what I've been saying!"

"And they want me to play this part because Consuelo Vanderbilt and I shared an ancestor ten generations ago?"

"At last! I was starting to wonder if you'd given away your brain and filled your head with pudding."

I ignored the slur and concentrated. Hard. "Why would an English TV company want an American with a tenuous—and there are probably millions of people who share the same relationship with Consuelo that I have—relationship to a long-dead heiress to act in their show?"

"You won't be acting, not really. It's one of those reality shows. Didn't I tell you that? They're filming everyone for a month, sort of a social history experiment to see how common people, nonactors that is, deal with living the Victorian lifestyle. There's a whole staff of sixteen to take care of you, servants you know, butlers and footmen and maids and all that. You'll love it. You won't have to lift a finger to do anything."

"A reality show?" I said slowly. "You mean like the one they did on PBS where people lived in a turn-of-the-twentieth-century house for a couple of months and a film crew followed them around as they went about their 1900-ish business?"

"Exactly!" Pierce's voice was replete with relief, but I was still confused.

"It sounds interesting and all, but I don't quite see why you think they'd want me to play the part of a duchess."

"Roger d'Aspry—he's the producer; we went to Oxford together—is trying for realism as much as he can. Everyone hired has some sort of link to the part they'll play. Max, for instance, he's the duke, and is he gorgeous! Girl, I wet my pants just thinking about him! Max is actually a descendant of the Duke of Bridgewater. Fifth cousin once removed or something like that. It was his ancestors who lived in Worston Old Hall, which is where the shooting takes place. Big old place, lots of oak and marble. You'll love it. Anyway, Roger told me to find him an American who was related to one of those American heiresses, the ones you were telling me about a couple of years ago when you were researching them, so immediately I thought of you."

"The dollar duchesses," I said, still trying to absorb everything he was tossing at me. It was a lot to swallow. So much, I started choking immediately. "All those American heiresses marrying English peers—it was fascinating research. . . . I'm flattered you thought about me for this, but there's two major problems."

He sighed again, a big, heavy, dramatic, long-suffering sort of sigh that was supposed to impart to me just how much I was trying his patience. I didn't pay any attention to it. "What problems?"

"First off, you never went to Oxford."

"Oh. That. I thought it sounded better saying Roger and I went to Oxford rather than he was my boy toy when we were both in L.A. What's the second problem?"

I hesitated to say it, but of all my friends, Pierce was the least judgmental. I might be uncomfortable with my appearance, but I knew he honestly didn't think anything about it, which just made it harder for me to explain to him why it wasn't at all possible for me to fly halfway around the world to pretend to be the wife of a man so gorgeous he made other men wet their pants. "Pierce, I just can't, I'm . . . I'm too big."

"No, you're not. Max is tall—taller than me—and I'm just a smidge taller than you."

I ground my teeth. I hated this. "Not tall . . . big. As in hefty. Chunky. Plump plus. *Beyond chubby into the land of fat.*"

He laughed—he actually laughed at me. I bristled and thought lovingly about slamming the phone down in his ear. "Don't be stupid, you'll have a corset! That and the long skirts will take care of anything you're worried about."

"But—"

"Just bring yourself and your glorious hair, and let the wardrobe people do the rest."

"But—"

"I'm overnighting you the rule book. Oh, and I thought of something to make this even more attractive! You know those journals you're always keeping about stuff happening to you? Start a new one today, and record everything that happens. I bet you'll be able to sell that later for oodles of money! The show is bound to be a hit, and I can almost guarantee you that publishers will beat down your door to find out all the behind-the-scenes happenings of a real-life duchess."

"But—"

"Must dash. Evan, that darling boy, just popped his head in and waved his hands around, which means one of the studio people is on the other line. I'll see you tomorrow! Toodle pip, and all that crap!"

The line clicked twice, then went dead.

I stared at the receiver in my hand for another minute before hanging up. Corsets? Long Victorian skirts? A duchess? *Me?*

And just who was Cynthia?

—⁓—

Monday
August 30
After dinner
Airplane over Canada

Well, I'm here. On a plane. Flying to London to meet an old friend who has arranged for me to take part in something I'm sure I'll regret. But damn, the money is just too good to refuse, especially for someone who makes a (pitiful and never enough to cover the bills) living finding baby boomers' roots for them. I'm taking Pierce's advice and starting a new journal, which you know if you're reading this, because that means I survived this "social history experiment," one I suspect is going to be nothing so much as hell for me.

I am *not* a corset-wearing sort of person, despite my avid interest in history. And a duchess? Ha! I bet there's not one single duchess who had to max out her credit cards to prepay her bills for the next month.

I will say that this Roger d'Aspry, television producer and former Hollywood plaything, is very well organized. The rule book that Pierce overnighted to me is utterly fascinating. I dug out a couple of Victorian etiquette books I bought on eBay (the researcher's best friend) and double-checked a couple of the items that jumped out at me, but they were correct. Which is kind of scary, considering the sort of stuff this show wants me and the others to do.

Pierce also enclosed a fact sheet about the show,

which filled in some but not all of the empty spaces he'd left in his explanation. It explained who Cynthia was (another person related distantly to American Old Money), but not what happened to her.

I didn't want to tell Pierce because his head is fat enough, but this was exactly the sort of thing I've always wanted to do. I love Victorian history, especially English Victorian history, and what dedicated Anglophile wouldn't jump at the chance to stay in a bona fide English stately home?

There is the corset issue, of course. But if I agree to do the job—I haven't signed anything yet, and won't until I talk more to Pierce and his friend Roger—I'm sure I'll find a way around it.

Then again, maybe Roger won't want me once he sees me. Well, if that's the case, I'll just hang around London for a couple of days, then go home. No problem. Nothing like a little vacation to brighten up a dull year, is there?

Oh, who am I fooling? I'll die of embarrassment if he turns me down. Why, why, why did I get on this plane? Why did I believe Pierce? No corset in the world is going to hide all my fleshy bits! The whole idea is ridiculous! No one is going to want a fat duchess. GAH!

—⁓—

Monday
Still August 30
Even later after dinner
Airplane over . . . um . . . polar cap, I think

How mortifying. The flight attendant turned vicious when I politely requested they turn the plane around, or at the least drop me off somewhere before they land in London. I mean, how hard can it be to find an airport between here and England? It can't take up that much gas or time! I *am* a paying customer, after all. Kind of. I didn't pay, the TV company did, but still, someone paid for my ticket and that's what really matters.

This doesn't bode well for the rest of the trip.

—⟋⟋⟋—

Monday—or maybe it's Tuesday now
August 30/31, depending on your time zone
Post-movie (Sleepless in Seattle)
Row 12, seat A, over Greenland, according to Bob the
pilot

I can't believe the sort of bullies they hire as flight attendants nowadays. I know they've cracked down on security and everything, but this has nothing to do with the safety of the airplane, its crew, or the passengers. Hilda Trentworth, flight attendant henceforth known to one and all as Hilda the Hun, is on my list. I'm going to formally complain about her not only threatening to take away my frequent flyer miles (she can't do that, can she?), but also the fact that she snapped at me *and* pushed me back into my seat when all I did was ask about the possibility of parachuting out of the plane so I don't have to be humiliated when Roger, after bursting into hysterical laughter upon seeing me, suddenly starts chanting "Fat, fat, the water rat!" as he dances around me.

I don't even think she even asked Bob the pilot about dropping me off somewhere. I'm going to ask one of the other flight attendants, the ones who aren't Hun-like, if one of them will ask Bob for me. He sounds nice. I bet he will.

Monday, Tuesday, who knows
August whatever
Middle of the friggin' night
Airplane from hell

Hilda the Hun just leaned over the old lady next to me
to tell me that if I bother one more flight attendant,
she'll see I get off the plane . . . in the middle of the
ocean, *without* a parachute.

    She is *so* going to get reported!

—⁓—

Tuesday (figured that out with the help of the guy sitting
in front of me)
August 31
Early morning U.K. time/middle of the night Seattle time
Chained to my seat, plummeting earthward from thirty
thousand feet if a certain flight attendant had her way

All right, so I've given up all hope of getting off the
plane before reaching England's fabled shores. I'm coping with the fact that I'm in for nothing but disappoint-
ment, embarrassment, and the sharp pain of rejection
once Roger sees me. I don't like it, but I'm coping, and
that's gotta give me some sort of cosmic brownie points.

    To distract myself from the horror that awaits me once
Pierce picks me up at Heathrow, I read a bit more of
the rule book. The first part basically covered the same
stuff the fact sheet does:

A MONTH IN THE LIFE OF A VICTORIAN DUKE

(snappy title, huh?)

Presented to you by U.K. Alive!, Britain's fastest growing television studio, this fascinating new series takes you into the lives of Victorians in a way that will startle and surprise you. Twenty-four volunteers from around Britain will join together to breathe new life into the stories of the wealth, glamour, and power that defined England's ruling class one hundred and twenty-five years ago.

Wealth, power, and glamour, huh? So far so good.

Historical Accuracy is a Must at U.K. Alive!

Filmed entirely at Worston Old Hall in Cheshire, one of the (now extinct) Duke of Bridgewater's many estates, a modern-day descendant of the duke brings his family to re-create life as it was for the landed gentry. How would you behave if you were suddenly whisked away from the stresses of everyday life and put down in a world where you had seemingly limitless power and wealth, a world where you only had to lift a finger to have any desire fulfilled? Maximillian Edgerton, an architect from Bristol, will soon find out as he assumes the role of the fifteenth Duke of Bridgewater, newly wed to a charming (and rich) American heiress. The role of the new Duchess of Bridgewater is assumed by Cynthia Towers, a descendant of the famed American Astor family. Joining Mr. Edgerton are his real-life daughter, twelve-year-old Melody, his sister, Barbara Edgerton-Slough, and his brother-in-law, Henry Slough.

Oh, great. He's bringing his whole family. Sure, he'll

have the comfort of everyone he loves around him, but what'll I have?

I don't know why I'm worrying. I won't fit into the corset. They'll send me home after just one look.

Damn my genes. This sounded like it would have been fun.

Downstairs Is a Much Different World

But what if you weren't born with the proverbial silver spoon in your mouth? What if you were one of the 1.5 million people in service in September 1879? Would you be able to accept life dominated by the complicated hierarchy and rules servants had to follow, not to mention working without modern devices? We'll join sixteen volunteers who come to Worston Old Hall with no experience of what it means to be a servant. Only the cook and coachman have actual working knowledge of what it takes to fill their jobs. Join Palmer the butler and Mrs. Peters the housekeeper as they struggle with the responsibility of turning the nine lower servants from modern, twenty-first-century volunteers into a team who work with Victorian precision and efficiency.

I couldn't help but wonder if I would be on the plane at that moment if the job I had been offered was that of scullery maid. . . . Well, that didn't take long to ponder. For ten thousand dollars, yes, I'd wash dishes for a month.

No Mobile Phones, No Toothpaste

(No toothpaste? GAH!)

For four weeks the entire household, from duke to scullery maid, will function just as houses of the nobility did in 1879. Each volunteer has foresworn modern machines and technology, agreeing instead to adhere steadfastly to Victorian standards of behavior, fol-

lowing with strict obedience the rules and manners of the time.

OK, so that meant what? No smoking if you were a woman, chaperones for unmarried women, couldn't mention anything remotely approaching a sexual subject without couching it in terms so obtuse that no one really knew what you were talking about, smelling salts and fans, and . . . Oh, those poor people playing the servants! From what I could recall reading about the Victorians, they really had a hard time. Oy. Maybe it's a good thing they needed an American to be the duchess . . . that's assuming I get the job, which I won't once Roger sees me.

Maybe if I slipped Bob the pilot a plaintive note and twenty bucks he'd stop in Ireland so I could sneak off?

Everyone in Their Places, and a Place for Everything

Toughest of all the rules for our brave volunteers downstairs will be the detailed and intricate hierarchy that governs the servants. How will our free-willed volunteers cope with being told who can speak and when, who must defer to whom, and how they must interact with the family above stairs? Most importantly, how will they deal with their loss of freedom?

If I do get the job (and I won't; I've seen pictures of Consuelo Vanderbilt and all the other dollar duchesses—almost all of them were skinny little things), I'm going to be extra-special nice to the poor people downstairs.

Everyone in Worston Old Hall has a place set down for them by hundreds of years of societal norms and mores—everyone from the duke in his smoking room to the third footman as he carries out the slops will keep to his place. Join us for four scintillating weeks as we examine how this group of modern-day freethinkers change into their Victorian counterparts. Will A Month in the Life of a Victorian Duke *prove to be heaven . . . or hell?*

"Holy cow!"

The woman next to me, a nice elderly English lady who chatted very politely with me for the first twenty minutes of the trip then pulled out a book and left me alone for the duration, moved restlessly. Most of the passengers on the plane were asleep by this time, the lights dimmed, blankies and pillows having been handed out, but I had remained awake to read the packet of info Pierce had sent. I angled my reading lamp away from my seatmate so I wouldn't disturb her while I read, but I guess my exclamation must have been louder than I thought, because she sat up and cast me a questioning glance.

I tilted toward her the eight-by-ten glossy that had been shuffled between consent forms.

"Is that your sweetheart?" she asked, making a little moue of appreciation at the photo.

I pursed my lips in a soundless whistle and shook my head. "Just a guy I might be working with."

Pierce was right; the man was gorgeous—black, black hair that waved back from a not-too-high forehead, startlingly light blue eyes that glittered from beneath his black eyebrows, a nice if slightly rueful smile, and a gently blunted chin that for some reason made my stomach flutter and my legs go a bit weak. For a moment I mulled over that reaction to a mere picture, then chalked it up to not having dated in the three years since Peter died. Lack of sex will sometimes make you a bit swoony.

There was also a photo of a woman; blond, pretty heart-shaped face, big eyes, and thin, thin, thin. In other words, as completely different from my brunette, freckle-faced, large self as she could be. It was Cynthia, the woman originally cast to play the part of wife to the drool-worthy duke, a woman who looked absolutely perfect for the part, a woman who would look even more perfect next to the black-haired Adonis. Seen together, it would be infinitely believable that the duke would have chosen her from all women to be his wife, the woman to bear his children, mother to his daughter, friend, help-meet, lover. She was, in a word, flawless.

I *really* want to go home.

—·m·—

Tuesday again
August 31
Nine in the morning U.K. time—post-breakfast
Still on the plane (will this flight never end?)

Breakfast was a dismal affair—potted meat and black bread and a pastry and yogurt. Not that I expect haute cuisine in tourist class, but still! Some fruit might have been nice. And of course, my breakfast tray was thrown to me over Mrs. Hargreaves (my elderly seatmate) by the Hun. She also deliberately tried to spill coffee on me when she poured it, but I was too quick for her. Ha! Triumphant at last. Just wait until the head of the airline gets my letter about her.

Mrs. Hargreaves turned out to be a gold mine of information. Seems when she was a "little gel," her parents had servants galore. She had a nanny, of course, and she remembers the housemaids smoking and chatting in the servant's hall. I asked her questions about how her mother dealt with the servants, but she was less help-ful there.

"What did you think of the servants?" I asked, and held up a photocopy of the cover for *The Glory of Wom-anhood,* a Victorian ladies' book that had been included in the packet of material from the studio. "This book says, 'Conduct toward servants should be always equal, never violent, never familiar. Speak to them always with civility, but keep them in their proper places.' Did your family treat them in that way?"

She raised one carefully penciled eyebrow. "Naturally. One is kind to one's servants, but one does not desire familiarity with them."

Well, that put me right in my place. And with great timing, too, since Bob the pilot just announced we're approaching Heathrow. Oh, lovely. My life is about to end. Fabulous.

Maybe I'll fall and break my arm in the airport and have to be taken to a hospital for lengthy arm-repair surgery, hence making it impossible for me to meet Roger.

Maybe Pierce will forget to pick me up, leaving me with no way to get in contact with him or Roger.

Maybe the passport guys won't let me into the country, and Roger won't have the opportunity to reject me in person.

Maybe I should just get a grip.

Still Tuesday
August 31
9:14 P.M., England time
Room 722, Hyde Park Hilton

Well. I'm still here. More than a little groggy and jet-lagged, not to mention bemused, but here.

Pierce was at the airport waiting for me when I came through customs. He looked the same as he always did— tall, good-looking despite the beginnings of a cute little beer belly, confident, with a smile that always made me think he was laughing secretly at something only he found funny.

"Tessa! At last! I've waited forever for you! Mwah!" He planted a sloppy wet kiss on my cheek then held me at arm's length to give me a brisk once-over. "You look like hell, honey, you really do."

My shoulders slumped as I crossed a protective arm

over my torso. "Thanks just oodles, Pierce. You sure do know how to make a girl feel good."

He laughed and waved his hands toward the luggage I'd set down to hug him. "Evan, be a lamb and take those, will you? Now, you know what I meant by *look like hell*. Your hair! Tessa, love, I've told you time and time again—a little color is not a bad thing! No one likes that dull shade of brown. A nice magenta cellophane, that's what you need."

"Auburn, definitely auburn," a slim young man with copious piercings said as he grabbed my two bags. "Auburn is much warmer. It would go with her skin tone better than magenta."

The two men eyed me for a minute, their heads tipped to the side just like they were symbiotic twins, then Pierce shook his head, *tsk*ed, and grabbed my arm to steer me toward the car park. "It's not important, honey. We can fix your hair up later, after the show is over. Now, you've read the rule book, yes?"

"No. Just some of it."

"Excellent," he said, obviously not paying the slightest bit of attention to me as he pushed me through the doors toward a dark tunnel leading to the parking. "Let's see, it's two now, and you have a fitting at four. . . . Yes, we have time for lunch. Evan?"

"Right behind you, Pee," Evan answered.

"We'll stop at the Cock and Cow for a bit of lunch, then go on to the studio."

"Pee?" I asked Pierce a moment later when Evan scooted around us, heading for a dark blue sedan.

"Isn't he delicious?" Pierce answered, his gaze resting with wicked intent on the younger man as Evan stuffed my luggage into the trunk. "Such a help, he is. You have simply no idea how useful I find him."

"Mmm," I said. "I bet you do. He's awfully . . . *pierced*, don't you think? I mean, even if he is trying to live up to your name, don't you think having his eyebrows, nose, ears, and lower lip pierced is going a bit too far?"

Pierce snickered and herded me to the side of the car, his voice low and soft as velvet as he whispered, "His tongue is pierced, too. I can't even begin to tell you how much I enjoy that!"

"Right. I think we're dipping into the realm of *too much information*, so I'll let that pass. About lunch—I couldn't possibly eat. I think I'm going to be sick as is. Could we just skip all the stuff and go straight to the part where I meet this Roger guy and he takes one look at my fleshy form and laughs hysterically, wiping his eyes just long enough to send me home?"

"Stop it. Roger's going to love you," he said as he shoved me into the backseat. I scooted over so he could sit next to me. "You're perfect for the job, just perfect! You have every quality he's looking for. You're intelligent—"

"Thank you," I murmured, flattered and disbelieving at the same time.

"—and you know just tons about history and all that stuff—"

"It *was* my major in college."

"—and you're American, of course, and related to the Vanderbilts—"

"Distantly," I pointed out. "Very distantly. And so are a lot of other people."

"—and most importantly of all, you're the only one who is free."

He went on for another minute, giving less and less believable reasons why Roger the producer would love me, but I was stuck on the last point.

"What do you mean I was the only one who is free? You said you moved heaven and hell to get me this job, and now you're saying the only reason I'm being considered is because no one else can do it? I wasn't your first choice?"

"Oh, look, we're coming into town. That didn't take long, did it? Traffic around here is normally the pits. How much farther to the Cock and Cow, Evan?"

I sat back and thought about giving in to a pout. The

way Pierce evaded my question was answer enough—
obviously, I was not the first choice as a replacement.
Of course I wasn't. What was I thinking?

Lunch looked good. I don't know if it was, because I
decided the only way I was going to get through the day
was if I had a little liquid courage, so accordingly, I
drank my lunch. I poured martini after martini down my
throat until a blessed numbness set in. Pierce stopped
me after the third one, which may not sound like much,
but trust me, for me it was. By the time Pierce caught
me sucking the last bit of gin from the olive's toothpick,
it was too late.

"I like olives. Don't you like olives? I really like olives. They're so olivey," I said to him as he hauled me
outside to where Evan was waiting with the car. "Olive.
Even the name is good. Ooooooooooolive. Isn't it
nummy? You're nummy too, Pierce. It's just too bad
you don't like girls, 'cause I bet a lot of them would
olive you. You have a really nice face." I gave his face
a pat, just to show him that I really liked it and wasn't
just saying it to be nice.

Pierce shoved me into the car, muttering under his
breath something about people who have no tolerance
for alcohol knowing better than to drink martinis.

"But I'm better now," I protested, wondering how one
of my legs had found its way onto his lap. "I never used
to be able to drink, but I can now. I've been practicing.
I can have a whole bottle of beer without getting silly
now, and I couldn't do that when we shared that
apartmen' on Queen Anne Hill. 'Member that apartmen'?"

"Remind me never to volunteer to help Roger again,
will you?" Pierce asked Evan. He pushed my leg off his
lap. "And as soon as we get to the studio, I want you
to find some coffee—black—and bring it to the wardrobe room. Six or seven cups of it."

I tipped my head back and started singing "Were-
wolves of London."

Pierce shuddered. "Make that twenty cups."

Thankfully, the buzz from the martinis lasted through the horrors of having to stand in my underwear in front of Pierce and a couple of wardrobe ladies while they measured every conceivable stretch of my skin.

They shoved a couple of dresses on me, but I don't remember much about them except they were scratchy and uncomfortable. Pierce let me have a little nap on a ratty old armchair in one of the wardrobe rooms while various people came up and held bits of material against my cheek to see what looked good.

The buzz, unfortunately, was gone by the time he shook me awake, and frog-marched me, dizzy and a bit queasy, down the hall, up a flight of stairs, and into a plush carpeted room dark with heavy mahogany furniture, lightened by a lovely view of the Thames.

Before I could open my mouth to protest Pierce's brutality of dragging me from a sound sleep, a balding man with dark red hair looked up from the massive desk I was pushed before. My stomach seemed to keep moving long after I stopped.

"Oh, there you are! Hello, Tessa, I'm Roger d'Aspry. Pierce has told me so much about you. I'm delighted that you're joining our team—relieved actually, because we start filming tomorrow and what's the story of a duke's life without his duchess at his side?" Roger came around the desk while he was speaking, his voice clipped in a manner reminiscent of expensive schooling. He took my hand in both of his to simultaneously pat and shake it. He was about four inches shorter than me; not terribly unusual, as I am almost six feet tall. "I know you'll have a grand time, just a grand time. You're going to love everyone and the house! It's glorious! Pierce tells me you're quite the devotee of history, so you should have no trouble adapting to the lifestyle. You've read the rule book and introductory material?"

I blinked at him and swayed just the tiniest bit while I let his words trickle through the fogged mass that was presently acting as my brain. "Um. Some of it."

"Good, good. We just need you to sign a few

releases—merely à legality, I assure you—then I'm sure you'll want to have a bit of rest before the evening's fittings, the audition, and, of course, you'll want to read up on the rest of the volunteers for the program."

Fittings? Auditions? He wanted me for the part? He saw me and he still wanted me? Maybe his eyesight was bad. I held up my hand and waved it before his face. "How many fingers am I holding up?"

Behind me, Pierce groaned. Roger frowned at me, then frowned at my fingers. "Three. Is there a reason you are asking me that?"

Oh, God, now I'd painted myself in a corner. If I said no, he'd think I was an idiot, the kind of lunatic who waved her fingers around and asked people to count them. If I said yes and explained that he couldn't possibly want me to be the duchess, I'd have to explain why, and if I had to discuss my overflowing abundance of flesh with one more person, I'd scream. My brain was still feeling fuzzy from the martinis, but I figured the truth was probably the best bet. I'd rather be thought self-conscious than a boob. "Um . . . it's just that . . . well . . ." I waved a hand up and down my torso.

"Honey, I've told you and told you that you're just perfect for this role!" Pierce hurried forward and grabbed my hand. "She has this idiotic idea that she's too fat for the part."

"PIERCE!" I smacked him in the arm. How could he come right out and say the word with no creative euphemisms or polite skating around the issue? "The word *fat* is politically incorrect. I'm skinny-challenged, thank you."

Roger eyed me up and down, from nose to toes, then back up to my head. "I don't see a problem."

I wanted to kiss him.

"Most of the aristocracy were pudgy. All that rich living, you know."

The kiss shriveled up on my lips. "Pudgy?"

He gave me a quick grin. "Sorry. Skinny-challenged. Besides, you have your own hair. I would hate to go through the wig trauma again." He shuddered delicately as he spoke.

I was hired because of my hair? Yes, it was long and fairly thick, but it also had a mind of its own and was an uninspiring plain old brown color. I toyed for a moment with the idea of being righteously indignant that it wasn't for my more meaningful qualities that I was asked to fill the role, then realized just how stupid that would be. I was getting the job! I'd be out of debt at long last! I'd get to be a duchess for a month! Best of all, I'd get to have that handsome blue-eyed man for a pretend husband for a month! A whole month! My stomach did another somersault at the thought, an action that left me swallowing hard to keep things where they belonged.

"And speaking of that, you've met the wardrobe people, yes? Wonderful team we have here, all experts in their field, and very keen on historical accuracy. I'm sure you'll be utterly delighted with the wardrobe they create for you, but if you have particular likes and dislikes, do tell them. Of course, you're absolutely free to pick and choose what you wish to wear each day. More authentic that way, you understand." Roger waved me toward a tall wine-colored leather armchair as he perched on the edge of his desk. I stumbled and half-fell into the chair. Pierce took the matching chair, sitting with an elegance and suavity that I felt far escaped my perspiring, rumpled, sleep-riddled, queasy slump. "Our goal with the *Month in the Life* project is absolute accuracy and authenticity in every facet of life. To that end, we're asking each participant to not only live without items that were created after 1879, but to live by the societal precepts of the mid-Victorian era. Manners, values, etiquette, social interactions—all must conform to the standards the Victorians lived by. Are you willing to do that?"

I blinked a couple of times and carefully cleared my throat. "I'm tolerably familiar with that period, so I don't imagine it will be a problem, although I'm not an expert by any means."

"That's why we included a copy of *The Glory of*

Womanhood in the project material. If you have any questions about how you should deal with servants, which fork to use when, how to have a tea for your friends, when you should go visiting, that sort of thing, it's all covered in the book. And just to get you started, we've made up a list of everyone's duties, from the duke right down to the scullery girl. That's in the packet, as well, and I urge you to become familiar with it, because as the mistress of the house it will be your duty to inter-act with the housekeeper to make sure the house is run smoothly. You are ultimately responsible for the ser-vants and their well-being."

I kept my eyes fixed on his left cheekbone and nodded slowly. If I looked anywhere else, the room seemed to dip and sway, taking my stomach with it.

"Now, regarding the filming—please, please ignore the presence of the cameramen and the sound people. They will do their best to be invisible—and, of course, you'll have absolute privacy in the bedroom and loo—so I'm sure that after a short time you won't even notice they're there. We want you to act just as naturally around them as you would should you be alone, strictly keeping within the guidelines of a Victorian duchess, of course," he laughed. "No turning your hand to a bit of dusting or putting a room to rights."

I gave him a weak smile. Did he honestly think I cher-ished housework to the point that I'd want to do it on what amounted to a monthlong luxury vacation? "That won't be a problem."

"Good. You may, of course, bring any cherished mementoes—black-and-white photos and the like—but we ask that everyone stick strictly to period reading. Worston Old Hall has quite an extensive library, which we've supplemented with reproduction and original peri-odicals and newspapers, so you should have a variety of reading material to choose from. Along those lines, we ask that you not bring any paraphernalia that is not period."

"Paraphernalia?" I asked, my mind more on keeping

my stomach in order than with what he was saying. "What sort of paraphernalia?"

He spread his hands wide. "Anything you can think of that wouldn't have been available to the Victorians— mobile phones, Biros, electric razors, hair dryers, that sort of thing."

"Oh. I have a journal and a couple of pictures, but that's it other than my clothes."

"A journal?"

"It's leather bound. I don't think it would stand out in any way."

He rubbed his jaw for a second, then nodded. "Just be sure you use the pens we provide. In fact, I think the idea of keeping a journal is an excellent one. Many ladies of the time did, I'm told. And as for the other things, we've engaged a variety of companies to supply items that you'd use everyday—sundries, toiletries, accessories—your entire wardrobe, of course, will be provided, including shoes and underthings. That goes for the stationery, dinner service, crystal, silver, wine, various supplies for the servants, as well and oh, did you read up on the masquerade ball? Wardrobe is creating a special authentic costume for you to wear to the ball. You can see that with so much effort being made to create as authentic a setting as possible, it's vitally important that you do your part in acting the part."

I gave him a brave smile, brave because I was suddenly struck with how unsuitable I was for this role— not only because of my weight, but because I simply was not raised by duchess standards. How would I eat with servants watching me? Then again, I doubted if Max the architect was brought up in a ducal household. "I'll do my best."

"I have every confidence you will." He tipped his head to the side for a moment, looking at me just as Pierce and Evan had earlier. "You'll quite enjoy yourself, you know. You'll be the mistress of the house. You won't have a care in the world except picking out what frock to wear and whether to go riding in the morning or in the afternoon. We have a lady's maid for you, naturally, a wonderful woman who is very experienced in the period. All you have to do is enjoy yourself and live a life most of the world would sell their souls to experience."

My stomach did a half gainer at that thought.

"Now, on the schedule for this evening is a brief audition—just an interview that we do on film for archival purposes—then I expect the good ladies in wardrobe would like you in for a second fitting, and then we're off in the morning, very early I'm afraid, but we wish to start filming with breakfast. Our film crew will go out to Cheshire later tonight, but they will primarily be filming the servants first thing in the morning, so we'll have time to smuggle you into the house and get you dressed before you make your first appearance." Roger looked up from a stack of papers as someone opened the door. "Oh, Sam, Max, what excellent timing. Come in, I want you both to meet our lifesaver. Tessa Riordan, this is Sam Everett, our head cameraman, and Max Edgerton, who'll be taking on the role of his grace, the Duke of Bridgewater. You'll be working very closely with Sam, Tessa, since he'll shoot all the principle photography, and, of course, you'll get to know Max very well during the next month."

Two men entered the room, the first a thin, wiry guy with carroty hair and wire-rimmed glasses. Behind him, a dark shadow flickered in the hallway, then Sam moved aside to allow the dishy man in the photo to enter. My stomach jumped and did a front somersault with a half twist as I got a good look at him—he was even more handsome in person than he was in a stiff, posed picture. His eyes were what most caught my attention. They weren't just light as the picture showed; they were a clear, crystal blue, a blue topaz blue, a summer sky in early morning blue, framed with sooty black lashes so thick I wondered if he had to comb them each morning to keep them from getting tangled.

Those beautiful eyes, a bit wary as they studied me,

suddenly warmed as he stuck out his hand, saying, "It's a pleasure to meet you, Tessa. I can't tell you how thankful I am to know you've agreed to take on the role. I hope you are free for dinner tonight. I'd like to talk about the project with you."

I opened my mouth to say hello, nice to be here, hope you like large women, would you like to have sex after dinner, but all that came out was olives. And three martinis. And the potted meat and black bread and . . . well, basically everything I'd eaten in the last five hours. It all came up, barfed ignominiously onto the plush carpet, a bit of it splashing up onto Max's neat brown loafers.

Pierce closed his eyes in horror and slapped a hand to his forehead as I stood hunched over, one hand clutching the back of the leather chair, the other hand twisted into the front of my thin gauze dress to keep it from dangling into the mess. I released the chair long enough to take the handful of tissues that Roger thrust from behind me, mopping my mouth as I straightened up.

Max looked from his soiled shoes up to my flushed, sweaty, tears-of-mortification-shining-in-my-eyes face and withdrew his hand. "I take it that's a no to dinner?"

―⁓―

Wednesday
September 1
2:50 A.M., Greenwich Mean Time
Bathtub, Room 722, Hyde Park Hilton

I can't believe I fell asleep while trying to write down what happened last night, but I did. Must have been all the energy expended on barfing on the handsomest man I've ever seen, not to mention dealing with Hilda the Hun, Roger, Pierce, the wardrobe fittings, the audition . . . everything. Gah.

I would also say I can't believe I barfed on another

human being, and then go into a five minute soliloquy about how embarrassed, humiliated, and disgraced I was that I did so, but I have every confidence that you're a smart person and can figure all that out by yourself. Take it as read, please, that the scene wherein I ralphed in front of everyone is one that will be etched in my mind for decades to come.

Pierce decided the best thing for me after throwing up would be to get some air, so accordingly he hauled me over to the window and threw it open, shoving my upper torso out the window until I had to clutch at the window frame to keep from falling.

"It's just jet lag, jet lag and the excitement of working on such a fabulous project, the poor dear," he rattled off, one hand firmly holding my head out the window, the other on the small of my back as I struggled to maintain my balance. "Tessa always pukes when she gets excited—it's something hereditary. Roger, honey, you just leave those releases with me, and I'll make sure she signs them before she leaves the studio. No, no, she'll be fine, just fine, it's just nerves and excitement and jet lag. You know how Americans are!"

Over the sound of the wind rushing past my ears, men's voices rumbled behind me. Mindful of the fact that Pierce had me doubled over the waist-high window, thus putting me in a position where the first thing anyone who looked at me saw was my butt, I began flailing my arms behind me, trying to catch any part of him that could be used to convince him to release me.

"Certainly, certainly, we'll be there bright and early! Five o'clock! No problem. Yes, I won't forget the releases, just as soon as she has a bit of air we'll get them signed, and then I'll trot her down to the studio to have the interview filmed. Yes, yes, not a problem. Evelyn promised she'll have the corset and all those other bits, as well as some of the dresses, done by tomorrow morning. The rest should be finished in a few days, so don't worry one little red hair on your head—you'll be able to start shooting tomorrow a.m. just as you planned."

"Pierce!" I gasped, my head buzzing as the blood rushed to my brain. "I can't breathe! Let me up!"

"Absolutely, one hundred percent. She is *completely* committed to the project. No, just nerves and excitement. I happen to know for a fact that Tessa doesn't drink. Hates the stuff. Wouldn't touch it with a ten-foot pole. You haven't a worry in the world as far as she's concerned, Rog. Would I lie to you?"

"PIERCE!" I grasped the window ledge with both hands and shoved backward as hard as I could. He suddenly released my head just as the door behind us clicked closed. I staggered backward two steps, then fell onto my butt, luckily well out of the distance of the puddle of guck. "You could have killed me doing that! I couldn't breathe!"

He stood over me, his hands on his hips, his nostrils flaring wildly. "Honey, there are times when I could just strangle you."

I pushed a chunk of my hair that had come loose from my chignon out of my eyes and glared up at him. "Do you honestly think I did that on purpose? Help me up. I feel awful."

He hauled me to my feet (grunting just a little, which was not nice of him), then walked with me to the ladies' room, giving me only a minor lecture on the wisdom of getting so plastered I vomited in front of the man who was in charge of a multimillion-dollar project that could make my life exceedingly pleasant. I ignored thinking too much about the barfing as I staggered into the bathroom to rinse out my mouth, wash my face, and twist my hair back into a reasonable facsimile of a smart hairstyle.

Pierce sent Evan running for fresh coffee as I sat in a tiny, soundproofed room in one of the studios, reading over and signing the documents that would commit me to behaving and thinking like a Victorian for the next four weeks. By the time I drank four cups of coffee, signed the papers, did a (thankfully brief) interview with one of the production assistants, and stood obediently turning this way and that while three wardrobe ladies swarmed me with some really lovely lace-topped linen nightgowns and chemises, I was more than tired; I was dead on my feet. Pierce offered me dinner, but I waved it away, wanting nothing more than the chance to sleep.

I have since then eaten, slept more, and am now having a bath. In a couple of hours I'll be on the train, zipping my way to Cheshire and the town of Worston, where I'll step a hundred and twenty-five years into the past. Me and twenty other crazy souls. And Max, the blue-eyed duke.

I hope he got the barf off his shoes without too much trouble.

—⁓—

Wednesday
September 1
5:31 A.M.
On the train, passing through . . . I have no idea where. About an hour outside London.

Well, this is going to be interesting. Not only do I have a head that feels like it's made up of shards of glass that have been dipped in acid and bonded to laser-mounted scalpels, but I just realized that in four hours or so, I'll be squeezed into a corset that wasn't completed enough for me to try on last night, stuffed into a Victorian dress, and trotted out to meet my lord and husband, stepchild, sister- and brother-in-law, and take over the reins of running a traditional country house in the manner of more than a century past, all while a couple of cameras film everything I do for millions of viewers to see.

Oh, joy.

Well, OK, everything but the part about my head and being filmed sounds like fun. I still can't believe I passed muster, but as I did, I've decided not to worry about my appearance anymore. I mean, Max didn't scream and yell and demand someone skinnier, and Roger didn't seem to find a problem with my pudginess (what a thing to say!), so who am I to point out to everyone that I'm on the hefty side? If they don't notice it for themselves, well, so be it.

Mind you, those millions of viewers are bound to notice. I bet the camera adds fifty pounds to me rather than ten.

So, to while away the train ride and to stop myself from fretting about something I can't do anything about (maybe the corset compressing all my excess flesh will make it disappear?), I looked over the rest of the project material. The photocopied etiquette book I'm saving for later since it looks pretty dense. Instead, since Roger said I was responsible for the servants, I read up on some of the other people who are participating, looked over the house rules, and then perused everyone's duties.

I figured a good mistress knows exactly what her staff is doing, so I started with Michael Lewis, who was taking on the role of third footman, the bottom rung of the male servants.

Third Footman Duties

The third footman rises at six o'clock, washes and dresses himself, makes his bed, and is present in the kitchen by six-thirty, ready to assume his morning duties, which are as follows:

1. Clean boots of the family and upper servants. Boots are to be collected the prior night just before going to bed. As the butler, cook, and housekeeper all rise at seven o'clock, their boots should be cleaned first. Family members rise no earlier than eight o'clock.

2. Empty and scour the chamber pots of all male servants.

Chamber pots? As in *chamber pots?* I started to panic over the thought of chamber pots, then realized that it was no doubt just the servants who had to use them (poor people). I know they had water closets by 1879; probably they were kept just for family use. Whew!

Still, poor Michael the third footman. Having to empty the slops—definitely an icky job. I can't imagine there being enough money to pay me to do that, but I suppose if you had rubber gloves and a clothespin . . . oh, wait, no rubber gloves. Hmm. I'll have to ask Michael later how he copes with this particular duty.

3. The table in the servants' hall is laid for breakfast at eight o'clock. Breakfast is served at quarter after eight. The third footman and second scullery maid clear the table afterward.

4. Attendance at morning prayers (quarter past nine) in the main hall is mandatory. The duke and duchess will preside.

Morning prayers? Hmm. Maybe I shouldn't say anything about being an agnostic.

5. At half past nine, breakfast is taken to Lady Melody and the governess in the day nursery. The trays are collected a half hour later.

6. Assist as necessary the scullery maids and housemaids as they clean the servants' quarters and servants' hall.

7. The table in the servants' hall is laid for tea at half after ten. Tea is served at quarter to eleven. The third footman and second scullery maid clear the table afterward.

So far the grunt footman's job didn't seem to be too bad. The chamber pots aside, that is. I mean, yes, it's a lot of running around, laying tables, taking up trays, but nothing too objectionable.

8. The tables in the servants' hall and housekeeper's room are laid for dinner at quarter to twelve. Dinner is served at noon. The third footman and second scullery maid are responsible for passing around the dishes for the upper servants in the house-

*keeper's room (also known as Pug's Parlor) before
returning to the servants' hall for their own dinner.*

Pug's Parlor! Too cute! I wonder if there really is a pug?
The afternoon duties looked much the same, hauling up
dinner, laying tables, cleaning up, and so forth. I riffled
through the papers until I came to the duchess' duties.

"Everything all right?"

I looked up. A portly young man with a blond goatee
and moustache stood in the door of the compartment. He
wasn't my idea of what a producer's assistant looked like,
but Kip seemed knowledgeable enough. He had met me
at the train station, taking charge when Pierce passed me
on. In addition to making sure I got on the right train, Kip
was also responsible for escorting that part of my wardrobe
that had been completed and several bits of expensive film
equipment that hadn't been sent down earlier. "Everything's fine. I'm just reading up on my duties so I'll know
what I'm supposed to do. It's all a bit overwhelming, you
know? I wouldn't want to screw up and ruin the show."

Kip frowned and gave me a look that was more than
a little jaded. "This project is very important, you know.
You shouldn't have taken it on if you thought you
couldn't do it. There's a lot invested in this, Tessa. More
than just money, time, and reputations. If you think you
can't do the role of duchess justice—"

"Wait a minute," I interrupted, laughing and holding up
a hand. "I was joking, Kip. You know, ha ha? I'm just a
bit nervous about the whole thing—I've never been on a
TV show before. When I'm nervous, I crack jokes."

He snorted, his lip curling in derision. "I told Roger to use
professionals, but would he listen to me? No, he wouldn't,
he just *had* to have common people doing the job. Well, so
be it. It's on his head. I've told Mark Tarvell that the whole
thing would fail unless we had professionals."

"Mark Tarvell?" I asked.

"CEO of U.K. Alive!" Kip snapped. "I know you're a
Yank and all, but that's no excuse for sheer ignorance."

"Whoa, Kip, what bee got up your bu . . . uh . . .

bonnet?" Why on earth was he jumping on my back? I
mentally reviewed everything I'd said to him for signs
of offense, but as that mostly consisted of me greeting
him and a few polite, breathless chitchat things as he
hustled me onto the train, I came up with a blank.

"I'm too busy to stand here and explain it to you. I
have to check on the equipment and your precious wardrobe. If I thought I'd ever see the day when I was nanny
to a bunch of sound equipment and a clueless Yank . . ."
He hurried off without explaining what it was I had said
that set him off.

"Maybe he's constipated or something," I told the
empty compartment, then went back to the duchess' duties.

*1. Crighton, the duchess' personal maid, will
awaken her grace at eight with tea, toast, and the
morning correspondence.*

Well, that sounds nice. I wonder if anyone will actually
send me letters or if someone on the show will write pretend letters to me? And would they film me in bed? The
dressing gown and nightgown the wardrobe ladies showed
me the previous night were gorgeous, all frothy lace and
ruffles and fine linen with white-on-white embroidery. I
thought about objecting to being filmed in such an informal
situation, then decided I might not look too bad sitting in
bed, leaning back against a plethora of silk pillows, lace
everywhere, elegantly sipping my tea and scanning one of
many invitations, my lady's maid hovering attentively.

I might just get the hang of this duchess business
after all!

Hmm. Where there was a bed, there was a bedroom.
I assumed I was to have my own room, since I wasn't
really married to that handsome devil Max, and also because aristocrats more often than not slept apart. Somewhere in the stack of papers was a floor plan of the
house, but I seem to remember seeing that the duke and
duchess had bedrooms separated by a shared bathroom.

Not that I expected a man like Max to be interested in

me in that sort of a way, you understand. Just because I lusted after him the second I saw his picture didn't mean that he'd feel the same way. I mean, I barfed on the man's shoes! Even if he *had* been smitten with a sudden, unexplained passion for me, throwing up on his shoes would have more or less killed any soft, squidgy feelings he had for me. Vomit is the ultimate relationship destroyer.

My face heated up just thinking about it. Since another round of mental self-flagellation would do me no good, nor would it erase Max's first impression of me, I concentrated on my duty list.

2. When her grace rises for the day, Crighton will arrange for a bath in the en suite bathroom, after which she will be available to help the duchess dress and attend to her hair.

That sounded pleasant. Might be nice to be coddled a bit, although I never really have enjoyed other people playing with my hair. Still, I'm sure it won't be that hard to get used to.

What am I saying? Having someone wait on me hand and foot won't be hard to get used to? Yeah, and maybe monkeys will fly out of my butt.

3. Morning prayers are conducted in the great hall at quarter past nine. It is traditional for both the duke and duchess to be in attendance.

4. Breakfast is served at half past nine in the breakfast room. Those partaking of breakfast help themselves from the row of dishes set on the sideboard. Traditionally, the duchess pours tea or coffee for those present.

5. The housekeeper meets with the duchess at ten to consult about the menus for the day and to discuss any other household matters that need the duchess' attention.

Hmm again. What sort of household matters would need my attention? Menus would probably be OK; I saw some when I flipped through the etiquette book. But other matters? Matters like when the sheets should be changed? Oh, well, if I do something horribly wrong, I'll just tell everyone we do things differently in the United States.

> *6. The butler should be informed whether or not the duchess wishes to receive guests (be "At Home"), if she wishes to take the carriage out during the day, or wishes to go riding.*

Oooh! Riding! I'd forgotten about that! There were going to be horses, not just for driving around in the carriage but for riding. Now *that* was going to be fun. I've always wanted to have a horse. I love riding. It sounds particularly aristocratic to go riding every day. Yes!

> *7. Luncheon is served at one o'clock in the dining room.*

Maybe I could work off enough calories riding so I could actually eat lunch?

> *8. Afternoon tea is served at five o'clock in the scarlet drawing room. Traditionally, the duchess pours the tea.*

Tea pouring, twice in one day. What a hard, hard life those duchesses had.

> *9. The dinner gong will sound at eight o'clock. Crighton will assist the duchess in dressing. Dinner is served at nine o'clock in the dining room.*

What? No tea pouring?

> *It is traditional that at the end of the meal, the ladies withdraw to the gold drawing room for coffee and await the return of the men.*

Ah, there it is, I just *knew* duchesses couldn't be let off the hook with only two pourings a day. The thought of those poor little skinny aristocratic arms straining to lift a full teapot three times a day just makes me want to weep. Not!

   10. Crighton will await the duchess in her bed-chamber in order to assist her undressing.

And so to bed, the end of a full and satisfying, if pointless and completely useless, day.
   Oh, yes, I think I could live that sort of a life for a month!

— ∞ —

Wednesday
September 1
9:02 A.M.
My bedroom

I can't breathe! I mean, I really, really can't breathe!
   Crap, late for morning prayers.

— ∞ —

Wednesday
September 1
10:18 A.M.
At the escritoire in the morning room

How long can a human being survive without being able to breathe? I think I see spots before my eyes. I think I'm asphyxiating. I think I'm . . . oh, double crap, I forgot Mrs. Peters, the housekeeper.

———m———

Wednesday
September 1
10:19 A.M.
Still at the escritoire in the morning room

LAST WILL AND TESTAMENT OF TESSA SEE RIORDAN

If I die before the day is out, I'd like all my worldly
goods left to my cousin Cyprian. I hope she sues the
wardrobe department for killing me.

———m———

Wednesday
September 1
12:50 P.M.
*Black-and-gold japanned desk in the scarlet drawing
room, with a candlestick, by Mrs. Peacock.*

Well. This day has certainly been different from what I
imagined it to be. I suppose I had better explain how
things happened in a coherent fashion, rather than jumping around (Corset! Max kissing me! The servants!
Being filmed while Max kisses me! No air! Max and
his lips! Annoying brat child! Max! Max! Max!) like a
deranged jackrabbit.

An aside: What is it with the English and their weird
breakfast foodstuffs? After my bath and a quick nap at
the hotel, I had trotted out in the wee hours of this
morning to find a quick breakfast since my stomach was
still on Seattle time, and found a place that served traditional English breakfasts, which, in addition to the normal eggs and potatoes, included grilled tomatoes and

beans on toast. I ate them because I like to try new things, but still, beans on toast? For breakfast?

Strange breffy notwithstanding, Kip got the luggage and me to the house by eight thirty. The front door was opened by a tall guy in lovely dark green livery with a hard collar and white bow tie, dark hair slicked straight back, and kind of an impertinent smile. I liked him right away. He bowed nicely when Kip, pushing his way past me, told him who I was, but I could see a gleam of rebellion in his eye when Kip ordered him out to the taxi to bring in all the equipment and the trunk containing my wardrobe.

"Just a second," I said, putting my hand on his arm as the man started for the door. "I'm sorry, but I have a terrible memory for people's faces, and an even worse when all I've seen is a picture. You're one of the footmen, right?"

He looked around us quickly, but Roger and his crew had been waiting for us, and they were busy talking to Kip. "I'm *the* footman, the first footman. Teddy Talbot is my name."

"Hi, Teddy, I'm Tessa."

He grinned.

"Oh yeah, Kip just said that, didn't he?" I made a face and waved my hand toward Roger and the crew. "So, how is it? Kind of strange to be filmed doing everything?"

"Not for me, no. I'm an actor, you see." Teddy flashed me another smile, a fake one this time, an actor's smile, the kind where there wasn't anything in his eyes.

"Oh. I didn't think they had any actors here."

He glanced toward the people at the end of the hall, still clustered together and talking quickly. "They don't know. I'm hoping this gig will be the break I need."

"Ah. Well, good luck. Oops. I mean, break a leg."

He bowed again and trotted out to the taxi. I took a quick look around the hall and had just enough time to take in the sights—a high, arched gray ceiling that reminded me of a cathedral, heavy chandelier that repli-

cated the ceiling's arches, marbleized walls of a soft blue
gray, dark wood medievalish chairs, a couple of tables
bearing bowls of flowers, and blue-diamond-tiled floor—
before Roger turned and waved me forward.

"Tessa, my dear, how are you feeling? Better? Good.
Now I would love to take you on a tour of the house,
but there's no time. You must go straight upstairs and
get into your things. Sam—you remember Sam—will be
waiting to film you at morning prayers. Quickly now,
upstairs and get changed. Kip, the sound equipment, you
did remember to bring . . ."

Roger hurried off, waving his hands and talking a mile
a minute. I turned to Sam the cameraman and smiled.
"Is he always like that?"

Sam rolled his eyes. "Always. How you feeling this
morning?"

"Much better. I'm really sorry about that yesterday. I
was . . . um . . ."

"Nervous?"

"That, too. And a bit worse for wear for a liquid
lunch."

Sam's eyebrows rose, but he did nothing other than
to gesture toward the others, still chatting next to two
tremendous metal storks that flanked either side of a
curved inglenook nestled beneath the stairs. "That's
Tabby there in the blue track suit; she's the other cameraman. Beyond her are Matthew and Wilma; they're our
sound crew. It'll be us four who dog your every step."

I grimaced and waved at the others when they looked
my way. They waved back. "Yeah, well, I'm still trying
to get use to that idea. I'm not exactly the sort of person
people want to film, so all this is a bit of a shock."

"You'll do fine," he said, slinging a camera up into
the harness he wore on his chest. "Just be yourself."

"TESSA!"

I turned at the shout. Roger stood in the doorway,
making shooing motions. I nodded and scurried up the
carpeted stairs, stopping when I got to the curved landing that bowed out above the inglenook, halfway up the

stairs. I leaned forward and called down, "I don't know where my room is."

"Down the hall to the left, third door on the left," Sam called back.

"Thanks! See you in a bit."

I barely had the impression of an intricately papered hallway before I found my bedroom. I hurried in, then stumbled to a stop. "Wow! What a room! This is gorgeous! Oooh, is that a fainting couch? I've always wanted to have a fainting couch!"

A woman appeared in a doorway across the room just as I was heading for the blue-and-cream striped fainting couch. "There you are! I've been waiting for an hour for you!"

"Oh, sorry, there was some sort of a delay with the train. You must be Ellis Crighton. Hi, I'm Tessa, and I'm—"

"Late. You will address me as Crighton. We don't have time for pleasant conversation, I have to get you dressed *now* in order for you to be downstairs in time for morning prayers. I assume your garments have arrived?"

Her lips were thinned into such a tight line it was amazing she could force words through them. Then again, maybe it was the way her nondescript sandy-colored hair was scraped back from her head into a meager little bun.

Whoops, my claws are showing. Saucer of milk for one, please.

"My wardrobe, the part that's done, is downstairs. I think—"

"It won't do you any good downstairs, now will it?" Ellis snapped as she bustled past me toward the door. She was wearing what I assumed was standard for a lady's maid in 1879—a black skirt that was draped around the front and gathered behind her knees in a poofy lump, and gray blouse with a high, uncomfortable-looking neck. Poor thing, I'd be snappish, too, if I had to wear such an awfully hot-looking outfit on a warm late-summer day.

"I'm sorry, the footman, Talbot, said—"

She spun around at the door. "Teddy. You must call him Teddy."

"Oh. I thought I was supposed to call him by his surname?"

She made an annoyed sound and held the door open wide. "Didn't you read the book? How do you expect to manage any form of convincingness if you do not adhere to the rules? You must read the book and follow the strictures in it to the letter. In here, Teddy. You took long enough with it. I shall be sure Mr. Palmer hears about this."

Teddy gave me a half-grin as he and another man carried my trunk in. "I had to unload the sound equipment, too, Crighton."

"That's Miss Crighton to you! Only Her Grace may refer to me without a title."

"Righto. My lady—" Teddy said, bowing with exaggerated obsequiousness as he spoke.

"You will refer to the duchess as Her Grace, as you well know. Such insolence does not become you, Teddy. If you continue it, you'll find your time here at Worston very much abbreviated."

Teddy's eyes narrowed and he dropped one end of the trunk as he turned to face Ellis. I decided to interrupt before someone said something they would regret.

"Whoa now, I think we're all taking this a wee bit too seriously, don't you? There's no cameras on us now, so what does it matter what Teddy calls me?"

"It matters a great deal! We have all taken a solemn oath to live just as the Victorians would, and I can assure you that no duchess would ever demean herself by allowing a lower servant to address her in anything but what was due her station. It is vital to this project that each and every one of us adheres to such standards. To do any less would be to destroy everything the rest of us are working so hard to achieve."

"Well, it is just a television show—it's not world peace or anything," I said, sharing a grin with Teddy and the other footman.

"Just a television show? *Just a television show?* It is not just a television show! This is a grand project, an important living history documentary that will provide much knowledge for scholars for years to come. That is, it will if everyone honors the contracts they signed, which, I might add, are legally binding."

I blew out a breath. "Hokay, what say we just let this go and move on. Thank you Teddy and . . . uh . . ."

"Bret. Bret Whitney, Your Grace."

"Hi, Bret. Thank you both for bringing up the trunk. I think you'd better leave now, Ellis—"

"Crighton!"

"Crighton has to help me get dressed, and I'd hate to be late my first day on the job."

Both men bowed again and snickered their way out of the room. Ellis closed the door in a manner remarkably akin to a slam, muttering all the while about people who did not have the proper attitude.

Five minutes later she had all of the undergarments and the dress laid out for me. I used the time to look around the room. The walls were painted a soft biscuit color that was picked up in a red-and-green cabbage rose rug. The bed was not as big as I expected, done in the sleigh style with gold claw feet at each corner. I gnawed my lip as I eyed the blue-and-gold coverlet, wondering if I would fit in the bed. It looked a bit on the short side. A pair of comfortable armchairs sat cozily before the fireplace, and long blue-and-gold draperies pulled back to reveal two full-length windows that framed the fainting couch. A huge mahogany wardrobe lurked in one corner, while an intricately patterned screen boasting a peacock and no less than four peahens hid the other corner of the room.

"All right, let's have you, then," Ellis said just as I was about to peek behind the screen.

"What? Oh, um . . . OK, just tell me what is the order of putting on this stuff, and I'll get right to it, and let you know when I'm ready for you to hook me into the dress."

Ellis' lips thinned even more. "We must first get out of our modern clothes."

I smiled, which was an effort, but I did it. I even kept my voice nice and polite. "Ah. OK, I see we have a little confusion here, so since time is of the essence, I'll just get right to it. You need to leave the room first, then I'll take my clothes off and get into the Victorian undies. After that, you can come back in."

"Your Grace, I am your body servant. That means I attend to your person, oftentimes your naked person. Please remove your clothing so I can dress you in the appropriate garments."

I crossed my arms over my chest. "I appreciate the fact that you're desirous of being as authentic as possible, but there is no way I'm going to take my clothes off in front of you, so the sooner you leave, the sooner I can get into those frilly things."

She took a deep breath, held it for about ten seconds, then blasted me. "Take off your clothes!"

"No!"

"TAKE THEM OFF NOW!"

"What are you, some sort of pervert who likes to see chunky women naked? No!"

"If you don't take off your things now," she said in a low, mean voice as she started toward me. I backed up nervously, eyeing the doors on either side of the room. "I will take them off for you, and I promise you, you won't like that."

"Are you threatening me?" I asked, stunned by the venom in her voice.

"Yes."

The back of my knees bumped up against the fainting couch. I put my hands on my hips and made the meanest face I could. "I am a duchess! You can't threaten a duchess! You can be beheaded or something for threatening a duchess. Hey! Let go of me!"

She yanked on my T-shirt so hard I stumbled forward. Her eyes bore into mine as she leaned forward, hissing. "Take. Off. Your. Clothes. Now."

"Fine!" I said, snatching the front of my T-shirt out of her claws. "I will, but not because I'm afraid of you, but only because I have to be downstairs in fifteen minutes. I warn you, though, if you make one crack, one little tiny crack about my weight, I'll deck you one. And don't think I can't, because I'm at least fifty pounds heavier than you and a good ten years younger."

She snorted, standing in front of me, her beady little eyes narrowing as I started to pull off my T-shirt.

"Well, don't watch me! I can't do it if you watch me!"

She snorted again and moved over to the bed, grabbing a lace-bedecked bit of linen. I peeled off my T-shirt, shucked my jeans, and glared at her defiantly, just daring her to say anything. She just pursed her lips and held the lacy combinations out to me. I took a deep breath and unhooked my bra and pulled off my undies.

I will give her credit. She didn't say anything, although I think I broke the land-speed record for getting into the combinations. For those of you not hip with Victorian undergarments, combinations were so named because they combined a chemise with drawers. My combinations were armless, with lace and a pretty pink ribbon at the bottom of legs (which ended at my knees) and around the neckline, and a line of buttons up the back. There were also buttons on the hips, to which the petticoat (a long underskirt) was fastened.

"Well, this isn't so bad. At least it covers everything important," I said as I looked myself over in the mirror on the dressing table. "Oh, stockings. Thanks. Are there . . . thanks." I took the black garters Ellis soundlessly handed me and pulled on the stockings and garters. "Um, about the shoes . . . the wardrobe people didn't have anything period in my size, so they're having some specially made. Until they get here, I'm supposed to wear those."

I pointed at the jazz shoes Ellis was holding.

She glared at them as if they had uttered an improper word. "These are dance shoes!"

"Yeah, but they took the taps off them. They're the best they could do until the shoes are made."

She huffed for a minute, then snarled that I'd have to be careful not to let anyone see my feet.

"What dress do you think I should wear?" I asked as she tossed the petticoat over my head. It also had pink ribbons and three rows of lace at the bottom.

"The green-and-black walking skirt. It's not entirely appropriate for morning wear, but it will have to do today. I hope the rest of your wardrobe comes tomorrow."

"You seem to be very knowledgeable about all this," I said as she shook out the corset. I held up my arms so she could hook the front together. "I know you normally work as a living history interpreter, but—OW! Hey, wait a minute, you're crushing my boobs!"

I slapped at her hands as she reached for my breasts. "OK, new rule—you're not allowed to touch my breasts. I'll do it."

She sighed the sigh of the heavily martyred while I adjusted my boobs so they weren't crushed in the body of the corset. "Are you finished?"

"Yes," I said with as much dignity as I could muster, which, I have to admit, wasn't a lot. There's just something about someone dressing you in underthings that strips away most dignity. I took an experimental breath as Ellis moved around to the back of the corset. "Well, you know, this isn't as bad as I thought it would be. It certainly does lift and separate the old—eeeeeeuggggh."

All of a sudden the breath was driven from my body. Ellis gave another pull on the cords at the back of the corset, and both my lungs collapsed.

"What are you doing?" I managed to gasp.

"Tightening your corset so you'll fit into the dresses," she grunted, then gave another hard pull on the cords. My ribs imploded into my organs and I staggered backward, trying desperately to get a single atom of oxygen into my now crushed lungs.

"This is ridiculous! I can't possibly go around with the corset this tight! I can't breathe! I know it's silly of me, but I *like* breathing!"

There was one more smaller tug, a tug that made my eyes cross as my waist compressed down to nothing. I thought I was seeing big spots before my eyes, but I realized when I looked down that they were my breasts, hoisted high by the pressure of the corset. "Jeezumcrow, look at that. It's like a breast shelf. I bet I could put a potted plant and a statue or something on them. Crighton, I'm sorry, but you're going to have to loosen the corset up. I can't—oomph!"

A patterned brocade skirt came down over my head. I tried to struggle my way through it, but lack of oxygen was making me woozy.

"It is as tight as it needs to be. You'll get used to it in time. Arms up."

Ellis finished hooking up the brocade and silk skirt (for you fashion mavens, the green-and-black brocade overskirt pulled back to reveal a pretty, patterned, silk pleated front. The bottom of the skirt was matching brocade that ruffled its way to the ground. The back of the skirt was a series of poofy gathered bits of the overskirt, looped and tied at the knees with a matching silk bow), then held out the bodice for me to slip into. The bodice was very pretty—a long-sleeved jacket of dark green with a narrow brocade panel at the front and sleeves, split at the top by waves of frothy ruffles that spilled out over the brocade front and cuffs. It was very feminine and I had to admit that about this, Ellis was right. The dress fit snugly. If I had been laced any looser, I doubted if she would be able to hook it closed.

Of course, that now meant that not only was I *not* going to be able to eat the entire month I was at Worston Old Hall, I would also not be breathing. Still, crushed ribs and not breathing seemed like an awfully small price to pay to have a nonleaking roof and no more hospital bills. Not to mention a month spent with Max the dishy duke.

Hubba hubba.

"Sit there and I'll do your hair." She pointed to the dressing table and blue-cushioned bench that was opposite the bed.

"Oh. Um. You know, I don't really like people messing with my—"

"Sit!"

I sat. Carefully. With extremely good posture—the corset wouldn't bend even a little.

"As you asked, yes, I am an expert on both the Victorian and Edwardian times," Ellis said as she grabbed a silver-backed brush from the dressing table. I pulled my hair out of its scrunchy and sat stiffly, gritting my teeth and hating the thought of her touching my hair. *Ten thousand dollars,* I reminded myself as Ellis tersely trotted out her qualifications. For ten grand, she could touch my hair.

"I should, of course, have been given the position of housekeeper since I am infinitely more qualified for that position than lady's maid, but that position was already filled." She spat out the words with a venom that made me stop thinking about her brushing out my hair.

"Perhaps Roger thought that your talents would be better used here rather than as housekeeper."

She snorted, which had me shifting uncomfortably, not just because I hadn't managed to get air into my lungs for five minutes now, but because her fingers tightened on my hair, pulling it painfully.

"You're hurting me. Do you think you could loosen up a bit?"

"I think a braid is suitable for this morning, around the back of your head, with an artificial rose tucked into it. I take it that will please Your Grace?"

"Yes, whatever, just leave me a little hair left, will you? Ow!"

She stopped yanking my hair through the brush, parted my hair down the middle, twisted either side back behind my ears with two big combs, then started braiding. "The position I deserve to have was not given to me because the woman who obtained it used methods to which I would never stoop."

"Really?" I eyed her in the mirror above the dressing table. "What sort of methods? Did she get naked with the company's president? Blackmail someone influential? Bribe her way into the coveted position of housekeeper?"

Her lips tightened until all that could be seen of her mouth was a thin slit. "Let us just say that she has knowledge of Mr. d'Aspry that could be said to be of a houghmagandric nature."

"Houghmagandric? What's that?"

"Carnal."

"Ah." I gnawed on my lip for a few minutes, wondering if she was unaware that Roger had been Pierce's boyfriend, then figured it wasn't anyone's business. Besides, she probably wouldn't believe me if I told her. It was obvious that Ellis had a bit of a jealousy issue with regards to the housekeeper, and since it was Ellis who would be responsible for doing my hair and stuff, it would behoove me not to irritate her any more than was possible.

Four minutes later she pinned my braid around the back of my head, took out a pale cream velvet rose from a drawer in the dressing table and tucked it into the braid, pinning it firmly into place with wickedly long hairpins.

"You hair is finished. Would you care to apply your own cosmetics, or would you rather I do it?"

I looked at the tray of objects she slid onto the table before me.

"Oooh, neat! Face powder! What's this?"

I opened a small metal pot and sniffed it.

"Rouge. As the author of *The Glory of Womanhood* so correctly states, 'although it is no longer considered vulgar to aid nature, good form does not permit that such artifices be noticeable.' "

"Is that so?" I asked, dipping my fingers into the rouge pot.

"Furthermore, the author reminds us that 'the lady

who feels the need for the bloom of roses upon her cheeks or lips must apply it with infinite care, and not slap it on as if it was mortar between bricks.' Wise words, do you not agree?"

I looked at my rose-blooming cheeks and blinked a couple of times. "Well, I'm colorful, I'll say that. Maybe a bit too colorful. Do you have a tissue or something I can use to take a bit of this off?"

She gave me a hard look and handed me a linen hand towel. I hated to soil it with rouge, but there was no other hope for it. I was running out of time.

Two minutes later I had applied a tiny bit of lip rouge (which came in a small glass pot with lovebirds painted on the top), brushed a bit of black onto my eyelashes in lieu of mascara, splashed on lemon verbena toilet water, and finished it all off with a big poofy powder puff loaded with face powder that unfortunately got all over my bodice.

"Thanks, Crighton," I said after she had finished brushing the powder off my boobs. I stood before the mirror and looked myself over, blinking a bit in surprise at what I saw. The dress was, as expected, very authentic, but the person in the dress—well, I might not be able to breathe, but I had to admit that the corset worked wonders on my figure. The way the dress was draped, along with the compression device, made my waist look much smaller than it really was. True, my boobs were hoisted up higher than they had ever been in their prime, but who was to know that? With my hair up and the ruffles framing my face, I looked . . . mmm, maybe not like a duchess, but at least presentable.

I leaned over sideways and snagged my journal off the closest armchair. The corset creaked warningly at such a foolish attempt at movement. "How much time do I have?"

"It is three minutes to nine. I will return with the jewelry box so you can select what jewels you wish to wear today." Ellis gave me a dirty look before she disappeared into a connecting room.

"Not necessary. The earrings I have on now came from a museum store, so they're fine, and I don't need to wear anything else," I called after her as I sat down with my journal, looking around quickly to see if she would notice I was using my favorite teal pen instead of the nibbed pen that sat next to a crystal ink bottle.

She came back a few minutes later and lit into me for being late for morning prayers, then saw the pen and confiscated that. I thought strongly about spilling my face powder all over the rug for her to clean, but managed, by dint of immense self-control, to simply thank her for her help, and creaked and wheezed my way out of the room and down the hallway to the stairs leading below.

As soon as I started down the stairs, I saw . . . oooh! I have to stop. Max the dishy duke wants me!

Wednesday
September 1
3:18 P.M.
Back at the Escritoire (sung to the tune of "Back in the U.S.S.R.")

It is impossible, impossible I tell you, to eat while wearing a corset. Worse yet, if you do, things happen. Unpleasant things. Embarrassing things.

Did I know that early this morning when I had a big breakfast? No, I did not. I know it now, though. I found out the sad truth when I made my appearance for morning prayers. My debut on film. The first time I met everyone, family and servants. My grand moment, my entrance, just me carefully walking down the front stairs, and about thirty people arranged on either side of the hall watching me descend with swanlike grace.

No, I did not fall down the stairs. How could you even imagine that I did? Sheesh! I walked very carefully and slowly down the stairs, trying to look serene and duchessy, while inside I felt like I was going to explode. Keep in mind that my torso from boobs to hips was compressed, squeezed, smooshed together, pushing everything that normally resided in that space either upward to where my boobs floated before my eyes or downwards to the depths of my pelvis.

I prayed that everything would return to normal once I took off the torture device, a thought that was soon driven from my mind as the camera lights suddenly came on and I realized they were filming me. I forced my lips into what I hoped was a pleasant, not in the least bit terrified, smile, and made it down the last couple of steps without tripping or stumbling.

"Ah, there you are, my dear," Max said, and came forward from where he had been standing behind a man and a woman. He held his hand out for me. "We have been waiting for you. You look lovely, as usual."

I stopped dead when I got a good look at him. In everyday clothes he was handsome, what with his black hair and light blue eyes and nice chin and stuff, but in Victorian clothes—black frock coat and pants, patterned waistcoat, snowy white shirt with high collar points, he was breathtakingly gorgeous. I couldn't keep from staring at him; just the sight of him melted my innards, or what was left of them.

He took my hand and bent over it, his back to the camera, his lips brushing my knuckles as he hissed, "Your mouth is hanging open."

"Gark," I said, staring down at the glossy black waves of his hair, then managed to drag my eyes off him. "Good morning, um . . . uh . . ." My mind was a blank, a total and complete blank. What was his name? Why couldn't I remember it? Come to think of it, what was *my* name?

"Max," he said out of the side of his mouth.

"Max. And . . . uh . . . good morning to the rest of you. Here I am! A bit late, but you know us women, always late!"

I groaned beneath my breath and closed my eyes for a few seconds, horrified by the words that had been chosen by my oxygen-starved brain. My first moment on film and what do I do? I stereotype my own sex. Lovely. Women the country over would now hate me.

"Shall we begin? My dear, if you would just stand here. Melody—"

Max had a lovely voice, not loud by any means, but deep and rumbly, the kind of voice that reverberated around in my bones and set up a kind of thrumming in my groin. Then again, it might have been the corset causing the lower half of my torso to go numb; it was hard to tell what exactly was causing all the gurgly feelings in my nether parts, but I'd rather think it was Max than something so mundane as gas.

I followed when he tugged me over to one of the metal storks guarding the inglenook, and stood there with my head bowed while Max's voice rumbled around the hall. The gurgly feeling increased until I had to admit that no matter how swoony I felt around Max, an attraction toward him couldn't possibly be responsible for the sharp intestinal pains that were at that moment stabbing through my lower torso. I bitterly regretted the beans on toast I'd eaten for breakfast and sent up more than one prayer of my own that Max would hurry up and finish so I could find the nearest bathroom.

A horrendous pain spasmed through me as Max droned on and on and on. I know the prayer only took a couple of minutes, but it seemed like an eternity as I stood next to him, surrounded by strangers, hot lights blazing off the cameras, bound and trussed, waiting for the torment to end so I could seek relief.

". . . May God so protect us. Amen."

"Amen," everyone said. There was a particularly loud rumble from my guts that I hopefully drowned out with my own amen.

Max turned to me and flashed a smile. "My dear, you would like to add something?"

I stared at him in horror, then realized he wanted me to add a prayer, probably something about the family and home. I switched my mind from the worry that I might make public the fact that I had gas to the panic that I was expected to trot out a prayer. Me, the agnostic. "Um. Why yes, Maximillian, I always do, as you know, ha ha. Uh . . . may the Lord bless all creatures great and small, and . . . uh . . . may we all live long and prosper."

"Amen," Max said, with an odd look on his face.

It was at that moment, as the last amens were whispering into nothing, that I wanted to die. A butterscotch-colored spaniel wandered forward from behind the man and woman I took to be Max's sister and brother-in-law. The dog's hindquarters were wagging in time with his tail as he snuffled my dress. For a nanosecond I forgot that I was wearing a corset, forgot that I had eaten beans that morning, forgot that my abdomen was cramping with the effort to contain the burbles of gas contained within, forgot that there were cameras trained upon me. I forgot everything as I bent over to pet the dog.

There issued forth from the pertinent part of my anatomy a noise that could not be mistaken for anything but what it was. I shot upright and turned five million shades of red as I looked wildly around. Utter, absolute silence filled the hall as everyone's gaze shot to me. Max turned to look at me with pure astonishment on his face. I thought briefly about fainting dead away, but I've never fainted before and don't know how to do it, and besides, there comes a time in everyone's life when you are tested, a moment when you learn exactly what sort of person you are. Either you triumph over such moments by sheer bravado and a sense of humor, or you sink into mortification and allow them to taint the rest of your life.

Evidently, my test was farting in front of what represented millions of viewers.

"Who knew they had barking spiders in England?" I called out gaily to no one in particular, then burst into laughter.

Max stared at me for a moment, his face frozen in a mask of disbelief, then his lips twitched twice, and he tipped his head back and howled with laughter. As if that was a signal, everyone in the room joined us, laughing and snorting and tittering and giggling. Even the camera crew was laughing, Sam wiping his eyes, Tabby doubled over, slapping her knee. I hadn't thought it was *quite* that funny, but I was just grateful to have survived the incident without actually dying of embarrassment.

"If you put that on the show, I'll kill you slowly with a pair of cocktail forks, a wedge of lime, and two double-A batteries," I swore to Roger through my own now lessening giggles. He grinned broadly and just shook his head.

"I'm so sorry," I turned to apologize to Max, who was also wiping at his damp eyes. "It seems every time I meet you I have some sort of bodily catastrophe. I can assure you that I'm not normally like this. It's the corset, you see. It's pushed everything around and . . . Well, 'nuff said, right? I mean, I don't really need to go into the mechanics of it all."

"Tessa," Max said, still chuckling. "I can't tell you how glad I am that you are here. You've made me feel a great deal better."

"By having gas? You're a strange man."

"I was a bit worried about today," he admitted. "I'm not used to all this, and . . . well, I was worried that it would be a month of solid tedium. I can see with you around that it won't be."

I grimaced. "Yeah, that's me, Tessa the icebreaker."

"Windbreaker would be more apropos," Max said and leaned close to me, his lips twitching, which of course meant we both went off again in gales of laughter.

"You're a very bad man," I told him, pulling the lacy handkerchief from where I had tucked it up into my sleeve so I could mop up my nose and eyes. "Which is probably why I like you."

He grinned, then glanced toward the cameras, waggling his eyebrows at them. I sniffed back the remnants of laughter, and was about to introduce myself to the others in the hall when Max suddenly grabbed me by both arms and swooped down to kiss me.

OK, now, let's not get excited here. It was a short kiss, a brief kiss, a perfunctory kiss, if you will. It was also a kiss that scorched my stockings off, and left me speechless with amazement, but you don't need to know that.

"Welcome to Worston Hall," Max said in a loud, clear tone, then tucked my hand into his elbow and announced that he was ready for breakfast. The servants scattered at that, the film crew dividing into two halves, one group hurrying after the servants, the other following as Max led us down a passage to a small, sunny room.

"Your mouth is hanging open again," he whispered as he pulled out a chair for me at one end of a table.

I snapped my teeth together, then muttered, "It's your fault. There ought to be some sort of a warning sign taped above your lips. They're too potent for their own good."

He chuckled a sexy chuckle that made my toes curl, then moved off to sit at the other end of the table.

There were four of us at breakfast: Max at the far end, a dark-haired woman who I assumed was Barbara, his sister, on my left, and a big guy with thinning brown hair and more than a little bit of a beer belly on my right. There were also three servants—Teddy the peacock, Bret, and an older man with a long lugubrious face and jutting jaw that I took to be the butler, Palmer. Behind Max's chair, Sam and Wilma the soundperson stood filming us. I fought down the brief spurt of pure nerves, knowing it would only make my gas problem worse, and smiled brightly at everyone at the table.

Palmer limped over and with a dramatic air of one who has completed a mighty task set down a tall silver teapot to my left. He offered me a beautiful china cup seated on an equally beautiful saucer.

"Are you all right?" I whispered to him, taking the teacup.

"As well as can be expected, what with my unfortunate affliction," he whispered back.

"You have an affliction?" I asked, surprised. I hadn't expected that Roger would have hired someone with frail health for such an onerous job.

He pulled his shoulders back and gave me a glare down the long length of his nose. "I have many, Your Grace. Currently, it is my lumbago that is causing me distress."

"Oh. I'm sorry. Is there something I can do?"

He sighed heavily, offering me a silver cream pitcher. "Alas, there is nothing to be done for it. I must bear this cross silently, even while my body is wracked with debilitating pain that would bring down a lesser man."

It was the grim satisfaction that was replete in his voice when he spoke that clued me in to his true nature. I knew a lot about hypochondriacs; I had been married to one . . . until he died of very real cancer.

Palmer turned from me and with one eye on the camera filming Max, quietly asked Barbara how she took her tea.

"Cream, no sugar. Mr. Slough prefers his with two lumps of sugar," she answered, her eyes hard as she turned to look at me. I blinked back at her for a moment, then remembered that I was supposed to pour everyone's tea.

By the time Sam swung the camera around to face me, I was pouring tea like I had been born to it. I even had enough wits about me to say, with much duchessness, "Thank you, Palmer, that will be all. I will ring if I need you."

"As you like, Your Grace. I shall go attend to the

many and varied duties which Your Graces have bestowed upon me."

He made a little bow to Max, one to me, and just stopped himself in time from making one to Sam and the camera.

Max smiled at me in approval of the tea pouring, I hoped. Whatever the source of the smile, it sent my spirits soaring as we all helped ourselves to the breakfast laid out on the blond oak sideboard. Yes, true, I had a few missteps, but all in all, I thought it was going very well. Life was definitely looking up. There wasn't much worse that could happen to me, right? "Oooh, this looks lovely. Peaches and cream, rice, um . . . fish? OK."

"That is Spanish mackerel, Your Grace," Palmer said as he left the room. "It is one of Cook's specialties."

"Num. Mackerel for breakfast, my favorite," I said, momentarily thankful that the corset would keep me from eating anything but the skinniest food.

"It looks very nice," Max said, one eye on the camera. He lifted a cover off a dish and blanched. I peeked over his shoulder, also very aware of Sam standing behind us with a camera waiting to capture every expression. Barbara and her husband (I couldn't remember his name) were scooping up herbed eggs and fried potatoes with little coos of pleasure.

"What do you suppose this is?" Max asked in a whisper.

"I have no idea, but it looks like . . . it looks like . . ."

"A turd."

"Exactly," I whispered, giving whatever it was a wary look. "I think I'll give it a miss."

One corner of his mouth curled up as he gently set down the lid. "I believe that is a good idea. Might I help you to the eggs?"

"Thank you ever so much," I said, parroting his plummy aristocratic tones, then had to beat down an unduchesslike giggle when Sam swung the camera around to me.

"Oh, look, Henry, rusks!" Barbara said as she lifted the lid to the poop pan. "It's been forever since we've had a really well-made rusk. What a clever cook you have, Tessa."

"Why, thank you, Barbara," I said as I took my place back at the table. I guess there is a bit of ham in me after all, because I smiled brightly for the camera and added, "Cook is a find, isn't she? Which is remarkable when you consider her history."

Barbara obviously didn't catch the wink I tossed her. She frowned at me over a forkful of Spanish mackerel. "Her history?"

I nodded as I nibbled at a piece of wheat toast. "Yes. Poor thing, she was raised by a pack of feral hedgehogs. When she was found by a kindly vicar, she was like a savage beast, naked and snarling at anyone who came within snapping distance. She never saw the inside of a house until she was twenty-four, which makes it all that much more amazing that she should have such a firm grasp on the proper way to form a busk—"

"Rusk," Max said quickly, his eyes laughing at me. *With me,* he was laughing *with me,* not at me.

"Thank you. We in the United States *of* America sometimes call them busks, depending on the region, and, of course, what day of the week it is. Regardless of that, it is amazing that Cook has such a grasp on rusk making. I personally have never seen finer specimens of ruskness in all my born days. Max himself was just commenting on the rusks. What exactly was it you said they reminded you of, Max?"

He dabbed at his lips with a snowy white linen napkin, slid a quick glance over to where Sam had turned to catch his expression, and sent me a look that promised retribution in the very near future. "I believe I said the rusks resembled the biscuits my sweet old nanny used to bake."

I smirked and sipped my tea, making a mental note to ask if I could have coffee instead. The tea they served was strong enough to strip paint off a barn. "Just so.

Cook's history is a tragic tale, albeit one with a happy ending, but still, we try not to mention it in her presence. She tends to have hedgehog flashbacks if we do, and as you can imagine, such a thing is not a pleasant sight. All those little grunting noises can quite turn one off one's feed."

Barbara stared at me in open-mouthed surprise for the count of three, then she took a deep breath and more or less ignored me for the rest of the meal.

Breakfast went pretty well, considering. I even forgot once or twice that we were being filmed, and due to the fact that I could fit no more than a teaspoon of food into my compressed stomach, I managed to breakfast without spilling on myself.

Afterward I followed Barbara to the morning room—trying not to wheeze and puff as I climbed the stairs, which wasn't easy, let me tell you!—while Max and Henry went out to examine the stables. Sam and Wilma came with us.

"I thought you might like my assistance with the menus," Barbara said smoothly, making sure she stood between me and the camera. She struck a dramatic pose and lifted her chin, enunciating her words clearly and with the languid drawl I had always connected with the British royals. "Since you are newly wed and have only arrived in England, I'm sure you will welcome a hand running the household."

"Oh, well, I—"

"After all," she said, stomping all over my words as if I hadn't spoken, "as sister to the duke, I have been his hostess since his dear, beloved first wife died, and I am most happy to place my experience at your disposal."

Now, call me catty, but there was just something in her voice that had the hairs on the back of my neck standing on end. Delivered of her declaration, she swanned into the room, waving her hand gracefully through the air as she chattered to the camera about all the (completely made up, unless Max lived well beyond the means of the average architect, and had a handy time-travel machine in his basement) parties and fetes and balls she'd hosted for him.

It was a bit disgusting the way she played up to the camera, and made me vow right then and there that I would not allow myself to do the same. I don't mind playacting a duchess and making up a few harmless details, but I wouldn't be a camera hog. That said, I had to live with this woman for an entire month, which meant I needed a little tact to handle her.

Unfortunately, tact has always been a bit of an elusive quality in me.

"And then, of course, there was the time the Prince of Wales and dear, dear Princess Alexandra—"

"Yes, fascinating, utterly and completely fascinating, so fascinating that I can quite honestly say that I'd rather have sharpened bamboo sticks shoved under my fingernails while red-hot pokers scorched the tender flesh of my inner arms than have you reach the end of such a marvelous tale, but alas, I must not be so selfish as to think only of my own pleasures."

She spun around from where she was pontificating to the camera and focused a glare on me.

I smiled and said politely but firmly, "Thank you so much for the offer of your assistance, Barbara. You are generosity personified, as ever, but I feel the time has come for me to take hold of the reins of management for dear Max's house."

I batted my eyelashes coyly for the camera, then turned to take a quick glance around the morning room, traditionally used by the ladies as an informal sitting room. The walls were done in a soft, muted shade of green, and the usual arrangement of overstuffed sofa, chairs, and at least one hundred and fifty-seven occasional tables dotted the landscape. I made my way through them and headed straight for a lovely dark writing table that I knew from reading lots of historical romances was commonly called an escritoire. Laid out before the intriguing little drawers with teeny, tiny shiny brass handles were stationery, pens, extra metal nibs, and four different glass jars of ink (blue, black, red, and violet). At the sight of the lovely pens and inks, my fingers itched for my journal.

"Pooh, I left my journal up in my room."

"Ring for it," Barbara said, sitting gracefully on the sofa and picking up a bit of linen stretched on a small embroidery frame.

That's right, I had servants now. But I knew from reading their duty list that they all had jobs to do, lots of jobs to do in the morning. I hated to make one of them wait on me, just as if I couldn't walk down the hall and get my own journal.

"No, there's no need, I'll get—"

I stopped when the door opened and Palmer the butler gave me a slight bow of the head, then turned to Barbara. "Mr. Slough has requested your presence, my lady. He is desirous of knowing which horse you would prefer to ride in the mornings."

"Oh, that silly man, he knows I trust his judgment when it comes to my horseflesh," Barbara simpered as she rose gracefully to her feet. I narrowed my eyes and examined her torso. She didn't look in the least bit like she minded wearing a corset. I was willing to bet it wasn't nearly as tightly laced as mine. "Palmer, Her Grace left a journal in her bedroom. Have one of the maids fetch it for her."

"Certainly, Lady Barbara. I will do it this moment—oh!"

Palmer staggered and grabbed the back of the chair, one hand to his chest.

I scrambled to my feet and hurried over to him. "Are you OK?"

"Yes, yes, I apologize for discommoding you." Palmer straightened up, giving me an apologetic grimace. "It is nothing; just my heart. A very minor heart attack, or perhaps a stroke. Nothing to worry about, I assure you."

"Oh, my god," I said, and turned to Sam, expecting that as a representative of the TV company, he'd take charge of emergency situations. Sam cocked one eyebrow at me and kept filming. Wilmà grinned. Clearly, they thought he was in no serious distress.

"Perhaps you should go have a lie down," I said, grasping his arm in case he needed my help.

"I've found that it doesn't do to coddle the servants," Barbara said as she swept out of the room, casting a glance that more or less ordered Sam to follow her. He hesitated and looked at me. I twitched my head toward the door and made shooing motions for him to follow her. He signaled to Wilma, and followed Barbara out of the room.

"Palmer, listen, if you're really feeling poorly, I can call for a doctor or paramedics or whatever you guys have in England. Roger said there's a doctor on call in town just in case someone gets sick. Why don't you go lie down and I'll get Roger and we'll call the doctor—"

He pulled his arm out of my grasp and gave me another down-the-nose look even though I was a smidge taller than him. "I wouldn't think of abandoning my duties."

"But, if your heart—"

"It is nothing I haven't tolerated for many years. If you permit, I will now go attend to Lady Barbara's request."

I opened my mouth to protest, but he stalked out with so much dignity, I figured he was simply enjoying a little martyrdom before the camera. I didn't want to make him look like a fool, so I let him go without comment.

Besides, I had more urgent matters to take care of.

"Bathroom!" I yelped as I dashed out of the morning room, down the hallway, across the landing, and into the next wing, where my room was. My faulty memory was right for once and I found the water closet where I had remembered seeing it on the floor plan.

A minute or two later I returned to the morning room and found one of the maids in there just setting my journal down on the escritoire.

"Hi, we haven't had a chance to meet. I'm Tessa."

The woman looked at me curiously for a moment, then gave a relieved sigh. Her whole demeanor changed from one of wary concern to a pleasant, relaxed stance. "Hello. It's nice to meet you. I thought you would be like the others. I'm Alice Bolton. I'm the head housemaid."

"Like the others?"

She gave a wry smile and tipped her head back so her nose was stuck in the air, affecting a very cultured tone. "Rather stuck on themselves."

I grinned. She did a pretty good job of mimicking Barbara's upper-class drawl. "Your job would be pretty hard to take if we really were living a hundred and twenty-five years ago, but I imagine it's horrible for you guys who are expected to jump every time one of the family snaps her fingers. If you don't mind my asking, what made you decide to do it?"

She hesitated for a moment, then bent over and pulled up her white apron, black skirt, and soft pink petticoat. Although both legs were wearing thick black stockings, one of them was artificial.

"Oh, geez, I'm sorry, I didn't mean to pry or anything. Do you need to sit down?"

She laughed, her hazel eyes twinkling with genuine humor. "You didn't pry, and no, I'm fine. I heard about the project and thought it would be a challenge to see if I have what it takes to tackle a demanding physical job. Ever since the accident that took my leg, I've set challenges for myself to overcome, just to prove to myself and my family that I'm no different than I was before."

"What a noble purpose!" I said, impressed to death. It made me feel horribly mercenary that the only reason I had taken the role was for the money. "That really is inspiring. What a great role model you are to girls everywhere."

She looked a bit embarrassed, then said with a flutter of a dimple in her cheek, "Well, the money also had something to do with my decision."

It was a bonding kind of moment, and by the time Alice left a few minutes later, I was feeling like I had at least one friend in the house.

Palmer interrupted me when I was just sitting down with my journal to ask if I'd see Mrs. Peters, the housekeeper, at that moment or later.

"Oh, shoot, I forgot. Um . . . send her up. Are you . . . uh . . . OK?"

He paused at the door, his left hand going to his right shoulder. "I'm quite well, excepting, of course, the pain in my sciatica."

I thought about pointing out that the sciatic nerve ran down the leg, but decided against it. Why ruin his fun? Instead I went over my list of duties for the day, making a couple of notes of what I wanted to get accomplished:

1. *Talk to Max. Alone. Without cameras. Apologize again for ralphing on him.*
2. *Ditto for the unfortunate gas leak at morning prayers.*
3. *Visit stables to see the horses. Maybe Max would like to go riding this afternoon?*
4. *Go up to day nursery and meet governess and Max's daughter. Maybe Max should be there, too, just to introduce us?*
5. *Ask Max to take me on tour of the house.*
6. *Check out library. Meet rest of servants. Cut corset strings. Go for walk by pond with Max.*

I frowned as I read over my list. The frown wasn't just for content, although I noted with some concern that Max's name popped up on every item, but also because the writing was hard to decipher. There were huge violet blots and splotches, and great big swoops of smeared ink where my finger had touched the wet scrawl. I glared at the pen and pulled the nib off it, replacing it with another one, but it didn't help. Clearly, writing with the pen and ink was going to take some getting used to.

"You wished to see me, Your Grace?"

The woman at the door was not who I had picked out in the hall assembly as housekeeper. This woman was petite with elegant hands, soft, curly light brown hair that defied her attempt to pin it into a bun, and a rather dreamy look in her eyes.

"Hi, you must be Mrs. Peters. You don't have to your grace me when the cameras aren't . . . oh, uh . . . I see. Right. Um, yes, I wished to see you about the menus for the day. Won't you sit down and tell me what you have planned to give us today?"

Her eyes widened as Sam and Wilma sidled around her. She turned with them so her back remained to the camera. Her eyebrows went wild, trying to semaphore something to me, but I didn't understand what. Finally, she nodded quickly toward the chair and made a negative motion with her hand.

I took it that meant that she wasn't supposed to sit in the presence of her betters, which I thought was too stupid for words, but I kept my mouth shut. For once.

"Luncheon will be stewed beef's heart, fried tripe, stuffed baked tomatoes, French bread, sponge cake, and peach cobbler."

I managed to get the look of horror off my face by the time Sam swung the camera around to face me. "Well, now, that sounds like just an indescribably . . . *lovely* menu, but silly me, I neglected to tell you that Max . . . the duke is allergic to beef's heart and fried tripe. Perhaps we could have some, oh, I don't know, chicken or salmon or something else?"

The housekeeper was shaking her head even before I finished speaking. "That wouldn't be wise, no it wouldn't."

"Wise? Why wouldn't it be wise?"

She gave me a pitying look. "The spirits wouldn't like it! They dislike change, you know. They're quite sensitive, and get most annoyed when changes are made harum-scarum."

I started to blink at her odd comment, then decided

I'd been blinking far too much of late, so changed the move to a cocked eyebrow. "Spirits? As in . . . ghosts?"

She nodded, her wispy hair forming a corona around her head. "This house has a great many spirits attached to it, and I would hate to see them upset simply because the duke can't eat the luncheon. There is, after all, dinner."

I tried to look like it was commonplace to be ordering meals around the whims of spirits. "And that would be . . . ?"

"Dinner this evening is beef soup with croutons, boiled fresh cod with Hollandaise sauce, roast partridge, mashed potatoes, spinach with eggs, tomato salad, stuffed aubergine, lobster croquettes, peach meringue pie, tutti-frutti ice cream, rolled jelly cake, and cheese, of course."

"Of course. It's hardly a meal without a great whopping wad of Stilton at the end."

Mrs. Peters bowed her head. "Exactly so."

"I take it this dinner has passed the spirit test?"

"Oh, yes, they quite approve it."

"Really? How do you know, exactly?"

She looked startled, which I thought was odd since I was the one who felt like I suddenly found myself in Wonderland. "They told me so."

I gave in and had a few therapeutic blinks.

"I held a séance last evening in the Pug's Parlor," she explained gently. "I plan to hold them every night. It was very successful. The spirits here have fascinating stories to tell, and they're very pleased to have someone to talk to."

Well, there just really wasn't much I could say to that, now, was there? Mindful of the camera, I just smiled and said, "Wonderful. Sounds like a very commendable project. An idle ghost is the devil's plaything and all that. Perhaps one day you will allow the duke and me to join the séance."

"Oh, I don't think they'd like that," she said with a sudden frown.

I kept the smile on my face even though my cheeks were starting to tire. "Oh? Why is that?"

She all but rolled her eyes. "You're American! Everyone knows English ghosts don't take to Americans! You fought a war against us!"

"Ah. Right. Silly me, what was I thinking? I'd assumed all that had been forgiven and forgotten."

She ignored that and instead said something about showing me around the house, but I wanted Max to do that. After all, it was supposed to be his house; he could do the honors. Right? Right. I'm so glad you're with me on this.

—✺—

Wednesday
September 1
7:40 P.M.
The fainting couch

I formally nominate today to be officially recognized as the longest day in recorded human history. It seems like it's gone on FOREVER and there's still dinner to get through. There's so much I want to do that I haven't had time (or the breath) to do. . . . Oh, well. It'll all be here tomorrow.

Sam and Wilma followed me around for most of the morning. They filmed us at lunch, which was not the success I'm sure the cook was shooting for, as no one but the Sloughs ate the tripe and cow heart. The rest of us—Max, Melody, and me—made do with the tomatoes (which were actually very good), bread, and desserts. I, of course, am now on the corset diet, so I didn't eat too much of anything that would either expand in my stomach or give me more gas. There's only so much humiliation a girl can take before she loses all dignity.

Melody, I hear you asking—what of this daughter of

Max's? I have two words to sum her up: spoiled brat.
Oh, all right, I'll be honest: smart spoiled brat. I met
Melody at lunch, but couldn't let on that I didn't know
her, of course, because the cameras were on. Instead I
just gave her a cheery smile, which she answered by
glaring at me and turning her back to the camera. After
Max helped me to my chair (which, let me tell you, is
something I could really get used to), he held out a chair
for Melody at the spot on my immediate right. She transferred her glare to him and huffed her way into the
chair, arms crossed, face set in a scowl that would have
warned off a rampaging bear.

I understood part of why she was so angry with her
father—she had a large port wine stain over the upper
half of the left side of her face. I sympathized with her
obvious desire to stay off camera . . . sympathized until
she opened her mouth.

"Who's that?" she asked her father, pointing at me.

Max gave her a look that most fathers keep for stupid
questions, and said calmly, "That is Tessa, Melody. You
know that."

"How can I know that? I've never seen her before."

Barbara, sitting across the table from her, tittered nervously. "Oh, now lamb, you know you've seen her, you
were at the wedding. Don't you remember it? It was
such a very grand affair—"

"She's not married to my father," Melody growled.
"He and my mom are divorced."

"Such a rapierlike wit, I can see why you all adore
her so. What a very clever child," I laughed gaily as
Sam, with Roger dancing around behind him, rolled his
eyes. Roger gestured something that I assumed meant
they would cut Melody's comments from the bits to be
aired on the show.

Teddy moved smoothly around the table offering various dishes of food, assisting Palmer. The latter's limp
notwithstanding, theirs was a beautiful ballet of service
made all the more impressive considering they'd only
worked together since the morning.

Melody's high, strident voice pierced my thoughts and the various nummy noises that Barbara and Henry were making as they loaded up their plates. "I hate it here. I want to go home. I'm not having fun at all. *You* said I'd have fun, but I'm not. I don't like Mademoiselle. She pinched me. And this dress is stupid."

Everyone started talking at once.

"I don't see why I can't have my computer. No one would see it. It's not like it would hurt anything to have it."

Max gave Melody another look, one that more or less told her to shut up. I said nothing, but smiled at her.

She threw down her fork and crossed her arms, her lower lip going out in as fine an example of a full-fledged pout as I've ever seen. "The only good thing about this place is the horses, but you won't let me near them. I hate it here! I hate you! I WANT TO GO HOME!"

Max set down his fork with great deliberation and frowned at her. "Melody, if you are finished eating you may be excused. I'm sure Mademoiselle will be happy to give you extra lessons to keep you occupied."

"It's not fair! I didn't ask to be here!"

"I believe I'll take a stroll out to the stables after lunch," I said, feeling more than a little sorry for the kid. A brat she might be, but I knew she must also be homesick. "If you like, Melody, you may accompany me. Perhaps we'll go for a ride."

Her lower lip sucked in just a bit as she turned her angry eyes on me. Her face was flushed red, making the port wine stain stand out in an ugly purple blotch. "I don't want to go anywhere with you. I don't *know* you."

"Melody is not to go riding; she doesn't know how," Max said. "She's not old enough to handle a horse."

"She's not old enough? She's twelve—of course she's old enough."

He narrowed his eyes at me. "In the hands of someone who does not possess the skill or strength to control them, horses can be dangerous. Melody has neither quality, therefore she will not be riding."

Tears glistened in Melody's eyes as she huffed in a way that foretold an explosion.

"There's nothing to riding," I said, trying to defuse the situation. I don't know why I wanted to defend the little brat, I guess it's just the peacemaker in me. "If she can ride a bike, she can ride a horse. I would be more than happy to teach her how to—"

"She is not going to ride, and that is my final word on the subject," Max interrupted, his jaw tense.

"But, I'd be happy—"

"There's no need for *you* to get involved."

"That's just stupid," I said, shaking a forkful of stuffed tomato at him. All of a sudden he didn't look nearly as attractive as he had before. Now he just looked like one of those annoying bossy men who think their opinion is the right one. They're inevitably wrong, of course. "It's obvious she's not happy. The least you can do is make this a bit more bearable for her—"

"It is not stupid, it is responsible. Horses can be dangerous, a fact I well know. I won't have my child endangered just because she's in a pout. Furthermore, I will thank you to keep out of my business. I certainly don't need advice from a woman who has never borne a child."

"I don't have to have given birth to know what's reasonable for a kid and what's not."

"Reasonable?" Max barked.

Barbara sucked in her breath in a manner that said she was both shocked and secretly thrilled.

"You're trying to tell *me* what's reasonable? You? A woman who's been here for less than—" He slid a glance toward the camera pointing at him. "—a few months?"

I slammed my fork down on the table. "Yes, I am telling you what's reasonable, since you seem to be too pigheaded or blind to see it. Melody is obviously unhappy—"

"I don't need you to tell me whether or not my daughter is happy—"

"I'm just trying to help, you annoying man!"

"We don't need your help!" he roared at me.

I bit my lip and ignored the fact that my cheeks were flaming as I stared down into my plate. There wasn't anything I could say. He made it quite clear that this pretend world was to go no further than what was displayed for the camera.

I just wished that knowledge didn't feel so much like rejection.

I didn't look up when Max cleared his throat and said, "My apologies, Tessa. I was out of line. As your step-daughter, Melody is—"

"She's *not* my mother! She's some stranger who is just pretending to be married to you!"

Within me indecision warred, an uncomfortable emotion that spawned a sudden epiphany. There are times in life when you face a point of no return and have to make a decision about how you are going to proceed— either wholeheartedly embracing whatever is facing you or sounding a judicious retreat, skirting the edges, keeping yourself safe from the dangers that the unknown can pose. I've spent the last three years since my husband died avoiding contact with friends and family, immersing myself in research of the dry, bloodless past, backing away from situations that challenge me to interact with others.

Clearly, I was at a point in my life where either I could push myself back into the world of the living—thus leaving myself open to the pain of rejection or worse—or I could step back to a safe distance and participate only on the most superficial level.

I glanced at Max and acknowledged that he held some sort of attraction for me, an attraction I hadn't felt for a very long time. If I wanted to see if it was reciprocated, I'd have to risk my own peace of mind. Did I really want to destroy the layer of insulation I'd managed to build around myself ever since Peter died? Was anything worth the risk of the sort of pain I knew one person could cause another? Could any relationship—assuming there was one to be had—be worth the heartache that could result?

Melody positively radiated anger, and oddly enough, it was that which ended up melting my heart. It was an odd feeling, this reawakening of my emotions, and at that moment I knew that what I had believed to be three years of insulation from the cruelties of life was really nothing more than a slow death. More importantly, the sight of Melody's angry face drove home the fact that these were real people, people whose lives I was touching for better or worse. They weren't just names on a piece of paper, they weren't puppets enacting a part, they were, all of them, people who had good qualities and insecurities and needs and desires and dreams, the same as I had.

Looking between the face of an angry girl and her frustrated father, I realized I wanted to live again, really live, I wanted to experience everything life had to offer to me—the good, the bad, and all of the flavors in between.

It was then that I realized I really hadn't taken this job because of the money; I'd been restless and unhappy for the last six months, fretting for a way to rejoin the world but not knowing how.

"Welcome back to the land of the living," I said under my breath, then used the opportunity of Barbara covering for the argument with tale of a marvelous story she'd read in the *Times* to lean sideways (ignoring the creaking of the corset) and hiss, "Listen, you little monster, either you play along with this setup, or I won't take you riding with me."

Melody's pugnacious little face achieved a level of obstinacy that I had heretofore thought impossible. "My dad says you're not supposed to take me riding."

"Yeah, well, I don't take orders from him, now do I? Either get with the program, or suffer. Those are your choices."

"I hate you."

"You're not my most favorite person on the face of the planet, either."

Her dark blue eyes narrowed until they were little slits of anger, misery, and frustration, all topped off with a huge dollop of self-pity. "My dad will never like you. You're fat."

She delivered the last words with the sharpness of a picador stabbing a bull. I bit back the retort that she was an annoying little snot and instead caught Sam's eye. As he turned the camera on me, I smiled and patted the monster on her head. "Why, certainly you can return to your studies! What an industrious little thing you are. Teddy, would you escort Lady Melody to the schoolroom? She's just itching to get back to work."

Lunch went much better without her, but I was aware the whole time of Max's less-than-happy eyes upon me. Brilliant Tessa, the master at relationships. Hour one of rejoining the human race, and I'd already angered the two people in whom I was most interested.

After lunching on the miniscule amount of food I was able to fit into my compressed torso, I headed out by myself to find the stables. I had no idea what the others were going to do—by that point Max was not saying much of anything, while Barbara did nothing *but* talk. To be honest, I preferred Max's sulky silence to her verbal diarrhea.

The house and grounds really were lovely. I knew it had cost the production company a packet to rent them for the month, not to mention hiding all of the electric fixtures, modern plumbing, and such that had been added over the passage of time, but I certainly thought it was money well spent. Since Max and family had scattered and I didn't know where the stable was, I figured the best bet was for me to ask one of the people in the servants' hall.

I slipped through the green baize door and felt like I'd entered another world. Rather than the rich carpeting, lovely wallpaper, bright paint, and highly polished wood that graced the public rooms, the hall leading to the back stairs was a dingy, depressing place with an ugly brown mat as carpeting, a horribly antiseptic pea-green paint on every available surface, and dark, age-spotted pictures of long-dead servants on the walls. My heels clattered loudly on the bare wood steps as I descended down to the realm of Downstairs.

Noise, billows of steam, and the nose-wrinklingly acid odor of a coal fire swept me into its embrace as I entered the servants' hall. I paused at the foot of the stairs, waiting for a quiet moment to introduce myself, but was immediately sucked into the drama that was being enacted before me.

"Raven, I need that large yellow bowl. Would you hurry up with it?" A large woman with a floury front waved equally floury hands at a small young woman at the sink. The floury woman would be Clara the cook, no doubt.

"Oy! Do I look like I have five hands? I'm washing it as fast as I can but it's not so easy without proper washing-up liquid, you know. And I've got that lot from upstairs to do yet."

A sharp-faced woman stood in the middle of the room with her hands on her hips. "What happened to my eggs? Did someone take my eggs?"

"I suppose you call this clean?" Palmer waved a limpid hand toward a silver salver sitting to the right of where Teddy was polishing silverware.

Teddy looked up. "Yes, as a matter of fact, I do call that clean."

Palmer sighed a long, drawn-out Eeyore sort of sigh. "Thought you would. It's not enough I have to drag my poor aching nerve up and down the stairs all day waiting on the family, now I have to do the silver, too. Ah, well, it's not as if I have much of a future, what with my nerve and the lumbago and the heart attack that's waiting to claim me. I might as well do the silver, as not."

"Eggs! I said eggs! Hello, can anyone hear me?" I gathered that was Sally the kitchen maid waving her hands around for attention, since she seemed to be preparing tea for the servants.

"That you will not do, Mr. Palmer," Mrs. Peters said as she bustled into the room, carrying a large red candle and a stick of incense. "It's Teddy's job to be doing the silver, and do it he will, or I'll be knowing why."

"Look, Peters, I'm not your slave—"

"You will refer to me as Mrs. Peters."

"I put a bowl of eggs down right here. A whole bowl of eggs. Now they're gone. Which one of you took them?"

Teddy ignored her and Mrs. Peters, instead focusing his glare on Palmer, going so far as to poke his finger in the poor man's chest, causing Palmer to stagger back a step. "The only reason I'm doing this is because my agent thinks it'll launch my career, not so you can go all toffee-nosed on me and think you can push me around."

"Toffee-nosed!" Mrs. Peters said, no doubt righteously indignant on Palmer's behalf. The frizzy corona of hair surrounding her head bobbed as she shook her head at Teddy. "How dare you speak to your superiors in such a manner?"

"Ow," Palmer said, rubbing his chest.

Clara the cook turned to where the scullery girls were washing up. "Raven, I can't make the pudding without that bowl."

"You're a bleedin' housewife from Manchester!" Teddy sneered at Mrs. Peters. "Superior, my arse!"

"People, if I don't get those eggs back, there won't be any tea, so whoever thought it would be funny to take them had just better give them back."

"Superior is as superior does," Mrs. Peters said with a testy sniff, then headed for a side door.

Alice the head maid entered the room (and the fray), a huge, shiny brass can in her arms. "Honey, what are you doing with the knives? They go to Michael; he's in charge of cleaning the knives."

A timid-looking young girl in a drab gray maid's outfit

almost jumped out of her skin at the words. "Sorry, Alice. I thought I was to do the knives, too."

"EGGS! Are you all deaf? Who stole my bloody eggs? I don't think it's funny at all, and if you think I'm going to be putting up with this sort of behavior, you can all think again."

"Ugh. Can we open another window? I'm sure breathing in all these coal fumes is toxic . . . oh, hello again."

Alice stopped midway across the servants' hall when she caught sight of me standing at the foot of the stairs. Silence fell like a week-dead flounder.

I rallied a smile and took a couple of steps into the room. No one moved a muscle; it was like they were all playing a game of statues. "I hope I'm not disturbing anything. Nice to see you all—I'm sorry I didn't have a chance earlier to meet you, but it's kind of awkward with the camera guys and all. I'm Tessa, and in case you didn't know, I'm playing the role of the duchess. I've met a couple of you—hi, Teddy, hi, Bret—but haven't had the pleasure of meeting the rest of you. I thought I would just pop in and say hi before I toddle off to the stable. So . . . um . . . hi!"

Palmer, looking faintly scandalized, limped forward. "Generally, it is understood that the lady of the house tells the butler or housekeeper when she plans on making a visit downstairs. I will, of course, take full responsibility for being downstairs here when you had need of me upstairs, and can give no excuse other than the sharp pain in the region of my kidneys—"

"No, no, you did nothing wrong, and heaven knows if you're having kidney pain on top of everything else you should probably be sitting down. In fact . . . er . . . maybe this job is too much for you. I mean, your health has to come first. If you like, I can talk to Roger—"

Palmer's shoulders straightened as he leveled an outraged look at me. "I assure you that I am perfectly capable of fulfilling my duties, Your Grace. If you have a complaint about my service, kindly address it to me and I will strive to do whatever it is you want of me."

"But—"

"What's going on out here?" Mrs. Peters asked as she reentered the servants' hall. "Your Grace, what are you doing downstairs?"

"She's trying to do Mr. Palmer out of his job, that's what she's doing," Raven the scullery tattletale said with a smirk thrown in my direction. "She wants to tell Roger that he's not fit to do the job."

"I am not, I just want Palmer to—"

"Well!" Mrs. Peters eyed me from the top of my head to my toes. "I'm sure the spirits will be most interested to hear about your attempt to do an honest, hard-working man out of his livelihood."

Oh, great, now she was going to sic her ghosts on me. "I am not trying to do him out of his—"

"It's difficult to please those who are in possession of perfect health," Palmer told Mrs. Peters. He had a certain morose sense of satisfaction about him that redoubled my conviction that he was shamming us all. "They don't understand those of us who are cursed with a more delicate nature."

"Shameful, that's what it is, completely shameful, Mr. Palmer," she agreed.

"OK, right, reality check time! First off, I'm not trying to get rid of anyone, I'm just worried about Palmer's health—" I held up my hand to stop both him and Mrs. Peters from interrupting. "—but if he says he's fine, end of story. I certainly won't say anything to Roger. Next, and more importantly, can we remember that this is all pretend, and that no one's livelihood actually depends on the month here?"

"That's not what my agent says," Teddy said, flicking a dirty linen cloth over a pair of candlesticks.

"Fine, I'll amend my statement to pertain to those of you who aren't using your time on camera as a means to finding another job. Now that I've been filled in on the proper etiquette of why it's wrong for me to come downstairs without making an appointment, can I please put some names to faces?"

Most of the indoor staff were present, with the exception of Mademoiselle Beauvolais, the governess, and Ellis. Mrs. Peters introduced the remainder of the staff in turn: Clara Billings, who was our cook (the flour-covered small woman with thick Coke bottle glasses), Easter, the second housemaid (tall, gorgeous, blond, could easily be a model—I made a note to talk to her later and find out why she had signed herself up to be a housemaid for a month), Honey, the third housemaid (shy-looking girl of about eighteen), Raven and Shelby, the two scullery maids who weren't looking too happy at the moment (could very well be the mountain of dirty dishes that they were washing), Michael, the third footman (nice eyes, going prematurely bald), and a weedy, unhappy-looking man sitting in the corner who was introduced as Reg Crighton, the valet.

"Crighton as in Ellis Crighton's husband?" I asked.

He bobbed his head a couple of times.

"Oh, how nice for you to be able to share this experience with your wife," I said politely. He murmured something about it being a thrill, and hurried off with one of Max's suit coats to press.

"It's lovely meeting all of you, and I'd like to say just how much I appreciate you taking on what I'm sure are perfectly ghastly jobs, and if there's anything I can do to make it a little bit less ghastly, just let me know."

Teddy grinned and Alice gave me a weak smile, but the rest of the staff just looked uncomfortable. I didn't know if it was because I was American or because I was representing Upstairs, or maybe they just didn't like me personally. Whatever it was, I felt as uncomfortable as they looked, so after asking directions to the stable, I hustled out of the servants' hall as fast as my corset would allow.

"Hello. You're not going to lecture me about what I should and shouldn't be doing, are you?" I asked the brown spaniel who was lazing about on a patch of sun-warmed cobblestones. His abbreviated tail thumped a couple of times. I wanted to pet him, but that would mean I had to bend over, and I wasn't sure the corset would let me do that. I ended up squatting down in a singularly ungraceful fashion and managed to give his head a few pats, as well as read the tag on his collar. "Ah. You're a Toby. Why didn't I guess? Don't tell me, you're owned by the Sloughs, right?"

"That he is." A man's voice came from behind me. I tried to turn as I got to my feet, but my skirt got tangled around my ankles and my corset objected strongly to me making any sudden moves, both of which resulted in me falling backward onto my butt. A pair of polished dark brown leather boots stepped into view. I followed the boots up to a pair of cocoa-colored breeches, up higher to snowy white shirt with gray suspenders, the sleeves rolled up to show strong, tanned arms, up higher still to a good-natured face topped by a thick mop of curly dark blond hair. The man grinned and stuck out a large hand to help me up. "Sorry, didn't mean to startle you. You didn't hurt yourself, did you?"

"Just my dignity, and that's taken a fairly big whack today, so nothing else can do much damage to it," I grumbled as I allowed him to pull me to my feet. It took a minute, not because he had any problems doing so, but because I had to first stop staring up at him. Max was breathtakingly gorgeous in his black frock coat and waistcoat and all, but this man was . . . seductive. Alluring. *Earthy.* He looked like he walked straight out of the pages of *Tom Jones.* I was willing to bet he could charm the undies off a nun. "You wouldn't happen to be Alec the coachman, would you?"

"In the flesh," he said, flashing me another one of those grins that made me very aware of the fact that I was a female and he was a male, and hoo, baby, was my girl equipment aware of his boy equipment.

I gave myself a brief, very brief lecture about lusting after a man who was probably young enough to be a really, really younger brother, and firmly told my uterus to stop twitching and behave itself.

"You're the Yank duchess. The one that . . . eh . . ."

"Yes, the incident at morning prayers. I was kind of hoping everyone would forget that."

"I thought it was pretty funny. It was a *gas*." He went off in a gale of laughter.

I smiled weakly. "Yes. Very funny. Ha ha ha."

"Ho, don't get angry, I'm just *pulling your finger*." Off he went again, holding on to his stomach while he laughed his guts out. I waited until the worst of it was over.

"Yes, thank you. I'm so glad you found it funny enough to laugh your spleen up. About the horses—"

"Well, you don't have to get *whiffy* with me about it!"

He doubled over, snorting in between howls of laughter. I resisted the urge to plant my foot on his extremely attractive behind. "Very clever. Truly, one cannot ever have too much flatulence humor. If you've finished, however, I'd like to talk to you about the horses. I'd like to go riding, and—"

"It's an *ill wind* that does no one good."

I sighed and waited patiently for the paroxysm to pass.

"Finished?" I asked as Alec wiped his eyes on his sleeve.

"Yes."

"Are you sure? I wouldn't want you to injure yourself by holding back a *cutting the cheese* comment."

He snickered for a minute, then took a deep breath. "Oh, God, that felt good. Haven't laughed that hard in a long time. You're wanting to know about the horses, then?"

"If it's not too much trouble."

"No trouble at all—that's why I'm here. Come along, we'll take a look at them. They're beauties, all of 'em." Alec stuck his hands in his breeches pockets and strolled off toward one of the outbuildings. I followed behind, thinking that *earthy* was exactly the right word to describe him and wondering how long it would take before the women playing the housemaids got into an argument over him.

Alec introduced me to the horses, all five of them. Two were used only with the brougham (the big carriage), but two of the remaining three did double duty as riding horses and horses that could be used with the gig and dog cart. The fifth horse was a particularly bad-tempered stallion named Abou who was intended for Max as his mount.

"Thanks for the tour, Alec. I think I'll go with Talisman, unless you think Penny would be better."

"You done much riding?" he asked, his curly blond head tipping to the side as he studied me.

"Lots. My brother-in-law has a cattle ranch. My husband and I used to spend our summers on it."

"Ah," he said, and absentmindedly scratched his crotch. At least I hoped it was an absentminded gesture and not some sort of subtle come-on. Not that he'd be coming on to me, since I was at least fifteen years older than him and probably a good twenty pounds heavier, but if he was, I hoped he wasn't, because I had no intentions on finding out just what exactly what he knew about *riding,* if you get my drift. If you don't, well, it's a double entendre, and we'll just leave it at that, shall we? "Penny was meant for any novice riders in the house. If you've experience, you'll like Talisman better. When you want to take him out?"

"Oh . . . um . . . probably tomorrow. Early morning? Before breakfast?"

He studied the tips of his boots for a minute with a puzzled frown. "I'm supposed to feed and groom the horses first thing in the morning."

"Oh, sorry, I forgot the schedule. I have one, too. Drat. I'm not supposed to get up until eight, but . . ." I gnawed on my lower lip for a minute. "Listen, Alec, I know how to saddle a horse. What say I trot down here about seven and take Talisman out for an hour? I'll have him back in time for you to make him look pretty, and then I can pop upstairs and be where I'm supposed to be. Does that work for you?"

"I can have him ready for you at seven," he said slowly, then he winked at me and nodded toward the house. "What they don't know won't hurt them, eh?"

I hated to enter into a conspiracy, on the very first day, against Roger and the team he had assembled but I have always loved early morning rides, and it seemed like a heaven-sent opportunity to get away from everyone for what I suspected was going to be a much needed sanity break.

I wheezed my way back to the house, making a brief stop to tour the front gardens, then played cat and mouse with Roger and Tabby, wandering around the house by myself, happily spending an hour in the library looking through the period magazines and newspapers Roger had provided. Tea was another filmed session. I had a slight tussle with Barbara over who would pour (I won by virtue of being stronger than she). She paid me back by ignoring me during the tea, chatting vivaciously with her husband (who looked bored), and Max (who wouldn't meet my eye), batting her eyelashes and sending sickeningly coy looks to the camera. Tabby rolled her eyes when I peeked at her over my teacup, which made me swallow my tea wrong. I hope Roger appreciates the five minutes of film of me coughing and hacking and trying desperately to get some air into my lungs while at the same time getting the tea out of them.

By the time tea was over, I knew I had to do something about Max. He was not just avoiding looking at me, he looked downright miserable. Yeah, I know what you're going to say—it was none of my business if he looked unhappy or not, but remember the epiphany I had earlier? Well that made it my problem, especially since I had a suspicion I had something to do with his grouchy look and refusal to look me in the eye.

"Can I talk to you for a minute?" I asked as we left the scarlet drawing room.

His lovely black brows pulled together in a frown.

"Oh, come on, Max, it's just for a minute. You can time me if you like."

He slid a glance over my shoulder to where Tabby was following Barbara and Henry out of the room.

"I'm afraid that's impossible. I have work to do. If you will—"

"Work?" I asked, grabbing his arm and hauling him into the alcove over the stairs so Tabby and Matthew couldn't pick us up on the microphone. "You're supposed to be a duke, what *work* do you have to do?"

His eyes met mine for the first time all afternoon. I didn't flinch at the look, although I wanted to. I swear there were little icebergs floating around the blue ocean of his eyes. "Regardless of what you think, I have work to do. I can't let my business suffer just because I'm doing this for a month. Then there's the estate accounts—Roger dumped the Worston's books in my lap and told me I have to run the bloody place for a month. If you have experience running an estate this size, you're welcome to do it. Otherwise, I must."

"Oh, geez, sorry, I didn't know."

"Yes," he said grimly, shaking off my hand from where it was gripping his sleeve. "There's quite a bit you don't know."

He stalked off, leaving me open-mouthed with surprise, anger, irritation . . . and a raging desire to grab his head and kiss the snarl right off his lips.

"Well, I wanted a challenge. I guess I have one," I said softly to myself as I watched Max's back disappear down the stairs.

"Tenner says she doesn't get him," Matthew said behind me.

I turned to glare at him. Tabby looked from the stairs to me, her dark gray eyes coolly assessing what she saw. I lifted my chin and looked right back at her, a slow smile curling her lips. "Fifty says does."

"Fifty? You're on." Matthew said with an obnoxious smirk. He looked back at me and smirked even more. "This ought to be good."

—ᴍ—

Wednesday
September 1
10:23 P.M.
Curled up in bed

Have I mentioned the toilet facilities? I figured there
was a bathtub behind the screen in my room, but it turns
out the connecting room between Max's and my room
is the bathroom. That's *bathroom* as in a room containing a bathtub and a sink and nothing else. The toilet
was an authentic water closet, situated at the end of the
hallway in a tiny little room that had probably originally
been a maid's room.

I discovered the WC earlier in the day, at the same time
that I discovered that Victorian ladies' drawers might have
been split for convenience, but managing skirt, underskirt,
petticoat, and drawers while corseted to the point that it
was impossible to bend does not make for a happy experience. The WC itself was actually very pretty, done overall
in a blue magnolia design with a polished oak seat, no
doubt worth a fortune to some antique collector, an irony
that didn't escape me as I put it to its traditional use.

Without putting too fine a point on it, I was thrilled
to find I was correct with regards to the WC situation—
it was for the family's use, and thus I wouldn't have to
use the commode that sat behind the screen in my room.
Ick. It just wasn't worth thinking about.

So here I am, all tucked up in bed, having spent a
good fifteen minutes scratching every inch of my torso
after that tortuous corset came off.

Ellis had been less than sympathetic after dinner when
I made my way back to my room and rang for her (I
have to admit it was a bit fun to ring for a servant).

"I take it Your Grace is ready to retire for the evening," she said sourly as she closed the door behind her a minute after I rang for her.

"How did you do that so quickly?" I asked, frankly astonished. "You had to run up two full flights of stairs and down the length of most of the house, and you're not even breathing hard! I had to take an air break coming up from the dining room."

Her lips turned up into what was probably a smile, although I wasn't willing to bet money on it.

"I am quite used to wearing a corset. I find that it improves my ability to function efficiently. The benefits of good posture on productivity have long been overlooked."

"Ah. Well, I'm more than ready to get this steel abomination off my body."

She grimaced at my word choice, but with only a minor lecture about how I'd get used to the corset in time, she removed the red-and-pink velvet evening dress I'd donned earlier. It took ten minutes to strip me down to my combinations, at which point I tried to dismiss her.

"Your Grace will please remember the discussion we had this morning," she said with more than a little menace in her voice.

I held up one hand, the other being used to scratch my stomach and sides. "OK, time for a deal—I let you dress me in the morning and for dinner, and you let me put myself to bed. I can get into my own jammies."

"But—"

"And I can comb my own hair. I've been doing it for years, now."

"I cannot allow—"

"Yes, you can," I said, haughtily looking down my nose at her. "If you don't agree to leaving me alone after you peel off the Compressor, I promise you that I'll get dressed by myself every single day."

Her nostrils, normally thin and pinched-looking, flared. I smiled. I knew I had her. "Do we have a deal?"

"It is not at all within the guidelines of what is permissible for a duchess—"

"Yeah, yeah, I know, but chalk it up to American eccentricities, OK?"

She took a deep breath. "Since you insist—"

"Great!" I said, pushing her toward the door. "Thanks! I'll see you tomorrow at eight. Have a good night!"

The serious scratching took place as soon as I closed the door and turned the lock (just to make sure she didn't come back in to force me into my nightgown). After peeling off the combinations and having a good scratch, not to mention a quick check of my ribs in the mirror to make sure they were still in the proper positions, I decided a bath was in order. Fortunately, the bathtub had taps, which meant I wouldn't have to bother anyone to bring me water.

I slipped into a filmy lace-and-ribbon-bedecked creation that my grandmother would have called a peignoir and spent a moment in appreciation of the wardrobe ladies. I twirled around the room a couple of times, feeling girly and feminine and sexy, then scooped up the matching (equally lacy and ribbony) nightgown.

I belted out a few stanzas of "I Enjoy Being a Girl," then danced a seductive dance to the bathroom, chuckling to myself. "This little outfit brings new meaning to Victoria's Secret."

"Do you think so? I'd say it leaves little left secret."

I spun around, my frothy nightie falling from where I was about to hang it on a hook.

Max was in the claw-footed bathtub. Naked. Wet. With one soapy knee showing above the rim. My tongue cleaved to the roof of my mouth as my eyes bugged out while they took in the magnificent sight of his bare chest. His wet bare chest. All if it, every blessed square inch of it, and there was *a lot* of chest.

"Um," I said, my brain having overloaded and gone into emergency shutdown at the first appearance of carnal thoughts about a man I'd met just the day before.

"Was that you singing?" One glossy black eyebrow raised in question. "You have a lovely voice."

"Um."

"I didn't recognize the song, although I agree with the basic sentiments."

"Gark," I said, just for variety.

Max's beautiful chest rose as he took a deep breath. My tongue swelled up and filled my mouth as one bead of water broke free from his collarbone, swept down the swell of his pectoral muscle, winding its way through the scattering of dark hair, pausing a moment to cling to the very tip of a little brown nipple nestled in the damp curls before it flung itself off the edge and rolled down his belly, finally merging into the soapy water that lapped at his belly button.

I seriously thought I was going to pass out from the desire that exploded to life within me.

"Is there something in particular you wanted, Tessa, or did you come in here just to ogle me?"

"Can I?" I asked breathlessly, gathering up the lacy peignoir in order to plop myself down on the curved corner of the tub next to the taps.

He stared at me for a moment, then waved a hand around at the water. "I'm taking a bath!"

"Yeah, I know. You do it really well."

He looked like he didn't know whether to yell or laugh.

"Laughter's better for you," I pointed out helpfully, then leaned over and snagged the sponge that was floating around his knee. "Want me to wash you?"

"What?"

"Wash, you know," I held up the sponge. "I'd be happy to do your back. And your front. And, um . . ." I couldn't help but study the water that hid his lap from me. It was too soapy to see through, drat it all.

"Tessa, I . . . I . . ." He blinked a couple of times, then made a helpless gesture with his hands and let them fall. "I don't know what to say. I've never had a woman proposition me while I was taking a bath."

"Oh, I'm not propositioning you," I said quickly. "I'm not suggesting we have sex. I'm a widow, you know."

Both his eyebrows went up. "I didn't know."

"I am, and although my husband's been dead for three years, and he told me over and over that last year that he wanted me to find someone else after he was gone, I'm not ready for that. Sex, that is. Well, I am *ready* for it, I mean. I'm only thirty-nine, and there's times when I'm really . . . Well, you can imagine. So I'm interested in it, and I like it and everything, but emotionally, I'm not ready to take that step. It's a *big* step, you know."

"I know," he said.

"Do you? Most men don't. Most men think with their penises. At least the ones I know do."

He leaned back in the tub, his arms stretched along the sides. I really liked what that movement did to his chest.

"You don't look thirty-nine."

"Really?" I looked down at myself and noticed that the peignoir was almost transparent where the water dripping off the sponge had dampened it. A little thrill went through me at the look in his eyes, leaving me feeling very naughty and wicked. "It's because I'm . . . um . . . you know." I waved a hand vaguely over my torso.

He frowned. "Brunette?"

I gritted my teeth. Did I have to point this out to every man I met? "Chunky."

He looked the available parts of me over. "You're not chunky."

"I am, but that's sweet of you to say I'm not. How old are you?"

"Thirty-four."

I dropped the sponge. "Oh, my god! You're five years younger than me!"

His eyebrows bobbed up and down as his soapy knee disappeared into the water. "Is that a problem?"

"You're just a baby! I can't think about seducing you if you're five years younger than me."

He opened his mouth to say something, closed it,

shook his head, then said, "I thought you said you weren't propositioning me."

"I'm not, but I can think about it, can't I? Except now I can't."

"Because you're five years older than me?"

"You don't have to say it like *that*," I said, frowning. "You make me sound ancient when you say it that way."

"My apologies. I can see that you're anything but ancient." His eyes dipped to where my breasts were thrusting themselves forward against the silk of the peignoir, demanding that I put them into his hands.

"Are you ogling me now?" I asked, aware of the warmth that started at my chest and rippled down to my groin, but ignoring both it and my breasts' demands.

"Yes, I am. I thought it was only fair."

"Oh. OK. I just wanted to know. I'm afraid I'm not as good to ogle as you are. I don't suppose you'd like to stand up and let me see the rest of you?"

He stared at me for a minute, then laughed. "Tessa, you are one in a million."

"Is that a no?"

"No, it's a compliment. If you want me to stand up, I will, but I will warn you, I might shock you."

"Really?" I looked him over, the parts I could see. Everything looked fine to me. "Why, do you have three balls or something?"

He laughed again, then suddenly lunged forward and got to his feet.

"Oh! I see! You meant I'd be shocked because you were—wow. It's been a long time since I've seen one of those. Hoo!"

"Three years?" Max asked, standing in the middle of the tub, water and soap caressing his flesh as it slithered down his body.

"Longer. Peter—my late husband—had cancer for two years before he died. He was sick most of the time. Boy, you're really . . ."

"Aroused?"

"Big." I eyed the rest of him, feeling it was only polite to ogle all of him, not just his chest and penis. "Are you really, or do you just have to pee?"

"Am I aroused?" Max looked at me like I had breasts sprouting off the top of my head. "Isn't it obvious?"

"Not if you mean I am the one arousing you. You've been mad at me all day, Max. You can't tell me you can be mad at me and be thinking naughty thoughts about me at the same time."

Max took another deep breath and closed his eyes for a couple of heartbeats. I liked what the deep breathing did to his chest. It also made the friendly part of him wave. I waved back. "Tessa, would you like to go into my bedroom and continue this conversation?"

I thought about it for a moment. "Are you propositioning me now?"

"Yes, I am."

"Ah. That's very sweet of you, but I'm going to have to say no. I'd like to, don't get me wrong. You're making all sorts of parts of me that I'd forgotten about do some lovely, warm things, but as I mentioned, I'm a widow."

"You want me."

"We just met," I pointed out. "And there's the age difference. I couldn't possibly sleep with someone so much younger than me."

He took a step forward, put both hands around my waist, and hoisted me up and into the tub, pulling me forward until I was pressed up against his warm, wet body. The sheer silk of the peignoir didn't stand a chance—it sculpted my flesh like a lover's hands.

"You want me," he said again, his voice a low rumble deep in his chest that I felt all the way down to my toenails.

"That, sir, is an understatement," I whispered as he started nibbling on my neck, his hands skimming down my back to my hips, pulling me tighter against him.

"Good. I want you, too."

"You can't want me," I gasped as his mouth found a lovely spot on the side of my neck. The steam of the bathwater was nothing compared to the inferno inside me, an inferno that he'd started without even touching me. My hands, of their own accord, I'll have you know, slid up the slick, wet planes of his chest. They did a little dance, enjoying the feel of him, the ripple of muscles as his arm tightened around me, the silken slide of his flesh as they swept higher, swirling momentarily over two adorable nipple nubs, then up to the long, sleek muscles of his shoulders. The smell of the soap mingled with something that I realized was a scent unique to Max, a spicy, tangy scent that made my knees turn to pudding. "You're angry with me, remember?"

"I'm not *that* angry," he said against my jaw. I turned my head until my mouth was almost touching his, his breath mingling with mine, his eyes no longer cold and chilly but burning with sapphire heat that fueled my inner fire even higher. I wanted to kiss him, wanted to do more than just stand in a bathtub, my hands on his shoulders. I wanted to touch him, to caress every wonderful sweep of muscle, to taste him, to welcome him into my body . . .

"Thank you," I said, swallowing back tears that came out of nowhere. I stepped carefully out of the tub, turning back to wring out the bottom six inches of my peignoir.

Max tipped my chin up, his thumb sliding to my cheek to wipe away one of the tears that escaped. "Why?" he asked.

"Why don't I want to go to bed with you, or why am I crying?"

His eyes were still warm, but there was puzzlement in them, too, and a touch of wariness that did much to cool the fire he'd started in my blood. "Both."

I tried my best to smile, but I doubt if it was very convincing. "I do want to go to bed with you, don't get me wrong, I'd have to be dead not to want that, but I've never been the *hop into bed with a sexy guy the second you meet him* sort of person, and it's too late for me to change now. I mean, sex is all well and good, but . . ."

"It's better when there's something else to it?"

I nodded, and sniffled back a few more tears before wringing out the front part of the peignoir. "I didn't think men realized that. I'm not interested in a fling, Max. I like you, and heaven knows my body is demanding an immediate and thorough introduction to yours, but I don't think it would be a good idea for us to, um, do anything."

His thumb stroked a line down my throat. "If that's the case, why are you crying?"

Tears immediately pricked the back of my eyes. I frowned down at the wet material wadded between my hands. "Because . . . because you're nice enough to get an erection over me."

"Tessa—"

I sniffled and looked up when his thumbs slid under my jaw. "Despite you being polite and all, I *am* chunky. I know men; they like skinny women. Even Peter, who was a wonderful husband, liked thin women. Which makes it particularly nice that you'd lie about liking—" I waved my hand around my stomach.

His fingers trailed a path down from my jaw to my collarbone, then down lower to the valley between my breasts where the first of five pearl buttons held the peignoir closed. I didn't realize what he was going to do until he had two of the buttons opened and was starting on the third.

"I don't think that's a good idea," I said, dropping my wet hem to grab his hand.

"Why?" he asked, tipping his head to the side in that cute way he had. "You wanted to see me naked, it's only fair I should see you."

"I'm not nearly as nice-looking naked as you are."

He leaned forward to kiss me, but I couldn't let him. I turned my head a little, just enough so that his lips were grazing the corner of my mouth. Beneath my hands, his fingers slid another button through the opening.

"Max—"

"Hush."

"No, I can't. I mean, you'll be disappointed, and then I'll . . . woobah!"

Max's hand slipped inside the half-opened peignoir and cupped my breast. Damp tendrils of his hair slid against my skin as he pushed the silk off my shoulders, his mouth following his hands as both trailed fire across my breasts. The peignoir gathered on my hips for a moment before a sweep of his hand sent it down to my ankles. I stood there naked, totally naked, naked in front of a man I'd just met, my fingers digging into his biceps as he kissed a path from one breast to another.

He stepped back and eyed me, all of me, every last bulge and curve. I thought momentarily of shoving him into the tub or throwing a towel over his head or clamping my hand over his eyes, but in the end I just stood there, my breath caught in my throat, my heart pounding with long-unfamiliar emotions.

He finished his examination and smiled, stepping close again. "I think you're lovely. I don't seen any part of you I'd describe as chunky. You're soft and warm and round in those areas that women should be round."

"That's the nicest thing anyone's ever said to me," I sniffled, then burst into tears. He held me, his arms a comforting strength behind me, his hands gently stroking my bare flesh. He was still aroused, still hard as he pressed against me, a fact that made my tangled, confused emotions that much more complicated.

He nuzzled my neck, nipping at my ears and scattering kisses along my jaw until I stopped crying. Twice he tried to kiss me. Both times I turned my head.

"There are times when I think I'll never understand women, and then there are times when I believe it's more fun not to. Are you going to tell me why you won't let me kiss you?"

"I can't," I said, wishing I had a tissue to blow my nose. It's really not fair—in the movies, women get to blubber all over their men without once having their nose fill up, but let a few tears form in my eyes, and whammo! I'm a walking snot locker.

"Why can't you?"

"I have to . . . oh, just a minute."

I grabbed the peignoir from where it was pooled around my ankles and wrapped it around myself as I hurried back to my bedroom. "You'd think the Victorians understood about tissues, but oh, no, they never had to blow their noses! Where did Ellis put that handkerchief . . ."

I grabbed the item in question and dodged behind the peacock screen, blowing my nose as quietly as possible. After buttoning the damp peignoir again, I stepped around the screen, only to find Max leaning in the open door. Naked.

"I really like you that way, Max, but you know, if anyone was to see you here—"

"No one will see me. Are you going to tell me?"

I sniffled and dabbed at my nose with a linen towel I found next to the washstand behind the screen. "I can't kiss you, Max. It's too . . . too intimate."

He blinked at me a couple of times.

"Don't let yourself get into the habit of doing that; it's a hard one to break," I warned him.

He looked confused. "What habit?"

"Blinking when you're taken by surprise. I know, I do it all the time, and it makes me feel like an idiot but I can't seem to stop."

He leaned against the door for another couple of seconds, his arms crossed over his chest, his happy part less happy. He blinked once more, then strolled forward and pulled me into a loose embrace, his hands slipping underneath my peignoir.

"Do you like this?" he asked, his voice low and a bit rough, like crushed velvet rubbing on my naked flesh.

"Oh yeah!" I said, swallowing the last of the tears.

"You don't mind standing naked in my arms, but you object to me kissing you?"

"It's not you I object to, Max. Not really. I thought you understood that. It's just that kissing . . . well, there's usually tongues involved with kissing."

"It's been known to happen," he agreed, a small smile flirting with the corners of his mouth.

"I'm one of those people who finds tongues more intimate than . . . well, seeing someone naked."

"And you're not comfortable with that intimacy?"

"No. It's just . . . difficult."

"I see." He looked like he really did see, like he understood what I was talking about, which was a miracle because I wasn't the least bit certain I was making any sense. "How would you feel if I kissed you without using my tongue?"

I looked at his lips. They looked like nice lips, lips I could trust, lips that weren't threatening in the least. "How about if I kissed you, instead?"

"If you like."

I pressed my mouth against his and waited for the guilt and pain and sickness to fill me, the same emotions that had to rush to the fore the two times I'd kissed a man since Peter's death.

It didn't come. None of it, none of the feelings of doing something wrong, of betraying Peter's memory.

"Wow," I said against his lips, my eyes crossing as I tried to look into his. His mouth was warm and soft and left me wanting more. "This is pretty good. I don't feel like I'm going to throw up."

"I am delighted to know that kissing me doesn't make you physically ill, especially after you vomited on my shoes yesterday."

"I'm really sorry about that. I was drunk."

"Ah."

Have I mentioned I like the smell of Max? I do. He smells spicy and male and very, very sexy. "I don't normally get drunk. In fact, the last time I was drunk was about eighteen years ago."

His lips caressed mine as he spoke. "You're changing the subject."

"I know. Is it distracting you?"

"No. Would you like to try the kiss again, this time with me in charge?"

"No tongues?"

"No tongues."

"Promise?"

"I swear it on my mother's grave."

I squinted up at him. "Is your mother dead?"

He gave me a crooked smile that melted all my insides into one big puddle of goo. "No, but my father is. How about if I swear on his grave that I won't molest you in any way with my tongue?"

I thought about that for a minute. "What if the day comes that I *want* you to molest me with your tongue?"

"Why are you making this harder than it needs to be?"

"I'm nervous."

"Don't be. I won't do anything you won't like."

That statement required another few seconds to mull over. "How do you know what I like?"

His lips thinned. "Tessa—"

"OK, but I'm trusting you on this."

"Close your eyes."

"Why? What are you going to do?" I asked suspiciously. "I'll know if you try to slip a little tongue in there, you know. I might be an idiot, but I'm not stupid."

His chest rumbled with laughter. "You can trust me. Close your eyes."

I gave him one last suspicious look, then did as he asked. His breath steamed my lips for a second, then his lips nibbled the corner of my mouth, first one side, then the other, then they caressed their way from one end to the other. My lips parted, allowing him to suck my lower lip between his, a little groan slipping out of my throat as his hands slid their way up from my behind, stroking a lovely serpentine path up my back just as he bit down very gently on my lip.

I froze for a moment, very aware that I was standing in an intimate embrace with a man who was not my husband, a man who I'd known for all of a day. My heart, already trotting along pretty fast by the nice things Max was doing to my mouth, kicked into a gallop when he said one word. "Relax."

I did. My legs went boneless under me, the scent and taste and feel of him melting away all the worries and concerns and nagging thoughts about smart women and how they conducted relationships, most notably that they did not throw themselves on men after knowing them only a couple of hours.

Max returned my lip to its accustomed location, and smiled down on me.

"Still with me?"

"Oh yeah." I looked around us, a bit dazed, and was startled to see that only a couple of minutes had gone by since I'd come in to blow my nose. It seemed to me like a short lifetime had passed. "Um. Somehow your lips disconnected my legs. Would you mind helping me over to the bed?"

"Is that an invitation or a request for help?"

I looked him dead in the eye, in both eyes, actually, both lovely light blue eyes. "You know, your eyes are just the shade of a blue topaz ring I have at home." His arm tightened around me as I stumbled over to the bed. "It's just a request for help, Max. I enjoyed kissing you, I really did. I don't think my legs would have gone off and left me if I didn't."

One ebony eyebrow cocked. I loved the way they did that. I had the worst urge to kiss them. "But . . . ?"

"But we just met, and I'm five years older than you, and although I really think it's sweet of your penis to be poking into my stomach, it's not fair to either of us to do anything else."

He traced my lower lip with his thumb. I returned the favor, but midway across his lip, his mouth opened and he bit my thumb. Gently.

"I'm still angry with you, Tessa."

I looked at my thumb for a second, surprised that a little bite on the end of it could send flames licking up my arm. "About Melody?"

"Yes. It's not easy to make me change my mind."

I couldn't help myself. I blinked a couple of times.

He smiled a slow smile, a wicked smile, a smile filled with all sorts of heated, sensual, seductive promises that made my uterus stand up and do a couple of back flips. "I look forward to you persuading me I'm wrong."

He kissed the tip of my nose, then left the room, closing the door to the bathroom very gently.

"Hoo," I said softly, then collapsed down onto the bed. "I am *so* in over my head."

Thursday
September 2
4:12 A.M.
Awake, although still in bed (darned time difference)

Spent the night dreaming about Max and his trained lips. Must stop. He's too young for me.

Thursday
September 2
4:19 A.M.
Lying on bed upside down with head hanging over the edge (bored, bored, bored)

He's FIVE WHOLE YEARS younger than me. He's still just a baby. Too young. Much, much too young.

—ɷ—

Thursday
September 2
4:33 A.M.
Floor next to bed, doing non-Victorian yoga

The age difference between us is just insurmountable. When I was a ripe, womanly twenty, svelte and full of seductive glances and appreciation for the manly form, he was a spotty, adolescent fifteen, gangly and hormonal. Nope. It wouldn't work.

In dog years, our age difference is thirty-five years. THIRTY-FIVE YEARS!

—ɷ—

Thursday
September 2
5:03 A.M.
On the fainting couch

Mmm. That *was* a dilly of a kiss, though. And he smells so good. And his eyes; I love the way they go all dark when he's aroused. He's mature for his age, too. Very mature. A lot of men wouldn't have understood why I couldn't just jump into bed, but not Max. He understood because of his inherent maturity. I like his jaw, also. He has a nice, firm, manly sort of jaw, the kind of jaw you want to investigate in more detail. And, of course, there are his lips.

Mmm. Those lips.

What *is* five years, anyway? Nothing, that's what it is; in the grand scheme of things, five years is nothing. When I'm seventy, he'll be sixty-five. It's a statistically documented fact that there is *no* difference between a man aged sixty-five and a woman aged seventy. It's something to do with biology. Women age slower than men—everyone knows that. So, if you look at it like that, when a woman is, say, oh, let's use thirty-nine as an example age, biologically she would be on par with a man who was roughly an eighth younger than her.

Which would mean a man who was chronologically five years younger than her would really be equal to her age.

Fascinating stuff, statistics.

—⁊—

Thursday
September 2
11:50 A.M.
At the escritoire (I love all the little drawers)

You would think that putting on a corset is something that someone with reasonable intelligence and the full use of all four limbs could accomplish with only minor setbacks, but I'm living proof that it ain't as easy as it looks.

I set the little brass and enamel alarm clock next to my bed for six thirty, assuming that would give me plenty of time to get into the green wool riding habit and make the stables by seven, but it took me almost half an hour just to get into the corset and get it tightened (I finally managed it by pulling the laces through the bedstead, leaning forward until it was tightened enough). The riding habit presented another challenge, although not nearly so daunting as donning the corset by myself.

I had to admit, I liked the riding habit the best of all the clothes I'd seen thus far. It was dark green, with a jacket cut high in the front that swooped down to cover my butt in the back, with a nonfrilly skirt. The only problem with the skirt was that it was longer on one side than the other. I didn't understand why until I raced (as quickly as possible while being in the clasp of the Iron Maiden) to the stable, huffing and puffing as I stopped to pat Talisman on his chestnut nose.

"Sorry . . . I'm . . . late . . . Alec . . . I . . . appreciate . . . you . . . saddling . . . him up."

Alec came around from Talisman's off side, the morning sun glinting off his hair as he squinted at me. "You all right, then?"

"Yeah, it's just this corset. Makes it difficult to do anything quickly."

"Ah. Want a leg up?"

"Please, unless there's a mounting block some . . . uh . . . Alec, that's a sidesaddle, isn't it?"

"That it is."

I looked at it with something akin to horror, gnawing on my lower lip as I considered what to say. I really wanted to go on a ride. I desperately needed to blow a few of the mental cobwebs away, especially the ones created when I thought about Max, and a ride sounded like the perfect way to do that. If I told Alec I'd never ridden sidesaddle, he might not let me go out on Talisman. I gnawed my lip a little more, then decided that it couldn't be that different than riding astride.

I am often so wrong about things.

Alec hoisted me up, but my dress got tangled around the curved pommel, with the result that I was stuck halfway up.

"What's the matter?" he asked, one hand on Talisman's bridle, the other on my behind as it waggled in his face.

"I'm . . . dammit . . . stuck! I think my dress is caught. Can you help me back down and let me try again?"

He untangled my skirt enough to let me jump back down to the ground.

"Sorry about that," I said as I wadded up all the extra material on the left side of the habit. It bared my legs to above my knees, but I had no time for niceties. "It's been a long time since I rode sidesaddle. I've forgotten that you have to gather up the dress first, then get on."

"You all right to try again?"

"Yeah. Sorry, Talisman! I'll do better this time."

Alec bent to give me a leg up.

"Stop grinning at my knees," I said, frowning down on his head.

He laughed, and I took a firm grip on the wad of material, another on the saddle, and stepped into his hands.

This time I made it all the way into the saddle, but Talisman, evidently tiring of waiting for me to climb aboard, decided it was time to go. Alec had dropped the reins to hoist me up, which was all the encouragement Talisman needed. He set off at a brisk walk just as I was in the awkward act of swinging my right leg over the curved pommel.

"Whoa, there," Alec yelled, which was the wrong thing to do around a high-strung, well-rested horse. Talisman flattened his ears and took off at a fast trot.

"What the—hey!" I yelled, and tipped over backward.

Before you shake your head and ask how a person can tip over backward while seated in a saddle, let me explain that if you are a woman of size (a.k.a. "chunky"), you have to lean back a bit to swing your leg up and over the horse's neck, in order to fit it next to the pommel, the proper position when riding a side-saddle. That plus the fact that I'd never ridden sidesaddle and was thrown off balance by having to have both legs on one side of the horse, not to mention Talisman taking off like he did, resulted in me lying flat on my back, my head bumping against his crop, staring up at the sky as he trotted off to God knows where. It couldn't have been comfortable for Talisman to have me like that, and heaven knows I wasn't having any fun bouncing around on my back, but in the end it was Talisman who stopped. Abruptly. When Alec (having realized chasing Talisman wasn't going to do any good) brought

out the grain bucket and rattled some grain around inside it.

Talisman and I parted ways at that point, he trotting
smartly back to shove his nose in the bucket Alec clev-
erly held out, me to fall to the ground like a sack full
of hams.

"Are you all right?" Alec called out to me as he led
a not very repentant-looking Talisman over to me. "Did
you hurt yourself?"

I got to my feet (not an easy thing to do when you're
wearing a corset) and brushed the dirt off my butt. "Just
parts of me that have lots of padding. You, sir, are a
very naughty horse, and I'm going to remember this!"

Talisman snuffled my front to see if I had any goodies
hidden away on my person, then blew his nose on me.

"Want to try again?" Alec asked, looking as if he was
trying hard not to laugh as I brushed the horse snot off
my lovely, if slightly dusty, habit.

"Stop it, it's not that funny."

He stopped trying not to laugh and chortled happily
until I socked him on the arm. "Sorry, Tessa."

"Oh, you are not. I don't suppose Max's stallion—"

A couple of leftover snickers escaped him. "Not broken to a sidesaddle."

"Crap. All right, we'll give this another go, shall we?
Talisman, if you don't want me to introduce you to the
local knacker, you'd better not move one single hoof
until I'm in place. Got it?"

I managed to get into the saddle properly, my habit
draped elegantly over the side, my right leg tight against
the curved pommel. Alec adjusted the stirrup for me,
checked the girth, then slapped Talisman on the rump,
and we were off.

I didn't go very far, worried as I was about not being
able to manage riding sidesaddle, but it only took me
half an hour or so to find my balance and begin to relax
as we trotted along the large pond north of the house.
Birds chattered noisily in the lovely crisp morning air as
we rode through a scattering of trees hugging the pond,

cars humming on a road distant enough that I could pretend it was the drone of Victorian farm machinery. It was a lovely spot, the last of the late summer wildflowers fighting with ferns for space around the base of the trees, the moist, rich scent of fertile soil laying a pungent overtone to the smell of sunshine.

Talisman had a rough trot that left my teeth chattering, but a lovely rolling canter. By the time we returned to the stable, I was feeling much more confident in my riding skills.

"You look like someone pulled you backward through a hedge," Alec grinned as we stopped in front of him. He was grooming one of the carriage horses, but came over to hold Talisman while I dismounted.

"There was a hat to go with the habit, but I didn't think it was worth the time to skewer it onto my head," I explained as strands of hair loosened by the ride drifted around my face. "What time is it?"

Alec pulled a pocket watch from his breeches pocket. "Getting on eight."

"Crap, I have to go. I was going to brush down Talisman. Hi, you must be Thom the groom. I'm Tessa. You won't say anything about my riding out so early, will you?"

A tall, skinny kid of about nineteen or twenty shook his head and went back to cleaning tack.

"Thanks, I appreciate . . . oh, good morning. I see you found your way down to the stable."

Melody, dressed in a horrible pink-and-blue print dress with three rows of ruffles and a big bow on her butt, came around from the far side of the horse Alec had been grooming. Her little chin set as her eyes squinted meanly at me.

"You're going to tell my dad, aren't you?"

I shrugged and brushed out the wrinkles in my skirt. "That depends. If you want to play nicely, I won't. In fact—hold on a second, Alec." I stopped Alec as he was about to relieve Talisman of his saddle. "In fact, I'm willing to make a deal with you. You play along with this whole Victorian thing when the cameras are on, and I'll teach you to ride."

"Dad said you're not supposed to." She frowned at me, a miniature version that was pretty darn close to her father's scowl.

"Yeah, well, your dad gave me carte blanche to change his mind, so that's what I'm going to do. Either you can wait around until he thinks you're old enough to learn to ride, or you can be a smart kid and realize that playing along with us won't hurt you, in which case I'll pop you on Talisman and give you your first lesson."

She looked at the horse, her lip quivering a bit as it prepared to commence pouting, but in the end she saw reason. "Only when the cameras are on?"

"Yep."

Her lips compressed into a mulish look. "I don't like it here."

"I got that impression. Needless to say, you're here, and your father doesn't seem to be entertaining the idea of sending you away. So you're going to have to make the best of it."

"It's not fair!"

I laughed, not at her but at the idea that there was any guarantee of life working out as it should. "There's not a lot in life that *is* fair, kid. You want to learn to ride or not?"

Her face was so sullen that I thought she'd refuse, but in the end her desire to ride was greater than her need to be miserable. "All right. But I only have to be nice when the cameras are on."

"Right. The rest of the time you can be your usual surly self." I pushed her gently toward Talisman's head. "First lesson, always introduce yourself to your horse."

Her lip curled scornfully. "It's a horse, it can't talk."

"No, but you can. Go up to him, give him a pat, and tell him who you are."

"That's stupid."

"No, it's not. There's more to riding a horse than just sitting on his back. You're not afraid, are you?"

Her little shoulders went rigid beneath the blue-and-pink ruffles as she glared at me for a second before marching up to Talisman, patting him on his nose.

Four minutes later I had her up on his back, giving her my best advice (which wasn't much) about how to ride in a sidesaddle. I led her around the stable yard a couple of times, showed her how to hold the reins, then walked beside her when she insisted on "driving" him by herself.

"Sorry to cut this short," I said as I grabbed Talisman's bridle and led him back to Alec. "But we're both late. I'm going to go riding again tomorrow morning. If you're out here early enough, you can come with me."

"My dad says I'm not supposed to go riding with you," she said self-righteously as Alec helped her down.

"What?" I cried, hands on my hips as I glared at her. "After I go to all the trouble of . . . argh! I'm going to be late because of you—you know that, don't you? I'm going to get a lecture from Ellis just because I was nice to you. What a little snot!"

"I am not a little snot!" she yelled, her face flushing with anger.

"You're worse than a little snot; you're a snot with hair on it."

"I am not!"

I turned on my heel and started back for the house, hurrying as fast as I could manage, which, admittedly, wasn't very fast, what with the corset and all.

"I don't think you're nice at all," Melody said, trotting after me. "I think you're worse than a snot. I think you're a big fat piece of dog poo!"

I muttered various things to myself that I didn't want to say loud enough for her to hear; gasping and wheezing I made my way up the steps to the French doors that opened into the scarlet drawing room, doors I had left unlocked on my way down to the stables.

"I don't like you at all, and I'm going to tell Dad that you gave me a riding lesson."

I threw open the doors and stormed through the room, the hellish little monster hot on my heels.

"He's going to be mad at you and won't let you stay here," she taunted. "And I'm going to laugh when he makes you leave."

I stopped before the door to the hall and smiled at her. "What a little tattletale you are. You'd better thank your lucky stars I'm not really your stepmother, kid, because if I was . . ."

"I have a mom, and she's nice," Melody spat at me. "She's not fat like you."

"Oh, really? Just where is this nice skinny mom of yours? Why is she letting your father keep you here when you'd rather be with her?"

I regretted the words the second I spoke them. Her jaw tightened, making me even more ashamed of myself for snapping at her—who knew where her mother was? Maybe she was dead and Melody didn't want to admit it. I was about to apologize when, with eyes hot with anger and tears, she said, "She's in Wales. She's having a baby. Dad said I can't visit her until the baby is born. She has to stay in bed because of the baby. I hate the baby. I hate it here! I HATE YOU!"

"Oh, boy, do I pick 'em," I said, leaning against the wall, watching through the door as Melody raced up the stairs. Poor kid, no wonder she was so nasty; she was obviously not coping well with life after divorce.

"Then again," I said to myself as I trudged my way up the stairs, waving to a startled Teddy as he emerged from the breakfast room, "who am I to throw stones? I certainly haven't coped well with life after Peter's death."

The library is my new favorite spot in the house. Yesterday when I zoomed through it, I didn't really have a chance to do more than glance at the newspapers and magazines Roger's people had left for us, but today I talked Max out of his breakfast *Times* and settled down this afternoon to read it. The front page alone was a fascinating amalgamation of personal notices ("If the LADY who arrived at New Croydon Station by the train from Victoria about half past eight on Saturday evening, twenty-third of August, and who then put an elderly gentleman into another train, which was waiting for Victoria, will kindly COMMUNICATE with Mrs. M., 4, Hill-place, Upper-hill, Richmond, she will greatly oblige"), vital statistics, notices of everything from funeral homes to concerts, obituaries, legal notices, advertisements of all sorts (my favorite was for a woman who wanted to get rid of a clock that chimed every quarter hour. There was a distinct note of desperation in her offer to take "any reasonable sum" for it), and wonderfully colorful "testimonials" of medicinal substances.

I know what you're thinking. "Max," you're saying to yourself. "What happened with Max of the Manly Lips, Tessa?" Don't think I'd forgotten Max's parting words to me the night before. I hadn't—far from it. They made a warm little glow of happiness inside me. I also looked forward to persuading him he was wrong. . . . But the trouble was finding the time to be alone with him to do the persuading. Among other things. I wanted to investigate his lips a bit more, too.

I fully expected him to be more than a little snippy with me at breakfast after Melody tattled to him, so by the time I finished hearing Ellis' lectures—on how a proper duchess behaves, why it's wrong to keep a lady's maid waiting, how my thoughtless actions of disregarding the schedule will ruin the project, and the ills sure to visit those women who improperly tighten their corset— and made it down to morning prayers only four minutes late, I was ready to take him on.

It turned out there wasn't a need to. Max smiled charmingly and held out his hand for me to take my place beside him. Evidently, Melody, pouting on Max's other side, decided to heed my warnings and kept quiet about her early morning jaunt around the stable yard.

"Max, do you have a few minutes?" I asked as we finished breakfast. "I'd like to . . . uh . . . talk to you. For a little bit. About methods of persuasions and such."

I swear his eyes darkened at my words. I know I blushed, which was idiotic; I hadn't done anything to blush about. Well, all right, if we're being strictly honest, I was thinking about things that would be worthy of a blush, but he couldn't know that.

"I thought maybe after breakfast?"

"You have to meet with Mrs. Peters after breakfast," Barbara pointed out.

"Oh, yes, very true. After Mrs. Peters, maybe we can get together—"

"This is your day to be At Home, isn't it?" Barbara asked, with a gay little laugh as Tabby, filming the breakfast, focused the camera on her.

"Is it?" I tried to remember what an At Home consisted of. I was pretty sure all it meant was that I had to be home if anyone paid a call, but who was going to pay us a call? We were the only people in the whole of Britain living in a time warp.

Barbara turned the smile on me, her eyes driving

home the point that I was to agree with her. "Yes, it is. Don't you remember, dear? Yesterday we decided that Thursday would be your day to be At Home, and Friday would be mine."

"OK. Sure. Whatever. So I'm At Home today. Can't Max be At Home with me?"

"I wish I could," he said before Barbara could answer. "But Henry and I have to check in with the tenants today."

"You're kidding," I said, wondering if that was just a fancy way of saying they were going off for a drink or something.

His right eyebrow made a lovely arch. I was amazed; he was ambi-eyebrowed. Not many men can cock either eyebrow to such effect. "No, I'm not. There are tenants, and it falls to me to make sure all is well with them. Henry offered to come with me."

"Ah. Right. Gotcha. Well then, perhaps this afternoon—"

"That's when you're At Home," Barbara said quickly. "This morning you will want to look over the household accounts. It is, after all, several days into the month. I would be happy to help you with them, but alas, I have the many tasks that you thrust upon my feminine shoulders to see to. And I simply must pay some calls this afternoon. What the neighbors—the landed gentry, of course—will think of my absence, I can't begin to imagine."

The smile she sent the camera was so cloying it could have choked a horse. A big horse.

"Um—"

"Good, that's settled, then. Max, be a love and tell Palmer that I'll want the open carriage this afternoon. Now, I must be off. I have so much to do this morning. I'm behind on my letters, and that housemaid did a perfectly appalling job mending a petticoat I tore last night, and I thought I would pop in and see how Melody is doing with Mademoiselle, and of course, I will do the flowers, as I always do, and oh, a million other things that keep us ladies busy. Such a slave driver you are, Tessa! Do let me know if you need my help going over the accounts with Mrs. Peters. I am, as you know, completely at your service with regards to those little things in managing a large and important household that might have escaped your training in the States. Somehow, I will find the time to assist you. Now, if you gentlemen will excuse me . . ." She rose gracefully from her chair, then stood for a moment, sending very pointed looks at the two men, until Max, with what I was willing to bet was a stifled oath, got to his feet. Henry lumbered to his as well, and Barbara, girlishly blowing her husband a kiss, bustled out of the room.

"Wow. She's good, isn't she?" I asked.

Tabby shook with silent laughter.

Max dabbed at his lips, those wonderful, warm, expressive lips, and came around to pull back my chair. "I will see you as soon as I can, my dear," he said loudly, for the camera's benefit, then lifted my hand to kiss my fingers. "I'll find you as soon as I finish," he added softly, for my ears only.

He kissed my fingers then, his eyes holding mine as he lifted my hand to his mouth. I knew it was just part of his ducal duties to make nice to the duchess, but I doubted if any Victorian duke kissed his wife's hand the way Max did mine. It wasn't so much a kiss as it was a tasting, the very tip of his tongue flicking between my fingers in a way that was utterly shocking, utterly . . . wonderful.

"Holy cow," I breathed, unable to take my gaze from his, a little tremor of pleasure rippling down my back.

"I just thought you'd like to know what my tongue can do when it puts its mind to it," he said, his eyes dancing wickedly.

"Gark." A wild desire to taste him—all of him—flared to life.

His smiled deepened as he made a little bow, then he nodded to the camera and headed out the door. Henry followed him out of the room, leaving me alone with

Tabby and Matthew. I looked straight at the camera and gave it a feeble smile.

"The duke is a *very* wicked man," I told the would-be audience of millions of viewers. Tabby grinned at me when I added, "It's one of the things I like best about him."

After breakfast I met Mrs. Peters in the morning room for menu planning and accounts checking.

"How are the spirits this morning?" I asked politely as I waved her toward a chair. She stiffened up and glanced back at Sam, who with Wilma was filming our consultation. "Please, Mrs. Peters, sit. I can't possibly do the accounts with you lurking over me."

"The spirits are most unhappy, Your Grace," she answered, perching warily on the edge of a blue embroidered chair. "The footmen mocked them last night. One of the spirits, Sir Ranleigh, was so offended that he wouldn't rap at all."

"Maybe he's into hip-hop instead," I joked, chuckling to myself.

She stared at me with eyes that resembled the boiled sweets in a bowl on a nearby gateleg table.

"Rap? Hip-hop? Get it?"

Evidently, she didn't.

"It is just such a reprehensible and frivolous attitude that the spirits find objectionable. They are *not* to be taken lightly."

I tried to look suitably chastised. I doubt if I succeeded, but I did try. "I would never want to offend a ghost."

"I should hope not," Mrs. Peters said, her hands folded nicely in her lap. "Not only is it extremely ill-mannered to mock someone just because he's dead, but the spirits have ways of making their displeasure known to their critics. I cannot imagine someone foolish enough to willfully incur their wrath."

I pushed down the snicker that was trying to free itself and forced my lips to stop twitching. "No, indeed, that would be the sheerest of follies. I myself live in perpetual dread of encountering otherworldly wrath. I imagine the titled ghosts, like Sir Ranleigh, are particularly vengeful."

She peered suspiciously at me to see if I was mocking her (I wasn't, although I was gently teasing her a bit). "That is to be expected, of course. The noble ghosts have a much finer sensibility than . . . you know . . ."

"The peon ghosts?" I asked helpfully.

Wilma made snorting, gasping, choking sorts of sounds indicative of someone stifling laughter.

Mrs. Peters tightened her lips. Her hair, I was secretly pleased to notice, was escaping its intended confinement, a fact that made me feel a bit better about my flyaway appearance earlier. "I wouldn't go so far as to call them peons," she answered. "They are simply not gentlefolk. Their manners are not quite as nice as those spirits of bluer blood."

"You know, I find this really interesting that you're so willing to perpetuate a class division, even among the dead. Certainly, you're not old enough that it was something you grew up with, and yet . . ." I glanced at the camera and decided that my observations would have to be saved for a less public airing. "Right, well—"

"You will find that there is little difference between the living and those who have passed over to the other side," she said primly. "Just as it is in the living, some spirits have that certain something, that innate sense of grandeur, that natural quality of superiority that sets them above lesser beings."

"You're kidding—ghostly snobs?" I couldn't help but ask.

Her hackles rose as she snarled out, "There can be nothing snobbish about the recognition of quality, be it among those of flesh and blood and those occupying less corporeal bodies."

"Er right." I glanced at the camera again and decided to change the subject before she went over the edge. "So, what does Mrs. Billings have planned for lunch and dinner today?"

She eyed me suspiciously for a moment, but evidently the innocent look I'd slapped on my face did the trick because she let her hackles deruffle. "Luncheon will be ragout mutton, oyster fritters, dressed cucumbers, French bread, Vienna twist, sponge cake, and blackberries and cream. Dinner will be dried pea soup, roast tame duck, browned potatoes, string beans, baked tomatoes, lettuce with mayonnaise, baked lemon tart, peach meringue, and feather cake."

"Ah. That sounds wonderful, although I wonder whose tame duck we're having for dinner?"

Mrs. Peters didn't rise to the bait. "I couldn't say, I'm sure."

The next hour was spent poring over the books with her, although by the end of the hour it was fairly clear that neither one of us really knew what we should be doing. That didn't stop us, however, and since the TV show was fronting the money to run the household for a month, I figured it couldn't hurt if I lavished a bit extra on things like additional helpings of butter and cream for the servants, as well as the purchase of new uniforms for all the servants, linens, mattresses, and copper laundry tubs. I knew that none of them would really be ordered, but I had fun indulging in a little make-believe Victorian shopping spree.

I don't think Mrs. Peters had fun at all. She didn't crack a smile once, and my suggestion that we could make up the difference between the monthly household allowance and the amount I'd been authorized to spend in my shopping spree by charging people to see an authentic English ghost was met with icy disdain and a chill "I think *not*."

Call it a hunch, but I get the feeling Mrs. Peters doesn't like me.

Max made an appearance at lunch but left immediately afterward, saying he had important work to do. I was more than a little bit disappointed by his defection. I had wanted to investigate his lips a bit more, not to mention explaining how, statistically speaking, he was as old as I was, but I couldn't very well do that while he was elsewhere. My At Home time was scheduled to begin at 3:00 P.M. and run through tea, so an hour before I was due to take up my spot in the gold drawing room, I escaped the house and went for a walk down by the small lake.

It was a fabulously gorgeous late summer day, warm but with enough of a breeze to keep it from being really hot, the sky a pure, perfect blue that inevitably made me think of Max's eyes, the birds doing their swooping, fluttering, chirping thing, the air filled with the scent of tea roses that lined the walk down to the lake . . . everything that would have made for an absolutely perfect day if I hadn't been strapped into a sadistic monstrosity of lace and steel, topped with about thirty-five pounds of pale blue-and-white cashmere.

I know what you're thinking—cashmere on a summer day? This is the very question I put to Ellis earlier in the day when she was dressing me.

"That's a lovely dress, but don't you think it's a bit too hot to wear in this weather? I'd hate to sweat all over that pretty cashmere."

Ellis is a woman without mercy. "You're having your first At Home today. It's important that you make the proper impression."

"Yeah, but I'll get all hot and sweaty if I wear that outside."

She slipped the dress—for you Victorian aficionados, it was a neo Greek design of a pale blue skirt draped over a white train, trimmed with gold embroidery done in a square Greek key pattern, with a blue bodice (square neck), and transparent white silk sleeves, edged with gilt braid, adorned by a pointed apron bit that layered over the skirt, finished with pleated white silk at the hem (whew! Say *that* three times fast!)—over my head, and basically ignored my objections. "Then don't go outside. You have no need to take your guests outside."

"I don't care about my guests, *I* want to go outside. I like taking walks. I need fresh air."

"You may request one of the footmen to open the window if you need air."

"I'm not a mole; I like to see the sun occasionally."

"The sun is bad for your skin."

"I don't care if I get sunburned. I just don't want to be lugging around a hundred pounds of dress on a hot day."

She did the narrowed lip–flared nostril thing at me. "Did you or did you not sign a contract agreeing to participate in this project to the utmost of your abilities?"

"Yes, but—"

"The dress is suitable for an At Home," she said, her lips closing tightly over the words as she snapped them out. There was a note of finality in her voice that told me that argument would not do me any good. I debated whether or not I wanted to go to Roger to complain, then decided that I wouldn't. I wasn't a wimp. I would just tough this out.

I glared at her as she tugged the pointy apron bit so it draped gracefully over my hips. "You are such a bully. I'm not going to forget this."

"Your opinions do not concern me in the least," she answered, then moved around to the back to hook me up. "My job is to see you dressed properly, and that is what I will do, regardless of your approval."

It was a very pretty dress, and I have to admit that Ellis did a lovely job twining gold cord through my hair in a way I'd never be able to duplicate myself, but even so, I seethed as I picked out the Etruscan gold necklace and earrings that she offered from the jewelry case.

By the time I strolled (elegantly, and armed with a parasol that Ellis insisted I take if I went outside), the sweat was rolling down my back beneath my corset, little snakes of perspiration trickling from behind my ears. I was hot. I was cranky. I was frustrated at my inability to best Ellis. In short, I was spoiling for a fight.

It's rather ironic that the first person I saw as I

rounded a dense crescent of trees was the last man I wanted to argue with.

"Hello. That's a very pretty frock. Greek, is it?"

I stopped in front of where Max sprawled on the grass, a fishing pole in one hand, a book in the other. "What are you doing out here? I thought you had tons of work to do."

He grinned up at me, an endearing grin, a boyish grin, a grin that was filled with conspiratorial glee. If I hadn't been so blasted uncomfortable, I would have grinned back at him. "I decided I needed a break. Are you out for a ramble?"

"Yes, despite Ellis' warnings that five minutes in the sun will result in inoperable skin cancer." I nudged his ribs with the toe of my shoes. "You could have told me you were going to play hooky today. I want to talk to you."

"Do you? How nice. I'd like that. Sit. If you behave yourself as a proper duchess and amuse me with witty anecdotes and amusing repartee, I'll even allow you to hold my pole."

The wicked glint in his eyes told me he was well aware of the double entendre of his comment.

"Do you go around offering pole holding to every woman you meet, or is it confined to just those of us lugging around two hundred pounds of cashmere?"

He tipped his head to the side and looked puzzled.

"Oh, stop it, that's only cute when my rib cage hasn't been crushed into powder. I can't sit, you boob. I'll get my dress dirty, and then Ellis will have the hissy fit to end all hissy fits. She's already told me that she had to spend hours cleaning the blouse of my riding habit, and I only had it on for a little bit."

Max set his book and fishing pole down, stood up, shook out his coat—lying over a branch—and laid it on the ground, gesturing toward it in the best Sir Walter Raleigh manner. "My lady, if you please."

"That's Your Grace to the likes of you, buster," I

said, a bit mollified. The thought of spending the next hour alone with Max did a lot to make up for being bound into a garment more suited to the outer reaches of Mongolia, and if I was a bit less than graceful as I sat on his coat, he didn't say anything.

"I thought you said I got to hold your pole?"

He grinned. "Shall I leave the choice of which pole you wish to hold up to you, or would you like me to choose?"

"You ought to have your mind washed out with soap," I answered, and held out my hand for the fishing pole.

He lay back on the grass, his eyes closed, his hands clasped behind his head. "Now that you have my pole firmly grasped, your fingers wrapped lovingly around its base as you caress its length with long, firm strokes, you may begin the amusing anecdotes and witty repartee portion of the afternoon."

I laughed and pinched a section of silk waistcoat that covered his side. "You're incorrigible."

"Yes, but that's what you like about me."

"You're also conceited."

"No, I just have a healthy appreciation for what a passionate woman can do with my pole in her hands."

His eyes were still closed, but he was smiling.

"How do you know that I'm passionate?"

One eye opened and stared at me in surprise. "You *are* passionate."

"I know I am, but how do *you* know that?"

"I'm a man. I know."

"Oh, right, it's one of those man things; thinking with your penis again. Ha. I scoff at your man thing."

He rolled onto his side and trailed a finger down the thin, translucent silk of my elbow-length sleeve. I shivered despite the heat of the afternoon sun. "You weren't laughing at my man thing last night."

I set down the pole and turned to face him. "Sirrah, are you trying to seduce me, a duchess, right here in the open, with scandalous talk of man things and poles and long, loving strokes of my hands and mouth thereupon?"

He tugged me down until I was lying next to him, our mouths an inch apart. "If I thought you would appreciate my advances, yes, I would seduce you right here where we are hidden away in our own little bower, with the sun shining down on those beautiful breasts of yours."

"You like my breasts?" I asked against his lips, unable to stop myself from taking little nipping kisses.

"Very much," he answered, his hand sliding down the curve of my hip, pulling me closer to him.

"How sweet of you. I've named them, you know."

His eyes widened. "You named your breasts?"

I smiled, allowing myself to melt into him as he rolled onto his back, holding me on top of him. "Well, no, I haven't really, but I might someday. Max, let me go. If someone came around those trees, they could see us. Besides, I'm way too heavy for you."

"No, you're not." His hand slipped down my thigh, tugging up my dress.

"Yes, I am. I'll squash you flat."

The fingers of both hands were involved now, underneath my skirts, sliding up my thighs, burning a trail even through the thin linen of my combinations. "You went riding this morning?"

"Yes," I answered, distracted by the sweet kisses, the heat of his mouth that seemed somehow to be connected to the fire his fingers were generating.

"If you sit up . . ." he said, his fingers discovering the slitted part of the drawers. I shivered with delight as he stroked his way up the last little bit of my thighs, more than a little surprised at the strength of my reaction to his touch. I *wanted* him to touch me, *burned* for him to touch me. ". . . you can go riding again."

I pushed myself off his chest a bit, moaning as his fingers found the sensitive little parts of me. "Maximillian, that was another proposition."

"Yes, it was. Do you like me doing this?" His fingers caressed my hot, humid flesh that had all but started dancing in its delight with his actions.

"Yes. Yes, I do. Do it some more."

He did. I melted.

"This is a very intimate act, Tessa."

I rocked my pelvis against his hand. One finger slipped inside me. "Holy cow! Yes, yes, oh yes, it's very intimate. Can you—oh, my!"

"This is surely as intimate an act as kissing with tongues."

It took a minute for his words to make sense, so caught up was I in admiration for the sheer brilliance of his finger work, but when they did, I shook my head. "No. That's more intimate. This is . . . oh, baby! . . . this is . . . I think . . . I think . . . good lord, man, your fingers ought to be illegal!"

It took some time—hours, maybe—but at last I had myself in control again. Max's fingers, his magic fingers, were quiet, one of them still inside me, solid among flesh quivering with delightful little aftershocks of pleasure. I looked down at his half-closed eyes bright with all sorts of naughty thoughts. "No one has ever done that to me. Well, I have, but other than me, I mean. Wow. You're good!"

He gave a little, one eyebrow cocked. "Your husband never . . . eh . . ."

I shook my head, then slid down his legs, reluctantly parting from his fingers. "No, he always said that all the womanly parts were a bit off-putting. Mind you, he would have if I'd asked him to, but I didn't. I think at heart he was a traditionalist, and I didn't want to shock him, so I never asked."

"He didn't know what he was missing."

"Oh, I don't know," I said, lifting the bottom of his waistcoat to get at the top button on his pants. "I have to say I see his point. I mean, have you ever looked closely at that part of a woman's body?"

"Yes. What are you doing?"

I paused. "Unbuttoning you. You like oral sex, don't you?"

His handsome blue eyes bugged out just a little bit. "Yes, yes, I do."

"Good." I resumed unbuttoning. "Anyway, if you've looked closely at all those labia parts and whatnot, you'll know. It's not the most scenic part on a woman's body. Oooh, you have red undies. Fun."

He jumped beneath my hand when I caressed the aroused length of him beneath his red cambric drawers. I started unbuttoning the tiny white buttons on them.

"Tessa, do you mind if I ask you a question?"

"Shoot." He was just as big and hard as I remembered. And hot—very, very hot.

"Are you planning on . . . eh . . . for lack of a more refined phrase, pleasuring me?"

I slipped the last button free and tugged the drawers down so I could expose his noogies, then looked up, suddenly worried. "Yes, I was. It's only fair. You . . . uh . . . pleasured me, so it's my turn to do you. You said you like oral sex, right?"

He blinked at me. I thought about reminding him about the bad effects that too much blinking has, but decided to save it for another moment. "Yes, but . . ."

"But what?"

"You don't think having my fingers inside you or taking me into your mouth is too intimate an act, and yet you won't let me use my tongue when I kiss you?"

"What is it with you and tongues?" I asked, wrapping my fingers around him. "Do you have some sort of a tongue fetish or something?"

"No," he said, his voice a bit rough. "I just wondered."

"OK. So we're a go to proceed."

"Uh huh," he said, a slight tremor shaking his body as I slid my fingers up to spread around the little bead of moisture crowning the tip.

He was hard and hot and velvety, and holding him in my hand I felt a surge of feminine power. I knew I could bring him pleasure, knew I could bring him ecstasy, and suddenly, I wanted that more than anything else. I wanted to give him something unselfish, a gift to show him that I respected him and liked him and found him incredibly sexy. What started out as a reciprocal gesture quickly changed into desire.

I smiled into his eyes for a moment, then dipped my head and touched the underside of him with the tip of my tongue. He twitched and moaned at the same time, his head lolling back, his eyes closed, one hand on my shoulder, the other fisted into the grass.

I touched, I licked, I squeezed, I caressed, desire and pleasuring mingling within me with every groan that escaped his lips.

"Be sure to tell me what you like," I said as I stroked my hand down him. His hips shoved upward.

"Whung."

I laved a serpentine path up the heat of him and smiled as his back arched beneath me. "I don't think that's English, Max."

"Snarg." He was shuddering now, his breath wild and rasping as both hands clutched convulsively at the grass.

"Do you know what you taste like, Max? You taste salty," I licked him in one long stroke from balls to the head. "You taste hot." I swirled my tongue around the flared tip. "You taste like a very sexy, very aroused man." He shouted something incoherent as I took him in my mouth, then pulled back slowly, gently scraping my teeth along his flesh as I reached lower to fondle the rest of him.

"Tessa!" he bellowed.

"Mmm? Oh! Wait, hold on, I have a handkerchief—oh, rats. Too late. Sorry. I'm sure that'll come out with a little club soda. Here, let me mop you up a bit."

He lay panting while I tidied him up, giving him a little pat as I tucked him away and buttoned his drawers and pants. With a low, exhausted groan he lifted his head enough to glare accusingly at me. "You can't tell me your husband didn't like that!"

"Well, of course he did. All men like that. Are you OK? You look a bit flushed. You're not going to have a heart attack or anything, are you?"

"I'm not sure. I might."

I watched him closely for a minute, then decided he was exaggerating. I have to admit that I was more than a little bit pleased with his response. "I've only had Peter to practice on. I'm glad I did it right."

His chest shook in a feeble laugh. "You did it more than right, Tessa."

"Good." I glanced back through the woods to where the roof of the house was visible. "I suppose I should get a move on."

"You could stay," he suggested, his eyes darkening. "There's that ride I mentioned. You'll have to give me a little bit to recover from your wonderful mouth, but I'm sure that I can provide you with an afternoon of enjoyment."

I smiled. "Well, my body is demanding I say yes, but . . . well, that's a big step."

He grinned and tugged me forward until I lay across his chest again, his lips teasing mine. "I'm a patient man."

"Good. I have more persuading to do." I kissed him, sucking his lower lip into my mouth before releasing it. "Oh, speaking of that, I wanted to tell you how great Melody did this morning."

"Did what?" he asked, nuzzling a hot line of kisses along my jaw.

"Riding. She's got a natural seat, Max. I don't think you need to worry about—"

"What?" He shoved me backward, sitting up as I slid off him. "What do you mean she's got a natural seat?"

"I meant that she's got good balance, that she can feel how to move on a horse without thinking about it. That's what having a good seat means."

He jumped up, his jaw tight, his eyes furious. "Dammit, you put Melody on a horse?"

I struggled to my feet. "Now, calm down, Max, it's

nothing to get upset or angry about. We stayed in the stable yard. I walked her around on Talisman. I didn't leave her alone, not for a second. She was just fine—"

He let out a string of invectives that stunned me not for their variety (which was breathtaking), but for the fury behind the words. "I told you not to! I specifically told you I didn't want her getting near a horse!"

"Yes, but—"

"Dammit, Tessa, she could have been hurt."

"Oh, don't be so melodramatic. All she did was walk around the stable yard. Besides, you told me you wanted me to persuade you."

He glared at me, his eyes burning a brilliant blue light. "Persuade me, yes. I had no intention of ever allowing Melody near a horse."

I bit back the oath I badly wanted to yell at him and bent to retrieve my parasol from the ground (an act guaranteed to squeeze all the breath out of my body). By the time I stood back up and could breathe again, I had regained my control. "Really. How nice to know that this is all just a game to you."

"My daughter's life is no game."

"No, it's not," I snapped, my control not as good as I thought it was. "But encouraging me to become physically and emotionally involved with you is. Thank you for making that crystal clear to me, Max. I would have hated to waste all that time trying to soften you up for *nothing.*"

I turned on my heel (not easy to do in the grass) and stormed off (also not easy to do, especially when you're wearing two thousand pounds of clothing in one-hundred-and-ninety-degree weather). Max called out something after me, but I ignored him. I didn't want to talk to him, didn't want to see his flushed, handsome face.

I didn't want him to see me cry.

—m—

Thursday
September 2
8:40 P.M.
Fainting couch

I wish I had more experience with men. I wish I had
dated lots and lots of men, broken up with them, made
up, been through all the ups and downs, rather than
having been married for sixteen years to a man twenty
years older than me, a man who was well settled into
his skin when I met him.

Experience, I feel sure, would be the only thing that
would help me figure out just what the devil was up with
Max. Obviously, he had some issues with the idea of
Melody going riding (issues? Ha! More like unassailable
mountains!), but somehow I didn't think a horse was
really what was bothering Max. Still, I didn't have
enough experience to tell if he was reacting to me, his
situation, or some other stimuli.

"It's a puzzlement," I said in my best Yul Brynner
voice earlier in the day as I entered the house.

"What is?" Teddy asked, opening the door to me. The
hall was empty, no cameras to be seen. Yay!

"Men. You have any sage advice for me on the
subject?"

"Yes. We're gods. Worship us appropriately."

I snorted. "Fat chance! How's it going? You holding
up under the strain of all that footmanning?"

He shrugged and looked at his reflection in the huge
gilt mirror hanging across the hall. "I thought I would
have more time on camera, but the work is all right. It's
a good sight better than what's going on downstairs."

"Oh?" I asked, pausing as I was about to enter the
gold drawing room. "Is there trouble?"

"You could call it that. *I'd* call it a revolt."

My heart sank. Two days and already there was trouble? "Crap."

He nodded. "Exactly."

I glanced toward the green baize door. "Do you think I should go down?"

"Might help," he said, shrugging slightly, preening a bit. "Then again, it might not. There's a lot of unhappy people down there."

"Maybe you should tell Roger that."

He rolled his eyes. "I did. He thinks it's great; says that conflict makes it much more interesting to the viewers. He doesn't care that old Palmer is guzzling beer, claiming it has healing abilities to clear up his lumbago, or that Michael is allergic to the tooth powder they gave us, or that the scullery girls are screaming bloody murder about washing up."

"Oy. Maybe Kip—"

"He's worse than Roger," Teddy said, straightening his waistcoat and tie before brushing a hand over his hair. "He told Michael that his hives from the tooth powder added reality to the show, and he'd just have to deal with the situation."

"Kip is a big old snotball," I said, gnawing on my lower lip. "Do you think I could do anything to help? I mean, I am supposed to be in charge of the servants."

He shot me a look from the corner of his eye. "You could talk to Roger. He'd listen to you."

"I doubt that, but maybe I can talk to the gang downstairs and see if I can straighten things out." The big grandfather clock interrupted me as it tolled the hour. "Poop, I'm officially on display. Maybe there's enough time for me to just pop downstairs and see—"

Roger, Sam, Kip, and Wilma burst through the green baize door.

"Drawing room, now," Roger ordered, shooing me before turning and snapping out some orders at Sam.

"Drat, I can't go down now," I whispered quickly to Teddy. "Do me a favor: Trot downstairs and tell everyone who's unhappy to give me the specifics, and I'll try to run interference for them later with Roger."

"Tessa!"

"I'm coming, I'm coming. I don't know what your knickers are in such a twist for; there's no one here yet."

Just as I spoke, a sharp hammering came from the front door.

Roger grabbed me by the arm and hustled me to the drawing room just as Teddy went to admit whoever had come to pay a call on the Duchess of Bridgewater. I had just smoothed my dress and struck what I hoped was an elegant and sophisticated pose when Teddy opened the door.

"The Reverend and Mrs. Hewitt."

I recognized the names from the info sheet as belonging to the local vicar and his wife. I assumed that Roger must have had some arrangement with them to pay me the obligatory visit, no doubt outfitting them in appropriate attire.

I assumed wrong.

"Your Grace, what a very great honor it is to meet you at last." A pleasant, round-faced man paused at the door and made a bow embellished by fanciful gyrations of a lace-cuffed hand. "I am Reverend Hewitt, the vicar for Worston. I am so delighted that at very long last the duke has brought home a bride worthy of the noble house of Bridgewater."

I stared at him. I couldn't help it, I honestly couldn't. From the top of his tricornered hat to the toes of his lavender satin, diamond-buckled shoes, the vicar was the embodiment of a late-eighteenth-century dandy à la the Scarlet Pimpernel. We're talking lacy ruffles at his neck, a salmon-colored watered silk coat that reached to his knees (opened to display a gold-embroidered long vest), tight satin knee britches of a mauveish color, and white stockings. He swept his hat off his head and made another bow, a ring-encrusted hand held to his chest as he waved the other toward the door. Reluctantly, I dragged my gaze off the pink-powdered wig that sent long tendrils of curls snaking down his shoulders to look at the vision coming through the door.

"Oh, lord," Roger muttered from where he stood in the corner of the room, one hand over his eyes.

"And this, of course, is my lady, Penelope."

Penelope had a bit of trouble getting through the doorway. "Good afternoon," she called into the room, her face red-cheeked and cheerful, a bright sunny smile on her lips. She grunted slightly as she pushed her huge, and I mean *huge,* Scarlett O'Hara hoop skirt through the door into the drawing room. The skirt's framework snapped back into its hemisphere shape with an audible *whoop.*

She came forward, holding out a hand covered in a netted glove, her skirt swaying and banging into the occasional tables as she moved. "What a pleasure it is to meet you. Oh, my, what a lovely dress. Greek, isn't it? Very stylish."

I stood up slowly, my eyes wide as I took in her big, floppy-brimmed hat decked out with cherries, silk flowers, a couple of stuffed birds, and what looked to be a badger's head sitting on the crown, the red-and-pink striped dress with matching white-and-red bolero jacket, and the lacy pink parasol that dangled by a cord from her wrist.

"Penny," her husband hissed. As she turned to see what it was he wanted, her skirt swung out, slamming into a small cherry wood table, knocking a lovely bust of Athena off the top. Wilma threw down the boom and microphone, flinging herself forward, down on one knee to catch the bust just before it hit the ground.

"You don't shake a duchess' hand unless she offers it first. It isn't polite."

"It isn't?" Penelope turned back to me, her skirt swinging the other way, sending her husband staggering a few paces to the side. Wilma replaced the bust and dragged the table toward her until it was out of danger. "Oh, I'm ever so sorry. I didn't realize it wasn't proper to shake your hand."

"It's a pleasure to meet you, as well," I finally said, getting a grip on myself and offering her my hand. She grinned and shook it, glancing over to where Sam was struggling to film without laughing. Roger had slumped down into a chair against the wall, out of sight of the camera, sitting with both hands over his eyes. Kip squatted next to him and whispered furiously in his ear, gesturing toward the Odd Couple.

That decided me. Clearly, the production company hadn't outfitted them, which meant they had decided to join the fun of their own accord. From the looks of it, they'd raided the local theater company for costumes. They looked like nice people, honestly thrilled to be there, and clearly they'd done their best to get into period costume for the show. That they missed by a century on his part and twenty years on hers was of no matter.

"How very kind of you to come to see me. I do hope you'll stay to tea?" I asked. They beamed back at me and nodded.

"Excellent, why don't you sit just here, Mrs. Hewitt." I patted the spot next to me on a the gold-and-black couch as I sat back down. She flashed me another smile, and with a self-conscious bob toward the camera, sat next to me.

Instantly, I was enveloped in hoops, crinoline, petticoats, and what was probably eight yards of pink-and-red striped material. The front part of her skirt swung upward, one of the hoops smacking me sharply on the nose.

"Oh, I'm so sorry, I had no idea it would do this . . . Kevin, can you help?"

The Salmon Pimpernel hoisted her to her feet, and with my help we managed to get her onto the couch in a way that it wouldn't expose her underfrillies. I had to sit on part of the hoop to keep it beaten into submission, but that was a small price to pay for the look of pleasure in Penelope's eyes once we got her settled.

"Well, that was a trial, wasn't it?" she laughed, her

cheeks a bit pink with embarrassment. "I never thought to practice taming my dress before I went out! Yours seems to be well behaved."

"My lady's maid, Crighton, wouldn't allow it to be anything else but well behaved. It is a bit warm, though, for the lovely weather we're having."

Penelope rooted around in her pink netted handbag, then extracted from its depths a large black-and-white fan. "We're having lovely weather, aren't we? So unusual. Usually, we have terribly wet Septembers."

Penelope chatted happily about the weather and the local area for several minutes, while Kevin the vicar sat in a chair across from us, his hat on his knee, on his face a smile that he shared between his wife and me as he sent shy little looks toward the camera.

"Well, it's a bit yet until tea, but I imagine you'd like something cool to drink," I said after Penelope had run out of small talk. "I'll just ring for some lemonade, and you can tell me all about what it's like to be a vicar in Worston."

"That would be lovely," Kevin said, tugging unobtrusively at his neckcloth.

I stood up to ring the bell situated next to the door, but I'd forgotten about the hoop skirt. It sproined up after me, smacking me on the butt as I stood.

"Bloody hell," said Penelope as her dress came to life again, then her eyes widened and she covered her mouth with both hands, looking with horror at the camera. "Oh! I mean *the devil take it*!"

I tugged on the bellpull a couple of times, then went back to the couch and sat on her dress.

"The duke is home today?" Kevin asked. "I had hoped to speak with him. I'd love for him to read a lesson on Sunday."

"Oh, yes, he's home. He's just out fishing and throwing temper tantrums, but I expect he'll return for—"

The door to the room was flung open suddenly.

"That's it, I've had it!" the dark-haired, aptly named Raven shouted, storming into the room with a dramatic sweep of her hand. Behind her followed Shelby, the second scullery maid. Both women wore dull gray dresses, stained dark with perspiration, sweat gluing their hair to their heads. Raven glared at Sam and the camera for a moment, then turned to me. "I'm not washing one more pan for you lot, do you understand? I didn't agree to become a slave, and that's what I am—nothing more than a slave. Look at my hands, just look at them!"

She shoved her hands, red and scraped and unhappy-looking, into my face. "It's not bad enough we have to wash filthy dishes and scour pots and pans. Oh, no, we're not allowed proper washing-up liquid. Well, no more! We're revolting!"

"Oh, I don't know," I said, trying for a moment of levity. "You're a bit sweaty and disheveled, but surely not *revolting*."

The joke went over like a rotting cow carcass.

"You're the duchess; you're supposed to be in charge. We want some changes around here, and we'd better get them or else!"

Shelby stood nervously behind Raven, nodding vigorously.

I glanced over at Roger. He waved both hands at me, clearly telling me it was my problem to solve.

"I'll see what I can do, Raven, but I'm afraid—"

The door burst open again. "My lady!"

"Your Grace," came a chastising response from the hall, delivered in Teddy's dulcet tones.

"Your Grace," Bret the footman amended, "we have an emergency downstairs."

He stopped behind the two girls, who swung around to glare at him. He winked at them both.

"I've already told her we're revolting," Raven said.

"Are you? I don't think you look that bad. Nothing a quick cleanup can't fix. If you'd like to meet me later at the dairy, I'd be happy to—"

"Oh, shut up, you randy git," Raven snapped.

"What exactly is the problem, Bret?"

Teddy stepped into the room, one hand outstretched

toward the door as he turned slightly to face the camera, lifted his chin, and said with perfectly clear enunciation, "Your Grace, the butler is stinking drunk."

"This is exciting," Penelope said, bouncing a bit as she wapped down her skirt so she could see what was happening. "Kevin, isn't this exciting? And we're a part of it!"

"Drunk?" I asked, astounded. "Palmer is drunk?"

"Very exciting," Kevin agreed, and turned eyes bright with delight back to me.

"Really drunk? Maybe he has heatstroke. Are you sure he's drunk?"

"Arseholed," Bret nodded.

"Wonderful," I said, trying to muster a smile for the camera and failing utterly. "I have two revolting scullery maids and an arseholed butler. Well, we're just going to have to sober him up."

"What about us? We were here first! You have to take care of us before you can coffee up that old souse."

"He's not an old souse," Teddy said with a flick of his head. "He's my father!"

"Your *what?*" I gasped. I didn't remember seeing that on the fact sheet.

"My father," Teddy answered me, making sure to keep his handsome profile well within the vision of the camera. He emoted for all he was worth. "I have kept this secret all my life, but now, when he needs me most, it is time I admit the truth. I am Ian Palmer's love child."

"He's good, isn't he, Kev?"

"Yes, very. I wonder if he'd like to join the Merry Minstrels? We could use someone like him for next year's Penzance."

Teddy made a subtle acknowledging movement of the praise before resuming a pose with head bowed to disclaim all the grief, anguish, and paternal pride a brave young man could feel for his love-child-spawning arseholed father.

It was all bull, of course. No doubt Teddy figured he'd try his acting skills for the viewing audience.

"Your Grace, if I might have a moment of your time?" Mrs. Peters sidled into the room, narrowing her eyes at the footmen and the maids, who were now standing sullenly with their arms crossed, glaring at Bret as he ogled them.

I took the Athena bust from the table and used it to hold down the part of Penelope's skirt I was sitting on, rising as gracefully as I could considering that my organs had been crushed together for almost three days. Roger had a hand on a furious Kip, holding him back so he wouldn't interfere. Sam's lips twitched as he looked around the room. Wilma was wiping back tears of laughter. Clearly, no one was going to take charge.

I guessed it was Tessa-to-the-rescue time. Oy.

"What is it, Mrs. Peters? Is Palmer all right?"

"I wouldn't know, Your Grace. He appears to be curled up sleeping in a coal scuttle. I have something of much graver importance to discuss with you."

"What would that be?" I asked wearily, wondering if the day would never end.

"Poltergeists."

I stared at her for the count of five. "Ah. I see."

"There are poltergeists in the west wing, Your Grace. As you are aware, the west wing houses not only the servants' hall, but the family's bedrooms."

"You're sure it's poltergeists? It's not just . . ." I waved my hand around vaguely. ". . . mice or something?"

Her brows drew together as she shook her head, her usual corona of fuzzy hair shaking vigorously with the movement. "Mice seldom rain down herrings, Your Grace."

I counted to ten this time, ignoring Roger's groan and Wilma's chirrup of laughter. "It's been raining herring in the family's rooms?"

"And the servants' hall," she nodded.

I looked around at the other servants. They all looked as confused as I did. "Have you guys seen it raining herring?"

"The herring were apports, Your Grace," Mrs. Peters said quickly before anyone else could speak. "They disappeared into their ethereal forms shortly after they made their appearance. Unless the spirits decide to reveal the apports to you, you might not notice them before they dissolved into ectoplasmic nothingness."

I gave in and had a good blink. "All righty. Um. I suppose—"

"*Merde!* Get out of my way. I must speak with the Duchess Tessa!" A young woman I recognized from the project information sheet as the governess, Mademoiselle Beauvolais, pushed her way through the fast-gathering crowd, the housemaid named Easter in tow. "Here she is," she said with a flourish, shoving Easter forward. "Here is the fire starter. You will now masturbate her!"

I stared at Mlle. Beauvolais in stark surprise. *"What?"*

"Masturbate, masturbate! Do you not speak the language? You must punish her!"

I wondered what new sort of hell had descended upon me. Where on the duchess' duty sheet did it say I was supposed to sexually pleasure the housemaids? "Castigate, you mean?" I asked slowly.

"Yes, yes, that is what I say! This one, she is always starting the fires in the day nursery. I tell her it is summer still, it is too hot, but she starts the fires, anyway. Each day I must put them out, deranging myself greatly to do so. This morning I say that I will bring her before you if she start the fire again. As soon as I went to discover where the *petite môme* has gone, she started the fire again!"

"Môme?" I asked.

"The unpleasant one, the child Melody. *Quel sale gosse!*"

I had a feeling she wasn't saying anything nice about

Melody, but let that go for the moment. I looked at the housemaid. "OK, Easter, dish. What's the story?"

She grinned. "I like to start fires."

I looked at her for a moment, then shook my head. "You know what? I think we're all going to take a time out—"

The door was thrown open again, but unfortunately Bret was in the way. It bounced off him and shot smartly toward the man standing in the doorway, his hands fisted, his eyes a blue blaze of sapphire, steam all but curling out of his ears. Max caught the door and took a step into the room. Before him, the crowd parted as if he was Moses, allowing him to stalk between their ranks until he stood toe to toe with me.

"That's the best glower I've ever seen," I said calmly, waiting for the axe to fall. "Does anyone else here feel like they're in a Marx Brothers movie?"

"Melody," he snarled through gritted teeth, his fingers twitching as if he wanted to strangle something. Or someone. I had a sudden horrible feeling I knew who that would be, too.

"Your daughter? That Melody?"

"My daughter has gone off on one of the horses."

I tried to look unconcerned. "Oh."

"Against my orders."

I dropped the unconcerned look and began worrying my lower lip. "Ah."

"Alone," he said, leaning toward me until I thought his gaze would scorch my flesh.

"Oy."

"She told Alec," he said, leaning even closer, "that she had your permission to do so."

"Oh, crap."

"I am going out now to look for her. If I do not find my daughter safe and unharmed, Tessa, I will know upon whose head the blame will rest."

Somehow, I don't think he was talking about himself.

"Er . . ."

He spun around and stormed back through the line of people, but pulled up when Clara Billings panted her way into the room.

"Kitchen's on fire," she said cheerfully. "Anyone have a fire extinguisher?"

The At Home kind of went downhill after that.

—⚏—

Friday
September 3
7:22 A.M.
Morning room

Max Edgerton is a poop!

—⚏—

Friday
September 3
8:57 A.M.
Alcove above stairs

I can't believe I let him put his fingers inside me. I can't believe I thought about him all last night. I can't believe I indulged in smutty thoughts about him. He's a poop and nothing but a poop.

Men!

—✺—

Friday
September 3
1:50 P.M.
Verandah

He's also a horrible judge of people. He doesn't deserve me. I hope he grows warts. *Everywhere.*

—✺—

Friday
September 3
10:33 P.M.
The room next to His Grace, the Duke of Poopy Pants

What a day! I wonder if life really was like this for the Victorian duchesses, because if it was, I take back all the smug comments I've made about them being useless little dolls. Let's have a little recap of all that's happened in the last twenty-four hours, shall we?

First, there was the kitchen fire. As it turns out, it wasn't really on fire; the pipe leading from the stove was clogged and belching black coal smoke into the kitchen. Roger, Kip, and Michael the third footman managed to get it cleared enough so that the smoke went up the stovepipe rather than into the kitchen.

Raven and Shelby were ready to walk out unless they got modern-day liquid dishwashing soap. Roger said no, it would ruin the project, but I sent Teddy into town today with orders to smuggle back a small bottle of liquid soap. What Roger doesn't know won't hurt him. I hope.

We found no signs of herring, ectoplasmic or otherwise. As far as Mrs. Peters goes, I have a feeling that there's a light on, but no one's home.

Roger took Easter the pyromaniac aside and told her to confine her fire starting to the stove until the weather turned colder.

Palmer slept off his binge in a heap of coal, and appeared this morning limping heavily and talking about the possibility of signing up for a kidney transplant, but with most of his dignity intact. Max supposedly had a talk with him about drinking on the job and the medicinal uses of beer. I wouldn't know, because Max isn't speaking to me, but that's another issue.

And last but not least, Melody was returned to her father's doting arms safe and sound. I'm the one who found her, having followed Max when he went out to hunt for her as the others ran downstairs to deal with the fire in the kitchen.

"Max, wait a minute, I can't run in this dratted corset," I yelled after him as he headed toward the stable.

"I didn't ask you to come along," he snapped over his shoulder, not even slowing down.

"I know you didn't, you obstinate man, but I'm trying to help."

"You've done enough to help today, thank you."

I thought for a few seconds of hefting a rock and throwing it at the back of his head, but decided that was childish.

Instead I stuck out my tongue at him.

"I didn't tell her it was OK to go riding by herself. I would never say that to a kid, especially one who'd never been on a horse before. Will you slow down?"

Max muttered something that I didn't hear, then he hallooed up Alec, who appeared in the doorway to the stables. "Has she returned?"

"Not yet."

Max swore. "How the hell did she get a horse without you seeing her?"

Alec looked like a blond Adonis in the late afternoon light, his hair burnished, his shirt a stark white in comparison to the tanned column of his throat, his eyes alight with his usual good humor, albeit now a bit clouded with concern. "Thom saddled up one of the mares for your sister. He said Melody came out, chatted him up a bit, and took the mare when he went in to check on one of the bays."

"Hell. She could be anywhere! Dammit, man, why aren't you doing anything?"

"Max, it isn't Alec's fault. Yelling at him isn't going to help."

He spun around and glared at me. "As this whole nightmare is your fault, would you prefer me to yell at you instead?"

I looked at him silently for a minute, weighing my options. I knew Max was overreacting about the danger Melody was in, but he really was concerned about her. "Fine, you think this is my fault. Well, then, I accept the blame."

Max looked surprised as I turned to Alec. "She took Penny?"

"Yes. She'll be safe on Penny, Max. A baby could ride Penny."

Max snarled an oath under his breath and spun around, scanning the area visible between the outbuildings.

"Which way did Thom go?" I asked as I went into the stable, Alec following behind me. I grabbed the bridle next to Talisman's stall and greeted the horse as I slid the bridle on.

"To the north. He thought she might be headed toward the lake."

"Right. Max, you take one of the carriage horses and go east, toward the town. I doubt if she'd go toward the road with all the traffic on it, but you never know. Alec, you go south. Talisman and I will head west, out to the farm."

Alec nodded and went to fetch one of the remaining horses.

Max looked like a thundercloud about to burst into a

downpour. "I am not getting on any damned horse. I'll take Roger's car."

I led Talisman outside and over to a barrel that would serve as a mounting block. "His car? Why, don't you ride?"

His jaw tightened. "No. What are you doing? You don't have a saddle on that beast."

"Nope, I sure don't." I hoisted my skirts up to my knees with one hand, holding the reins with the other, and managed to get onto the barrel with only minor flashing of my combinations. "So you have horse issues as well as a tongue fetish. It's good to know you're not perfect. I was beginning to wonder."

I swung a leg over Talisman's back, settling myself and gathering the reins. My dress was hiked halfway up my thighs, but I doubted if anyone but Ellis would care that I was riding in a dress created to do no more than a little gentle promenading.

Max's storm cloud darkened even more. "You could be hurt riding without the proper equipment. I'll have Alec bring you out the saddle. Stay there."

I rolled my eyes and nudged Talisman forward. Max backed up quickly. "Don't be ridiculous. I've been riding bareback for years. Besides, I'm not terribly comfortable with the sidesaddle. Don't forget to check along the drive. She might have figured that was the safest area to ride."

His jaw worked for a minute, his blue eyes cloudy with emotion as he hesitated, the full measure of his worry and concern for Melody visible. I bent down and pressed a kiss crookedly to the corner of his mouth. "Don't worry, we'll find her safe and sound. You'll see."

I pressed my heels into Talisman, heading out of the area at a fast canter, leaving Max yelling warnings behind us.

Twenty minutes later I came across a bedraggled and dirty Melody stumbling through a field left fallow, leading Penny. Her face was streaked and splotched where she'd been crying, her yellow dress stained with grass and dirt, but she was in one piece.

She looked up when Talisman cantered down the field toward the farm that bordered the estate. For a moment I thought she was glad to see me, then her habitual scowl darkened her face.

"You OK?" I asked, pulling Talisman up. She held her right arm tight to her body, but other than that she seemed to be OK, despite having obviously taken a tumble.

"My arm hurts," she answered sullenly.

"Ah. Fell off, did you?" I asked as I slid off Talisman's back into the long grass.

"Are you always so clever?" she retorted.

There were still tears in her eyes, so I ignored her mutinous lower lip and gently took her arm. "Hmm. Looks like a sprain. Can you wiggle your fingers?"

"Yes."

"Let me see you do it." Her fingers wiggled. "Good enough. It's not too bad, it'll probably just be sore a couple of days. If I get you back up on Penny, can you ride?"

She glanced over at where Penny was cropping at the grass and hesitated.

"OK, how's this: We'll both ride Talisman, and I'll lead Penny."

"You don't have a saddle," she replied, frowning. "You're supposed to have a saddle when you ride a horse."

"Like father like daughter," I sighed, turning to Talisman. "All right, let's see if I can still do this."

It took me a few minutes of jumping, but at last I managed to hoist myself up onto Talisman's back and get a leg over him before he started off. "Come on, give me your good hand."

Melody looked at my offered hand, and shook her head, backing up. "No."

"You're not afraid, are you?"

That stopped her, but it didn't get her to come forward. "I'm not afraid. It's not safe to ride like that."

"Sure it is. I used to ride bareback when I was

younger than you. Took a lot of spills, too. The thing is to not let the fear take over. Come on, you can use my foot as a stirrup. I won't let you fall."

"I'm not afraid," she repeated, chewing on her lower lip for a minute. She must have decided looking like a coward was worse than possibly falling again, because eventually I got her up in front of me.

"You're not going to go fast?" she asked, her nervous voice belying the nonchalance she was so earnestly striving for.

"No, we'll go at a nice sedate walk. Can you feel the rhythm of how Talisman moves? You're too stiff, you're fighting the movement. Just relax, and let your body move with his. You won't fall."

Max was the first one to see us as we headed back toward home. He was driving down one of the side roads next to the field. I waved when he stopped the car, getting out to peer across the field at us. I doubt if he could hear me bellow that we were going straight to the stable, but evidently he figured it out because he got back into the car and went roaring off toward the road that led to the house.

"Dad's going to be mad," Melody said.

"Yup. Probably wasn't the smartest thing going off on your own, huh?"

"I wanted to go riding, and you already showed me how. I knew he'd never let me."

I couldn't see her face but her voice held a familiar sullen tone.

"There's a lot more to riding than just walking around a stable yard, squirt, but I guess you found that out."

She turned around enough to scowl at me. "I'm not a squirt."

"It's that or a spoiled brat. Take your pick."

Her back stiffened as she faced forward again, indignity visible in every line of her body. We rode in silence for a few minutes before she said, "Dad's going to be mad at you, too, because you showed me how to ride, but you didn't do it good enough and I fell off and now my arm is hurt. He's going to yell at you. He'll probably hate you."

I looked down at the top of her head, the yellow ribbon tying back her braid smudged with dirt and leaves. A sudden pang of sympathy reminded me how unhappy I was when my parents divorced. It wasn't enough to keep me from wanting to make her walk the rest of the way, but it was enough to keep my comment confined to a simple, "And I'm sure that'll make you delirious with joy."

"Maybe," she answered, her back straight, her thin little shoulders rigid as she stared forward.

I grinned at the back of her head. She was just as obstinate as her father, a realization that for some reason amused me greatly.

Until we got back to the stable and met Max.

He came unglued when he found out that Melody had hurt her arm, hustling her off to Roger's car without even waiting for me to tell him it was only a sprain, without even saying thank you for finding his daughter. He just shouted something about the hospital, and off he went.

They were gone for several hours, and when they did return (it was only a sprain, and a pretty mild one at that, or so Roger told me), Max spent the rest of the evening in the nursery with Melody.

I wanted to talk to him, to explain again that I didn't tell Melody to go riding, but the way Max cut me out brought home the fact that I had no real right to interfere. Max and Melody were just my pretend family, and no matter how much I wanted to help them, I couldn't.

"This is what happens when you get involved with people," I told my sad reflection that night as I was preparing to go to bed. "No matter how much you want to make things better for them, sometimes you have to leave them alone."

My reflection stuck her tongue out at my words of wisdom.

The following morning, which, in case you're keeping

track of these things, is this morning, I was downstairs at the stables promptly at seven.

Imagine my surprise when the first thing I saw was Max.

Imagine my surprise when the first words out of Max's mouth were "I thought I'd find you here."

"Yeah, well, you wouldn't have to be the Amazing Kreskin to figure it out. I told you yesterday I was going to go riding this morning."

He ignored my smile and glowered down into my hopeful little face. "I wanted to say something where no one in the house could hear us."

"Oh, really? How very interesting. Is it something naughty? Were you having smutty thoughts about me all night? Do you want to do wicked things to me with that intimate tongue of yours?"

His eyes blazed sapphire. "I don't want you to see my daughter again. Clearly, you're a bad influence on her. You incite her to reckless and dangerous acts. You are a threat to her well-being."

"I didn't incite her to do anything, Max." His scowl grew. I hurried on before he could storm away without letting me say what I had to say. "Look, I'm sorry I put her on Talisman's back and walked her around the stable yard the other day. I didn't think it would hurt, but I realize now that you have every right to do what you think is best for your child. In the future, I promise to respect your orders."

His brows rose in surprise for a moment before descending into their familiar scowl. "You're apologizing? Admitting it was your fault?"

"I'm apologizing, yes, although I truly did not encourage or incite Melody into going off on her own."

"Oh. Good. Just so you know my feelings."

"I know. I understand. I swear I won't ever take her riding without your permission."

His jaw tightened. "That won't be an issue, since I have forbidden her to be alone with you."

Frustration mingled with something a whole lot

warmer. I ground my teeth for a moment, fighting the simultaneous urges to argue with him and kiss the scowl right off his face. "I know you're upset, and I understand why you're upset, and I've apologized. I've turned over a new leaf. But, Max, Roger said it was just a little sprain. Melody's not seriously injured. Maybe you should lighten up this overprotective father bit just a smidge?"

"Maybe you should mind your own business."

Ouch. Now, that one hurt. I took a step away from him, my heart compressing into a painful lump. He wasn't my husband. I didn't have any right to interfere. But oh, how I wanted to make things right between them, between us. If I could just get him to see how much I had to offer them both. That's what my brain was thinking—unfortunately, my mouth bypassed all those deep thoughts and went straight to what it wanted. "Do you know that you're incredibly sexy when you're angry? It's too bad you're so mad at me, because I've been rethinking my objections to intimacy, and I've decided I really want to know what you taste like."

He stood impassive for a moment, his eyes cold as the North Sea, then heat shimmered in them, a blue flame that licked along my skin until it stirred an answering fire deep within me. "I can't leave you alone," he growled, his jaw as tense as his words. "God knows I try, but I can't. Do you have any idea what you do to me, woman? Do you have any idea how you make me feel?"

"Other than furious, you mean?" I asked, a brief little flicker of hope stirring inside me.

Max ran a hand through his gorgeous hair. "Part of the time I want to strangle you, the other part I want you writhing beneath me, and all the times in between I just want to . . ."

He wanted me writhing beneath him? That was a good sign, wasn't it?

"What do you want to do?" I asked, wondering about the way anger was so often mixed up with sexual desire, even if the two had separate origins.

"Kiss you," he snarled, crushing me up against his chest.

I don't know what I was expecting, but it certainly wasn't the kiss he gave me. His mouth took possession of mine in a dominant, *I'm going to check and recheck every tooth in your head, and you have nothing to say about the matter* manner, his tongue not even pausing to ask permission, just pushing its way in and immediately taking over, ordering my tongue around, conducting a check of the perimeter, doing an amazing tongue dance all around my mouth that had me moaning and clutching Max's shoulders because my legs once again gave out on me.

I rubbed myself against him as his tongue twined around mine, then swallowed his groan of pleasure when I sent my tongue out on a little exploratory mission of its own. He made a seductive, primitive noise deep in his chest that pushed me over the edge, making me wild with the need to get closer to him, to join with him, to feel him not just in my body, but in my blood and soul and all those hidden little areas of my heart.

He pulled back for air and we stood, panting, staring at each other. My lips felt wonderfully abused and swollen, the taste of him still on my tongue.

"Does this mean you forgive me?" My words were jerky as I struggled to regain my breath and calm my madly beating heart.

His jaw worked for a few seconds, his eyes dark with unreadable emotion. "No."

Without another word he turned and went back into the house. He left me, he walked away and left me standing there, all breathless and bemused by his kiss and frustrated as hell. He just left me.

"You rotter, Max!" I yelled after him. "You can't kiss me like that and walk away!"

He kept walking, never once turning around to look back at me.

"Fine! Have it your way! That's it! This is war!"

There was a noise behind me. I spun around, ready to give whoever had been spying on us the lecture of a lifetime. Matthew and Tabby stood next to the door to the kitchen.

"Double or nothing?" Matthew asked Tabby.

She frowned and considered me for a good minute or so, then she nodded. "You're on."

I pointed a finger at Matthew. "You're going to lose that bet, buster. I just hope you can afford it."

He grinned.

Max pretty much avoided me the rest of the day, which was spent going over the linens with Mrs. Peters (who extolled the virtues of all the ghosts who wandered the halls of Worston as we counted sheets and towels), meeting Barbara's cronies, who all came for her At Home dressed in excruciatingly correct dress, a fact she didn't hesitate to point out often, and trying to settle arguments downstairs that seemed to be breaking out with increasing frequency.

Roger was of no help, telling me I was mistress of the house, I had to handle the servants' problems myself—as long as I didn't break the rules, of course. I thought guiltily about the bottle of dishwashing soap, but dismissed it as not being worth the trouble to fret over.

Max was polite but distant at meals. I thought about his kiss all day. I tried not to, but it kept coming back to me, and finally I just gave in and sat on the verandah and thought about it for a long time. I've come to the conclusion that although Max is pigheaded and obstinate and doesn't know a good thing when it's kissing him, I wanted him. I wanted all of him, not just his lips and his body, but all of him. I wanted him to trust me, I wanted him to talk to me, I wanted to know what he was thinking about, what he was feeling, what sorts of silly things made him laugh, and where all the tender spots of his heart were located.

I wanted his tongue to ravish mine again. And more. I wanted the whole enchilada, and everything that went along with it, all the emotional ties and the baggage and the heartache. Well, hopefully not the heartache.

I have a plan. I'm putting it into action tonight. Wish me luck.

Saturday
September 4
6:14 A.M.
Fainting couch in my bedroom

Mmmrowr!

Saturday
September 4
6:16 A.M.
Dressing table

Is it possible to die of happiness?

—∞—

Saturday
September 4
6:25 A.M.
Bed

Oh, baby!

—m—

Saturday
September 4
11:47 A.M.
The darling, darling escritoire

VERY IMPORTANT NOTE TO SELF: REMOVE THE
FOLLOWING SMUTTY ENTRY WHEN HANDING
THE JOURNAL OVER TO ONE OF THE MANY
PUBLISHERS PIERCE SWEARS WILL BE BEG-
GING FOR IT.

I've had some really good sex in my life. There was
the time that Peter tried Viagra, and he turned into the
Energizer Bunny and just kept going and going and
going until I wanted to knock him on the head with
something big because I mean, really, there *is* a limit to
the number of times you can make love during one
night.

However, last night with Max . . . well, let's just say
he brings new meaning to the word *sated*.

It didn't start out all that well, however.

On the way upstairs to get dressed for dinner, I ran into
Max, apparently doing the same thing. He said nothing but
waited for me to precede him up the stairs. I stuck my
nose in the air and marched up the stairs.

"This is stupid," I said as soon as I reached the top.
"I don't want to be mad at you, and I really don't want
you mad at me. I want to kiss you again. Can't we call a
truce? I've apologized. I've promised not to take Melody
riding without your permission. Can't you forgive me so
we can move on to the point where we do wicked,
naughty things to each other?"

His beautiful eyes narrowed. "There can be no truce."

Lord, how I wanted to shake him! "Why, because you

are afraid to forgive me? Is that it, Max? You're afraid of intimacy, and you're using your anger to mask the real reason you don't want to move on?"

"I am not the one with admitted intimacy issues," he said in a low growl. "My anger is justified. Any father would feel the same. The fact that I desire you and dream about you and want to touch every inch of your body until you're squirming with pleasure, those delicious breasts of yours heaving up at me as I thrust myself into your fiery heat again and again, your muscles rippling around me, gripping me in velvet fire, tightening and tightening until I know I'm going to explode deep within you . . ."

I stared at him, swallowing hard, my mouth suddenly dry. Max blinked a couple of times, a look of horror dawning as he realized what he said.

"Good god, what have you done to me? You've bewitched me somehow! Well, I won't let you do it! You can take away your lush, tempting, delectable body with all its glorious curves, because it will have no effect on me! My mind is made up. My daughter's life is more important than a few fleeting moments of pleasure."

It took me a moment, but at last I had a grip on my tumultuous emotions. Aware that Teddy was watching us from the hall below, I turned and walked down the hallway toward our rooms, Max following behind. I paused before the door to my room and looked back at him. "A few fleeting moments, huh? Doesn't sound like you are overly confident about your staying power."

He opened his mouth to say something, but I just smiled sweetly and slipped into my room.

Ellis was there waiting for me. "I thought the navy blue faille dress would do for this evening—"

The door to the bathroom was thrown open before she could finish the sentence. "Just so you understand, if I were to make love to you, *I* am not the one whose staying power would be in question."

"Oh!" I said just before he returned to his own room, slamming the door behind him.

Ellis looked at me strangely for a minute, then silently went around to my back and started unhooking the dress. I let her slip it off me, then, while she was turned to get the evening dress, I marched over to the bathroom, flung open the door, stomped through the bathroom, and threw open the door to Max's room. He was in the process of taking off his pants, Reg Crighton standing next to him with a pair of pants hanging over his arm, and an extremely shocked expression on his face.

Max scowled when he saw me.

"Are you implying that I can't keep up with you sexually? Because if you are I have one word to say to you: ha ha ha ha ha ha ha!"

I turned on my heel and flounced my way back to my room, feeling wonderfully vindicated.

"What—" Ellis said, then stopped when Max appeared in the doorway sans pants.

"That was seven words, not one. You might try using your fingers to count next time."

I was right behind him as he stormed back into his room.

"I did use my fingers, buster. On you! Not to mention my mouth. And you *loved* it! So don't give me that line about me not being able to keep up with you. If we were to have sex, I'd wipe the floor with you!"

I turned, but he grabbed my arm before I could make it out of his room, hauling me up close to him, his eyes burning into mine. Ellis stood watching us from the open doorway of my room, while Reg was gaping behind Max.

"Right, that's it, take off your clothes!" Max ordered.

"What?" I will admit a few blinks slipped in there as I looked up into his stormy eyes.

"Take off your clothes. I'm making love to you, right here, right now. We'll just see who wipes the floor with whom."

I goggled at him for a minute, then started chuckling. He really was adorable. How could I resist such a man?

"Max, we can't."

"Sure we can," he said, stripping the tie from his neck and unhooking his collar. "I'm an adult, you're an adult, and we both have the requisite set of equipment. You've challenged my manhood. I'm not going to take the sort of insinuations you've been bandying about lying down. So to speak."

The chuckles worked their way into a full-fledged laughter. "Yeah, but . . . but . . . oh, man, you're making my sides hurt. I can't laugh in a corset."

His nostrils flared with outrage as he shot me a look that should have knocked me down cold. "You're *laughing* at me?"

"No," I said, laughing even harder, wrapping my arms around my stomach. "Well, OK, I am, but you're so funny! One minute you're furious with me, the next you're ordering me to strip. Max, Ellis and Reg are both standing here. I know we're not supposed to really notice the servants, but I draw the line at going to bed with you in front of an audience."

He looked around, narrowed his eyes, then leaned forward until we were nose to nose. "Eleven o'clock. Right here."

"Are you challenging me to a duel of sex?" I asked softly, rubbing my nose on his.

He inhaled deeply. "Yes."

"I thought you weren't going to forgive me? I couldn't possibly do anything so intimate with a man who was so angry with me."

"I'm not angry," he snarled.

I raised an eyebrow.

"Perhaps just a little. But it's something we'll work out."

It was an olive branch; there was no doubting that. Max was acknowledging that there was something powerful between us, and if he wasn't willing to forgive and forget, at least he was offering us a chance to build on the shaky ground we stood.

"Very well, I accept your challenge. I suggest you dine

well, Your Grace. You're going to need every ounce of energy you can rally."

Max's eyes darkened a couple of shades. I smiled and kissed him on the tip of his nose, then returned to my bedroom and a sour-looking Ellis.

Dinner that night was . . . oh, my. I'm trying to think if there are enough synonyms for the word *arousing*. There aren't, so I'll just confine myself to saying that dinner was most definitely an experience.

Max fired the opening salvo in our little war of seduction when he helped me into my chair. As he stepped away from scooting me in, his fingers trailed from behind one ear, along the nape of my neck, to the sweet spot behind my other ear. Immediately, my whole body went up in flames.

"Dinner at last. I know it's not at all the thing to say, but I am simply famished! Max, Henry and I went to see Bunny Watkins today, you remember her, don't you?"

"Oh," I said softly enough so that no one else but Max could hear over Barbara's chatter. "You are not playing fair!"

"She and I went to school together. I'm sure you remember her; she looked a bit rabbity when she was younger, but thankfully she's grown out of that."

Max just smiled at my comment and took his seat at the opposite end of the table. I was a bit surprised to see that we weren't going to be filmed, but remembered that Sam had offered to film Mrs. Peters' nightly séance instead. No doubt Tabby was filming the servants doing their evening chores.

This was all to the good, of course, as it gave me free rein to torment Max without the camera's unblinking eye upon me. While I contemplated what form my answering shot would take, Max lifted his glass of wine to me in a silent toast, drinking deeply as he gave me a look that could steam drapes.

"Well! She married one of the Ffinchwattles—you know, the marmalade Ffinchwattles? They have a lovely home just outside of town, although it's not in an entirely desirable neighborhood, if you know what I mean."

I inclined my head slightly in acknowledgement of the toast, then made sure he saw me lick my lips—slowly and with much tongue action—before taking a spoonful of soup. I pursed my lips with exaggerated care, and blew gently across the spoon, then slowly tipped the spoon up to my lips, licking it clean with long, loving strokes of my tongue.

"Shops, of course, shops everywhere. I realize we must have them, but in our neighborhoods? It's just not at all the thing. Still, it's a lovely home, and I won't hear anyone say a word of criticism about her choice of decorators."

Max's eyes widened, then narrowed into icy blue slits as he reached for his wineglass. He played with the stem of the glass, the tips of his fingers running lightly over ridged design cut deeply into the crystal. My breathing got a bit shallow as his fingers swirled around the glass, higher and higher in a widening circle, dancing along the rim until suddenly he plunged one long finger deep into the liquid.

"Although I have always said that one really can have too much plaid. Haven't I said that, Henry? Be that as it may, Bunny has a lovely home, and of course, the children were there, which meant they all had to give their Auntie Babs a big kiss."

A shudder of pure and utter desire swept through me as his tongue flicked out and caught the bead of wine from the tip of his finger.

I licked my lips slowly, carefully. The look in Max's eyes promised payback, a payback that was thankfully delayed until the second course.

"What's this?" Max asked, leaning forward as if he was peering into the dish presented to him, but really he was shooting me looks that would have done Valentino proud. "It looks like roasted chicken."

"It is orange chicken, Your Grace," Palmer said.

Max picked up the serving forks and slid me another

glance. "I believe I'll have some breast. I've always found breast to be succulent, divinely succulent, perfectly suited to my mouth and tongue. I do so love the taste and texture of a really firm breast. Although I like thighs as well, especially well-rounded, soft thighs, long thighs, thighs a man can really sink his . . . teeth into."

Beneath the table, I crossed my legs.

"Oh, now, you see, Henry is just the same way. Dark meat, that's all he ever eats, dark meat. He's never so happy as when he's eating duck."

"Why look, it's buttered asparagus," I said, taking a piece in my fingers. "I haven't wrapped my tongue around a piece of buttered asparagus in years."

I licked my lips and sucked the tip of the asparagus into my mouth, sliding it in and out, opening my mouth just enough to allow Max to see my tongue as it caressed the underside of the stalk.

Max sat perfectly still, a forkful of chicken frozen halfway to his mouth.

"Oh, it's so *good*," I cooed, then started loudly sucking the butter off the asparagus.

Max's fingers tightened around his fork until I thought he was going to bend it in two.

"My very favorite part is the tip, where it flares out and captures all the silky goodness of the butter." I slid the length of the asparagus into my mouth, then pulled it out slowly, baring my teeth to show them grating along the stalk.

Max's hand trembled.

With a wicked, wicked smile I keep for just such an occasion, I laved the head of the asparagus with my tongue, then snapped my teeth closed, biting the asparagus in two.

There was a loud clatter of crockery as a silver salver, ceramic plate, and several pieces of asparagus hit the floor.

Bret the footman stood next to Max, staring at me with bulging eyes as I dangled the remains of the well-pleasured asparagus between my fingers.

"Something the matter, Bret?" I asked innocently.

Max choked.

"No," Bret gurgled, then stiffly got to his knees and cleaned up the mess.

I won't go into how Max ate grapes at the end of the meal. I'm sure it's illegal in at least three countries, possibly more.

After dinner, I went immediately upstairs, not even hanging around the drawing room with Barbara, as she insisted I do.

"Sorry, I really, really need a bath," I told her, and escaped before she could make any protests. Max and Henry were still in the dining room, having their port and cigars. I figured I had at least half an hour before Max would come upstairs, which left me a half hour after that to get ready for the sexual showdown.

"Bath!" I said to Ellis as I burst into my bedroom.

She gave me a jaded look.

"Oh, don't start that bit again about fraternization of cast members," I said, shooing her out the room. "Just go ask the girls if they'd bring up the hot water for my bath."

"Sexual congress between individuals—" she started to say.

"Yeah, yeah, yeah, you said all that earlier. I know Max and I aren't really married, but hey, you're always after me to up the realism for the project; me jumping Max's bones is about as real as you can get. Water. Please. NOW!"

I had anticipated a lot of stuff the night before I joined this project, mostly things related to wearing a corset and long dresses all the time. What I hadn't considered was the aspect of time. Time to the noble classes of the Victorian age was a much different beast than time is to us today. Even though the bathtub in the connecting bathroom was equipped with taps, Roger had the water turned off so we couldn't cheat and take a quick bath, saying that the indoor plumbing was added after 1879; therefore, we couldn't use it.

I hadn't known that my first night here, when I walked

in on Max having his bath, but by now I was well aware that bathing was no longer a solitary sport. No more could I disrobe, turn on the water, and take my bath. No, bathing for the Victorian upper class meant sending down for water, waiting for suitable amounts of water to be heated on the coal stove, then carried upstairs by a parade of maids and footmen, who slowly filled the tub until the desired depth and temperature were reached. No longer was a bath a ten- or fifteen-minute task; now it was an undertaking that stretched out over the course of an hour.

During that time Ellis helped me out of my dress and corset, then went in to oversee the delicate process of filling milady's bath. I combed my hair out from the intricate curl and braids that Ellis had arranged, tying it up in a loose knot held together by one easily removed comb. By the time I did that, donned a sturdy red velvet dressing gown (which, unlike its lacy counterpart, did not reveal anything), and marched into the bathroom, the water had arrived.

"No, this is not hot enough. Stupid girl, go down and bring up another can of hot water this time."

Alice's face was red, but whether it was from the exertion of carrying heavy cans of water up three flights of stairs or whether it was from anger was impossible to tell.

"Hey, hey, hey! I don't think we need to be calling anyone names, Ellis."

"You are to refer to me as "

"Crighton, yeah, I know. My mistake." I dipped my fingers into the water in the tub. "It's fine, thank you, Alice. And thank Honey for me, too."

Ellis sighed noisily as she bustled around with a towel and soap. "A lady does not thank her servants."

"Well *this* lady does." I turned back to Alice and smiled. "I appreciate you guys slogging water up here at this time of night."

"You're welcome," she replied, shooting Ellis a victorious glance.

"Thank you, Crighton, I won't need you anymore tonight."

She sniffed in that annoying way she had. "It is my duty to assist in your bath."

There was no way I was going to let her bathe me! "Thanks, but honestly, you're really working too hard. I just know I must be a horrible trial to you, so why don't you go relax? I'm just going to go to bed after the bath."

Her gaze shot to Max's door. "Yes, but whose bed?"

I grinned. "That is the question, isn't it?"

"Your Grace—"

"Night, Crighton!"

With thinned lips and flared nostrils (one of her better looks), she left.

"Geesh, what a sourpuss. How are things downstairs?"

Alice paused on her way out of the room, giving me a rueful smile. "How are things? Let's see . . . Mrs. Billings told Palmer she had a recipe for a posset that would cure his migraine."

"Ah, he's on to migraines now?"

"Yes. All would have been well, except the posset is made up of equal parts of brandy, rum, and claret."

I made a moue. She nodded at it.

"Yes, you can imagine just how many possets he's had to take to get rid of his"—she made air quotes as she said the last word—"migraine. In addition, Raven is threatening to hide most of the dishes because she's tired of washing them, Mrs. Peters insists that Sam stay with her all night filming the Pug's Parlor because she thinks that's the center of the poltergeist activity, and Bret keeps disappearing with the scullery maids and my second housemaid."

"Disappearing? As in, they're out having a quickie?"

"Exactly."

I stared at her open-mouthed. "All four? At the same time?"

She laughed. "No, not all at once, but the girls are starting to get a bit snarky with one another over him."

"Oy. I'll have a talk with him tomorrow. Or maybe I'll ask Max to. Bret might take a request to rein in his libido a bit better from a guy."

She smiled, then tipped her head toward the door to Max's room. "So that's true, then? Bret said you and Max were all but tearing off each other's clothes during dinner."

A little blush swept up my cheeks. "Yeah, we got kind of carried away."

"You don't mind everyone knowing?"

I made a face. "Of course I mind everyone knowing, but honestly, Alice, is there anything I've done here in the last couple of days that the entire house doesn't know about?"

She thought about it for a minute, then shook her head. "I see what you mean."

"Between the cameras and having a servant everywhere, I figured there was no way we were going to be able to hide it. So why fight the inevitable? However, I really didn't know that Bret was watching us until he dropped the dinner. You should have seen his face!"

Alice chatted for a few minutes longer, then toddled off while I got into the lukewarm water, washed quickly, and was back into my room trying to decide just what armor I needed for the upcoming *engagement*.

I was just dabbing a bit of perfume behind my knees when I looked up and caught my reflection in the dressing table mirror. At the sight of my pudginess visible through the thin silk of the frothy lace nightgown, my doubts and insecurities reemerged in a tidal wave of disgust. I slumped down into the bench in front of the dressing table and glared balefully at myself. "This is stupid. What am I thinking? I'm too old and too fat. Max doesn't really want to have sex with me."

"You're absolutely right," Max's voice said from behind me. "I don't want to have sex with you."

I stiffened at his words, refusing to look at his reflection. It was bad enough I knew the truth; for him to come right out and say it was . . . devastating.

"I know," I said, hoping to forestall any further revelations. I mean, a girl can take just so much before she breaks down and bawls. "I'm sorry, I just got carried away by everything. You don't have to be here, Max. I understand completely. After all, I'm five years old than you. I could have baby-sat you!"

"Silly," he said, coming closer and nuzzling the back of my neck, his lips hot enough to send little rivulets of fire licking down my skin. "I don't want to have sex with you, Tessa, I want to make love to you. There's a difference, as you so wisely pointed out to me that first night."

Now I looked at him. I turned around on the bench and stared up at him, hope and desire and a healthy dollop of lust blossoming within me. Age difference be damned, he was *mine!* "You do? Really? You're not just saying that because I called your bluff in front of the Crightons?"

He grimaced as he pulled me up against him. "I apologize about that. I wasn't thinking very clearly when I shouted that I wanted to make love to you." He dipped his head and started nibbling on my ear. "You truly have bewitched me. I forget everything but what I want to do to you."

"But you're angry—"

"Not now," he said, his mouth a whisper against my skin. "We'll talk about it later."

I hesitated, hating for there to be anything between us, but his mouth was just too insistent. *This is a start*, my inner voice told me as I melted against him. *Take what he's offering without demanding everything at once.*

"Hooo," I said, my fingers digging into the dark blue wool of his dressing gown. "What sort of things has your busy little mind been imagining?"

He told me. I sagged against him, my legs having gone

utterly and completely boneless under the effect of words like *plunging* and *deep* and *lick every inch of you.*

"Now, can we get started, or do you have a few more objections to make?" he asked, turning slightly so he could slide his arm behind my knees.

"Hey, wait a minute! Max, you can't pick me up, I'm too heavy. I'll give you a hernia! You'll break your spleen or something."

Bent over as he was, his head was right at nipple level. He nuzzled his cheeks against my left boob for a moment, then opened his mouth and sucked me right through the nightgown. A streak of fire shot down from my nipple to my groin.

"You're not too heavy," he said, then scooped his arm behind my legs and straightened up.

He grunted when he did so.

"Hey!" I yelled, then smacked him on the shoulder.

He grinned and started toward the bathroom. "What?"

"You grunted! I heard you! That was definitely a *picking up a heavy object* grunt."

"No, that was a *I'm in a bad way sexually and can't wait to bury myself in you* grunt."

"Oh, right. Do I look like I just fell off the stupid wagon? Put me down."

He walked through the bathroom, into his bedroom beyond, pausing to kick the door closed behind him. "Why?"

"Because you challenged me to a duel. Duelists do not haul each other around. Put me down so we can count off ten paces."

"My sort of duel requires you to be much closer than ten paces," he said as he deposited me onto the biggest bed I'd ever seen. I don't know how I missed noticing it before; it was roughly the size of Rhode Island.

"Good lord!" I gasped, looking up at a blue-and-gold embroidered canopy. "This thing is monstrous."

"It is, isn't it? It does, however, have one benefit."

I dragged my eyes off the canopy to look at Max. "What's that?"

He slipped out of his dressing gown, his skin a lovely bronze in the diffused light of the oil lamps. "It has you."

My tongue cleaved to the roof of my mouth at the sight of him.

"You, sir, are absolutely gorgeous." I got onto my knees. "Look at you! Just look at you! You were nice before when you were taking a bath, but now you're even better. My lord, Max, you're perfectly formed! Abso-bloody-lutely perfect!"

He made an embarrassed little face and started toward me until I held up a hand. "No, stop. I want to look at you."

He humored me. What a sweetie—was it any wonder I was enamored with him?

"You've got nice feet," I said, figuring I'd start at the bottom and work up. "Big, but nice. And I like your legs, too."

"Thank you."

"You don't have turkey legs, like so many men have, you have nice legs, really defined muscles in your calves. Do you run?"

"Swim. Five miles every morning."

"Ah. That would explain your thighs, too. I mean, those are not the thighs of your average architect; those are thighs that get out and do things. You have lovely, lovely thigh contours, Max."

"That's nice of you to say so."

I dragged my eyes up from the bulge of his thigh muscles to a bulge of a different sort. He was hot and hard and ready for action. "I've already admired your penis, but I'll be happy to do it again. Do you have a pet name for it?"

"Er . . . no. Should I?"

"No, it's not necessary. It's just that some guys do. I just wondered."

He cleared his throat and said with great deliberation, "Tessa, I can honestly say that I don't care what you call it, just so long as you hurry up and finish this damned examination, because I'm about at the end of my tether. I don't know how much more of this I can stand without pouncing on you."

"Really? How very flattering. Moving on . . . You have a lovely stomach, Max, you really do, but I have a complaint."

Max looked down at his stomach. It rippled with muscles. "What?"

"You need a little softness there. You need a little belly. I've always had a thing for men with a belly."

He unfisted one of his hands long enough to run his fingers through his hair. "You want me to have a belly?"

"Yeah, just a little one, just a tiny one. Just a teensy, tiny little itty-bitty belly. Not a beer belly, just a little smoodge of softness there. It would melt me completely. What do you think?"

He rubbed his hand over his jaw. "I'll see what I can do. Are you done? Is it my turn now?"

"No. Your chest . . . Well, Max, your chest is the chest of a god. It's lovely, all bulgy with muscles without being too muscley, if you know what I mean, and I really like that you're not obscenely covered with chest hair, and yet you have enough to keep you from looking like a skinned Chihuahua. *And* you have sexy nipples."

"I'm glad you think so. Tessa, could you hurry this up? I really can't stand much more of it."

"Almost done. Turn around, please."

"What?" His eyes, which I admit were starting to show more than a hint of desperation, were wide with disbelief.

"Turn around, I want to see the back of you. Oh, never mind," I said, climbing off the bed, my lacy silk nightgown swirling after me. "You don't have to move, I'll just go around behind you to see—whoa, Nelly! Hoo!"

"What?" Max tried to look over his shoulder. "What are you hooing at?"

"You have the nicest butt! It's just absolutely adorable! I love the swoopy indentations on either side.

Wow. Fabulous butt muscles. Do you have to do a special exercise to get them? I just want to bite it all over."

"No," Max said firmly, turning around and picking me up again. Three long strides and he was at the bed. "I'm first. I get to bite first. You've had your turn; now it's mine."

His hand slid up my calf as he set me down on the bed, pushing the frothy nightgown confection up before him.

"Um. Maybe this would be better if I stood up."

Max, climbing on the bed to straddle my legs, looked down at me. "I can assure you it will be much better in bed, my fabulous butt muscles notwithstanding."

"No, I wasn't talking about that, I was talking about this. Foreplay. I think it's better if I stand."

He lifted my foot to his shoulder and began kissing my ankle, dipping his tongue into the little hollows around my anklebone. "Why?"

"Because I look fatter lying down." He stopped laving my ankle long enough to look at me. I fluttered a hand around my torso. "Lying down, everything smooshes out to the side and makes me look broader. I don't want you to see me all smooshed."

He blinked. "Would you like me to turn out the lamps?"

I gnawed on my lip for a moment, my heart warmed by such a generous gesture. Tempted though I was to say yes, I had to admit that I wanted to see him, all of him, every glorious inch. "No. But promise me you won't hold my smooshedness against me."

"I promise," he said solemnly, then kissed a trail up my calf to my knee, pausing to repeat the process on my other leg.

"Thank you."

"The only thing I plan on holding against you . . ." He shot me a look that could have melted glass. ". . . is me."

"Oh, yes, please!" I breathed, then my eyes rolled up in my head and I fell back into the featherbed mattress, all soft and gooshy beneath me, with Max all hot and hard above me. His mouth and hands on my flesh were a feast of sensation sending little tendrils of fire up my thighs, tendrils that erupted into an inferno as he kissed a line up one thigh, the silky brush of his hair against my sensitive skin sending shivers down my back.

"You, my fair duchess, are not wearing your drawers," Max said as he pushed my nightgown up to the top of my thighs. I stiffened for a minute, a stab of doubt dimming my pleasure, but I forced myself to relax. It was time, I was committed to this, I wanted it, and if he was repulsed by me . . . well, so be it. I'd die of humiliation, but so be it.

"I've seen you before," he mumbled against my thigh as he kissed higher, pushing the nightgown up over my hips. He avoided the part of me that was just about doing back flips to get his attention and kissed a hot, wet trail along the curve of my hip. I shivered again, my nipples tightening in anticipation as he nipped a side path across my belly.

"I know, but it wasn't like this."

He tickled my belly-button with his tongue, then looked up.

"Now there's something else at stake than just sex," he said—a statement, not a question. My heart did a happy little flutter that he understood me so well.

"Exactly."

He scooted up, capturing my thighs between his knees, his head dipped low to lick a path to my breasts.

"This has to go," he said, tugging the nightgown over my head.

Once it was off, I tightened my arms alongside my body.

"You see, this is a perfect example of what I was talking about," I said, a bit breathlessly to be truthful, as he nibbled a line up my breastbone. "If I weren't flat on my back, my boobs would be just where they should be, arranged in the traditional breast layout on my chest, but lying like this they've swooshed to either side. Any day now I'm going to wake up and they'll be in my armpits."

Max laughed and leaned forward over me. I wrapped my arms around him and tried to pull him down, but he resisted.

"Don't move."

"I just want to feel you—"

"No. You made me stand there and let you look at me with that deliciously wicked glint to your eyes. Now it's my turn."

"But you're touching me," I gasped, my back arching as his mouth found the underside of my left breast. I clutched the bedspread beneath me to keep from grabbing his head.

"You could have been touching me if you'd wanted to." He sucked an ever shrinking circle around my breast.

"I want to now," I shrieked as his teeth closed very gently over my nipple. "I want to rub myself all over you! I want to touch you and taste you and feel every bit of you. Oh, god, Max, I'm going to die if you don't do the other breast."

He lifted his head and smiled at me with wicked delight, then lowered himself slowly so that he was propped up on his elbows, his chest hair teasing my now perky breasts. His legs clamped my thighs together as he rubbed himself lightly along me from groin to shoulder, raining hot kisses along the side of my neck. I bucked beneath him, my arms trapped next to my body, unable to move except to arch myself against him.

"Max?"

"Mmmrf?"

His teeth scraped along the spot beneath my ear, until my body was as tight as a drawn bow.

"If you're not inside me in five seconds, I'm going to spontaneously combust and then you'll have to explain my charcoaled corpse to Roger."

He sucked hard on the shivery spot on my neck, then lifted his head, his eyes a brilliant blue. "I love a woman who gets demanding with me."

I bit his lip. "NOW!"

He chuckled a chuckle that I felt all the way to my toenails and shifted, sliding a hand between my thighs, pushing them apart. I skimmed my newly released hands up his arms, over the muscled shoulders and down the wonderful planes of his strong back, digging my fingers into the firm muscle of his rear as he settled between my legs.

He flexed the muscles beneath my hands and grinned when I laughed with the sheer joy of the moment, capturing most of my laugh in his mouth when he bent down for a kiss. His tongue was just as hot as the rest of him, swooping in to dance around mine, tasting me, letting me taste him, a wonderful, wild erotic dance that matched the movement of his body as he slid forward, his hardness pressing against me, parting me, pushing himself into my tingling core.

"Oh, hell!" I said into his mouth, and pushed back on his shoulders.

His eyes were wild. "What?"

"Condom!"

He stared down at me for at least ten seconds, the very tip of him still sitting snugly inside of me, my muscles cramping with the need to wrap themselves around his hot, hard length.

He swore.

"I'm sorry," I said, almost sobbing with need and desire and frustration. "I'm not on any birth control because . . . well, because I didn't think I'd need to be. I don't suppose you've been snipped?"

He just looked at me.

"Vasectomy?" I clarified.

"No." Slowly he edged out of me, then rolled off me to lie on his back, his chest heaving.

"I'm sorry, Max. You don't have any condoms?"

"No," he said again, his voice hoarse.

A tear leaked out of my eye. "I don't have any either. If I did I'd get them, but I don't—"

He shot up off the bed suddenly, diving for the dressing gown he had stripped off a few minutes before. "Stay there. I think I know where to get some."

He stopped at the door, looked at me oddly for a moment, then came back and kissed me. Hard. "Don't move a muscle. Not one single muscle."

"OK," I said, more than a little stunned by the heat clearly visible in his eyes. I smiled at the door as he left, stretching like a cat, digging my toes into the bedspread, burying my head into the pillow. It smelled like Max, all spicy and male and Maxish. Soon *I* was going to smell like Max. Well, parts of me were.

I frowned into the pillow and sat up, looking down at the parts in question.

"What if he doesn't find any condoms?" I asked my crotch. It was horrified at such a suggestion, and urged me in no uncertain terms to make sure that there were condoms a-plenty, because it had plans for Max that called for his parts to come visiting often.

"I'll settle for one to start," I said grimly, climbing out of bed to get my nightgown. I pulled it over my head, grabbed a night candle and lit it from one of the oil lamps, and hurried out of Max's room, my hand in front of the candle to keep it from blowing out. I hesitated at the stairs, trying to remember where everyone's rooms were. Max, I was certain, would have gone downstairs to where the footmen slept, figuring that Bret, at least, was sure to have a gross of condoms lying around.

I turned and raced back down the dark hallway I'd just come from, turning right at the end and continuing down a shorter passage to the back stairs that led up to the attics, where the maids slept.

"I feel like something out of Victoria Holt," I grumbled as I caught my image reflected in an uncurtained window, a white-clad, ghostly figure darting through the dark shadows of the hallway. "If a dog starts howling, I'm going back to my room."

I hurried barefoot up the uncarpeted back stairs, stumbling over my nightgown at the top step.

"Damn," I swore softly, the candle having fallen and

gone out when I tripped. I didn't stop to bemoan the situation; I didn't have the time. I wanted to find a condom and make it back down to Max's room before he came back. I didn't want to risk having him there with his motor all revved up and me nowhere to be found.

The window at the far end of the hallway was unshuttered, allowing a faint haze of moonlight to drift in. It was enough to let me see the dark shapes of the doors.

"Let's see. . . . Alice has a room to herself at the far end, I think. Or is it this end? No, it's the other end. Which means that Mrs. Peters and Cook are in the middle, then the two housemaids together, so that means *this* room should be the scullery girls'."

I leaned my ear close to the door and tapped softly on it, hating to disturb them if they were sound asleep. A giggle met my knock.

"It's just me. Tessa," I said, then opened the door and peeked in. "I'm sorry to bother you guys, but I just wanted to know if you had any condoms you could spare—oh. Hi, Sam. Fancy meeting you here."

"Tessa?" Alice pulled the covers up over her chest as Sam rolled off her, grabbing for the blanket to cover his lower parts. Her eyes were big in the dim lamplight.

"Hi, Alice. I'm really sorry, I thought your room was at the other end, but I must have gotten them mixed up. I wouldn't have disturbed you for the world—not that I knew Sam was with you to be disturbed. I just wouldn't . . . have . . . um . . . oh, blast. Never mind. Just go back to what you were doing."

I started to close the door.

"Tessa?"

I peeked around the edge of the door.

Sam reached down to the ground, then sat up, tossing something that flashed silver in the light. I caught the condom package and saluted him with it. "Thanks. You're a lifesaver. By the way, Alice, your fake leg is very cool."

She looked from me over to where her prosthetic leg was leaning against the chair. "Thank you."

"Night!"

I closed the door and felt my way down the hall, stopping briefly to swear at my stupidity. I could have lit my candle on their lamp. Oh, well, the condom was all that mattered. I clutched it to my chest and edged down the hall to the stairs, taking them slowly, feeling for each step with my bare toes.

The windows on the floor the family slept on were shuttered and dark, no moonlight at all coming in. Palmer must have roused himself out of his drunken stupor enough to put out all the house lights, because there were none lit in the hallway. It was black, blacker than black, a veritable black hole of blackness in that hallway. I had a nasty suspicion that the pounding of my heart had nothing to do with the arousal Max had generated, and everything to do with the age-old fear of things that couldn't be seen.

I remembered with sudden clarity everything Mrs. Peters had said about the house being haunted, and stood shivering for a moment at the end of the hall. Only the thought of Max could get me to walk blind into that abyss, but walk into it I did. I took a deep breath and, with the condom clutched firmly in one hand, the other outstretched to warn me of any of the chairs or tables that lined the hallway, I headed down to where Max's room was, counting as I passed them the faint black outlines that were all that was visible of the doors. Just as I tiptoed past the shared bathroom and was almost to Max's room, my hand brushed against something soft and warm, something that froze at my touch.

I blinked in the inky blackness, visions of American-hating, vengeful ghosts rising before me as I reached out with a shaking hand to determine if I'd gone too far and come up against the beautiful upholstered chair that sat beyond Max's room.

My hand touched flesh—cold, icy lifeless flesh.

"Aaaaaaaaaaaaaaaaack!" I shrieked, and threw myself backward, away from the ghostly thing that guarded Max's door.

It shrieked right back at me, a parody of my high-pitched, horrified sound. I stumbled backward, running into a half-moon table that hugged the wall.

"Dammit!" I swore as both the table and I tumbled to the ground.

"Tessa?"

The word came soft and breathless out of the darkness, making my blood run cold as I struggled to extricate myself from the yards of silk that wound around my legs. It knew my name! Oh, God, the ghost knew who I was!

"Tessa, is that you?"

I stopped trying to pull the table on top of me to keep me from the ghost's horrible claws, and peered up into the darkness. "Max?"

There was a thud and a grunt of pain. "Damn. Where's the bloody door?"

He found it a second later, the blessed, wonderful soft glow of the oil lamp spilling out into the hallway.

"Oh, Max, I thought you were the ghost," I said as he pulled the table off of me and helped me to my feet.

"What were you doing running around in the pitch black?" he asked, pushing me inside the room, locking the door behind us.

"I went to find a condom, and my candle blew out. You felt like a ghost! How come your skin is so cold?"

He held up a strip of condoms. "Had to go out to the stable to get them."

"Alec?" I asked, rubbing my calf where I had whacked it on the table.

He nodded.

My lips twitched as I looked at him. His black hair was tousled, his dressing gown buttoned crookedly, and there was a smudge of dirt on the side of his nose. I rubbed it off with my thumb, saying, "I'm sorry, but I may have to rethink you and me doing this."

He looked at me like I had condoms coming out my ears. "Why?"

I nipped his lower lip and tucked the condom Sam

had given me into the breast pocket of his dressing gown. "When I touched you in the hallway you screamed like a girl." I shook my head in mock sadness. "It just wasn't manly, Max, and if there's one thing I insist on in all my lovers, it's that they be manly."

He stared at me for three seconds before whipping the nightgown off me, pulling the dressing gown off himself, and tossing me onto the bed, following me down into the soft down of the featherbed.

"Now we will address the subject of manliness," he growled, rubbing himself along me.

"Oh, yes, address it, address it long and hard," I moaned, grabbing a condom and tearing the package open with my teeth as he went straight for my nipples, licking them into a frenzy. "Address it like it's never been addressed before! Max, if you . . . oh, baby! If you . . . if you . . . yes, yes, right there! If you slide up I can put this on you—" The word trailed off into a moan as the licking turned to sucking. I gathered together enough parts of my mind to reach between us and unroll the condom onto him even as I squirmed against him.

Max bucked under my hands and peered down at me, balanced on his hands. His eyes were brilliant blue, blazing with need and desire and all the things that I knew were visible in my eyes, but it was his voice that sent me over the edge; rough and hoarse, it set something inside me thrumming. "Tell me you're ready. If you have any mercy in your soul, you'll tell me you're ready for me. Please, Tessa!"

"I was ready half an hour ago," I answered, pulling him down onto me and sliding my legs up over his. "Oh, geez . . . no, to the left . . . no, that's too far, you need to go down a little. Stop! Wrong door! Just a second, let me get you started . . . aaaaaiiiiieeeeeee!"

Max lunged into me with one hard stroke, pulled back a smidge, then lunged even deeper and harder, filling me with his heat. I shook with the intensity of feeling him inside me, joined with me, his body plastered against mine, his breath ragged and hot in my ear as he stroked in deeper. I clutched his back, my body tight and tense, pulling my legs up higher on his hips to take him in deeper, and then everything within me exploded, blinding me with a miracle of such beauty that I wept with the joy of it all. Max yelled something that sounded suspiciously like a yodel as he pounded into me, his back arched and sweaty beneath my hands as he found his own moment of rapture.

He collapsed down onto me, and I welcomed his weight, nuzzling his neck and stroking my hands along the damp planes of his back, still quivering with wonderful little aftershocks of pleasure and feeling the same running through him. It felt right being with him, being joined in the most elemental way, almost as if there was no end to him and no beginning to me. We just *were*.

Sometime later, after his chest stopped heaving and I could breathe without gasping, he propped himself up on one elbow and looked down on me. His eyes were a pure, brilliant blue, a sated blue, a blue that was tinged with more than a little bit of masculine smugness. "Was that manly enough for you?"

I smiled and reached one hand out to hold up the long strip of condoms. "To be honest, you haven't convinced me yet. I think we need to go through a few more of these, then I'll know for sure."

"You're not sure?" he asked, looking at the eight or nine condoms contained in the strip. "How many is few more?"

I let my smile go naughty and tightened every muscled I had around where he still lay snugly within me. He twitched twice, then dipped his head down to plunder my lips, growling into my mouth as he did so, "Prepare to be convinced, woman."

By the time dawn streaked the morning sky pink and gold, he had convinced me. Oh, man, how he convinced me!

—〰—

Sunday
September 5
4:01 P.M.
Lake, watching Max teach Melody how to fish

Max is a boob. Let me qualify that—he is an extraordinarily warm, drool-worthy, handsome-as-sin man, but still a boob.

I twirled my parasol and glanced over to Sam, who was filming our little threesome. He raised his eyebrows. I rolled my eyes.

"Dad, I can do it."

"Just wait a moment, Melody. I don't want you to hurt yourself."

"I'm not a baby. I can do it."

Max frowned at her. "Most girls wouldn't want to. You don't see Tessa playing with worms, do you?"

"That's only because I get other ideas once I get a pole in my hands," I said, trying to look as if I didn't mean exactly what I did.

Max shot me a look that let me know he was on to me. I wiggled my toes at him, enjoying the pleasant tension that hummed through me whenever he was near.

"Dad, it's *my* worm. I can put it on the hook!"

"Come on, Max, it's just a fishhook. She's not going to cut her arm off with it. Let the poor kid spit her own worm!"

"It isn't ladylike," he answered, his dark head bent next to Melody's as he sacrificed a worm on the altar of fishing.

I bit back a retort, mindful of the camera. I had a feeling that Victorian daddies didn't think it was at all nice for their daughters to skewer worms, so I let it go. There would be time later for a little lecture about just how outdated the term *ladylike* was, not to mention the bad effect an overprotective parent could have on the development of a child.

I closed the parasol and leaned back against the tree trunk, pleasantly warm but not too hot in the shade, watching quite contentedly from the blanket Max had spread out as Sam and Wilma filmed him showing Melody how to cast. The gentle tingling that hadn't seemed to leave me since the night he and I spent frolicking on that big bed of his provided an undercurrent of desire that grew as I watched him. I marveled over the fact that I was privy to all the secrets his stuffy Victorian clothing hid, all the sleek lines of his body, all the warm spots, his ticklish armpits, the wonderful muscles of his thighs, the way his hair curled at the back of his neck. I marveled even more that he was my lover, a status that meant I had the right to touch him whenever I wanted. I could just walk up to him and slide my hand up his chest, and he would accept the caress.

Tempted as I was to do that very thing, I sat on the blanket and kept my smutty thoughts to myself. Everyone in the house might know what was going on with Max and me, but I didn't need the viewing public of Great Britain to be in possession of that knowledge.

"I thought this morning went very well. We got some wonderful footage of everyone watching as the carriages arrived at the church."

Roger squatted next to me, out of sight of the camera, his voice low so it wouldn't reach Wilma and her sound equipment.

"It was a bit strange going through town with cars whizzing around us and everyone staring," I said, my eyes still on Max and Melody. "But yes, I think it went well. Although someone should have a talk with the guys about falling asleep in church."

Roger raised an eyebrow at me.

I sighed. "Fine, I will, although I really don't like being the heavy all the time. They're your rules; you ought to be the one enforcing them."

"I wouldn't want to deprive you of the opportunity of chastising your servants," he said righteously. I pinched his arm. He grinned and nodded toward the foursome at the edge of the pond. "I take it things have worked out between you and the duke?"

"Worked out? Well, let's see. . . . he refuses to allow me to visit Melody in the nursery unless he's with me, he refuses to go riding with me in the morning, he refuses to talk about the fact that he's stifling the poor kid when he should be encouraging her to spread her wings, he refuses to talk to me about anything but . . ." I let the sentence trail off, a small blush pinkening my cheeks.

"Things you talk about in bed?" Roger guessed.

"Mmm," I agreed. "Well, no, not really even that. Max won't pillow talk with me. Every time I try to, he distracts me. It makes me feel . . . oh, I don't know. Cheated. Insignificant. Unimportant."

Roger considered me with a thoughtful look. "It sounds to me like you are falling under the spell of our handsome duke, Tessa."

"I know," I said, admitting it for the first time. "Which is only going to lead to heartbreak, because in exactly three weeks and four days the filming will be over, Max will go back to being an architect in Bristol, and I will be just another American tourist visiting a foreign country."

"You don't think . . ." Roger inclined his head toward Max in an unasked question.

"No. He's not looking for someone permanent in his life, and even if he was, I'm not sure I am. Or that we'd be right for each other. We spend most of our time arguing, Roger. It's hard to build a solid relationship on argument."

"You'd be surprised," he said with a smile. "The fact that you're arguing means that you're both comfortable with each other. Lots of couples I know won't argue for fear of breaking up the relationship. You're already way ahead of them."

I looked at Max, now sitting at the edge of the pond, giving Melody pointers on her casting. He glanced back toward me and smiled, a smile that reached his eyes and thawed the icy blue in them. Roger was right, I realized with some surprise. I might have only known Max for a few days, but we were comfortable together. I could tell him anything.

"Maybe so," I said slowly. "But comfort has to go both ways, and as Max's reticence to talk about anything but things pertaining to lovemaking has shown, he doesn't feel the same need to talk to me."

"He wouldn't be a man if he did," Roger said dryly.

I shot him a glare. "Oh, you're a fat lot of help. Thanks."

He grinned and patted my shoulder, then stood up. "Give him time, Tessa. And speaking of that, I wouldn't mind if you two were to show your affection a little more on camera. You know, a peep or two into the intimate relationship of the duke and duchess. A few kisses, a bit of fondling, that sort of thing. A little sex never hurts the ratings."

"Oh, sure, Roger, no problem. I'm sure I'll be happy to destroy what might turn out to be the best thing in my life just so you can bring in a few more viewers with the promise of some smut."

My sarcasm was wasted. His mind was already on other things. "Thanks, Tessa, I appreciate it. What the devil is Kip doing now. . . ." He hurried off to where Kip was pushing Tabby and Matthew into the formal garden.

Max came over after a while and plopped down next to me. Sam and Wilma went off for a break, leaving the three of us alone. Melody kicked at a few ferns and stopped in front of us, her hands on her hips.

"What are we going to do now?" she demanded.

"I am going to sit here and talk to Tessa for a bit. You can go play," her father replied.

She glared at me. "No, you're not, I know what you're

going to do. You're going to kiss her. I saw you this morning, before prayers. You had your hand on her chest and you were kissing her."

"Melody, it isn't polite to spy on your elders—"

"I don't like her," she said, stomping her foot. "She made me hurt my arm!"

"Which, I notice, is well enough for you to go fishing," I pointed out. "And don't be trying to blame me for spraining your wrist. I never told you to go out riding alone—"

"You're supposed to be spending time with me, not her," Melody said, interrupting me. "*I'm* your daughter!"

"I know who you are," Max said evenly. "I also know you're being rude to Tessa and me. You can start by apologizing to her, then you may return to the house if you're bored here. We'll talk later about the rest of your behavior."

"Dad—"

"Now, Melody."

"No! I won't! You can't make me. I hate her! Why can't we go home?"

"Because I agreed for us to stay here for the month. I'm waiting for your apology to Tessa."

"I won't do it!" she shrieked, then took off for the house, running flat out. Max watched her for a moment, then turned back to me with a wry smile.

"That went well," I said. "How long have you been divorced?"

He pulled me down so I was draped over his chest, his fingers busily tracing out the contour of my corset. "Seven years. You look overly warm to me. I had better remove a few articles of your clothing to cool you down."

"Oh, no you don't," I said, struggling out of his grasp. I scooted to the far end of the blanket. "I want to talk to you, Max."

He waggled his eyebrows and looked down at his lap. My mouth started watering at the bulge located therein. "No," I said, grabbing my parasol and holding him at bay with it. "Don't you try to seduce me with your manly wiles."

"You like my manly wiles," he said, crawling forward slowly. I scooted back until I was at the very edge of the blanket.

"Yes, but that's not the point."

"Oh?" He tipped his head in that adorable way he had. Kind of like Lassie, only cuter. "What is the point?"

"The point is that we're not hidden by the trees like we were in that other spot. Anyone who looks out a window will see us, and besides that, I'm—Max!"

He sprang forward, knocking me backward, his arms hard around me to keep me from smashing into the ground. "And now, Your Grace, I am going to ravish you."

"No, you're not." I struggled to free myself, but he was too strong. I stopped fighting him and gave in to the shivers of enjoyment that rippled through my body when he claimed my lips. I waited until he'd checked every filling in my mouth and came up for air before saying, "Max, please. I want to talk to you, and I can't talk when you're touching me."

Max sighed into my mouth, then hauled himself off me, holding out his hand to help me back up into a sitting position.

"All right, go ahead, I'm willing to talk." I opened my mouth to speak but he stopped me before I could get the words out. "Unless you want to talk about my parenting skills with Melody, in which case I will just ravish you instead."

I got to my feet without wheezing or grunting (a minor miracle considering that dratted corset), and scooped up the parasol as Max stood up. "Come on, Maxikins, let's go for a walk."

Both his eyebrows rose as he took my offered hand. "Maxikins?"

I shrugged. "Max doesn't lend itself to well to nicknames. It's the best I can do."

"Try again."

"You were married awfully young, weren't you, Maximillie?"

He flinched. "Maxikins it is."

I smiled. "So, how long have you had custody of Melody?"

He stopped and glared at me. "This smacks of a discussion about my relationship with my daughter."

"Or it could just be my way of trying to get to know you."

"Hmrph." He didn't look like he believed me, but resumed our stroll nonetheless. "I've always had custody of her. My wife was busy with her career, and I work from home."

"Ah." We walked around the house, avoiding Barbara and a few of her friends playing dress-up in the garden, complete with tea table, attendant servants, and film crew. The afternoon air was filled with jasmine from a nearby bush, the low drone of traffic in the distance, and sounds of hammering from the stable yard, where the farrier had come to shoe the horses. Times such as this made it very easy to forget the outside world and believe that we really were living a hundred and twenty-five years in the past. "That would explain why you're so overprotective of her."

He stopped again, dropping my hand as he turned to face me, a scowl firmly in place. "I'm not overprotective of her! The very fact that she's here proves that point."

"Oh, really? Is that why you told Roger the only way you'd do this stint was if he made sure Melody was filmed only on the right side, so her birthmark wouldn't be seen?"

"It may come as a surprise to you, but I love my daughter. Is it so wrong to want to keep her from being ridiculed?"

"Ridiculed? Over what? Her birthmark? That's silly."

His jaw tightened as he turned and marched on. I grabbed his hand and laced my fingers through his. He didn't squeeze them in return, as he usually did. "You may find her defacement trivial, but I do not."

"Well, you should."

He stopped and gave me an outraged look.

"Oh, don't be stupid. I don't mean that it's unimportant, I just mean that you should be teaching her that it doesn't matter *what* she looks like."

"This from a woman who has such a very fine self-image?"

It was my turn to drop his hand. I poked him in the chest instead. "Yes, Max, this from a woman who knows what it's like to be anything but perfect, and who found happiness despite it. Or have all your compliments and sweet words been meaningless and shallow?"

"Of course they haven't been—"

"Then where's the difference? Max, she has a spot on her face. It doesn't mean she's more vulnerable than anyone else. All it means is that she's got a spot on her face. If you give her the support she needs to deal with how other people react to it, she'll be fine."

He walked around me, heading for the stable. "You don't know anything about what she has to deal with. You haven't been there during the nights she cried herself to sleep because her classmates made fun of her."

"Max." I grabbed his arm and stopped him. "No, I don't know exactly what she's gone through, although I think I have a good idea. I didn't have a terribly happy childhood, either. I was the fat kid in class, so I *know* what it's like to be ridiculed and poked fun at, what it's like to feel different. But I also know that you trying to keep her from experiencing life—the good along with the bad—is going to backfire on you. Rather than sheltering her from hurt, she's going to end up neurotic and even more unhappy than she is now."

"Thank you, Doctor Riordan," he snapped, and continued around me. "I suppose your solution to keep her from being neurotic and unhappy is to let her run wild and encourage her to take dangerous chances?"

I trotted behind him. "Not dangerous, no, but—"

He stopped and spun around to face me. "Riding horses, for instance."

"Yes, that is a perfect example of what I mean." I put a hand on his chest, over his heart. "Max, I know you've got something against horses—I don't know if you were scared by one when you were a kid or you just haven't been around them or what—but I can assure you that it wouldn't be dangerous for Melody to learn how to ride. She is crazy about horses, just like every other little girl her age. What can it hurt if you lighten up a bit and let her learn to ride?"

He grabbed my wrist in a hard grip, pulling it from his chest. "What can it hurt? She could end up dead!"

"Oh, now you're just being ridiculous—"

"Am I? Tell that to Trevor Benedict."

I wiggled my fingers to let him know he was hurting my wrist. His eyes were bright with anger, but he didn't seem to notice. "Who's Trevor Benedict?"

"My friend. We grew up together, went to university together. He was the best man at my wedding, and I at his. He's dead now."

Uh oh. I didn't like where this was heading. I swallowed. Hard. "I'm sorry—"

"You don't think horses are dangerous? Neither did Trevor, until the day he fell off a horse and broke his neck. He lived for three years after that, lived in a hell where he was completely paralyzed, unable to do anything for himself, unable to care for his wife and baby. He wasted away—slowly, bitterly, his body destroyed— but his mind lucid to the end. He died cursing himself. Tell me again how horses aren't dangerous, Tessa. Tell me, because I'd like to go to Trevor's heartbroken wife and fatherless son and explain it to them."

Tears slipped down my cheeks. There was so much pain in his eyes, I wanted to cradle him to my body and keep him safe. I understood why he was so adamant about keeping Melody from hurt, but I knew that it was wrong. "Oh, Max, I'm so sorry. I had no idea. I see now why you think riding is such a bad idea, but you have to understand that for every tragedy like the one that happened to your friend, there's thousands of other people who ride without once hurting themselves. Trying to shelter Melody from the pain that comes with being a member of the human race isn't the answer."

"Being a member of the human race doesn't break your neck."

"No, it doesn't, but it can break your heart. Oh, Max, don't you see, you're doing more than just trying to keep her physically safe; you're trying to protect her from everything, every hurt, not just physical, but emotional pain, too. You're trying to wrap her up in a protective cocoon of your love so nothing will harm her, but if you do that, you also cut her off from the things she needs from people, things like companionship, and friendship, and loving and hating and all the emotions in between. I know what it's like to live emotionally withdrawn from the world, and I wouldn't wish that sort of limbo on anyone, especially not a young girl ready to step out and make her life what she wants it to be."

"You don't understand, do you?" Max's voice was low, throbbing with pain. "She's all I have. Her mother has started a new life for herself and doesn't want to be burdened with an awkward twelve-year-old with a ruined face. We only have each other, and I won't allow her to endanger herself over some foolish childhood desire she'll grow out of in a few years. I won't allow her to throw away her life the way Trevor did his."

"You're not alone, Max," I said softly, moving closer to him despite the warning his body language was screaming. I traced my thumb along his tight jawline, willing it to loosen up a bit. I knew what I wanted to say, what my heart wanted to say, but to say it would be to risk the sort of anguish I hadn't felt since Peter died. I looked into his angry eyes filled with so much agony, and the last little barrier around my heart crumbled away to nothing. "You're not alone—you have me, too."

He didn't say anything. He just looked at me, then

slowly, finger by finger, he released my wrist and walked past me toward the house.

I stood there for a minute, so overwhelmed with pain that I couldn't draw a breath, then slowly I turned and headed back to the lake.

Max's issues with Melody went much deeper than I had imagined, and now they were tangled up with both of us. I knew it wasn't going to be easy untangling them, but I couldn't let things stay as they were. It might destroy everything between us, but I had to try. I had to help them both.

I sat back against a tree overlooking the lake, and thought about things for a long, long time.

—⚏—

Monday
September 6
8:40 P.M.
Fainting couch

I have a plan.

—⚏—

Tuesday
September 7
7:33 A.M.
Library

The plan is good. Which is nice, because nothing else in my life is good right now. Well, except the nights. The nights are breathtakingly splendiferous.

—w—

Wednesday
September 8
10:57 A.M.
Linen closet

Tomorrow the plan goes into effect. It is simple, it is straightforward, and I'm praying it works. Because honestly, I don't know how much longer I can go on spending wonderfully warm, sensual, erotic nights in Max's arms but have a cold, unforgiving stranger wearing his face during the day. I want more from him than just his body. Why can't he see that?

The last three days have been very hard for all of us. I haven't been writing because . . . well, I haven't felt like it. Who wants to write about life when it's so sucky? Not surprisingly, Max's bad mood has seemed to trickle down to everyone else in the house. Barbara and Henry had a rousing spat over something he did with one of her friends—I'm not quite sure what; she won't say—and now they're not talking to each other. Frankly, I wouldn't think that was the end of the earth except Barbara needs an audience, and without Henry, she's turned to me. She's worse than a limpet. I've taken to hiding from her.

And then there's Max. . . . Ah, Max. Such a nummy but frustrating man. I didn't know quite how to take his noncomment on Sunday—you know, when I told him he had me if he wanted me, and all he did was walk away. At first I figured it was a rejection, then I decided I wasn't going down without a fight and if he wanted to reject me, he'd have to do it with words right to my tear-stained face.

His actions that night also gave me pause.

I had allowed Ellis to get me ready for bed, something

I hadn't done to that point because I really felt like I needed some privacy, and bedtime was the only time I had it.

"How long have you and Reg been married?" I asked Ellis as she unbuttoned the rich brown-and-gold dinner dress that for some reason made me feel very pretty despite the fussy kilted underskirt and draped panniers.

"Mr. Crighton and I have been married eighteen years."

"Wow. That's a long time. I was married for sixteen when my husband died."

She peeled me out of the dress and shook it out, peering closely at it to see if she had to clean any spots.

"Oh, I'm sorry, I spilled Hollandaise on it. And there's a spot on the bodice that's lobster salad. And a tiny dab of orange cream on the sleeve. I tried to wipe it off as best I could."

She just glared at me.

"I said I'm sorry!"

"Some people can feed themselves without throwing their food around."

I turned around and let her strip the corset cover off. "Yeah, well, I've always been a messy eater. I'll try to confine my food to my plate tomorrow."

"That would be a pleasant change."

She loosened the corset. I gave a sigh of relief and scratched myself through my combinations. "So, if you've been married such a long time, you must have learned something about men, right?"

Her nostrils flared as she handed me the frothy silk nightgown. I skimmed out of my combinations and into the nightie.

"The same might be said of a woman who was married for sixteen years."

"It might be, except for the fact that my husband was twenty years older than me and he'd worked out all of his emotional issues by the time I met him. So with regards to men with baggage, no, I haven't learned a lot. Oh, that's not to say that Reg has baggage," I added quickly, seeing her eyes open wide in affront. "I just meant that he is your age and that you guys probably grew together."

Ellis conceded that was so as she started brushing out my hair.

I gnawed on my lower lip for a minute, trying to think how to come right out and ask what I wanted to know. There was certainly no love lost between us, but I trusted Ellis to tell me the truth, no matter how painful I might find it. In fact, I was sure she relished those sorts of truths more than anything flattering to my ego. "Do you . . . do you think I'm all wrong for Max?" I finally blurted out.

She stopped brushing for the count of three, then resumed. "It's not my place to speculate about my superiors."

"Oh, come on, Ellis, it's just you and me here. I know you don't like me, and I know I make your life a living hell, and I'm sorry I'm not the duchess you envisioned for the job, but I'd really like to know what you think. You're smart and . . . and . . . well, to be honest, I have a feeling you see more than you let on. I'd appreciate you sharing your thoughts. Am I just fooling myself that I can help Max? Is the whole relationship going to end in disaster? Do I stand a chance of succeeding with him?"

She tied my hair back at my neck with a satin ribbon, gathered up the dinner-stained dress, and headed for the door, pausing for a moment before leaving. "No. That's up to you. Yes."

The door closed quietly behind her, leaving me a bit stunned. Did she just say something nice to me, in a roundabout, Ellis sort of way?

I curled up in bed, thinking about what I was going to do with Max. Male voices rumbled from the shared bathroom, indicating the man in question was taking a bath. I toyed with the thought of trotting in there and offering to scrub his back, but the cold, icy depths of anger visible in his eyes earlier when he'd turned away from me had my heart in a frigid grip. I didn't need to add rejection of my body on top of everything else he'd decided he could do without.

I was just snuggling down to read the *Illustrated London News* when there was a brief tap at the bathroom door. I stared at it in surprise. "Max?"

My heart did an interesting combination of somersaults as he came into the room. His hair was still damp from the bath, curling wildly at the bottom. He wore his blue dressing gown, the one that emphasized his broad shoulders and long legs. I immediately started drooling.

He frowned down at me, then shucked the dressing gown and got into bed.

"Um. Max? I thought you were angry with me. Again, I might add."

"I am, but it's not an all-consuming anger." He rolled onto his side to glare at me.

"I see. Would you care to tell me why, if you're angry with me, you're in my bed?"

"You didn't come to mine."

He didn't touch me, just lay there and looked at me, a furrow between his silky black eyebrows, his eyes hot with emotions that made my skin flush.

"Do you know that you have eyes that my Irish grandmother called *being put in with a smutty finger?*"

He blinked. "Why are you telling me this?"

"Just trying to make conversation. Do I take it that your presence here, especially since you're all suited up and ready to romp, means that despite the fact that you have behaved in a dastardly and cruel manner to me, don't want to listen to my opinions, and are angry at me for trying to help you, despite all that you'd like to make love?"

He didn't bat an eyelash before he answered. "Yes. That's what it means."

"I see." I thought about this for a minute, coming to a sad conclusion. "Much as I desire you, and want to do all sorts of wickedly wonderful things to your lovely body, I don't want you when you're angry at me."

His face was a study in discomfort. "If I am willing to put aside our differences until such time as we can find a resolution, would that be acceptable?".

He sounded so pompous my lips twitched, but I kept them serious as I considered his offer. He wanted to find a resolution to the problem—that was promising. He was reaching out, trying to find a common ground—or in this case, bed—and far be it from me to refuse his offer.

"How noble of you. Very well. I won't kick you out of my bed, and instead will be the understanding, caring woman you need."

He made love to me with his mouth and hands, not allowing me to participate, not speaking except to murmur little bits of praise against my skin. I cherished every word, every stroke of his fingers and lips on my body not because of the fire and need and something profound he stirred within me, but because I knew that he was just as moved as I was. He made love, not gratified himself, he sang a siren song of wordless desire with his entire body as it moved over mine, clearly needing something more than just a physical outlet for sexual tension. I realized that he truly wanted me, a thought so sweet it brought tears to my eyes . . . until I realized what he was doing.

"Um . . . Max?" He pushed my legs wider and kissed a very intimate path up my inner thigh. "Max, what are you doing down there? Why don't you come back up here where I can touch you? Look! I have breasts! Come and get 'em!"

He shook his head, the silk of his hair brushing against my intimate parts sending little zaps of electricity through me. "Relax, Tessa. You'll enjoy this."

"No, I don't think I will. That's not a terribly scenic vista down there, so why don't you just come back here and you can play with my breasts some more. They're lonely, Max. They want you back. Look, I'll even smoosh them together and you can do naughty things to them with your penis."

"Later," he said indistinctly, his mouth being busy at

the moment with kissing closer and closer to the part of me that had plans for entertaining one particular part of him.

"Later is too late! Now is better. Max, I'd really rather you came up here than—holy Mary, mother of God!"

He found a very, very sensitive spot and gave it a quick flick with his tongue, then went to work arousing me to a fever pitch.

"This is embarrassing," I gasped, clutching his hair and trying to tug him closer. "This is horribly embarrassing. Not even my gynecologist has stared eye to eye with my personal parts, let alone shoved her face in them, which is good because I'm not in the least bit turned on by her, whereas you make me break out into a sweat just looking at you. I can't even begin to tell you what you do to me when you're going to town down there. How can you stand to do that, Max? How can you breathe with your face buried in me like that? Oh, my god, not the fingers again! I can't hold out against the fingers, Max, not when you're nibbling and sucking and doing that wonderful swirly thing with your tongue, you've just got to stop, yes, yes, stop right now, because if you don't stop, I'm going to—"

His tongue swirled over me again. I bucked, thrusting my hips upward, clutching his head even harder. "You're going to make me sing again! Dear heaven, where did you learn to do this? Do they teach this to men, or is it something you're born knowing?"

Max gently pulled my fingers from where they were entwined in his hair. "Tessa?"

"What?" I cried, almost blind with the ecstasy he was bringing me with just two fingers and a tongue. "You're stopping? Now? Right now? As in, you're stopping? Max, you can't stop now! Not now! Maybe later you can stop, maybe in three or four years you can stop, but not now, Max, please God, not *now!*"

"You're babbling."

"Yes, yes, I know that," I answered crossly, pushing his head back down to where I wanted it. "Now is not the time for trivia, Max. Now is the time for paying attention. Now is the time for taking pride in a job well done. Do that swirly move again. And the sucking. And the thing with your teeth, I really liked that."

He chuckled a hot, steamy chuckle into my crotch and did everything I demanded and more, many more things I couldn't begin to identify in my mind as separate touches because they all blended together in one harmony of bliss. He pushed me higher than I had thought possible to go, and just when I was sure I was going to fracture into a zillion little (extremely happy) pieces, he rose up over me, grabbed my hips, and thrust into me hard and deep.

I was the one yodeling now, screaming my pleasure in his ears, biting his shoulders, kissing his neck, trying to pull him closer, deeper into me as I went over the edge in a wonderful, blinding haze of rapture. I felt the tension in his back and knew he was about to go over the same edge. Muscles I didn't know I had tightened and rippled along him as he shouted hoarsely into my neck, his body shaking and spasming with the force of his climax.

I have no idea how long we were there, bound together, our hearts beating wildly against each other, arms and legs entwined, our bodies damp with mingled sweat, but eventually, at some point I became aware that Max rolled off me and lay panting at my side. I lay thinking wonderfully muzzy, warm, satisfying thoughts about the man I just realized I'd given my heart to, the man who touched my soul in a way no one else had, the man who filled me with the joyous feeling of being a part of someone's life . . . and then he went and ruined it all.

"Good night," he said, and got up and left the room.

I stayed in bed for exactly three minutes and twelve seconds (I know because I was staring in complete and utter shock at the door to the bathroom reflected in the mirror and the clock was right next to it) before I gathered my wits.

I grabbed the peignoir and without even donning it, marched through the bathroom to his room.

"You bastard!" I yelled into the darkness of his room as I headed straight for his bed. "You scum-sucking pig of a man! How dare you treat me like that!"

"Tessa—"

A match flared to life as Max lit the candle next to his bed. I threw my peignoir at his head. He pulled it off and glared back at me. "How dare I treat you like what? You liked me going down on you! You're the one who was yelling me on!"

I looked around for something else to throw at him. Something *hard*. I found a book on the armchair next to the fireplace and threw it. He grabbed it before it could hit him on his pigheaded head. "You treated me like a whore! You can't just come into my room and make love to me like that and then leave! I'm not just a convenient vessel to get your rocks off, you know."

Max propped himself up on one elbow and fired up his really potent scowl, the one that can strip the hide off a mule. "I got your rocks off, too, if you hadn't noticed, and I know you did because you damn near squeezed my penis off when you came."

"Yeah, well, maybe life would be much easier if I did!" I bellowed, and plucked his hairbrush off a tall bureau, throwing it straight at his fat head.

He caught the hairbrush easily, too (I don't have a very good throwing arm), and took a deep, long breath. I ignored the way his wonderful chest expanded as he did so.

"Tessa," he growled. "Is there something in particular you wanted, or is this just your idea of postcoital fun?"

"Is there something in particular I . . . oh!" I threw a second hairbrush, a handful of thin black neckties, and his wallet at him, then marched over to where he sat surrounded by the debris of my fury. I fisted my hands on my hips, for once completely unconcerned that I was stark naked.

"Yes, Max, there is something in particular I want to say to you."

His jaw tightened. His eyes narrowed. His chin lifted. "Go ahead, then."

I leaned down until I was nose to nose with him. "It just so happens that I love you."

With a style and panache I doubt I'll ever again achieve, I whisked my peignoir from beneath his hand, tossed it over my shoulder, and sauntered nonchalantly out of his room.

He was in my room before I could close the door.

"You do not love me!" He looked outraged, utterly outraged, mad enough to spit. "I'll thank you to take that back!"

I smiled to myself. Somehow I had known he wasn't going to take the news with good grace. With great care and deliberation I donned the peignoir, shivering when the cool material hit my overheated skin. Max's eyes greedily followed my hands as I buttoned the five buttons down the bodice. "Make me."

"What?" His gaze shot back up to my face. "What did you say?"

Deep within me, in my feminine core (and no, I'm not talking about my crotch, for those of you who have smutty minds), a celebration of self-awareness broke out. I've never felt particularly powerful with a man sexually, but the desperate, hungry look in Max's eyes spawned an epiphany, filling me with the knowledge of what it meant to hold a man in thrall. Only the fact that I loved him with every ounce of my being kept me from becoming some sort of sexed-up dominatrix who spent her days stomping all over her man just for the enjoyment of seeing him squirm.

Not that I wasn't in favor of making Max grovel, but now was clearly not the time for that particular bit of fun.

"I said, *make me*. Make me take it back." I stepped forward and ran my hand down his beautiful damp chest, his muscles tightening beneath my fingers as they caressed his warm flesh. "Come on, you're bigger than me, you're stronger than me—make me do what you want."

He stood stiff as a board, his eyes blazing with a myriad of emotions, too many to put names to. I licked the corners of his mouth, my hand stroking down the slick line of hair on his belly to where his penis was beginning to show new life. "What's wrong, Max? Afraid you can't prove me wrong?"

He made that noise again in his chest, the primitive, earthy noise, a mating noise, a noise a man makes when he is driven past endurance and stops thinking with his head, instead allowing his heart to take over. He snarled something unintelligible as he scooped me up in his arms and hauled me into his room, his eyes burning over my flesh as he threw me down onto the bed and literally ripped the peignoir off me. I had hoped to goad him into revealing his own feelings for me—despite the fact that I wasn't entirely sure that he felt anything approaching what I wanted him to feel—but the hard, merciless expression that settled on his face was *not* what I was expecting.

"Eep," I said, deciding that the better part of valor was discretion and all that as I tried to squirm out from under him when he leaned over me.

"It's too late for eeping," he said, wrapping one of his ties around my wrist, knotting it on the headboard. I stared at my bound wrist, unable to believe what he was doing, all the while he was tying my other wrist down. "You wanted me to dominate you. The least I can do is satisfy your desires."

"You tied me down?" I looked from one arm to the other, testing the bonds. They held firmly. He hadn't stretched my arms out—my elbows were close to my body—but still . . . "You tied me? This is bondage, isn't it? I've never done bondage before. I've never known a man who got into that sort of thing. There are unseen kinky depths to you, Max, depths I had no idea existed."

He smiled a hard, cruel smile, a smile filled with all sorts of wicked promises of retribution as he slid down my legs to my feet, running his hands down my legs as he parted them. "Do you still claim to love me?"

I looked from one bound hand to the other, then down to where he sat at my feet. I shivered at the hard look in his eyes. "That depends. What are you going to do to me? Are you going to arouse me with your hands and your mouth the way you did before? Are you going to drive me wild with need, but not give in and fulfill that hunger until I'm begging and sobbing for relief? Are you going to torment me by rubbing your body all over mine, making me arch beneath you, desperate to feel you, mad with longing and passion? Are you going to touch me and tease me until I'm half insane with the need for you to plunge into my body, again and again, harder and faster and deeper, your body slamming against mine over and over and over again until we share a screaming orgasm to end all orgasms?"

Max leaned forward on his hands, his eyes positively burning my flesh as he raked a gaze down my body so tangible, I swear it left scorch marks. "Yes, that's exactly what I'm going to do. I warn you, Tessa, I am feeling merciless."

"Oh, good." I sighed, a ripple of pure pleasure skimming down my back. "I like you merciless. Go ahead, Max, conquer me."

A long, long time later, after I had been conquered and done some conquering of my own, I kissed Max's salty shoulder and snuggled closer to him. "Ah, Max, you are the perfect man."

His sigh parted my hair. "I'm not perfect, Tessa."

"You are in all the important ways," I said sleepily, my fingers curled over his bicep. "I don't know of any other man who would voluntarily lie in the wet spot just so I wouldn't have to. That's perfect in my book."

"Go to sleep."

"I love you."

"Good *night,* Tessa."

"I'll always love you, no matter how pigheaded you are."

He didn't say anything, but his hand continued its long, gentle sweep up and down my back. I smiled to myself as I drifted off to sleep. Sooner or later, he'd see the light. Sooner or later, he'd realize that I was the only woman who could make his life truly happy.

Right? Right. Thank you for agreeing with me.

Later that night, we were woken up by an incoherent Easter.

"You've got to come," she gasped, clutching her night candle as Max struggled to light the lamp next to the bed. "It's Mr. Palmer. He's gone berserk! He's attacked Mrs. Peters!"

Max and I looked at each other for a moment, then scrambled out of bed, slipping on our respective dressing gowns as we raced up the dark stairs after Easter.

"Oh, thank God you're here," Alice said, as we lunged into Mrs. Peters' room. She sat on the bed next to Mrs. Peters, one arm wrapped around her. "I've sent Sam off to alert Roger, but I didn't want to leave her alone, so I sent Easter for you."

"They saved me," Mrs. Peters said, her eyes wild as she trembled in the aftermath of her attack. "They saved me from him! I knew they would, for I am a true believer, but never did I imagine I would have my belief tested in such a manner! *Never!*"

Max knelt down next to where Palmer slumped, dazed, against the wall, blood smeared across his forehead. "Palmer? What happened here?"

Palmer lifted his head, frowning as he tried to focus on Max's face. "Oh, it's you. I thought you were that she-devil, come to bash in my brains again."

"The spirits saved me," Mrs. Peters said, clutching the sleeve of my dressing gown. "He came in here, intent on having his wicked way with me—me, a married woman!—and the spirits of Worston Old Hall rose up and smote him!"

"Did they? How providential," I said, looking back at Palmer. He didn't look to be in any state to ravish Mrs. Peters. He looked bleary-eyed and very sleepy.

"What happened?" Max asked again.

Palmer belched. My nose wrinkled at the sour smell

of wine. "Don't quite know. Thought this was my room. Was having my bedtime constitutional—very good for the spleen, y'know—and decided to take myself to bed. Next thing I know, that woman is cracking my head open with a chamber pot."

"He attacked me! The spirits saved me! The chamber pot rose of its own accord and smote him on his lecherous, alcohol-befuddled head! It is the proof of spirit intervention I have been seeking for so many years! No human hand could have wielded such a weapon, nor dealt such an unearthly blow!"

We all looked at a broken chamber pot that lay next to Palmer, one edge of its curved rim red with blood. It didn't look unearthly.

"Tricky things, spleens," Palmer bobbed forward to tell Max. "You have to exercise them or they go bad on you."

The wisdom of his words was put into doubt when he pulled from his ratty silk bathrobe a thin silver flask. Max plucked it from Palmer's fingers, ignoring the latter's whine of complaint. "Need a jot of m'medicine. Suffer from migraines, you know. Bad spleen and migraines always go together, they do. Am having a hell of a migraine now. Bad for the spleen, that. Need m'posset."

By the time Roger arrived and took Palmer off to get his head x-rayed, we had a pretty good idea of the events of the evening. Palmer—more than a little bit squidgy on his potent posset—evidently managed to climb three flights of stairs in his evening spleen stroll. Although Mrs. Peters refused to admit that he entered her room with anything but nefarious intent on his mind, we assumed he simply got confused and was trying to find his own bed.

There was little doubt that any spectral hand had been raised in the staving off of the (supposedly) lecherous Palmer, since Mrs. Peters bore a cut on her right hand that corresponded to a sharp edge on the cracked pottery. She claimed it was due to ectoplasmic backlash from the spectral hand that manifested to save her, but we all attributed it to the more mundane act of beaning a man on the head with a ceramic pot.

I'll say this for Palmer—he has staying power. He was back on the job the following morning, having been given a clean bill of health from the emergency room doctors. He did, however, swathe his entire head in a particularly dramatic bandage, and made sure the camera was pointing at him both times he crumpled to the ground, moaning and clutching his head.

Max has forbidden Mrs. Billings to make him any more possets.

On Monday I had to send Bret and Michael into town to bring back some illicit supplies: rubber gloves, more washing-up liquid, and filtered cigarettes for the scullery girls, who swore they were going to leave if they had to roll any more of their own ciggies.

On Tuesday, Honey and Easter, two housemaids, had a huge fight over Bret and refused to sleep in the same room. Alice and I had a talk with them without the cameras present, and they agreed to stay on if they could sleep in separate rooms. Roger didn't like OKing that, but he did when I told him he'd have to bring in new servants if we didn't separate them.

This morning . . . oh, drat, I hear Barbara. Must go find another hidey-hole.

—⁓—

Wednesday
September 8
4:02 P.M.
Bathtub

Barbara is positively psychic, I swear. She routed me out in the linen closet, where I'd gone to hide from her. As I mentioned, Barbara without Henry as an audience means she's glommed onto me as her new best friend.

She's not a bad woman, you understand, just a bit wearing. She's found the last three of my hiding spots, flushing me out to force me into listening to her many confidences about how insensitive and uncaring men in general were.

I didn't agree with everything she said, being heels over ears in love with her brother and all, but I did agree that there were times in the last forty-eight hours when I was convinced Max was too stubborn to admit a few commonly known facts.

Take, for instance, the fact that I loved him.

"You don't love me," he announced dramatically Tuesday, just two days after the very titillating Bondage Night. I was sitting in the morning room, having just done the menu with Mrs. Peters (still flushed with righteousness over the beaning of Palmer), trying to decide whether or not I should write to my sister in North Dakota with lavender or emerald ink.

"I don't, huh?" I answered, turning around in the chair to look at him. He was wearing a dark green frock coat, gold waistcoat, and black pants. I allowed my eyes to play over his figure for a few seconds, mentally stripping the clothing off him and exposing every delicious bulge.

"No, you don't, and stop looking at me like that."

I let a wicked smile curl my lips. "Like how?"

"Like you're a cat and I'm a bowl of cream. You don't love me. You *can't* love me."

I licked my lips, just to tease. His eyes widened. "Why can't I?"

"Eh?" His fingers flexed as I ran my tongue around my lips again. His eyes, beautiful in their icy disdain, melted into hot pools of shimmering blue. He cleared his throat. "Erm . . . oh, yes, you can't be in love with me because I'm too young for you. You said so yourself."

"Did I?" I tapped my finger against my mouth, then sucked on the very tip of it for a moment. Max twitched. The fun part of him, that is. "I was wrong."

"No, you weren't. It's not right you being so much

older than me. As you said, you are old enough to have been my baby-sitter."

"Yes, but I wasn't. I've changed my mind. Now I see the benefit of a younger man. Just think: I'll have all those extra years of a young, virile, stud muffin of a man to satisfy my deepest yearnings, and, Max, I have *a lot* of yearnings. Thus, it makes perfect sense for me to be madly in love with you."

Max opened his mouth a couple of times to object, but in the end he just snarled, "Damn!" and stomped out of the room.

I smiled as the door slammed behind him. I wasn't worried about him trying to convince me I didn't love him. If he didn't share any of those wonderful, warm feelings that I had for him, he would be behaving completely different: He would be kind and gentle and very, very sweet as he broke it to me that a relationship with him had no future. The very fact that he yelled and ranted at me and stormed around demanding that I admit I lied simply confirmed the fact that he felt the same things, only he had to take the typically male route of fighting the feelings for as long as he could, rather than just admitting to them like any sane person (read: woman) would.

"All right, how's this," he whispered later that day as I handed him one of the beautiful thin green china cups painted with willows and graceful swallows that we used at tea. Tabby and Matthew were filming us, but they were focused on Barbara sniping away at Henry. "You can't love me because we've only known each other a week. That's not nearly enough time to find out everything there is to know about me, therefore, what you're feeling is a common garden variety of lust and not love. You're in lust with me, Tessa. That's all. It's not love."

"I fell in love with Peter the first day I met him," I whispered back. "I'm a firm believer in love at first sight, and I can assure you, I'm very much in love with you."

His frown darkened to epic proportions. "No, you're not."

"Yes, I am. Sugar?"

He reared backward, splashing tea everywhere. I grinned as Tabby swung the camera around to catch me innocently offering him the sugar bowl.

He muttered what I was sure were oaths under his breath.

"Lust is quite easily confused for love," he said some six hours later, holding out his arm so I could tie his wrist to the bedstead. "It happens all the time—you shouldn't be embarrassed by that fact. I'm quite willing to admit that I myself am in considerable lust with you. I feel no shame about it; it's a perfectly natural emotion to be shared between two adults who have a mutually satisfying sexual relationship. In addition to being fun and enjoyable, a lust-only relationship has the benefit of not tearing people's lives apart the way the other can."

"Love, you mean," I said as I knotted the black necktie and tugged on it to make sure it was tight enough that he couldn't get his hands free, but not so tight it cut off circulation. Tonight was my turn to be conqueror, and I very much looked forward to tormenting him until he begged me for mercy.

"Yes."

"Hmm." I sat back on my heels and looked at him spread out before me, a vast panoply of flesh, his arms stretched above his head, his chest rising and falling with quickened breath, his long, long legs tense with the knowledge that I was soon going to have him delirious with pleasure. "Don't tell me you're one of those men who holds a bad relationship with one woman against every other woman in your life?"

"Erm . . ."

"Because if you are, I'm going to have to punish you," I said, reaching for the drawer of the nightstand next to the bed. "I expected better from you, Max, I really did. Just because your ex-wife was a vindictive shrew doesn't mean I am."

"She wasn't a vindictive shrew," he said, watching with interest as I withdrew a small bottle and a black scarf from the drawer. "What's that you have?"

"Lick Me Lemon massage oil. And this"—I tied the scarf over his eyes—"is a blindfold."

"A blindfold? Blindfolds are not in the rule book," he said, tipping his head back so he could see alongside his nose. I adjusted the scarf so he couldn't peek.

"Sure it is. It's in Appendix C of the rule book. Don't tell me you didn't read the appendices?"

His head did a little blind thrashing from side to side thing. "I don't like being blindfolded. I like to see you while you torment me. Take it off."

"So sorry, busy at the mo. This darn cap . . . ah, there it goes. Mmm, lemony. So, your ex-wife wasn't a shrew? Was she a heartless, self-indulgent bitch?"

"No. What are you doing now? Where did you get the massage oil? Take off this damned blindfold!"

"Nope, it's there for a purpose—I want you to feel totally at my mercy, bwahaha! The massage oil is from Teddy. I asked him to get it when he was making his covert whisky-and-cigarettes run to town. Was she mean to you?"

"Carol? Not in the sense you mean. What do you plan on doing with that oil?"

"Use it on you, silly." I rubbed the bottle between my hands, warming it up a bit as I considered him. "Was she a spoiled rich brat who couldn't live the life of a poor architect's wife, betraying you with your best friend, the postman, and the kid who mowed your lawn?"

"No. Use it on me how?" He pulled at the ties, his brows pulling together in a frown above the blindfold as he realized I hadn't used a slipknot as he had during our previous round of Bondage Love-o-Rama.

Even though he couldn't see it, I gave him my very best leer. "You'll see. Or rather, you'll won't see, but you *will* find out, heh heh heh. If your ex wasn't a shrew or a bitch or mean or a spoiled rich kid, what was she?"

He pulled on the ties again, his frown deepening. "A soulless succubus who chewed men up and spat them out when she was through with them. What sort of knot is this?"

"Fisherman's knot. Peter used to take me sailing," I said as I flipped open the lid of the massage oil, and drizzled a line down his chest, inhaling deeply. The sharp scent of lemon blended perfectly with the spicy smell of Max.

He sucked in his breath. "Do you think we can get through the evening without mention of your late husband?"

"Why?" I asked as I scooted forward and let my fingers dance around the oil. "Does it bother you to have me talking about him?"

"Yes," he gasped as I oiled up one adorable little nipple nub, and gave it a friendly tweak before lowering my mouth to it. He squirmed as I flicked my tongue across his nipple, sucking it into my mouth so I could scrape it gently with my teeth.

"Really?" I blew across the nipple and spread oil on its mate. "It doesn't bother me. I'm not comparing you to him, if that's what you're thinking. Peter wasn't at all into games; he was a very white-bread guy when it came to sex. He never would have let me tie him up, blindfold him, and bring him seven times to the point of coming before finally letting him blast off."

I swear Max's eyes bored holes through the thick black cloth over his eyes. He started struggling against the ties. "Seven times? Is that what you have planned? SEVEN TIMES?"

I smiled and drizzled more oil on him. "I got the jumbo economy size. I thought seven has a nice sound to it."

"Oh, my gaaaaarg!" he said as I slipped my oily hands around his arousal, rubbing a little extra on the very tip of him, then slathering it around with my tongue. His hips thrust upward, his hands flexing convulsively as I spread the oil everywhere I could lick.

"Now, let us discuss these issues you have with women, and how we can overcome them," I said, smiling as I found a rhythm that had him thrashing around on the bed, moaning nonstop.

In the end, I only managed to bring him to the verge of ecstasy four times before I gave in to his pathetic pleadings and sobbed entreaties and impaled myself on him. It was a wild, sensual experience riding him when he was bound, and although I threatened to just please myself and leave him wanting, our shared joy was a million times sweeter than had I really done so.

"I love you," I whispered, kissing the slightly reddened flesh along his wrist where he had struggled against the ties.

The blindfold was askew on his head, exposing one eye. He cracked that open to glare a blue-eyed glare at me, his chest heaving madly, his breath loud and harsh as he sucked in great quantities of air. "Tomorrow," he croaked.

"Tomorrow?" I asked, sliding across his sweat and oil-slicked body to release his other hand. "What's tomorrow, Maxikins?"

He pushed the blindfold off his other eye, pinning me back with a molten blue gaze that threatened to ignite my still simmering blood. "Retribution."

That thought has been the only thing that's kept me going through the day.

Today, as anyone consulting the *A Month in the Life of a Victorian Duke* calendar will know, is Tennis Day. I have been dreading this day for two reasons: one, I don't play tennis, and two . . . well, I don't play tennis. Oh, the day started out well enough—me draped over Max, him lying on my hair, the two of us squished together sleeping the lemon-scented sleep of the exhausted, our legs entwined, that first thin, drowsy awareness as warm and comforting as the heartbeat of the man lying beneath my cheek, but then life, as it usually seems to do, took a turn for the crappy.

"Dad, I don't feel well, I have a stomachache, and Mam'selle says I have to wear this stupid dress and play tennis—oh!"

I pried myself off Max's chest to peer over his arm at Melody. Unfortunately, she was not alone.

"Looks like you owe me a hundred pounds," Tabby said to Matthew. He peered around her and Melody, scowled furiously at me, then stepped back muttering to himself.

"Max," I hissed, trying to pull the blanket out from under his arm so I could crawl under it and hide.

"Mmm?"

"Dad! You're in bed with her! Naked!"

"Max, wake up," I whispered louder as I slid to his side, yanking madly on both the blanket and my hair.

"Tessa? Love, give me a few minutes. You wore me out last night with your wild, lustful demands," he mumbled.

I swore into the pillow, damning his lovely English accent. "You're the only man I know who can mumble understandably enough for a microphone to pick you up clear across the room. Max, *wake up!*"

He rolled over to face me, one sleepy hand tugging me toward him. "Insatiable wench."

"MAX!" I pinched him on his side. Hard!

He opened his eyes. "Tessa, I'm not at all interested in rough sex. I don't mind tying you up as I did the other night—"

"Oh, god," I moaned, and tried to crawl under him. I wondered how much it was going to cost me in blackmail money to get the film from Tabby.

"—nor did I mind it when you had your turn tying me up, but I draw the line at hurting you, or vice versa. Now, if you'd like me to spank you, why, I think I could see my way clear to indulging—"

"MAX!" I shrieked, slapping a hand over his mouth, then forcibly turned his head until he could see who stood in the doorway.

"Bloody hell," he said indistinctly around my fingers.

"In a nutshell," I said, and tried to summon up a smile for the camera. I failed miserably, Tabby told me later.

"Do you want me to talk to her?" I asked Max in a whisper when Melody spun around and ran out of the room, her eyes bright with tears.

He rubbed a hand over his eyes. "No, I'll do it. Later."

By the time he promised to pay Tabby and Matthew roughly the sum it would cost to build a small house if they would conveniently lose that bit of film, there was just enough time for me to dash to my own room, have a quick wash, allow a tight-lipped Ellis to dress me in a dress of white batiste and blue satin damask with silk rosebuds down the front of the bodice, and make it downstairs for morning prayers.

Melody was noticeably absent. Tabby and Matthew had enormous grins on their faces, which I did my best to ignore. Barbara latched on to me on the way in to breakfast, and rattled on and on about how popular she had been before she sacrificed her life to marry her husband while we plowed our way through a breakfast of grapes, oatmeal, broiled beefsteak, tomato omelet, potatoes, crumpets, and toast. That is, everyone but me plowed through it. I ate about two bites of toast, sick with worry about what had happened that morning. I knew Tabby and Matthew could be counted on to keep the film from ever reaching Roger's grubby little mitts, but I worried about Melody as I poked at my toast and omelet.

Yes, she could be an obnoxious little beast, but she was also still a kid, and no kid wants to see her father in bed with a naked woman, especially when that woman is someone she loathes.

I tried to get a private word with Max before he left to do the morning rounds of the estate, but Barbara grabbed my arm and wouldn't let go, talking and playing to the camera, with occasional digs at Henry, who followed us as we went to the morning room.

I endured an hour of it, then managed to escape by pleading the need to use the toilet. I hurried up the stairs as fast as I could bound in the white-and-blue dress, heading straight for the nursery. I knew Max had said he was going to talk to Melody, but I shared the responsibility for being in his bed, so it was only fair I should take some of her anger.

I found her curled up on the window seat in the nursery, alone except for Barbara's old spaniel, who was asleep on a faded cushion, a couple of dismal-looking Victorian kiddy books, and a ratty teddy bear that looked like it had been in the house when it was originally built.

"Hey, Melody, how are you doing?" I asked, closing the door carefully behind me. No need for everyone to hear her when she started in on me. "Where's Mademoiselle?"

"She's out mooning over Bret."

"Her, too? Hmm. It's just as well she's not here. I wanted to talk to you for a bit about your dad and me."

"Go away," she said, her knees under her chin, her cheek pressed against the window.

"Look, I know you're angry and hurt and probably a lot of other things because you think your father has betrayed you, but you have to believe me when I say it's not true. Your dad has a big heart, and he will always, always have room for you in it."

She looked at me with acute hatred. "I don't care about that. Leave me alone. I want to be alone."

"Melody, I'm sorry that something we've done has upset you, but you know, both your father and I are adults, and as such, we interact on an adult level. I know you're a bright girl, so I don't need to spell it all out to you, but I wanted you to know that just because Max and I like each other a whole lot, that isn't going to affect your relationship with him—"

"Go away!" she yelled, then suddenly hunched her knees tighter to her chin, her face set in a pained grimace.

I stepped closer, wanting to comfort her but not daring to do it. "Are you OK?"

"Yes. Go away. I'm fine."

She didn't look fine. She looked pale and clammy. I felt even worse than I had before, knowing that there were a million better ways for her to find out the truth about Max and me.

"All right. I just want you to know that if you want to talk about it or ask questions or . . . oh, I don't know. If you need someone to help you figure things out, I'll be happy to help."

She didn't say anything, just grunted and stared out the window.

I hesitated for a moment, but when she didn't look back, I turned and started for the door.

"I'm having the painters in," she said in a rough whisper just as my fingers closed around the doorknob.

"You're having what?" I asked, looking over my shoulder. She kept her face turned toward the window.

"Having the painters in."

I made a *I'm totally lost* motion with my hand. She turned to glare at me. "I'm having my period."

"Oh," I said, the light finally dawning. "Oh. I'm sorry. Do you need anything?"

She looked back out the window and wrapped her arms tighter around her legs. A stray thought wafted through my mind, sending me forward even though her body language screamed for me to go away.

"Melody, this isn't by any chance the first time you've . . . er . . . had the painters in?"

She shrugged, which I took to mean yes.

I moved the ratty teddy bear so I could sit down in a raggedy wicker chair that bumped up against the window seat. "Oy. You really have had a heck of a morning, haven't you?"

She blinked fast a couple of times and twitched her shoulders. The sympathetic route was clearly not going to be welcome.

"OK, let's take this from the top. You know about

periods, right? I mean, they've taught you about it at school?"

Her face was pale, making her birthmark stand out even more. "Of course. I'm not a baby."

"Obviously not. In fact, a lot of cultures would consider you a woman today, although I think there's a bit more to it than just cramps. Right, so I don't need to tell you what's what. Now, you'll probably want some ibuprofen or aspirin, and you'll need tampons, which, luckily, I smuggled in because there is no way I'm going to use the rags that Victorian women used."

She wrinkled her nose. "Rags?"

"Ucky thought, huh?" I stood up. "Come on, squirt, we'll go down to my room and I'll get you a few things. No one will see you."

She got to her feet slowly, her face suspicious. "Why are you being nice to me?"

I smiled. "Because no one deserves to suffer through Mr. Monthly Visitor without a little pampering."

"Mr. Monthly Visitor?"

"Yeah. It's what my mother called having the painters in."

She hesitated at the door. "You won't tell anyone?"

I crossed my heart. "Nope. Not even your father, unless you'd rather have me tell him than tell him yourself."

She thought that over while we went downstairs. I gave her a quick course in tampons, gave her the tiny cache of ibuprofen I had snuck in with the tampons, and advised her to ask her governess for a hot-water bottle. "Sometimes heat helps. Does your back hurt?"

She shook her head, one hand on the door.

"Good. If you need something else, let me know."

Her jaw worked for a minute, then she blurted out, "You were having sex with my dad, weren't you?"

"When you saw us in bed? Not right that moment, but yes, if you're asking if your father and I have slept together, we have. Does that make you angry?"

She shrugged again, a brittle, tense movement that said a lot more about her emotions than she knew.

"Why?"

"Why what?"

"Why do you want to have sex with Dad? It's . . . it's ugly."

"You mean your dad's penis is ugly?"

Her right shoulder twitched.

"Ah. Well, I admit that as a rule, penises aren't the most amazing sight I've ever seen, and sometimes they can look downright funny, especially when you're—well, we'll let that go for now—but you're just going to have to take it from me that I don't think anything about your father is ugly."

Her face wasn't pale now, it was as red as a ripe apple. "I think it's just gross. I wouldn't want anyone touching me with one."

"Don't worry about it, Melody. You have a few more years before you'll see if you want to change your mind about boys and the men they grow into. Is there anything else?"

She shook her head and faced the door, opening it just a crack so she could peek out and make sure no one saw her.

"Would you tell him?"

"About you and the painters? I might, if you said the magic word."

Her whole body tightened, curled in on itself, but she managed to get the word out. "Please."

I laughed and gave her a gentle push out the door. "The magic word is Tessa, squirt. Remember, only two ibuprofen at a time. Any more and you'll make yourself sick."

She nodded and dashed out the door, thundering up the stairs before I could blink. A second later the thundering returned and she came back down a few steps.

"Tessa," she yelled, then turned around and raced back up the stairs to the safety of the day nursery.

"Oh, poop," I said, sniffling back a few tears as I

made my way downstairs. "She had to say it. Damn it, now I'm going to end up *liking* the little snot. I just hate it when that happens."

—⚏—

Saturday
September 11
8:10 A.M.
East terrace

So much for my plan. I didn't get to put it into effect yesterday morning because of my hair. If I thought it would help, I'd cut the blasted stuff off!

My great plan, my fabulous plan, my clever plan hinged on getting Max and me up early and out to the stables, but my hair ruined it all.

When you have waist-length hair and a bed partner who gets turned on when it slides across his panting, heaving body, you tend to wake up with it all over—in your eyes, glued to the side of your mouth, and usually a good quantity of it lying underneath some part of the aforementioned bed partner.

Max loved my hair, which was the only reason I didn't braid it for the night as I usually did. He liked my hair draping around us when I rode him, he liked it sliding along his belly when I kissed him all over, he liked grabbing fistfuls of it when he pounded hard and fast into me. I liked it all, all except for trying to pull my hair out from underneath him when he was sleeping.

Yesterday morning he had most of it under him, and when I tried ever so carefully to pull it out without him noticing, he woke up and immediately got that *you're touching me with your hair* look in his eyes, the same look that I knew presaged absolute ecstasy for me, but for once I didn't want ecstasy.

I wanted Max on the back of a horse.

Unfortunately, my mind and my body had different priorities, so when Max rolled over onto me, murmuring sweet, erotic words into my hair as he nuzzled my neck, my body stayed where it was and enjoyed itself to the fullest, telling my mind it could enact the plan another day.

It'll have to wait until Monday, unfortunately. Tonight we're having a dinner party, a real dinner party, the kind where people come and mingle and have drinkies, and then sit down to an elegant eight-course dinner, all while pretending to be Victorians. The servants have been gearing up for the party for two days.

"Just who are all these people who are coming to dinner?" I asked Roger late last night.

"Friends of Barbara's, friends of mine, and some members of Ellis' historical reenactment society."

"Oh, lovely, a bunch of snobs, wacky television types, and experts who'll pick apart everything I do. That ought to be fun."

"It will be, don't worry," he said, patting me on the shoulder. "You'll be fine, just fine. Think of it as a rehearsal for the other events."

The other events, in case you don't have the Victorian Duke calendar handy, include a garden party the middle of next week (during which family members are allowed to visit the servants), a shooting party for Max a couple of days after that, the servants' ball the week following, and the pièce de résistance, the masquerade ball on the last day of the month.

A word about tennis: Never try to play it if you a) don't know how to play, and b) have to pretend you do while wearing a ridiculous Victorian tennis costume.

"This is silly, Ellis," I said as she buttoned me into the cream merino bodice. It had long sleeves (just what I wanted in warm weather when running around a tennis court) with some lovely embroidery, a matching skirt with deep kilting over which fitted an old gold silk tunic with short, wide sleeves, looped back above my knees. "There's no way on God's green earth I'm going to be able to play tennis in this. For one, I can't draw enough breath to actually breathe, and you know, breathing is an integral part of playing any sport, and for another, the only part of me that can move freely is below my knees. Doesn't leave me much scope for a successful round of tennis, now does it?"

"It is an authentic tennis costume from Messrs. Jay, dated 1879. I provided the wardrobe personnel with the details on the costume myself." She plopped a large straw coal-scuttle-type hat down on my head. "I think it's very fetching. You will mind the syllabub?"

I looked down at the expanse of delicate white-and-gold fabric and gave a mental shudder. "Yes, absolutely, I'll be very careful not to spill anything on this. Ellis, do I really have to wear this—"

"Yes. And my name is Crighton."

I sighed heavily. I knew that look she was giving me. It was the *it's all for the good of the project* look.

In the end, the tennis was enjoyable. Max partnered me against Barbara and Henry, with predictably disastrous results. I only fell three times, all of which were caught on camera (such is my luck), after which I announced my retirement and designated Melody as my replacement. She brightened up quite a bit with Max as her partner, even giggling at one point when Max's lob knocked Barbara's hat off.

Drat, it's almost time for the morning prayers. I still don't know what to say at them. Ellis told me I was supposed to add something for the good of the servants, something motivating. Yesterday I quoted Buddha ("Do not dwell in the past, do not dwell in the future, concentrate the mind on the present moment."); today I'm going for Confucius ("Our greatest glory is not in never falling but in rising every time we fall.").

Thank heavens for that book of quotations in the library.

—᙮᙮᙮᙮᙮᙮᙮᙮᙮᙮᙮᙮᙮᙮᙮᙮᙮᙮᙮᙮᙮᙮᙮᙮᙮—

Sunday
September 12
2:43 P.M.
Willow tree next to the pond, with Max the scrumdilly-
umptious (who is currently dozing)

Well, we survived the dinner party . . . barely. I can't help asking myself, Is this project doomed? Cursed? Is Worston built on top of some sacred Druidic burial ground? Because there's not a lot else that can explain why everything that can go wrong does go wrong. Maybe it's me. Maybe Mrs. Peters is right and the ghosts are objecting to having an American playing a duchess. Maybe it's sunspots. I don't know, and I'm not sure I want to find out.

The evening started out on a note of disaster and just kind of went downhill after that. The first problem was the dress Ellis stuffed me into.

"No," I said when she brought it out of the wardrobe. I stood in fancy lace combinations, shaking my head just in case she didn't understand the word no.

"Yes. It is the evening gown created for this dinner party. You will wear it."

"Nope, not me. It's awful. It looks like something out of a tart's boudoir. A tart with extremely bad taste."

"Nonetheless, you will wear it."

"It's hideous!"

"A great deal of money was spent on making this dress for you," she said, her nose pinched in that way she had. "You will wear and will look quite lovely in it."

I clutched the corset to me and glared at her. "I will not; I'll look like some horrible pink-and-white bonbon box."

She took the corset and wrapped it around me. I quickly adjusted my boobs so she wouldn't crush them as she tightened the torture device. "The dress is directly from the pages of *Le Journal des Demoiselles*. The *Journal* was the very height of fashion in the Victorian era. I can assure you that the garment will not make you look like a bonbon box."

I sucked in my breath as she pulled the laces tight. "I'm the duchess here, and I get to say what I wear."

"No, you do not."

"Ellis—"

"You will wear the dresses the production company has created for specific events. On other days, days in which you have no social events, you may choose what you wish to wear."

"But—"

She slipped the corset cover on, adjusted it, then got the frilly pink-and-white horror and started toward me. I made a last ditch effort to save myself from looking like something that would have given Marie Antoinette nightmares. "It's white," I said, ignoring the distinct whining tone to my voice. "You know how I am with white clothes! I spill things!"

"You will not spill, and you will wear it. Arms up."

"I'll pay you," I said, unable to resist the look in her eyes. I held up my arms so she could slide it over my head. "I'll pay you a lot. I have a credit card. I can pull some money off it and we'll just forget about this particular dress."

"A proper duchess does not bribe her lady's maid."

"But I'm not really a duchess!" I yelled in frustration, obediently turning when she gestured for me to.

"You're more of a duchess than many ladies were," she said, her voice muffled as she bent down to fasten some extra froufrou to the back.

I half turned to look at her, my mouth agape in surprise. She grabbed my hips and turned me around so my back was to her as she fussed with the train.

"You're not playing fair, Ellis. That was a compliment. That makes two in one week. What do you mean I'm more of a duchess than other ladies?"

She squatted and reached for her pincushion, doing a spot of repair work on a bow that had broken free at the bottom of the dress. "You care about people. Most duchesses were oblivious to their servants and family, sometimes even their children. They thought of nothing but themselves and what was owed them." She looked up. "You're not like that. You care."

I blinked back a few tears, touched by her kind words.

"Mind, I could do with a bit less sniveling and arguing on your part. You certainly could be more serious about this project. And then there's the way you throw your food around when you eat—"

Now, that was the Ellis I knew. I sniffed back a few more tears and stood patiently while she arranged the dress to her satisfaction.

It really was an abomination. Ellis told me it was what was called a princesse dress, which just meant fussy bonbon box, as far as I was concerned. It was made up of pink faille and white mousseline, the body of the dress being pink with a long train in the back, and an overdress of the white mousseline. There was Valenciennes reproduction lace down the center front, flanked on either side with pink embroidery. A big pink bow adorned the front of my chest and either elbow, below which more lace spilled out (the lacy sleeves were the only thing I approved of). But it was the body of the dress that was so appalling. Starting at my left hip and spiraling down the dress until it formed part of the train was a huge ten-inch gathered ruffle topped with lace, dotted every foot or so with a pink bow, with one really massive bow in the rear at calf height, right above the train. At the bottom of the dress, peeking out from under the train, was pleated pink faille. It was awful, completely awful, but by the time Ellis finished with my hair (pink roses crowning a blob of curls on top, long curled strands hanging down my back—I looked like Mary Pickford after having been dipped in a wedding cake), I had no time left to get on my knees and plead for anything else to wear.

As I tottered from my room, trying not to trip over the train, Melody jumped out at me from the morning room. She eyed me from foot to head, curling her lip derisively. "That's ugly."

"Yeah, it is, isn't it? Can you imagine thinking this was pretty? How are you feeling? Everything OK in the painting department?"

"Yes." She transferred her perpetual glare to my waist.

"I'm glad to hear that." She looked uncomfortable and unhappy, and for a moment my heart went out to her. She must be bored to death all by herself in the nursery. "Hey, I have a thought. Would you like to come down to dinner with us tonight?"

"Tonight?" She looked up, interest clearly sparking her blue eyes that were so much like her father's. "At the party?"

"Well, maybe not for the later part, but for the dinner, yes. You do know how to eat with a bunch of forks and stuff, right?"

She made an annoyed *tch*. "Mam'selle says I had to learn that, but it's stupid because no one eats like that anymore."

"Yeah, I know what it's like to be under the thumb of a martinet."

Her brows pulled together. "What's a martinet?"

"Someone who tells you what to do all the time. There's still a half hour before people are supposed to arrive. Why don't you run upstairs and tell Mademoiselle that I said both of you could come down to dinner."

"All right." She didn't go running off like I expected her to. I raised an eyebrow in silent question. "My arm feels better. It doesn't hurt at all."

"Ah. Good. I figured it wasn't bothering you too much by the way you played tennis yesterday."

Her face lit up for a minute, then she scowled again and looked anywhere but at me. "I want to learn how to ride. Properly, I mean. So I won't fall off again."

I pursed my lips and pushed her into the morning room, closing the door behind me. "Oy. See, the problem is your father has a thing against horses."

She nodded. "Because of Uncle Trevor."

I raised my eyebrows. "You knew him?"

She rolled her eyes and plumped down in a chair, her arms and legs akimbo in that boneless way girls have. "Of course I knew him; he was Dad's best friend. Uncle Trevor died two years ago. A horse killed him."

It was only two years ago? I thought it had been much longer from the way Max had been talking. No wonder he was so manic about the subject.

"Right, well, because of that, your father doesn't think it's safe for you to go riding."

"You think it's safe. You said it was. You said you used to ride when you were younger than me."

"Er . . . yes, that's true, but—"

She sat up straight, her scowl miraculously melting away. "Then you'll teach me how to ride?"

Oh, man, talk about a rock and a hard place! "Melody, I can't promise that."

She jumped up, her face once again stormy, but before she could run out I grabbed her arm. "Look, I'll talk to your dad about it, OK? I have a plan, a plan that I hope will make him change his mind, but you have to let me do it my own way. Until I can get his permission to teach you, you'll just have to be patient."

"I'm tired of being patient! I'm tired of living here! You're just like everyone else," she snarled, jerking her arm out of my hands and running to the door. "You say you'll do something, but then you won't. You say it's for my own good, but it's not. It's stupid. I'm not a baby! I can do whatever I want!"

The door slammed behind her.

"One step forward, two steps back," I muttered, and

headed downstairs to inform Palmer and Cook that two more people were added to the dinner roster. Possibly. Maybe Melody would change her mind.

"You've what?" Mrs. Billings bellowed when I slipped into the Pug's Parlor to tell her.

"It's just two more—that shouldn't be a problem, and possibly they won't come, although I'm willing to bet they will, so you should count on two more. The menu I picked has enough food to feed an army—"

"Argh!" Cook screamed, and threw down her napkin as she jumped up from the chair.

"What?" I cried, confused.

"The shrimp! There is just enough for twelve people, and now you want me to have shrimp for fourteen? Argh!"

"I don't like shrimp, you can use mine—" I said.

"Girls! You'll have to eat later, we have a crisis of major proportion on our hands," she called as she bustled into the servants' hall.

"No, wait," I said, desperate now. "Sit down, everyone, and finish your dinners. I'm sorry, Cook, I didn't mean to cause any problems, I just thought it would be a nice change for Melody—"

She didn't listen to me.

"Raven, I'll need you to help me. Fetch the clams I was saving for tomorrow. I can stretch those out farther than I can the shrimp."

"Cooking isn't in my job description," Raven yelled as Mrs. Billings raced by her.

Palmer, the white head bandage inexplicably replaced by a black eye patch (he had conjunctivitis, I found out later) limped by me in the doorway to the servants' hall, sighing heavily, his long face filled with morose satisfaction. "Come along, boys, our toil is not yet at an end. Her Grace wishes us to work, and work we shall. Neither lack of food nor near fatal head injuries shall keep us from attending to our duties. Teddy, we'll need two additional places set on the table. You'll have to readjust the spacing on all the settings. Bret, you'll need to polish more silver. Michael, go and fetch the extra dining chairs from the attic."

"No, no, no," I pleaded, following Palmer out into the steamy kitchen. "Please, sit down, all of you, and have your dinner. Oh, god, I'm so sorry I did this. Teddy, sit! Eat! Palmer, please go back and finish your dinner. Raven, put the clams down, and finish your dinner. Cook—"

It was instant chaos, with everyone talking at once, Cook yelling and giving instructions, Palmer alternately giving the footmen orders and taking his pulse while murmuring his doubts concerning the strength of his heart, and the maids running around trying to do half a dozen things at once. No one paid the least bit of attention to me, no one but Alice, who patted me on the arm and gently pushed me toward the stairs. "Don't worry, it'll all sort out."

"But I feel so bad—everyone is missing their dinner—"

"It won't hurt any of us," she said, a smile on her lips. "Go on, you have entertaining to do."

"Alice, I'm really sorry—"

"I know. Off with you, now."

"But—"

She didn't hear me; she had turned around and bustled off to help Cook.

I told myself off all the way up the stairs, swearing I was going to make it up to everyone. I pushed open the green baize door (which was white on the servants' side—I have no idea what the significance of that is) and had just gone through it when my train got caught in the door. I gave it a yank, but instead of the door swinging open, the train tore off with a reverberating *riiiiiiiiiip!*

I stared in horror at the bit of ruffle and lace and that god-awful big pink bow wadded up in the doorframe, and I knew fear. "Oh, crap! Ellis is going to kill me! Quick like a bunny, Tessa, think! *Think!*"

My mind gave a terrified little whimper and closed up

shop for the night. I grabbed the train and started off to my bedroom, praying that Ellis had left her tiny sewing kit on the dressing table.

Eighteen minutes later I descended the stairs carefully, my tacked-on train whispering along the floor behind me.

"Ah, there she is. Tessa, you remember Barbara's friends Mr. Evans and his wife, Dorie?" Max stood in the hall, smiling up the stairs at me.

I greeted the couple (dressed with excruciating accuracy), and made polite chitchat with them for a few minutes. Barbara came down sans Henry and took over for her friends, who were nervously eyeing Sam and Wilma. She sent me a pointed glance that had me saying, "Well, shall we go into the drawing room and have an aperitif?"

I turned to lead the way, but I didn't get very far.

Riiiiiiiiip!

"Good God, Charles, what have you done to the duchess' dress?" Dorie gasped. My shoulders slumped as I turned around. The train lay in a heap on the floor.

Charles' face was bright red as he stuttered out an apology.

"Think nothing of it," I laughed with forced gaiety as I scooped up the annoying bit of fabric. "It happens to me all the time. I'll just go have my maid tie this on again. Barbara, would you—"

"Oh, yes, certainly, of course I will, Tessa. Dorie, darling, you and Charles come this way. Max! You are the host, you must come with me."

Max leaned close to me as the camera followed a chattering Barbara and her mortified friends into the drawing room. "Are you going to be all right with that?"

"Yeah. Hey, would you happen to know if they had a stapler in 1879?"

"Stapler? Yes, there's a fastener in my office, but—"

"Great! I'll be along in a mo."

Max shot a quick glance over to where Teddy was opening the door to more guests. "Tessa, you can't staple your dress together. Ask Crighton to—"

"Are you kidding?" I hissed, pushing him toward the front door. "You want me to die? She'll kill me if she finds out. Just go deal with the guests and I'll be back in a couple of minutes."

I ran off before he could protest any more. The fastener, a big black steel monster that looked somewhat like an old-fashioned sewing machine that had been on a diet, was on the desk in his estate room. It took me a couple of minutes to figure out that the fastener used only one staple at a time, which slowed me down some, but eventually I managed to get the train reattached by means of a straggly line of brass staples.

Barbara gave me a curious glance when I slipped into the drawing room, but no one else seemed to notice my by now somewhat mangled train, and the next half hour was spent playing hostess to a bunch of people I didn't know. Roger's friends turned out to be not at all the brash, life-of-the-party sort of people I'd always imagined "show folk" to be. Instead, Neil and Harry were two quiet, witty men dressed in impeccable black-and-white dinner clothes. Neither, it should be mentioned, came close to being as devastatingly handsome as Max was in his dress blacks.

Max, oh, my Max. The brilliant white of his starched shirt and collar set off the black of his hair and coat. He wore a white waistcoat, white tie, and blue studs in his cuffs. He looked absolutely gorgeous, and I had to struggle to keep from flinging myself into his arms and kissing the breath out of him.

The other couple was from Ellis' historical society, and were polite but a bit reserved in front of the camera. I was wondering where the fourth and final couple was when, just a few minutes before we were due to dine, Teddy opened the doors to the drawing room and announced the vicar and his wife.

I glanced over to where Kip (standing in for Roger) was hiding behind Sam and Wilma. He shrugged and mouthed something at me. The historical society couple gasped when Penelope Hewitt sashayed into the room with a rustle of satin. She'd traded in her Scarlett O'Hara outfit for a Gibson girl dress, a very pretty, very low-cut dress in champagne satin. Unfortunately, it was also a dress that would have been worn about twenty years after the date we were supposed to be living.

"Reverend Hewitt," I said, getting to my feet to greet them, which occasioned another horrified gasp from the society couple. Duchesses, I remembered from the etiquette book, were not supposed to trot over to meet people; they were supposed to stand in stately elegance and allow the lesser folk to be brought to them.

Well, not *this* duchess. "How nice to see you both. Mrs. Hewitt, you look absolutely stunning in that dress. Gown. Frock. Whatever it is, it's simply gorgeous. Max, isn't it gorgeous?"

"Very fetching," he agreed, bowing over Penelope's hand.

She giggled when he brushed his lips over the back of her hand, and elbowed her husband just in case he missed Max's smooth move. "Oh, do you like it? It shows a terrible amount of my chest, doesn't it? But I told Kevin that we simply had to dress up, because it's just not every day one's invited to such a posh dinner party. But you look lovely, Your Grace. You look just like the picture of a shepherdess on a box of face powder my grandmother had. She was ever so pretty, with her big white wig and the panniers and pink everywhere. The shepherdess, that is, not my gran."

It sounded awful, but I knew well what I looked like. I thanked her as she smiled happily at everyone, the outstretched wings of the stuffed dove that had been worked into an intricate hairdo bobbing in time with her movements.

The vicar was in formal dress, this time the standard dress blacks that gentlemen in the late-Victorian era favored. He beamed at me, shook hands with Max, and seemed quite happy just to watch his wife chat as I introduced her to everyone.

"Lady Melody. Mademoiselle Beauvolais," Teddy said as Melody and Mademoiselle swept into the room.

"We are come," Mademoiselle said grandly, looking very pleased with herself in a green-and-blue patterned brocade with small silk ribbon and rose clusters gathered along the tulle edging at the bottom of the dress. She pirouetted for the company. "Do we not look extremely beauteous? This frock, it is very friendly to my coloring, yes? I do not look like at all the mousy governess."

Max frowned at his daughter, then turned to share the frown with me. Before I could explain the situation to him, Teddy's graceful exit from the room was ruined when instead of backing out of the room, he stumbled forward as if he'd been shoved. Henry stomped in behind him.

"Erm . . . Mr. Slough," Teddy said, giving Henry a dirty look before quickly replacing it with his usual suave expression.

"Ha! Thought I wouldn't make it back in time, didn't you?" he snarled at Barbara, who had leaped to her feet with a horrified, "Henry!"

"It is a very *fine* frock," Mademoiselle said firmly, a smile fixed to her face as she moved to stand between Henry and the camera. "It has boys, yes, but they do not march as the boys of the duchesse in the manner of the drunken stupor around her body. The boys on my dress are most orderly."

Everyone ignored her except Kevin the vicar, who helpfully whispered, "Bows, not boys."

Henry turned to the rest of us and spread his hands wide. "She tried to get rid of me! Sent me off on some wild hare's chase for a certain type of pomade she said she had to have, but I know the real reason she tried to get rid of me. Well, it won't work. I'm here, and now you're going to hear the truth, whether you want to or not!"

"Um," I said, watching nervously. Behind Henry, Palmer slid open the connecting doors to the dining room. I couldn't help but notice the eye patch had been supplemented by the return of the head bandage, complete with what looked to be artistically dabbed splotches of tomato sauce.

"Naturally, the ladies, they are jealous of my frock," Mademoiselle told the camera. Sam stepped sideways so he could film around her. She followed him. "It is to be understood, however, for I am of the temper most amiable. I do not mind their jealousy, not in the very least. This is why I was hired for such an important position. I have a very fine understanding of the English peoples."

Sam scooted around her, focusing on the three men in the center of the room.

"Henry, perhaps this would be better left to a less public time—" Max said, putting his hand on Henry's arm.

"No," the latter snapped, jerking himself away from Max and pointing at Barbara. "You're her brother; you'll side with her. I'm going to say my piece. I'm due a little consideration for putting up with her all these years."

"Henry!" Barbara shrieked.

"You cannot film my very beauteous frock if you stand with your back to me," Mademoiselle complained, but Wilma kept her from rushing in front of Sam.

"Oh, look, there's Palmer," I said, waving at him. "And he's got his bandage on; his head wound must have opened up again. How tragic. However, his appearance indicates that dinner is ready, so why don't we all go into the dining room—"

"I'm in love with Dorie Evans. We're going to Barbados together, and there's nothing you can do to stop us!" Henry announced to the room, setting his jaw.

That is, it was set until Charles' fist hit it, and then both the jaw and Henry crumpled.

"You damned bounder! That's my wife you're talking about!" Charles roared as he stood over the fallen Henry.

Kip was almost dancing with delight behind Sam, who was trying to catch everyone's expressions at the same time.

"It will not hurt," Mademoiselle said, peering down at where Henry lay. "His clothes, they were not of the very best quality."

"That's enough, Charles," Max said, starting forward.

"Stay out of this, Edgerton! This is between your brother-in-law and me."

"I will not stay out of this. This is my dinner party, dammit."

Charles straightened up from where he was glowering at Henry, still lying on the floor, rubbing his chin, and glaring back at Charles. "If you think I'm going to allow any man to insult my wife like that without beating the life out of him—"

"No one is going to beat anyone while I'm around," Max said.

Charles' nostrils flared as he challenged Max. "Right. I'll take you down as well."

"Are they to fight the duel of honor?" Mademoiselle asked Kevin, who looked confused and shook his head. "It is most exciting. I hope they do. I greatly enjoy the manly pursuits such as that."

Max rumbled ominously.

"DINNER IS SERVED!" I bellowed, throwing myself in front of him.

Everyone turned to look at me. I glared at each one of the men, pinning them back with a look they couldn't possibly mistake. "Now, we are going to walk into that dining room like civilized people and we are going to sit down and eat our dinner, because if we don't, the entire staff is going to rise up as one body and kill me, and I very much want to go on living. This is a polite dinner party, not a barroom. If you want to brawl, you can do it on your time. Got that? Good."

"Tessa—" Max said. I turned my glare on him.

"If any one of you so much as *thinks* about starting something, I'll castrate you. Slowly. With a grapefruit knife. Now." I took a deep breath and lifted my chin. "Shall we have our dinner?"

Things went fine after that, at least with regards to Henry and Charles, although Barbara managed to get a kick in to Henry's ribs while he was getting to his feet. The look she gave him probably could have peeled paint from a barn, but that was his concern, not mine. My concern was to get us through this wretched dinner party without anything else happening.

"Oooh, look, Kevin, little menus in French," Penelope said as she took her seat, picking up one of the individual menus Mrs. Peters had written up earlier. "Goodness, look at the wonderful treats! Salmon and bass and saddle of lamb and duck, and good lord, is that calves' sweetbreads? How very elegant!"

Mademoiselle snorted disdainfully at the menu. "It is not the very correct French, you understand."

I frowned down at the card set between two crystal wine glasses. I didn't care about how good the French was; I had told both the housekeeper and cook that they were *not* to include baby cow parts in the dinner unless they wanted to see me throwing up. Clearly, they hadn't taken that threat seriously.

"What's sweetbreads?" Melody asked, her scowl firmly in place.

"Nothing you want to eat, trust me," I said.

"I'll have some," she said defiantly.

She really did bring new meaning to the word *pugnacious*.

"You won't like it," I warned.

"I will so!"

"Melody," Max said from the opposite end of the table. "Children should be seen and not heard at dinner."

"That's just stupid. I can talk if I want to!"

Sam had positioned himself so he saw only Melody's right side, which meant he could film with impunity. He swung the camera back and forth between Melody and Max, capturing every scowl of hers and frown of his.

"Turtle soup," Kevin the vicar said with obvious delight as Palmer began ladling out the soup, happily putting an end to what could have been another argument. "My godmother used to serve that every New Year's Eve when I was a boy. What a treat it is to have it again."

I hadn't the heart to tell him it was mock turtle soup.

Despite the poor beginning and the tension rife in at least half of the members of the dinner party, things actually went very smoothly until the last course.

Neil mentioned the upcoming shooting party, having been asked to be a member. "I'm very much looking forward to a quiet weekend in the country. It's a shame we won't be able to hunt, but I do hope you'll let me take out that handsome stallion I saw."

"Yes, of course, if you'd like to, you're welcome to ride him," Max said, looking not at all happy with the subject.

"How come he can ride and I can't?" Melody asked, just as I knew she would. I tried to send her a little eyebrow semaphore that warned her off that subject, but she ignored me.

"Because I said you couldn't, and that is the end of that discussion. Eat your desert."

"You're always telling me what to do. It's not fair!" Melody glared at her father, slumping back in her chair, her arms crossed over her chest.

"Melody, darling, I've warned you before about making such a terrible face. You wouldn't want it to freeze that way, now would you?"

Melody stared in outraged fury at her aunt.

"Oh, clam up, Barbara. Let the poor girl have her say. It's not often she can get a word in around *you*."

"Oh!" Barbara gasped, shooting her husband a look that promised horrible tortures the minute she got him alone.

The threads of civility that had held us together during the dinner began to unravel.

"A man shouldn't speak to his wife that way," Charles said, his eyes narrowed on Henry, who sat across from him.

"Don't tell me how to treat my wife," Henry snapped back, half rising from his chair.

"I'll bloody well tell you anything I want—" Charles also started to get up.

"Gentlemen, I have a grapefruit knife, and I'm not

afraid to use it!" I said loudly, brandishing the small serrated piece of cutlery.

Both men sank back into their chairs, the hostility between them palpable enough to cut with a . . . well, a grapefruit knife.

For a moment there was silence. Peace reigned. Everyone turned their attention to their plates of champagne ice and pears with raspberry sauce.

It was a very *brief* moment.

"You're just as bad as she is," Melody told Barbara, pointing at me. "You say you'll do something, then you go back on your word."

"Now, dear, you know that's not true. I have only your best interests at heart, and I'm sure Tessa has the same."

"This is the best champagne ice I've ever had—" Kevin started to say.

"She does not!" Melody stood up, her hands fisted at her side as she faced her aunt, her face almost as red as her birthmark. "All she wants to do is have sex with my dad."

Barbara gasped. "Tessa!" she said, shooting me a look that should have killed me on the spot. I was a bit surprised by her reaction, having assumed she knew that Max and I were doing the bed tango together—everyone *else* seemed to know.

"I saw them together. They were both naked, and she said she likes him to touch her with his thingie! She's just trying to be nice to me so Dad will have more sex with her. She doesn't care about me at all—none of you do. I hate it here! I want to go home!"

She threw her napkin onto her plate, the lovely white linen immediately staining red in the raspberry sauce as Melody raced out of the room in her usual tears-in-the-eyes fury.

Max sat back with a groan, one hand over his eyes.

"Since when have I ever been nice to her?" I asked under my breath, then smiled as Sam swung the camera around to face me. I looked around the table. Henry was smiling smugly at Barbara, who was glaring at me. Neil and Barry were watching the floor show with bright, interested eyes. The society people looked shocked to their back teeth. Mademoiselle was making eyes at the camera. Kevin looked embarrassed, Penelope had a worried frown, Teddy and Bret were biting their lips to keep from laughing, and Kip was making furious notes behind Sam's back.

I scooted my chair back. "Well, ladies, I believe we'll retire to the drawing room and let the gentlemen have their port and cigars. Barbara, perhaps you would play for us?"

As I stood, a horrible sound filled the room, the sound of expensive lace and material being ripped asunder as the brass fasteners that held it together gave way. I bent and pulled the train out from under the foot of the chair, throwing the devastated bit of material to Teddy.

"Burn the blighted thing for me, would you, Teddy? Ladies, shall we?"

Trainless, head held high, I led the way to the drawing room, praying all the while for the evening to end with no one being beaten, castrated, or killed by their furious lady's maid.

Wednesday
September 15
8:49 P.M.
Library, waiting for morning prayers

The last three days have been pretty peaceful, considering. You wouldn't think they would be, what with Henry mad at Barbara; Barbara mad at Henry, Max, and me; Melody mad at Barbara, Max, me, and just about everyone else she knew; Roger furious that he missed the showdown at the dinner party; Ellis in a huff about the pink-and-white party dress; Teddy mad at Henry; Max annoyed with me telling Melody she could come to dinner without first clearing it with him; Mademoiselle pissy because she wanted to be the center of attention and wasn't; and the entire kitchen staff ready to burn me in effigy for screwing up the dinner plans.

Still, things have gone pretty well. I'm beginning to worry. It's not like life to suddenly be kind to me.

It was touch and go there on Monday morning, the morning after the dinner party from hell.

"Max, wake up; we don't have a lot of time. We have to be down at the stable in ten minutes."

"Hmm?"

I grabbed a shirt, braces, and pair of pants from the wardrobe, crossing the room to find socks, a pair of the long red underwear that the wardrobe had given Max, and his boots.

"Come on, sleepyhead. Boy, you are a sound sleeper aren't you?" I plopped down on the side of the bed and kissed Max's nose. He squinted groggily at me.

"Woman, are you after my manly body again? I thought I satisfied your lustful desires last night."

"Oh, ha ha ha. You're the one who wakes up in a playful mood. Come on, we don't have time to swap sexual innuendoes. You have to get dressed. Do you need to go to the bathroom first?"

Max sat up, outrage clear in every line of his body as I got off the bed and poured some water for him to wash his face. "Why are you dressed? You always wait for me to wake up so we can play. Why do you have my clothes out? Why are you wearing—" He sucked his breath in as he realized I was in my forest green riding habit. "No!"

"Aw, come on, Max, it won't hurt you. I promise I won't let you break your neck and die a slow, horrible death."

He glared at me, his eyes quickly changing from the heated blue that blared his desire to the cold, pale blue of an iceberg. "I don't find the subject amusing."

"Max—" I set down the ewer and took his hand. "I'm

sorry, I wasn't trying to make light of your friend's death. I just want you to see that horses aren't necessarily the great evil you think they are."

"I never thought they were, however, involvement with them can lead to tragedy and destruction."

"It can also lead to pleasure. Come on, let's get you dressed."

"I am not going riding, Tessa."

"Fine. But you have to come down to the stables with me."

"I do not," he said, allowing me to pull him to his feet. "Why do I have to go to the stables?"

I gave him a quick kiss and handed him his red underdrawers. "Because last night I had Sam film me telling everyone in the U.K. that you accused me of being afraid of horses, and that you dared me to go out riding with you this morning. If we fail to show up at the stables in four minutes, the whole country will think I'm a complete and utter coward."

"You *what?*" He stopped in the middle of buttoning the drawers.

"That's a humdinger of a glare, Max, but it's not going to change the fact that Sam and Wilma are waiting down at the stable to see if we show up or not."

"No. I won't do it." He snatched the pants out of my hands and with fast, jerky motions, pulled them on. "That's an underhanded trick, Tessa. If you had said it was me who was afraid of horses—"

I handed him his shirt. "—you wouldn't care, I know. But you're too much of a gentleman to let me look bad, aren't you, Max?"

He grumbled something as he buttoned up his shirt.

"What?"

"I said how do you know that I'm *not* afraid of horses?"

"Don't be silly," I said, and handed him his boots. "You're just a teensy bit afraid of emotional commitment, but I have every confidence we'll get you over that hurdle, too. Your issue with horses doesn't have anything to do with them, it has to do with protecting the people you love."

"I am too afraid of horses. Deathly afraid!" He shoved his foot into his boot. "I'll probably faint if I get too close to one."

"Oh, right, you're afraid of them like I don't love you."

His beautiful eyes narrowed as he shoved his other foot into the second boot. "I've told you, you're in lust with me, not love."

I took his face in my hands and flicked my tongue across the very tip of his nose. "Max, my darling, I'm so madly in love with you that I will do whatever it takes to make you realize that I'm the best thing that's happened to you since . . . well, since your daughter was born."

He grabbed his jacket and stuffed his arms into the sleeves. "I'll get you for this, Tessa."

I smiled and grabbed my dashing riding hat with the long green veil. "You mean you're going to punish me? Will you tie me down for the punishing, Max? Will there be massage oil involved?"

He gently shoved me through the door, taking my hand in his as he stalked down the hallway, his boot heels clattering loudly on the uncarpeted back stairs. "Your punishment will be not knowing what your punishment will be."

"That doesn't make sense."

"I know it doesn't." He held the door of the laundry room open for me. We stepped out into the fresh morning air filled with the noisy chatter of birds, sounds of crockery and voices coming from the kitchen, and the distant low of cattle from the neighboring farm.

"Tessa," he said, holding me back as I was about to cross the stable yard. He turned me until my breasts brushed up against his chest.

"I promise you that you won't get hurt," I said, brushing a lock of hair off his brow.

His eyes all but spat outrage at me. "I'm not concerned about *me*," he said.

"Oh, sorry. I promise you I won't get hurt either. Is that better?"

"No. Why are you doing this?"

I gnawed my lower lip for a moment, just long enough for his eyes to lock onto my lip. The second they fired up with steamy blue passion, my innards, all the squished bits, started cheering. I decided the moment had come to lay it all out on the line. No, not my innards, my cards. So to speak. "You have a tender heart that you've learned to guard very well against pain. Part of that guarding is your need to protect the people you love, to keep them from being hurt, and hurting you in turn."

He sighed. "We've had this talk before—"

"Melody is being strangled by your well-meaning but stifling protection," I continued, ignoring his comment. "More than anything she wants to make you proud of her."

His eyes flared open wide. "I *am* proud of her!"

I shook my head. "By denying her the opportunity to experience something new, you're telling her that you think she's going to fail before she even has a chance to try."

He ran his fingers through his hair. "I don't think she's going to fail, I just want to keep her from being hurt—"

"I know." I leaned against him and wrapped both arms around his waist, breathing in his wonderful spicy Max scent. "I know why you're doing it, but the very fact that you won't even let her try sends the wrong message. It tells her that you don't have any faith in her, any confidence in her ability to learn something new. You may be protecting her from a few bumps and bruises, but you're tearing her self-esteem to shreds."

He stood stiff against me, not saying anything, his hands resting lightly on my back. I kissed his chin and pulled away, catching his hand and pulling him toward the stable. "Come on, we have to go show England I'm not a coward."

"Tessa, I . . ." His lovely eyes were filled with pain. "I know, it's not easy, is it? We'll just take this in baby steps, OK? Today you go riding with me, tomorrow we'll go riding with Melody."

He glowered at me as we rounded the corner of the stable, Sam and Wilma chatting with Alec as he saddled up Talisman and Abou, the handsome but bad-tempered stallion. "Those aren't baby steps."

I grinned. "Yeah, I know, but I thought you might be distracted enough by thoughts of punishing me with the Lick Me Lemon that I could slip it by you."

His hand slid down my back to my bottom, giving me a none-too-gentle squeeze. "Don't worry, sweetheart, you'll be punished. And I promise you it'll be a punishment you remember for a very long time."

"Oh, man, I hope so." I breathed, my toes curling in my riding boots at the throb of passion in his voice.

Sam filmed us mounting up and riding off with nothing untoward in the least happening. Max was, of course, not afraid of horses. In fact, he did very well keeping control of the feisty stallion. I began to suspect that he had a lot more riding experience than he let on.

"Shall we have a gallop across the field?" I asked as we left the stable yard.

"No."

"How about a lively canter down the lane leading to the farm? That doesn't get a lot of traffic."

"No."

"A spirited trot to the far side of the estate?"

"No. We'll walk. From here to that telephone pole."

I looked at where he was pointing. "Max, that's six feet away."

"I know."

"Would you feel better with a riding hat? I bet Alec has one tucked away somewhere."

"No. I would feel better being back in bed."

I shot him a disgruntled glance. "Max, sweetie, you know I love you, and you have to know how I feel about the things you to do me in bed—as well as on the fainting couch, and of course, there was last night in the bathtub—but you know what? I like to do other things with you, too, nonsexual things, things like just be with you and talk to you and have you talk to me."

"We're talking now," Max said, his jaw as tight as his fingers on the reins.

"If you loosen up a bit on Abou, he won't fidget so much," I said.

Max gave Abou a bit more rein. I watched him for a minute as the horses ambled across the fallow field. "You've ridden before."

"Yes."

"I thought so. You're using your legs, and your hands are low, and you keep your seat even when Abou shies. Have you ridden a lot?"

"Some."

I pulled Talisman to a stop. "OK, let me explain something—a conversation is when two people talk together in an interacting format. One person talking and the other person answering in one-word grunts is *not* a conversation. It's an interview."

Max's brows pulled together. "I'm here. We're riding. What more do you want?"

I nudged Talisman forward into a walk. "I want you to relax. I want you to enjoy yourself. I want you to realize that because your friend suffered a horrible tragedy doesn't mean you or Melody or I will, too. Most of all, I want you to forgive your friend for dying."

He stared at me like I had just told him to dance stark naked on Abou's back. "What are you talking about? I don't have to forgive Trevor anything."

"Don't you?"

"No, I don't."

"You're not angry at him for dying and leaving you without a friend?"

"I have other friends."

"Not like him. You said he was your closest friend, that you grew up together. The fact that he was partially responsible for his own death must have made you furious."

"I've had enough conversation," Max snapped, reining

Abou back, turning him to face the way we'd just come. "And I've had enough of this ride."

"Do you know that every time you get mad at me, you run rather than confront that anger?" I called after him. Abou stopped suddenly, tossing his head as Max tightened his hands on the reins. "Obviously, that's an attempt to escape any sort of self-analysis. You'd rather avoid the issues than take a good, long look at what's really happening inside you."

"And I suppose you're bloody perfect," Max snarled as I rode up beside him. His eyes flashed ice and fire at the same time.

"Far from it. I, too, have layers of self-protection I've built up over the years to keep from being hurt, and just as many, if not more, faults, but there's one thing I am that you aren't—I'm willing to be honest with myself."

Max just stared at me, his eyes blazing, his fingers white with strain as they gripped the reins.

I sighed. "Maybe I'm all wrong, maybe I've totally misread everything about you, but if that's the case—" I turned Talisman to face the direction we were originally headed. "—you're going to have to tell me so to my face. And to do that, you're going to have to catch me."

I dug my heel into Talisman as I leaned forward, shouting my encouragement. He leaped forward in a textbook example of how to go from standing to a gallop in three seconds flat. I didn't look behind me to see if Max followed; I knew he would. He had a protective streak a mile wide in him, and despite the fact that he wasn't willing to admit that I had touched his heart, I knew I had.

"You fool woman, slow down. You're going to get yourself killed," he shouted from just to the rear of Talisman. Abou was half Arabian and had the deep chest of a horse with some serious speed, something that Talisman lacked.

"I might be willing to slow down to canter if you admit that you are angry at your friend."

"All right, fine, have it your way. I'm furious at

Trevor, I'm sick with anger, I'm galled that he could have been so bloody stupid, now PLEASE SLOW DOWN!''

I eased Talisman back to a slow canter and made a wide circle toward the direction of the stables, slowing down even further to a trot. "Did you say that just to make me slow down, or did you really mean it?"

Max rolled his eyes. "I don't stand a chance with you, do I?"

I grinned. "Nope. Did you mean it?"

"Yes, but not in the sense that you think I did."

"Oh, really?" Talisman settled into a walk, Abou tossing his head and snorting in protest when Max slowed him down. He danced sideways for a few steps until Max got him under control. "What were you angry with him about?"

"He shouldn't have been riding that day. The horse he took out was mine. I was supposed to ride at the local cross-country meet, but both Melody and I had been sick with the flu, so Trevor took my place in order to keep the local stable represented. He went down halfway through the course."

Max's face was hard, set in a mask of indifference, but I could see the anguish in his eyes. "Oh, how awful. He died taking your place, leaving you filled with guilt—"

"Not guilt!" he growled, his gaze holding mine. "I told Trevor not to take Galileo out. He'd never ridden him and had little experience on the cross-country course, but the damned fool had to prove something. He didn't listen to me, ignored my arguments, brushed off my concerns that he or the horse could be injured, and went ahead and took out a young horse he'd never ridden on a course he'd never seen . . ." Max's voice broke. A muscle in his jaw twitched. "And for what? To prove he was as good a rider as I was. No, Tessa, I don't feel guilt over Trevor's death. I'm angry that his family mattered less to him than his pride."

I blew out the breath I had been holding. "Boy, when you have baggage, you *really* have baggage."

"Now perhaps you understand exactly why I object to Melody riding."

I nudged Talisman closer to Abou, who was cropping at the long grass, and curled my fingers around Max's hand. "You're not Trevor, Max. I know you put your child's welfare first. I know you would never do something foolish that would leave her without your love and support. I honestly don't care if you ever ride another horse again. All I want is for you to understand what this stranglehold you have on life is doing to Melody . . . and to you."

His eyes held the question that didn't reach his lips.

"Me," I said in answer to that question. "I want you to see what you're doing to me, to us, to our relationship."

I thought he was going to run again; I was certain he was going to simply leave me sitting there in the middle of a field, but sometimes people surprise you.

Max slid his hand out from under mine and grabbed the back of my neck with his strong fingers, pulling me sideways to him until his mouth took possession of mine, his lips hard at first, then softening to a caress so sweet it brought tears to my eyes, tears that were dried in the heat of the passion he fired within me when his tongue swept past my lips and into my mouth. It was a hard kiss, a dominating kiss, a kiss that claimed absolute possession, but behind all of that it was also a kiss that begged for understanding from me. I clutched his shoulder and gave him every ounce of myself, let him into every corner of my heart, and prayed it was enough.

We rode back to the barn in silence, only the early morning scoldings of the birds disturbed by us marking our presence.

Melody's face was a thing of joy to behold when I told her that night that her father had given his permission for her to go riding with us.

"He said yes?" she asked, her eyes wide with disbelief before filling with sheer, unadulterated happiness. I wished Max was there to see it. "He really said yes?"

"Yep. Mademoiselle, she'll need a sturdy dress and boots for riding."

Mademoiselle, buffing her already perfect fingernails, made a little gesture of compliance. "It is possible. You do not expect for me to get on the back of a so smelly animal?"

"No, not tomorrow. If you'd like to go riding you certainly may, but there are only three saddle horses, so you'll have to do it another time."

She shuddered delicately. "*Non.* If you are here to amuse the little one, I will visit with Bret for the short while. *Il vachement bandant.*"

"What did she say?" I asked as soon as Mademoiselle took herself off to flirt with Bret.

Melody shrugged. "She said he was very sexy. Can I ride every morning?"

"Well—"

"Do I have to ride sidesaddle?"

"Probably, although for safety purposes your father might prefer—"

"Can I ride your horse?"

"No, Penny—"

"Will you teach me how to jump? I want to know how to jump. Dad used to do it and he promised me he'd teach me when I was older, and then Uncle Trevor hurt himself and died and he went back on his promise. You promised me I could go riding with you tomorrow, you can't go back on it now."

"Whoa! Can I finish a sentence, please?" Her lower lip threatened to commence immediate pouting. "First of all, I'm not going to teach you anything—your father is. I'm just going along to keep him on an even keel, so to speak. He's a much more experienced rider than I am, but I have to say your chances of learning to jump now are slim to none. However," I said, holding up my hand to forestall the protest I could see her about to make. "That doesn't mean he won't ever teach you. You have to be a good rider before you learn to take jumps and such, so you'll have a lot to do before you're ready.

And I'm not going to go back on my word; I try very hard to never do that. So just calm down and keep your nose clean so your dad won't yank his permission."

She glared at me. Why was I not surprised? "My nose is *always* clean."

The following morning we took Melody with us. The ride itself was pretty much a nonevent since Max absolutely refused to allow Melody's horse to go beyond a walk, as well as insisting that we flank her in case Penny spooked. We walked the horses all over the field while Max instructed Melody in the proper seat (she wasn't riding sidesaddle, the lucky puck), how to hold the reins, and so forth. Pretty tame stuff, but she was thrilled to death. Max looked like he'd rather have his fingernails chipped out with an ice pick than be there, but he survived the experience.

Oops, time for the morning prayer thing again. Loads to do today; it's the much anticipated garden party. Everyone's family members have been invited. The thought of the party has been the only thing holding everyone downstairs together. I'm worried about what's going to happen once it's over. Will they make it another week to the servants' ball? Gah.

—✦—

Sunday
September 19
11:10 A.M.
Bed, with a hot-water bottle, a stack of magazines, and a pot of cocoa

The cramps woke me up this morning.

"Oh, no," I groaned as a bad one hit, forcing me into a fetal ball.

"Hmm?" Max murmured sleepily above me, his voice muffled because curled up as I was, my head was level with his stomach. It was warm beneath the blankets and smelled of a marvelous blend of Max and the faint, lingering odor of sex, but even that wonderful mixture couldn't distract me from my agony. "Tessa? What are you doing down there?"

"Cramps," I groaned, trying to relax even though every muscle wanted to tighten up against the pain.

"Cramps?"

"CRAMPS!" I yelled at his belly.

He pushed the blankets down until my head emerged. "Oh. I'm sorry. Is there something I can do?"

"Yes. Go ask Melody if there's any of my ibu left."

"Ibu?"

"Ibuprofen. Are you going to repeat everything I say?"

"No, I'm sorry, it's been a while since I lived with a woman." Max slid out of bed and grabbed his dressing gown.

Another gripping cramp hit and I groaned my way through it.

"Are you normally in that much pain? Carol—my ex-wife—didn't seem to suffer as much as you are."

I clutched my abdomen and glared at him. "Look, either you go find me some frigging ibuprofen, or I disembowel you to show you what it feels like. The choice is yours."

Wisely, he decided to find me some ibuprofen. Melody had used all of my precious stash, and all Alice had was a couple of aspirin that didn't do much but take a bit of the edge off the cramps.

Ellis offered to prepare a willow bark draught, which I refused. "Not unless it's laced with codeine."

"Of course it's not," she said as I crawled into my own bed. "That wouldn't be authentic, although if I had some laudanum, I could give you that. I doubt, however, that Roger is able to acquire that, since it contains opiates. Would you like some cocoa?"

"Yeah. And something salty, too. Can you rustle up a hot-water bottle, do you think?"

She could and did. By the time Max and the shooting-party guests and the rest of the house went off to church, I was as comfortable as I could be, which isn't saying very much. I have no idea how women the last few thousand years have survived without heavy medication during their monthlies, and you know what? I don't care. All I care about is that I survive the next twenty-four hours. I think I stand a good chance of that, thanks to Max. When he returned from church, he carried with him a bottle of ibuprofen he'd sent Teddy for at the local Boots (drugstore). I'm starting to feel human again, thank heaven, and am planning on making my grand reappearance at the al fresco luncheon in a couple of hours.

Before I get into the shooting party, let me backtrack a couple of days and detail the happenings at the garden party.

Everyone, especially the younger members of the staff, were really looking forward to the party, as it would be the first time they were allowed to see their families since the filming started.

All of the maids' families came—mostly parents, although I did meet Alice's sister and Easter's elderly grandmother, who was in service when she was a young girl.

"She's a good girl, our Easter," Granny Chester said. The wardrobe department at U.K. Alive! had raided their sister film studio's costume department to outfit everyone, and Granny, a tiny little woman with curly white hair and two of the biggest chin warts I've ever seen, very much enjoyed wearing a shiny black bombazine dress and frilly white widow's cap that bobbed as she spoke.

"Easter is a delight—we love having her here. And she's just a whiz with fires."

"Aye, gets that from her granddad, she does. Always lighting fires, my Harold was. Burned down the local church once." I must have shown my horror because she hastened to add, "No one was hurt in the fire, and the church was rebuilt bigger than before with the insurance money, so in the end, 'twas a good thing Harold did."

I refrained from commenting on that, and made a mental note to myself to have another talk with Easter.

Alec the handsome coachman strolled by, his hands in the pockets of dark green breeches, an old gold waist-coat topping his usual snowy white shirt, the sleeves rolled back to show the fine sprinkling of golden hair on tanned arms. I leaned out over the tea table, where I was presiding over a huge tea urn, and called to him. "Alec, would you like some tea? Lemonade? There's ale, too, if you'd prefer that."

Alec gave me a curious glance, then smiled his daz-zling smile. If I hadn't been so madly in love with Max, I would have swooned at the effect of that smile. Well, OK, I swooned a little bit, just on the general principle of the thing, but quickly overcame my swoony tenden-cies by reminding myself that not only was Alec much younger than me *and* had a proclivity to flatulence jokes, but I had Max. Max just wasn't ready to admit that state of affairs yet. "You must be Tessa. I'm Julian, Alec's brother."

My jaw dropped. "My God, there's two of you? Twins?"

His cheeks dimpled as he grinned. "That we are."

"God help the women of England."

He laughed and spent a few minutes chatting with me about his job. Unlike his horse-obsessed brother, Julian favored fast cars, and spent all his spare time working on rebuilding a racing car.

Later, Mrs. Peters introduced her husband, Barry. "Barry is the president of the All England Ghost Hunt-ing Society," she said proudly. "It was he who did all the historical research into Worston and determined the identities of the ghosts who presently haunt its halls."

"How very fascinating," I said, smiling at the short, round man. His eyes, greatly magnified behind big glasses, and the fringe of shaggy gray hair with two little odd tufts that stood on end reminded me of a scholarly owl. "Mrs. Peters has had great luck with the resident ghosts, what with them manufacturing ghostly herring and stuff. I'm hoping she invites me to a séance before the month is out."

Mrs. Peters dragged her husband away before he could answer, mumbling something to him about not wanting to upset the ghosts.

"Tessa, there you are. I've been looking all over for you."

I turned at the sound of Barbara's cooing voice, more than a little surprised at her pleasant tone, not to mention the fact that she'd sought me out. Ever since the dinner party from hell, she'd been giving me the cold shoulder. Oh, not when the cameras were around; then she'd be just as gushing as ever, although I could tell from the hard glint to her eye that she was still mad at me for sleeping with her brother. Why, I had no idea. Maybe it was just the general principle of the thing, but she made it clear she did not approve.

Why is it that everyone, male or female, always blames the woman when it comes to an affair? You'd think that women would be supportive of their sex and take the female's side, but no, Barbara treated me like I was the biggest hussy of all time. The only time she'd willingly spoken to me in the last few days was to complain about Mrs. Peters hunting ghosts in her room—it seemed that Barbara's boudoir was particularly high in ghost density. Barbara's irritation with me even stretched as far as allowing her to take Henry back into her good graces, although I suspected by his hangdog air that she was keeping him very subdued, poor guy. I wanted to ask him what happened to Dorie, but never had the chance to catch him alone.

Back to the garden party. Barbara had, as was usual with her, a camera trailing behind her. She oozed up to me, all smiles and graceful gestures of her hands, Tabby and Matthew hot on her tail, along with a very pretty blond woman in an elegant red-and-white striped dress with matching hat and parasol. No shiny black bombazine for her; this lady screamed nobility.

"Have you seen dearest Max?" Barbara asked, not introducing the striped lady. She looked vaguely familiar, but I couldn't put my finger on who she was. She certainly wore the Victorian dress with a panache that I lacked, her graceful figure positively hourglass under the effect of the corset.

"I think he's down at the lake with some of the guys, doing a spot of fishing."

Barbara made a face, which she quickly changed into an acid smile. "Is he? Did you hear that, Cynthia? He's fishing. You love to fish, don't you? We'll stroll down there."

Cynthia, who had been giving me a cool appraisal, smiled. "Yes, it would be lovely to see Max. I've missed him."

An icy chill shivered down my spine at those last three words.

The blonde's smile deepened, but none of it touched her steely gray eyes. "How are you doing as duchess? I imagine by now you're settling down well into the role. I must admit, I feel the tiniest morsel of regret that I didn't see the job through, but Max agreed that although I was imminently suited as his duchess, losing a month of time would be too great a sacrifice to my career."

Cynthia. Blond Cynthia. The woman in the picture. "Oh. You're the Cynthia who walked off the job four days before shooting."

"I had to, I simply had to. You have no idea the dreadful frocks Roger insisted I wear." She eyed my white-and-green-ivy batiste gown. "Or perhaps you do. Regardless, I simply could not tolerate his demands. They would have crushed my artistic spirit."

I remembered then that the bio sheet on Cynthia said she was a sculptor.

"It's been lovely chatting with you. Tess, is it? I do hope you stay for the entire show, despite the many trials you must be enduring. Barbara, shall we go to the pond? I simply must see Max. The poor lamb has suffered enough without me these last few weeks, don't you think?"

Remember the icy chill going down my spine? It had turned into glaciers, big fat glaciers that moved into my bloodstream and froze my blood solid.

Barbara laughed gaily, then waited until the camera turned to follow Cynthia as she strolled across the rose garden, nodding graciously to clusters of people just as if she was the one playing the duchess.

"Isn't she lovely? Cynthia is Max's girlfriend. They're engaged. Didn't he tell you? Tsk," Barbara said, her mouth stretched wide in a cruel smile. "That brother of mine. Always breaking hearts."

As Barbara hurried after Cynthia, quickly catching up to her and sliding her arm through the blonde's, great warning claxons went off in my head to alert my entire body to the horrible surprise attack that had just been leveled at me.

Girlfriend? An engaged girlfriend? To Max, my Max, the warm, adorable, sexy Max who woke me up that very morning in a manner that kept a smile on my face until Cynthia started her bombing run? *That* Max?

"No," I said aloud, setting down the teacup that I absently held, moving around the tea table, purposefully striding toward the lake. "Not that Max. It has to be another Max, some other Max entirely, because I know my Max, and he wouldn't play Cowgirl and the Randy Stallion with me if he was engaged to someone else."

"No, of course Max wouldn't," Alice said as I passed her.

"Do what?" her sister asked.

"Play Cowgirl and the Randy Stallion with Tessa."

"Why not? I'd play it with him. He's gorgeous." Their voices drifted back to me as I marched onward.

"He wouldn't, he's not that kind of man at all. He's a good man, a caring man, even if he is a bit stubborn and pigheaded at times, still, stubborn and pigheaded is not a two-timing scumwad."

I pushed my way through the family members gathered around the servants, grabbed my skirts, and ran down the incline to the lake.

"He's not like that, he's not like that, he's not like that," I chanted as I ran. A crescent of trees hid most of the lake from sight of the house, but as I rounded the curve of trees I could see a group of several people clustered together, all looking at the same thing.

"I love him. I have faith in him. I believe in him. He wouldn't hurt me," I ground out through my clenched teeth as I shouldered my way through two footmen, three family members I had been introduced to but promptly forgot, past Matthew, past Tabby, past Barbara to where Max stood with his hands on the red-and-white hips of Cynthia while she sucked the tongue from his head.

"Tessa," Max said when she finally released his lips (with an audible wet, sucking noise, I might add).

"Damned right!" I snarled, and shoved him into the lake.

I didn't even stay to see him get soaked; the loud splash and resulting gasped "Oooh!" from the crowd was enough to tell me he went under. I took three steps, decided I was just as much a hypocrite as Barbara was, and turned around, marching back to where Cynthia was watching a waterlogged Max try to get to his feet.

I put both hands on her back and shoved her in, too. She slammed against Max with a shriek that could have pierced leather, a shriek that got even louder as both she and Max went down into the mud and slime and dirty water of the lake.

I smiled sweetly for the camera, dusted off my hands, then turned and walked back up to the house.

It would have been a very satisfying moment had my heart not been breaking.

Ironically enough, it was Melody who found me. I had assumed Max would come storming in with some slick explanation on his lips, which is why I shoved the wardrobe up against the door to the connecting bathroom.

But Max wouldn't tap hesitantly on the door to my room, so when the knock came, I unlocked the door and opened it to see Melody.

"How come you're wearing that?" she asked, pointing at my legs.

I looked down at my jeans, then moved back and waved her into the room, locking the door behind her. "Oh. Uh. Well . . . I was going to go home, but I've changed my mind."

"Because of my dad?" she asked, her brows pulled together in a manner so much like Max's puzzled frown that my heart gave a lurch and tears pricked the backs of my eyes.

"It's a bit complicated, squirt. I'm not leaving, though. That wouldn't be fair to everyone else."

She just looked at me with her blue imitation-Max eyes, eyes that seemed to be a lot older than they should be. I fidgeted around with pulling out a skirt and bodice, shaking out the corset I'd managed to get out of just twenty minutes earlier, and getting a clean pair of combinations. "Why do you think they say 'pair' of combinations, just like a 'pair' of underwear?"

Melody shrugged. "I don't know. Are we still going riding tomorrow?"

"Did your dad say tomorrow was a riding day?" Max told Melody he would teach her riding three days a week, the days to be negotiated.

"He said I had to ask you. Were you going to leave because Cynthia was kissing Dad?"

"No. Tell your father that he can take you out whenever he wants; I won't be going with you anymore."

"Oh," she said, her face placid.

"Well, don't get upset about it or anything," I said, slamming the bureau drawer after pulling out a pair of garters. I knew I was being childish, but dammit, my heart was broken. Max destroyed everything I had believed and hoped for and wanted so desperately with one wrestle of his lips on that blond she-devil.

"I won't," Melody answered snappishly.

"Good," I said. "I'm glad you don't care."

"I don't."

"Good," I repeated. "Because I don't either. Care, that is."

I ruined my tough front by bursting into tears, a real flood, the kind of sobbing that shakes your whole body. I crumpled up onto the floor and grabbed my knees and bawled and bawled until I thought I was going to throw up.

Melody watched me for a couple of minutes, then she left without saying one single thing, which made me cry harder, if that was humanly possible.

That's how Max found me, lying on the floor, surrounded by stockings and petticoats, heaving into the chamber pot I never used.

"Tessa," he said, in what would have been a soft voice if he was still the love of my life, but he wasn't, so it was just a plain, old, ordinary voice that just *seemed* to be velvety soft and warm and wonderful.

"Go away," I said, wondering if any more of my lunch was going to come up.

"Are you all right?"

"Yes. Now go away."

"You don't look like you're all right. Melody, go ask Ellis to bring Tessa something to settle her stomach."

Melody? She'd gone to fetch Max? I looked up. She stood beside him in the doorway, her face peaked. I had the worst urge to hug her, which I promptly squelched. I might have given in to it earlier, B.C. (Before Cynthia), but not now. It would just hurt that much more when we went our separate ways.

"I don't want anything to settle my stomach, and I don't want you, Max Edgerton. So please just go away and leave me alone."

Max gave Melody a little shove out the door, then turned back to me. "I'm not leaving until we've had a chance to talk, Tessa."

I clutched the chamber pot. "I'm throwing up! Can't

you see that? What are you, some sort of barf fetishist that you want to stay and watch?"

He went behind the screen to the washstand and poured me a glass of water, handing it to me with the command, "Rinse."

"No."

"For god's sake, Tessa, just do as I ask."

I rinsed out my mouth and spat into the chamber pot. He took it from me, stuffed it behind the screen, then came to stand over me.

I looked at his shoes. "Your feet don't look like the kind of feet that would two-time me. I guess feet can lie, huh?"

He squatted next to me and tried to take my hands. I sat on them, instead.

"My feet would never lie to you."

"Oh, really?" I looked up at him, at that handsome long face with the silky black brows, at the little mole on his left earlobe that he loved for me to suck, at his nose that was just a little bit too big, at his obstinate jaw, and the lush curve of his lower lip that could turn a saint into a sinner, and the last few ounces of liquid in my entire body rushed up to my eyes to squeeze out as a few hot tears.

"Tell me you're not engaged to Cynthia, Max."

He put his hands on my knees. They felt warm even through my jeans. "I'm not engaged to Cynthia. I never was. I never thought of marriage with her."

"Tell me you weren't kissing her."

"I wasn't kissing her. She kissed me. She took me by surprise."

"Tell me she's not your girlfriend."

He tucked back a strand of my hair that had come loose from the elaborate curled mop that Ellis had spent half an hour creating with two pairs of heating tongs. "She's not my girlfriend. She hasn't been for months; we broke up earlier this summer."

He looked me dead in the eyes when he said it, his

lovely eyes shadowed with emotion. I wanted to believe him. I *did* believe him.

Kind of. Almost. No, I believed him.

"Tell me you love me." The words were out before I even knew my brain was thinking them, but by then it was too late. They just hung there in the air between us.

Max looked at me for a minute and life as I know it came to a grinding halt while I waited to see what he would do. He sighed, then pulled me onto his lap, leaning back against the bed. "I love you, Tessa."

"You don't sound very happy about it," I said into his neck, breathing in the wonderful Max scent, wrapping my arms around him, allowing his warmth to sink into my bones.

"I'm not."

I pulled back and glared at him. "Thanks oodles."

He gave me a half a smile and brushed a tear off my cheek. "I didn't intend for this to happen, Tessa. It complicates things."

"Well, I've been called worse than a complication, but still, that's not quite the lover's talk I was hoping for." An odd, pained look crossed his face, and I realized that I must be too heavy. "Am I crushing your balls?"

"Yes."

"Sorry," I said, and started to scoot off him.

"No, just let me move you . . . there." He hoisted me a little to the side, then pulled me tight against his chest. "Tessa, you have to understand, Melody and I have been by ourselves for a long time. I never thought I'd find someone I wanted to share my life with."

"But now you have?" I asked, feeling it was better to beat a dead horse than to misunderstand.

"Yes."

"Are you by any chance proposing to me?"

He grimaced. "I guess I am."

"That was a grimace. You grimaced. I saw it."

"I'm sorry."

"You're not supposed to grimace when you propose;

you're supposed to look joyful and happy and thrilled to death by the wonder that is womanhood."

"Ah. Can you give me a minute? I'll try to look joyful and happy and thrilled to death then."

"All right. Where's your watch?" I pulled back so I could pat his waistcoat, following the gold chain to the small gold pocket watch that was tucked into a pocket. "You changed your clothes."

"I had to—the other ones were covered in mud."

"Oh. Um. Sorry about that. OK. You have one minute. I'm timing you."

He laughed then, hugging me tight, his breath warm on my ear as he pressed gentle kisses to the shivery spot behind it. "Tessa, you are a delight. What would I do without you?"

"Continue on as you are, I suppose."

He started nibbling on my neck, which sent wonderful shivers of delight down my back and arms.

"Max?"

"Mmm?"

"Your proposal—it *was* for marriage?"

"Of course."

"Good, because I like being married, and although I'd just shack up with you if you insisted, I much prefer it being legal and all."

His lips kissed a line along my jaw, then headed for my mouth.

"Max!"

"What?" he asked when I slid my hand between our mouths.

"You can't kiss me, I just threw up. I have barf breath."

"Oh." He looked at me for a moment with those lovely blue eyes that sparkled like blue topazes in the snow. "Would it prove my undying love to you if I were to kiss you despite your barf breath?"

"No," I said, wiggling out of his embrace and getting to my feet. "It's just too gross to think about. I have to brush my teeth and my tongue and everywhere else in my mouth. I feel the need to kiss the pants off of you, and I can't do that with barf breath."

By the time I came back around the screen from brushing my mouth, Max was standing stark naked in the middle of the room. "Wow, I guess you really take that *kissing the pants off you* thing seriously."

Max frowned. "It's not going to be easy, you know."

I looked at his arousal. "Oh, I don't know, we haven't had too much trouble so far, except last night when you got that wild hare to try stuff out of the *Kama Sutra* that you found in the library."

"Tessa—"

"I mean, the Union of the Tiger was fun, but that Donkeys in the Third Moon of Spring thing was a bit harder to manage."

"Tessa—"

"All the blood ran to my head. I thought I was going to pass out at one point."

"That's not—"

"Still, it was fun. I've never been a wheelbarrow before."

"TESSA!"

I looked at him in surprise. He yelled at me! "What?"

"Will you let me say what I want to say without interrupting me?"

"You're naked, Max. I always get a bit rattled when you're naked and your penis is waving at me."

"Waving at you? It's not wav—" His eyes went a bit wild around the edges. "You're doing this on purpose, aren't you? You're trying to drive me mad purposely, willfully. Aren't you?"

I smiled and stepped forward, leaning against him, sliding both my hands up his fabulous chest to his fabulous shoulders and his fabulous neck. "Do you know what you are?"

"Barking mad?"

"Fabulous," I said, my lips teasing his.

A half an hour later I collapsed onto his chest and

gasped into his sweaty neck, "OK, so that's three *Kama Sutra* positions we've done. Are we going to work through the whole book? Because if we are, we're going to have to save the more strenuous positions for last. I think I'm going to have to build up my stamina for them. This one almost killed me."

Max grunted as I slithered around on him. "If you can still talk, I must not be doing something right."

I kissed the wildly pounding pulse beneath his jaw and pushed back just enough so that I could smile down at him. "*Au contraire!* You're doing something very right."

He grunted again and tugged me back down onto his chest. I sucked on his chin for a few seconds. "I love you when you grunt. It's such a primitive, *I've been sated with sex* sort of sound. It's earthy, but not unattractive when done in the right way at the right moment. Now, if you were grunting while you were picking your nose, well, that would be gross, but a grunt of satiation, a grunt that says you've been sexed nigh unto oblivion is a good sound. I like it. You may grunt freely."

He narrowed his eyes at me. "Why is it that you can talk, putting actual words together in a way that makes sense, when I can't even work up enough strength to move my leg even though a muscle in my calf is cramping?"

I sat up. "Which leg?"

"Left."

I slid off him with a slicky wet sound that was almost as good as his grunt and adjusted his legs, rubbing his calf.

"What happened to Cynthia?"

"She left."

"Ah. I guess she was pretty mad at me. What does Barbara have against me being with you?"

"I have no idea. Barbara is . . . a bit odd at times."

I decided to let that go. "I suppose we should get dressed and go back down to the party."

"Mmm."

"Although they were having fun without us. Maybe they won't notice we're not there."

He didn't say anything to that, but his toes flexed as I worked his calf muscle. "Better?"

"Yes."

I ran my hand along his leg, just a little pet, really, nothing sexual, although somehow my hand ended up at his fun zone. He quivered. "Again?"

I giggled at the desperation in his voice. "No, don't worry, you can just lay there and recover. Here, let me just peel this off. Ew. Gooshy."

I toddled over to the screened-off area, disposed of the condom, had a quick wash, and came back around the screen, snagging my combinations en route. "So, before we did the Utkalita, what was it that you wanted to say to me?"

Max's chest rose and fell a couple of times.

"Max? What was so important that you had to say?"

A gentle snore answered my question.

"Poor guy," I said softly, pulling the blanket up over him. "All tuckered out. Looks like we'll need to work on your stamina, too."

———— ⁓⁓⁓ ————

Sunday
September 19
7:01 P.M.
Morning room, at the escritoire

There's just one more dinner to get through and then breakfast tomorrow morning, and the Shooting Party will be officially over. Whew. Never thought it would end. Yesterday wasn't bad because people (Neil, Harry, and Jean and Dennis, another couple from Ellis' historical society) didn't start arriving until just before teatime.

I've been dreading this weekend for a couple of reasons—the first is because I don't like blood sports of

any kind, hunting in particular, and the second is because things are dicey below stairs again.

Alice knocked on my bedroom door as Ellis was
dressing me for lunch. "Tessa, do you have a—oh. Sorry,
I didn't know you were busy."

"Not a problem. Come on in," I said, turning so Ellis
could button up the back of the blue linen skirt (not too
terribly fussy a costume, but with more frills and ruching
than I care for).

Ellis froze, giving Alice a look of dislike. "A servant
does not refer to her employer by her Christian name."

"Yeah, yeah, we know that servants and family aren't
supposed to talk to one another, but this is just us, Ellis.
No one will know if we've breached the almighty class
barrier by actually behaving like human beings to one
another."

"I will know," Ellis said righteously, her nostrils going
immediately into flare mode.

"You're making this much harder than it has to be,"
I said, turning to face her, my hands on my hips. "I
know we're supposed to be the very model of Victorians,
but that's just for the cameras."

"No, it's not. The agreement that you and every one
of us signed states that we would live just as our counterparts would in 1879—all day, every day, no exceptions."

"You're really cheesing me off, Ellis, you know that,
don't you?"

"My name is Crighton," she said through gritted teeth.

"Fine. You want to play it strictly by the book, we'll
play it strictly by the book. You're fired."

She stared at me in dumb surprise. "What?"

I crossed my arms. "You want me to be the imperious
duchess, someone with no consideration for her staff?
Well, you got it. I'm firing you. You're no longer my
lady's maid."

"You can't do that! Only Roger d'Aspry can fire me
from this project."

"Ha!"

"You can't possibly manage without a lady's maid," she hissed.

I looked at Alice, standing silent as she watched us. "Alice can be my lady's maid. You can take her place. Effective immediately. Alice, would you finish buttoning me up, please? I believe I can do my own hair today."

"You can't do this," Ellis cried as Alice buttoned up the skirt. "It goes against every rule. You cannot simply switch our jobs like that!"

"I can do anything I want to do. I'm the duchess, remember?"

She ground her teeth in frustration.

"You know, it doesn't have to be this way. You were the one who pointed out that I care about the servants—I want to get along with you, Ellis, I really do. But I refuse to make nice only to the upper servants and ignore the rest. I'm not going to be chatty and friendly with you and treat the others like they are dirt under my feet. So if you want your job back, it's going to have to be on my terms."

Alice rubbed her nose, keeping her hand in front of her mouth. I suspect it was to hide her smile.

The veins in Ellis' neck stood out. "Very well," she spat out, shouldering Alice aside. "I will say nothing about your manner of conducting yourself with the servants when you are not on camera, but I will lodge my protest with Mr. d'Aspry. Such an attitude is in complete disregard of the rules, and is no doubt responsible for undermining the power structure below stairs."

"Viva la revolution," I said, then gave in to the urge to grin. "Sorry, Alice, looks like you're back to head housemaid."

She laughed. "I prefer it that way, thank you."

"Good. What was it you wanted to see me about?"

She sighed and sat when I waved her toward the overstuffed armchair before the fireplace. Ellis pushed me to the bench and began to yank a comb through my hair.

"People aren't happy downstairs."

Ellis sniffed but didn't say anything as she started to

twist my hair into a complicated coil that would sit low on the back of my head.

"Still? I thought things improved with the garden party?"

"It did, for a bit, but Raven and Easter are at each other's throats over Bret, Michael has a cold, Mr. Palmer started drinking again, which means Mrs. Peters is a positive hag to him, which in turn means he's moping around like a melancholy Eeyore, not getting a single thing done. Sally has decided that meat is bad for us and is making us all vegetarians. To top it all off, Teddy, Bret, Shelby, and Raven have all disappeared. We're running mad downstairs trying to get everything ready for the luncheon with only half the help we need. We have no butler—Mr. Palmer is sleeping off the effects of a bottle of posset he found. We have no housekeeper— Mrs. Peters claims she is expecting some sort of enlightening message from her ghosts and has locked herself into the Pug's Parlor and won't come out until the spirits speak to her. What's left of the staff and I are trying to get everything ready for the luncheon, as well as our normal chores."

"Oh, geez. It sounds like things are awful down there."

"It is beyond awful, it is a nightmare, but it's not just this morning. You have no idea because you get your tea when you ring for it, or your hot water, or whatever, and the rooms are cleaned without you ever having to lift a finger, and you don't see any of the work we do. You can't possibly understand just how horrid it is to feel trapped in this job without any hope of getting anything better "

Alice stopped her unexpected outburst by covering up her face with her hands, her shoulders shaking.

"Oh, Alice, I'm so sorry," I said, going to kneel at her feet with only half my hair coiled. "I know how hard it is for you guys, I truly do know, and I'm deeply appreciative that you all took on such demanding jobs. I can imagine how frustrating it is to be working so hard and yet be expected to blend in to the scenery. What can I do to make things better?"

She pulled a handkerchief from her sleeve and mopped up the waterworks. "Nothing. I'm sorry, I didn't mean to rail at you. It's not your fault—you and Max are the best of everyone. It's just that sometimes it gets to me, the way we're treated. Everyone else is so rude to us, like we don't have any feelings. Sometimes it's a little hard to take."

"I bet it is. I wouldn't have been able to take that sort of treatment. Would you like me to talk to everyone upstairs?"

Behind me, I could feel Ellis stiffen.

"No, that wouldn't be right. Ellis has a point—we did all agree to live our lives like the Victorians, and for the servants, that means we have to take being treated like we are nothing and deal with it."

I gave her knee a pat and returned to the bench so Ellis could finish my hair. "That doesn't make it right. OK, so let's brainstorm this—we need to do something to make everyone happier, but it has to stay within the guidelines of the rules. Any ideas?"

"No," she said, dabbing at her eyes and blowing her nose discretely. "If I had, I wouldn't have bothered you with the situation."

"It's no bother. Well, I'll think about it. Maybe Max will have an idea. In the meantime, just keep telling everyone there's only eleven more days left, and only four days until the servants' ball."

"I will, but I'm not sure even that will keep people from walking out."

It didn't help that we had four extra people staying the weekend, which dumped even more work on the servants. I didn't have time to think very hard on the problem before I had to go downstairs and play hostess to the ladies while the men were out shooting innocent birds.

I didn't have a chance to remind Max this morning that although I would not be a demanding and domineering wife, if he killed so much as one bird I would never speak to him again. So it was with much trepidation that I joined Barbara, Jean, and Mademoiselle and Melody in the open barouche, to be driven out to join the men for an al fresco luncheon (a.k.a. picnic).

Jean stared hard at Alec as he jumped down from the coachman's seat and flipped down the steps, holding the door open for us to climb into the carriage. "That's the coachman?" she asked in a whisper as Barbara (still ignoring me except when the cameras were pointed at us) grandly ascended the three metal steps.

"Yeah. Isn't he dishy?"

"You can say that again. He's just stunning." Jean breathed, and I knew that unlike her predecessors, I'd like her.

We rode out in style to the north edge of the estate, where the men had tramped out earlier to slaughter the bird life. Melody rode up front with Alec, and Sam sat facing back across from me, with Wilma clutching her sound equipment and hanging on for dear life to the groom's seat at the rear of the carriage.

Although I'd been to town twice for church, it was a bit strange riding along in a carriage while cars zoomed around us. Many of them tooted their horns politely and waved. We all waved back, smiling and nodding at the people who stopped to stare. A few people pulled over to take pictures of us. Barbara loved that.

Most of the road was paved, but after fifteen minutes, Alec turned off onto a dirt road and we rattled our way down it until we reached the designated picnic spot.

The servants, of course, had been out since the return from church, setting up the picnic. This was no simple *blanket and a basket of goodies* picnic; this was a proper Victorian picnic, and that meant green velvet cushions, lots of rugs, pillows, two small tables covered in beautifully snowy-white tablecloths, several folding chairs for those people who didn't care to lounge on the rugs, and huge, copious amounts of food.

The main part of the picnic consisted of cold roast beef,

two roast chickens, a duck, ham, two pigeon pies, salad, tomatoes and cucumbers, a large cheesecake, two fruit pies, blancmange, and jam puffs. Of course, there was champagne, wine, and lemonade to wash it all down, and tea and coffee in flasks for the less libationary souls. As if laying all that out on a table wasn't enough, Alice (acting in the passed-out Palmer's stead) also oversaw the arrangement of wineglasses, tumblers, silverware, plates, teacups, and saucers, as well as all the condiments and spirits (so the gentlemen might refill their hip flasks, because everyone knows it's thirsty work shooting sweet little innocent birds).

"What a very elegant setting," Jean said as she stepped out of the carriage. "This is utterly fantastic. I can't believe how authentic it looks. It's like stepping through a magic door and finding yourself a hundred years in the past."

"It is pretty fantastic, isn't it?"

"Oh, goodness, just see where they've set that table—that won't do at all. Alice! You must move it, it's below a tree. Any number of horrid things could fall out of the tree into the food. No, to the right, that way. Oh, I see I shall have to take charge once again. I can't *imagine* allowing my servants to get away with murder the way yours do," Barbara said, shooting me a nasty look as she hustled off to have the table moved two feet to the right.

I gave Jean a look that fell just short of being an actual eye roll. A little giggle slipped out of her lips.

"How do you keep from laughing?" she asked behind her hand, one eye on Sam as he filmed Barbara overseeing the table move.

"It's not easy, let me tell you, although sometimes . . ." I looked out over the lovely green meadow, dotted with wildflowers and sunny dandelions, butterflies dancing on the afternoon breeze. ". . . Sometimes, it's very easy to forget that this is all just a temporary life. I can see why people fought to retain the privileges of the upper class. It has its discomforts, but for the most part, it is a very easy lifestyle to fall into."

My gaze fell onto Alice and Easter, dressed in clean

white pinafores over their somber black maid's dresses, the long white streamers from their caps playing in the wind behind them, as they staggered a little while hauling the heavy table the prescribed distance. "Then again, I can see why the lower class demanded a revolution. It certainly wasn't a life of ease for them."

"That's true, but I have to admit, I'm enjoying myself greatly. I know I should feel guilty for lolling about, having servants waiting on me, but it is a wonderfully delicious life."

I smiled as Max stepped into view, his shotgun broken over his arm in the traditional manner as he chatted with Barry and Neil. "It has its moments."

Behind them the two Hs (Harry and Henry) followed, looking rather glum, while trailing them were Michael and Thom, both acting as beaters for the hunters, and three rangy dogs loaned from a nearby sportsman. Michael and Thom, I was unhappy to see, each had a string of dead birds.

I wasn't the only one unhappy to see the proof of their day's *sport*.

As Max walked toward us, a smile on his manly lips, a popping noise came from the left. I stared in disbelief as red exploded on Max's chest.

"Oh, my God, he's been shot," I screamed, and started running toward him. *"MEDIC!"*

Max looked down at his chest, his shotgun hanging limply from his hand as he touched the bloom of red on his chest.

"Don't move! Don't touch anything! Stop breathing, you'll just make the wound worse," I yelled as I hiked up my skirts in order to run faster.

Another pop sounded. He jerked as a second blast of red formed on his side.

"Dear God, someone call the police. Max is being murdered before our eyes!" I yelled.

"Tessa, no—" he said.

"Stop talking," I bellowed. "You'll just make it worse."

"No, stop—" he said just before I threw myself at him, knocking him flat on his back. The impact effectively stripped us both of breath, but I didn't bother with paltry concerns like breathing when Max was dying in front of me. I fumbled with the buttons on his waistcoat, the blood making everything slick.

"Oh, God, how badly are you hurt? No, don't talk, just answer me. Oh, my god. There's blood everywhere! Dammit, Max, you can't die on me now! It's not fair! I'm not going to lose two husbands before I'm even married to the second one! I refuse to let you die! I'll kill you if you die now, do you hear me?"

Another popping noise and a shout from behind me warned that the horrible assassin was still out there. I lunged over Max's body to protect him from any more bullets, my hands now soaked red with his blood.

"Tessa," Max said, trying to pry me off his chest.

"Stop talking! You have to save your strength!"

"Tessa, I'm not hurt."

"Yes, you are. You've been shot, Max. Really badly, too. I think your whole chest is gone. You're delusional. You probably have a fever or you're in shock or something due to your massive chest wounds. Just stay still. I'm going to make sure you don't die. You don't have anything to worry about. I'm right here. I'll save you."

Beneath me, Max's chest rumbled.

"Oh, dear God, he's doing the death-rattle thing," I shrieked, turning so I could clutch his dear, adorable head in my bloodstained fingers. I dug my fingers into his hair and shook him. "Max, my love, my darling, hang on. If you see a light, don't go toward it, OK? Promise me you won't go toward the light! The same goes for a tunnel. If you see any tunnels, just turn around and go the other way, all right? Max? *Max?*"

With remarkable strength considering he'd been shot twice, Max heaved me off his chest. "Tessa, I'm not hurt, I haven't been shot. That's paint, not blood."

Two more soft pops followed his words, but I ignored both them and the shouting to look down at my hands.

They were covered in red, a bright red, a really *red* red, not at all the color of blood. "Paint?" I said, staring down at my hands, then over at his chest. I touched the soaking red spot on the middle of his brown waistcoat. It was cold and wet, almost slimy. "Paint?"

"Paint," Max said, his eyes narrowed as he scanned the surrounding trees. "There—see them? They're in black."

He jumped to his feet, pointing to the line of trees bordering the road as he yelled to the others. "They're over there, in the trees."

"He's not going to die?" I asked my hands, then jerked back as someone punched my shoulder. Only there wasn't anyone there—Max and the other men were running off toward the trees. I looked down at my front, the lovely blue-and-cream bodice stained red from Max, now also marked with a huge yellow blotch on my shoulder. I touched it. It felt just like Max's red.

Someone was shooting us with paint balls.

"The bastards!" I screamed, furious. How dare anyone shoot us? Didn't they have the slightest idea of what Ellis was going to do to me when she saw the paint on me? She'd skin me alive! "That's it, I've had it. No more nice-guy Tessa! Melody, stay with Alice. Ladies, get behind something!"

I grabbed Max's shotgun from where it had fallen, jerked my skirts up over my knees, and took off running toward where Max and the guys were about to disappear into the woods.

To the left of them, where the woods tapered out to the verge along the road, a half-dozen people dressed completely in black—black pants, black shirts, black ski masks—ran out of the woods and headed for a Range Rover parked close by.

"Stop right where you are," I yelled at them as they ran for the car, stopping to snap the shotgun together. I pointed it at them. "I've got a gun and I'm not afraid to use it."

"It's not loaded," Sam said breathlessly as he raced by me, the camera held tightly to his chest.

"It's not?" I snarled and threw the gun to the ground. "Damn!"

Max and his posse ran at a diagonal angle to off cut the black-clad assassins. I followed Sam, who was heading straight for the Rover, but veered off when I caught sight of something blue in the grass.

It was one of the paint guns.

"Bwahahahah," I laughed. It looked very similar to the kind of paint ball guns my brother used to play with. A dozen or so green balls showed in the little window along the tube atop the barrel. I jumped up on a large rock sitting at the edge of the field and held the gun with both hands, pointing it slightly ahead of the closest person in black. "Listen up, you scumwads! I'm packing heat, so you'd better stop right now or else! Hands up! Spread 'em and assume the position!"

No one paid the slightest bit of attention to me. They all kept running for the car, Max and his gang behind them, Sam coming in at an angle. I started firing, missing everything for the first few shots as the gun bucked in my hands, but once I got used to it, I began to hit things. Sam, unfortunately, was the first object I nailed. He stumbled as green paint splashed across his back, turning to look at me.

"Sorry! Go on, I'll cover you," I yelled to him in my best SWAT-team manner, and took aim again. A patch of grass, a fence pole, a tree, and a cow standing across the road were the next victims, but finally I yelled with triumph as green erupted on the side of one of the black figures. I shot two more of the assassins, one on the head (I was aiming for the person in front of him), before I ran out of ammo.

Max had almost reached them as they piled into the car but wasn't quite quick enough. One of them yelled something out the window, throwing out a white piece of paper as they sped off in a cloud of dust.

"Damn," I huffed as I ran to where Max, Sam, and the guys were clustered around staring at the Rover as it disappeared down the dirt road. "Did someone get the car's license number?"

"It was covered up," Max said, turning toward me. He held up the piece of paper that had been tossed out. *"Turn the hunters into the hunted."* I read the words printed in big, blocky red letters. *"Save our birthright from domination and destruction by the upper-class terrorists who would rape our land!"* I looked up. "Huh?"

"It's an animal-rights group," Sam said, peering over my shoulder. "Freedom Against Rural Terrorists—yes, that's the group. They used to show up at foxhunts and the like. Looks like they're targeting private hunting parties now."

I started snickering. Max looked at me like I was crazy. "They have a heck of an acronym." He gave me a look he usually reserves for Melody. I stopped snickering and tried to look dignified, despite the fact that I was covered in paint.

We made our way back to the picnic and tried to clean off as much paint as we could with the hot water carried in for tea. Max, Neil, Barry, and I had all been hit by the animal-rights group, and Sam carried the mark of my paint ball on his back, but no one else had been hit, although a paint ball had smashed into a couple of teacups, breaking one and staining the others nearby.

All in all, we had a pretty good time at the picnic (those of us who weren't waiting hand and foot on the others). We spent an hour eating and talking about what we should do with regards to the attack.

"I don't see how we can do anything if we don't have the number of their car, nor do we know who the people are," Neil said. "Lord knows I'd like to string them up by their toes—this is a hired suit, and I'll be damned if I have to buy the blasted thing because someone objects to a little grouse hunting but what can we do?"

"I wonder if club soda will take this out?" I asked, trying with a fresh napkin to clean the yellow off my bodice. "How am I supposed to face Ellis?"

Sam, who'd turned the camera off so he and Wilma could eat lunch, snorted into his champagne. "You've got a bigger problem to worry about than your lady's maid, Tessa."

"Are you kidding? I'm going to be dead meat if she sees me like this. She darn near strangled me yesterday when I got a bit of soup on my dress. The rest of you might have a bigger problem, but I can assure you that the only catastrophe on my horizon stands five foot four and has a glare that can strip aluminum siding off a building from fifty yards."

"Can I have some champagne?" Melody asked.

"No," her father and I both said at the same time. I got a lump in my throat. It was such a *family* moment.

"What problem?" Jean asked Sam.

"Roger," Max answered, looking a bit sulky.

"Why not?" Melody asked me.

"Because you're just a little squirt, and little squirts aren't allowed to guzzle champagne."

"Surely he can't be upset about what happened," Alice said, taking one of the chairs and sinking exhaustedly into it. Once Sam turned off the camera, we declared a time-out for the servants so we could all discuss the attack. Barbara had several snarky things to say about that, but we overruled her and told the servants to help themselves to the lunch. "No one could have foreseen that this would happen."

"I'm not a squirt, and I don't guzzle. Please, Tessa?"

I handed her my glass. It had about two teaspoons of champagne left in it. She sipped it, her nose wrinkling at the taste (it was *very* dry champagne). "Ick."

"That's exactly it," Sam said. "No one outside of you lot, the servants, and the interested persons in the production company—that's Roger, Kip, and Roger's secretary, Sarah—knew that the shooting was scheduled for today. The calendar hasn't been made public in order to keep crowds away while we're filming."

Alice's eyes grew round.

"Oh, lovely, what you're saying is that someone, probably someone inside the house, very probably one of the four servants who conveniently disappeared this morning—four being the exact number of paint ball assassins—is responsible for the attack?" I asked.

Max and Sam nodded.

"Where *is* Roger?" Harry asked.

"Off taking an important conference call in town. Kip went with him. They didn't think there would be any need to be present for the lunch," Max said. I dabbed at the paint on his waistcoat. Yellow from my shoulder smeared across his red.

"Sorry," I muttered in response to his outraged look.

"If it was one of my girls that did this, I'll have her head for it," Alice said grimly. "The same for the lads."

"What I'd like to know is who is going to explain all this to Roger?" Sam asked. Wilma, ever silent, nodded and crammed a jam puff into her mouth.

We all looked at Max.

"Oh, no, I'm not going to tell him his project is being sabotaged by one of the participants," he said quickly.

"Sure you are. You're the duke—you have to," I said, cheerfully passing the buck.

"You're the duchess; you do it."

"I can't do it. I'm going to be dead once Ellis sees this dress. You're just going to have to buck up and do it, Max. Where's all that *the sun never sets on the British Empire* spirit, eh?"

"The sun went down on that a long time ago," Neil said, a bit waspishly to my mind, but I didn't feel privy enough to British politics to make a comment on it.

We talked a bit more, then the servants got back on their tired feet and started packing everything up, Sam and Wilma fired up the equipment to film them, and the lazy slobs of the group (that is, the rest of us) patted our tummies and made comments about how a nap was just the ticket for rounding off such a trying day, and toddled off to the two carriages that were waiting for us.

—ᴍ—

Monday
September 20
11:22 A.M.
Comfy chair in the library

All right, so Ellis didn't actually kill me when she saw the dress. I attribute that fact to the outrage she felt over the group of demonstrators—she was so aghast that they would try to ruin one of the project's events, the little matter of my paint-splattered dress slipped to minor importance. I hope that's what it is. If I she suddenly pops up with an axe or a very sharp knife, I'll know I was wrong.

I won't go into the details about what Ellis *did* say other than noting that I had no idea she knew those sorts of words. Roger had a talk with everyone this morning, off camera. He held it in lieu of morning prayers (which was a good thing, because I'm running out of Victorian inspirational sayings), when everyone was gathered in the hall.

"Right, first thing I want to know is what the bloody hell you lot think you're trying to do," Roger said, pointing at the four truant servants as he paced along where they stood lined up against one of the dark paneled walls. "Do you have *any* idea how much money is invested in this project? More than any of you little gits will see in a lifetime, I can promise you that! You're just damned lucky that stupid little stunt of yours didn't do any serious damage. I don't know which one of you came up with the bright idea of sabotaging the project, but I am going to know before anyone steps foot from this hall, and this I promise you—when I find out who is responsible for it, you're going to pay. Oh yes, you're going to pay!"

"Um, Roger?" I stepped forward. "I talked to everyone last night, including Easter, Raven, Bret, and Teddy, and none of them know anything about the animal-rights group."

Roger spun around and glared the hair right off my head. Or he would have, if I hadn't been clutching Max's hand for strength.

"What?" he snarled.

"I talked to them last night—the four who were missing yesterday—and it wasn't them. They weren't involved."

"That's right," Teddy said, nodding and looking especially virtuous, which was ridiculous, considering what he was doing yesterday while we were dodging paint balls.

"What the hell do you think gives you the right to talk to anyone?" Roger bellowed at me.

"There's no cause to yell at her, Roger," Max said, sliding his hand around my waist. I gave him a quick little appreciative smile before turning my attention back to where Roger paced before us like a tiger who'd been drinking triple-shot espressos all day. "You've told Tessa more than once that she's responsible for the servants. She was simply doing her job."

"If she was *doing* her job, they wouldn't have had the time to lark off and try to ruin my bloody show," Roger yelled, the little hair he had standing on end.

"No one would try to ruin the show," Barbara started to say, but Roger snarled at her and she (wisely) decided not to continue.

"Max is right, Roger. I was just doing what you've told me all along—to keep everything together as far as the servants and house go."

"Fine," he said, coming to a halt in front of me, his face red and furious. "Then you tell me, mistress of the bloody house, if those four weren't out trying to ruin my show, what were they doing?"

"Um . . ." I glanced over his shoulder. Teddy looked bored, Bret had a smug look on his face, Easter watched Alice nervously, and Raven glared at Roger.

"Well?" he demanded, his breath puffing around me as he leaned in.

"Er . . ."

Everyone looked at me, waiting expectantly. Max, who knew what I'd found out, tightened his fingers around in mine, for support, I hoped.

"Dammit, Tessa, I will not have this! If you won't tell me—"

"They were having an drunken orgy in the dairy," I said quickly, then gave the four an apologetic grin. "That's where I found them last night. They were sleeping it off, and before you ask, yes, I'm sure they were both drunk and . . . er . . . had been doing what they later admitted to doing. It was pretty obvious. I'm sorry, Roger, they aren't your culprits."

"Then who the hell was it?" Roger bellowed, turning around to look at the rest of the group gathered. "Which one of you was it? *TELL ME!*"

"No one's going to tell you if you stand there screaming at them," Tabby said. Sam, standing next to her, nodded as he fiddled with something on his camera.

"No one is leaving this room, do you hear me? No one is leaving this room until one of you confesses. That means no meals, no toilets, no sitting down, nothing. I am in deadly earnest! I will have no mercy—none whatsoever! You're all going to stand here until . . . *What did I just say?*" I thought Roger was going to burst a blood vessel he was so furious.

Mrs. Peters leveled a cold, disinterested glance his way, unfazed by being screamed at by a man who was looking very much as if he was a few onions short of a tuna salad. "You cannot possibly think to include me in your accusations. I have devoted myself wholly to the success of this project. And now I have work to be done. The spirits are uneasy, and I must reassure them that no suspicion will be cast upon them."

"You're crackers, do you know that?" Roger asked her.

"Spirits are often the first ones to be blamed for practical jokes such as this. They are very sensitive to atmosphere. I must reassure them that they are welcome here."

"Practical jokes?" Little bits of spittle went flying as Roger barked out the two words. "You're not just crackers, you're stark, staring mad!"

Mrs. Peters straightened up to her full height and would have responded, but Raven beat her to it.

"We can't stay neither, we have a shitload of pots to clean," Raven said.

Shelby poked her in the ribs. "Rave! It's not polite to say that."

"Sorry," Raven said, with a grin that decried her apology. "We have a shitload of *dishes* to clean."

Melody snickered. Max gave her a squinty-eyed look. She giggled even harder when I grinned at her behind his back.

"Our appointed duties—many as they are—await us as well, lads, although how I'm supposed to do anything with my sciatica burning, and my brain tumor making me see spots whenever I bend down, and the vertebrae in my neck fusing . . ." Palmer said, adjusting the neck brace he was sporting this morning, evidently the accoutrement of his injury du jour.

Everyone drifted toward the green baize door.

"You can't leave, none of you can leave. I just said that you have to stay here— Bloody hell, they're leaving. Kip! Stop them."

Kip looked at the servants as they filed out of the hall. "What would you suggest I do, throw myself in front of them?"

"Christ, doesn't anyone here care about the project but me? Doesn't anyone realize how serious this is?"

Max sighed, gave my fingers one last squeeze, then let go of my hand to put his arm around Roger's shoulders. "Come into my office, Roger. We can talk about it in there."

"Yeah, you know, maybe if you did the country-house murder thing, you could figure out who the guilty person is," I said, my tongue firmly in my cheek.

"The what?" Roger asked, pausing to look back at me as Max led him out of the hall.

"You know, the country-house murder thing. What they do in all those Agatha Christie books. Interview the staff one at a time, draw up a timeline, list everyone's motivation, check their alibis, and bingo! You have yourself a culprit."

Sam groaned behind me, but Roger brightened up immediately. "That is the first sensible thing you've said this morning, Tessa. Interrogation! That's the ticket! Come along, Max. You can help me. I've always fancied being a detective. I wonder where I could find some really hot lights?"

Max shot me a look that told me I was going to hear about this later, turning to follow Roger as he went down the side hallway. I blew a kiss to his back and smiled at everyone who remained standing around like statues in the hall. "Hungry, Melody? You and Mademoiselle can eat with us this morning if you'd like."

"Interrogation?" Mademoiselle snorted and raised her chin, glaring down her nose at me. "I am not a common servant, I am the governess most supreme. I dine in the Pug's Parlor! I attend teas and dinners! I do *not* carry water to fields!"

"Don't worry," I said, patting her on the shoulder as we followed a silent Barbara and Henry into the breakfast room. "I doubt if Roger's irrigation will last too long. You'll be back in the nursery in next to no time."

I met Sam's eye as he fired up the camera, and smiled innocently. "Although you never know what may happen if Roger finds a rubber hose."

I hope the interviews don't last too long. Max and Melody and I plan to do an informal picnic today for lunch. On horseback! I'm thrilled at this breakthrough with Max. It only took two hours of solid wheedling last night before he finally caved . . . er . . . *agreed* to let us ride out to the stream at the other end of the estate. He was a little peeved because I wouldn't let him use the Lick Me Lemon on me, but his promises of not touching me anywhere south of my belly button fell on deaf ears. He cheered up once I pointed out that *he* wasn't crampy and bloated, and thus I could oil him up and clean him off. It was after I had him squirming that he agreed to do the picnic on horseback.

Such is the power of a really good massage oil.

—m—

Thursday
September 23
3:03 P.M.
Verandah with the love of my life

The servants' ball—a bit of a misnomer since there weren't hundreds of other servants from neighboring estates to join in the fun, only a handful of locals and some friends of the staff—went off without a hitch despite the great seething and unrest below stairs. Roger has been less than brilliant in his handling of the servants, treating them like . . . well, *servants.* Real servants, not people who hired to play the part for a month. Since it's my job to keep everything running smoothly with them, I'm about ready to strangle him. If he conducts just one more interrogation . . . gah!

The servants' ball was really a trial run to see how the staff will handle the masquerade ball coming up next week. The huge, echoing ballroom was cleaned and dressed for the occasion, with tables set up along one end to hold party food and beverages and a hired four-piece band at the other end. I really liked the band; they were a local Celtic group who had a killer fiddle player. She had everyone's toes tapping, and kept them tapping all through the evening.

"Houston, we have a problem," I said to Alice the morning of the ball. She was giving the morning room a quick dusting when I wandered in.

"Oh, god, no, what now? I've already dealt with Honey's attack of nerves, Mrs. Peters' wailing that the spirits don't want the ball to be held on the night of the full moon, and Mr. Palmer's quality checking the ale. I don't think I can handle much more!"

"I hate to add to your burden, but I don't know how to dance."

She stared at me stupidly.

"The rule book says that Max and I are supposed to open the ball by dancing with Mrs. Peters and Mr. Palmer, respectively. I've got two left feet, Alice, and I'm sorry, but my nineteenth-century dance skills are a bit lacking. I can Frug if I absolutely have to, and can twist with the best of them, but that's about it."

"Oh, lord," she whispered, her eyes going dark with worry. She slumped into a chair, making me feel awful for dumping this on her. She was more or less managing the entire ball by herself since Mrs. Peters was spending almost all her time in consultation with the spirits, locking herself into the Pug's Parlor for long hours while she communed with them. "The dancing, I hadn't thought of that. No one will know how to dance properly, of that I'm sure. The girls are too young, and the lads—you know what they are."

I nodded. They didn't seem to me to be the type of guys who were very hip on the two-step and polka, let alone waltzing.

"Damn Roger! Why isn't he thinking of these things? He's supposed to be in charge of the project, he should have enough insight to know that no one here is going to have any experience with . . . with . . . whatever it is they danced back then."

"Waltzes, mazurkas, polkas, schottisches, quadrilles, country dances, and two-steps," I said. "At least, that's what my handy-dandy *The Glory of Womanhood* book mentions as appropriate dances to have at a function. And before you ask, no, it doesn't tell you how to actually do them."

"We're sunk," she moaned, clutching her head in her hands.

"You watch way too much American television. Don't panic yet. I'll talk to Roger. Maybe we can rustle up someone local who can teach everyone a step or two."

"Before this evening?" she wailed.

"I know it's tight, but hey, what's life without a challenge?"

"Enjoyable?" she shot back.

I grinned at her glare. "I wouldn't know. I'll go hunt down Roger. If I know him, he's probably trying to lift fingerprints from the paint ball gun."

The dance situation resolved itself easier than I had expected—Roger, promptly claiming that this was yet more proof that everyone was against him and his wonderful project—dragged Kip off to find a local dance instructor. By the time he returned with a middle-aged lady who was prepared to teach us the polka and two-step, we were all in the ballroom with Palmer the butler, tripping the light fantastic. Kind of. It turned out that Palmer knew how to do a couple of dances on the list.

"A quadrille is danced in a square, two couples per square. Confusing isn't it? It gets worse. You'll have to listen carefully, my voice isn't strong enough to carry for long—I believe I'm suffering from a touch of walking pneumonia. Are we set? Leading couples, turn to your right; sides, you go to the left. Very well, here we go." Palmer started clapping out a beat, calling out instructions in a low, mournful walking pneumonia sort of voice. "Four steps advance, four steps retreat, advance again, and turn opposite with two hands."

Our square, composed of Teddy and me, Alice and Alec, converged together into one solid lump.

"No, no, no!" Palmer moaned and clutched his head. "Lead couples to the right! Sides to the left!"

"Sorry, forgot that," Teddy said with a grin. "Who's the lead again?"

"I *told* you it was confusing. You are the lead. Now you turn to the right, the others to the left. Look over there; they are doing it correctly."

Max and Easter and Bret and Honey were moving

back and forth and twirling like clockwork, smiling smugly at us as they did.

"Try it again." Palmer sounded the beat, and we all advanced and retreated, advanced and turned with dignity, if not grace.

"I suppose that is the best you can do. Now head couples take inside hands and cross between the side couples as they cross, and when you return, side couples take the lead spot inside while the head couples pass outside."

We all looked at Palmer like he was insane, which he was if he thought we understood his instructions.

"Right, who's up for a waltz instead?" Teddy asked. Everyone's hands shot up.

Palmer's waltz instructions were only slightly less convoluted than his quadrille instructions, but by the time Roger, Kip, and the local dance teacher arrived with a portable tape player and an armload of tapes, we had at least the rudimentary elements of the waltz down. I had a nasty habit of stepping on my partner's toes whenever it came to a turn, but I figured that was just going to be an occupational hazard, and Max's feet would have to fend for themselves.

The ball went off well, by all accounts. Max and I were the only family members attending, and then only to kick the thing off, whereupon we left everyone to have fun without the specter of the upper class dimming their enjoyment.

"That was kind of fun! I'm looking forward to the ball when we can dance together. How are your feet?" I asked Max as we climbed the stairs, the strains of "The Dashing White Sergeant" following us.

He looked a little startled. "Fine, why do you ask?"

"Palmer said he thought I had broken one of his toes," I said thoughtfully, then unable to resist, did a little polka down the hall to his door, polkaing back to twirl around Max. "He said something about me possibly crushing his instep, too, but I'm pretty sure he was just exaggerating. You know how he is. And besides, high arches are overrated."

Max's eyes widened as I danced around him. "You're going to practice dancing every day between now and the masquerade ball, Tessa. Every single day."

I grinned at him and kissed the tip of his nose. "Come on, Mr. Astaire. I need your assistance getting out of the torture device while Ellis is downstairs having fun."

"I mean it, Ginger! Every single day!"

"Yeah, yeah, whatever. I wonder if the Victorians had arch supports?"

Max shuddered in faux horror, then followed me into my room to play lady's maid. I smiled to myself as I watched him in the mirror loosening the cords to my corset. Life had turned out pretty well. The servants' ball appeared to be a success, Roger had finally given up trying to find out which of the project members—if any; I was beginning to have my doubts about that now—had told the animal-rights group about the shooting party, and there was only a week left before I'd be out of the corset for good and into Max's arms (also for good).

Ah, yes. Life was looking very pretty indeed.

—⁓—

Saturday
September 25
10:47 A.M.
Morning room

What a morning. The scullery girls have once again called it quits. I ran downstairs as soon as I was dressed to see how bad it was.

"Just give me one good reason why I shouldn't walk out of here today," Raven asked, not even trying to hide the rubber gloves Teddy had smuggled in to her. "I'm sick and tired of washing up after everyone! No one appreciates the scullery maids, no one! Well, that's it, I've had it. I'm not going to wash one more pot."

I glanced over at Tabby. She turned off the camera.

I gave her a quick smile, then turned back to Raven. "Look, I know you don't think you're appreciated at all, and I realize that you have the yuckiest of all the jobs—Michael's chamber pot duty aside—but you've got to hang in here. There's only six more days to go—just six! Then it'll all be over."

"So what?" Raven asked, unrolling her sleeves. "That's just six more days of washing up to do. I don't see any reason why we shouldn't just leave now. We've done more than our share of the work."

"Where's your pride?" Ellis asked, coming down the stairs into the servants' hall. "You agreed to stay for the duration of the project, just as the rest of us have done. We've all worked hard, all sacrificed much in order to make this work. It's not just you, you selfish girl."

"Besides," Alice said, "if you quit now, you'll prove to everyone that you weren't up to the job, that it was too hard for you. Is that what you really want?"

"What I want is to take my five thousand pounds and never see another dirty pot again."

"If you leave now you won't get paid," Teddy said, looking up from where he was polishing a salver. "That's in the contract. You have to stay to the last day in order to be paid, otherwise all you get is five hundred pounds."

Several of the others nodded their heads.

"Raven, maybe we should stay," Shelby said, tugging on Raven's sleeve. "I need that money. It's only six more days—"

"Shut up," Raven hissed, her hands on her hips as she narrowed her eyes on me. "You're the one in charge of the servants. You tell Roger that Shelby and me want more money. If he wants us to keep on here for another six days, he can bloody well pay us what he's paying you."

"Look," I said, spreading my hands. "I don't have anything to do with the money part of the project—"

"It's not right that you should get twice what we get when all you do is swan around upstairs and stuff your face and act all toffee-nosed to us. *We're* the ones really working around here, *we* deserve the money. So you just tell Roger that unless he wants to be up to his oxters in dirty dishes, he'd better double our salary."

"Raven, I don't think—" Shelby bleated, but stopped with a harsh look from her scullery mate.

I took a deep breath. I needed to keep the girls going, keep everyone held together for just a few more days. "No, Raven, I'm not going to tell Roger that. You agreed to a price. You're either going to have to tough it out for another six days or you can leave now. Those are your only two choices. Pick one."

"Oh, like that's going to be hard," she sneered.

"Tessa, we need them," Alice said apologetically. "I'm sorry to say it, but it's the truth. No one else here wants to add washing up to their list of duties, and Roger couldn't hire someone in time . . ."

"We'll find a way," I told her with false bravado. "If they don't want to hang on for all the glory and fame and all that stuff that's sure to follow the end of the project, well, then, there's nothing I can do to keep them."

"Fame? Glory? All of what stuff?" Raven asked, her lip still curled up in a sneer.

"Are you kidding?" I gave an insouciant little laugh and half a shrug. "Everyone is going to be gaga over this show, which means they're going to be massively interested in the people who participated in it. Roger is already talking about a book to be published after the last episode airs—can you imagine the press *wouldn't* want to talk to people who lived the lives we've lived the last month? They pay for those interviews, you know. Job offers, endorsements, magazine articles, maybe even offers of acting jobs, or something on TV.

Who knows? They did a show like this back home, and two of the people went on to have a movie career, one ended up hosting a TV show on historic houses, and a couple of the others wrote books about their experiences. Made lots of money, too, but that's something you're obviously not interested in."

"That's right," Teddy said quickly. "All my mates say that this job will be the break I need to get a proper acting job. We'll be celebrities—and I for one intend to stay on and prove to everyone that I have what it takes."

Several of the others murmured their agreement.

"I'm sure you'll be justly rewarded," I told Teddy. "All of you will, of that I have no doubt. Well, then, I'll go tell Roger that you two are the only ones who are quitting. I'm sure he'll be pissed, but there's nothing we can do about that."

Shelby bleated again and poked at her friend. I made a show of standing up and brushing out my skirts, peeking from the corner of my eye to see whether or not Raven would take the bait. Her face was a portrait of indecision, anger mingling with greed and uncertainty.

"All right, we'll stay. But you had better be right about all the things you're promising, because if you're not, you can be certain I'll make you—"

"You'll what?" Max asked, stepping into the room with Roger. Raven's black eyes almost spat at him as she clamped her lips together.

"What's this?" Roger asked, frowning at Raven. "What's going on? Why are you all here doing nothing? Tabby, why aren't you filming?"

"We were just having a little crew meeting," I said, worried by the light in Max's eyes. "It's over with now. Everything's peachy keen, right, guys?"

Everyone but Raven nodded.

"I want to know what Raven thinks she's going to make Tessa do," Max said, his voice low and even and *incredibly* menacing. His hands were fisted, his eyes narrowed on Raven as he walked forward. Slowly.

Even antagonistic Raven decided it wasn't a good idea

to finish her threat. She snarled under her breath and turned her back on us to stalk over to the sink, where a mound of crockery and pots was heaped to the side.

There's something to be said for the protective instincts in a man, even when they're a smidge *over*protective. I patted Max's fist and pried his fingers apart. "Deruffle your feathers, Max. You've made your point."

He slid a glare my way. I kissed his chin.

"If you're all quite through with your plots to destroy this project before it even sees airtime, would you mind terribly continuing on with your appointed tasks so my crew can film you? Ta ever so," Roger said in a veddy, veddy upper-class voice.

"Snideness ill becomes you, Roger," I said as Max hustled me upstairs. "Hey, speaking of that, what did Kip find out in town? Anything on the paint ball assassins?"

"Nothing, not one single thing. No saw the Rover on the road, no one knows anything about the group, there've been no attacks anywhere else in the immediate area. It's apparent they came down here specifically to ruin the shooting party. Now, tell me that's not an inside job."

"It's not an inside job," Max and I said at the same time.

"Maybe it's a rival TV producer trying to ruin you professionally," I suggested, then added when both men looked askance at me, "Hey, it was just a suggestion."

"Not a very good one," Roger growled as we entered the hall. He stopped in front of the two cranes and stared sightlessly into the cold fireplace.

"Makes more sense to me than blaming one of the people who've slaved away for the last four weeks, unless you think Max or I or Melody is behind it."

"No," Roger said, tugging on his lip and looking thoughtful. "Not you, but possibly—" He shot a quick look at Max, then shrugged.

He meant Barbara and Henry, of course. I had to admit, that thought had crossed my mind once or twice, as well.

"No," Max said, shaking his head at both of us, obviously following Roger's train of thought. "She wouldn't do it. She's enjoying herself too much. She can't wait until the show's on the air and she can lord it over all her friends."

"Henry?" I asked.

"Doubtful. He's very much under Barbara's thumb. She'd have his balls on a platter if he did anything to ruin her coming glory."

"There was Dorie," I pointed out.

He smiled. "And you saw how that turned out. Henry might have the desire to ruin the show just to prick Barbara's pride, but he doesn't have what it takes to carry out such a plan."

"You have a point. Hmm. Well, I guess we're back to the rival producer theory."

"I'm going to find out who's behind it," Roger vowed, his voice tight and strained as he stared into the fire. "Just you wait and see. I'm going to find out, and then there will be hell to pay."

—⁓—

Thursday
September 30
3:20 A.M.
Fainting couch, one last time before returning to Max's arms

Mrs. Peters has gone off the deep end. She's so quiet, it's hard to see that, but the second she starts talking, it's pretty clear that she's more than one candle short of a candelabrum.

"The spirits of Worston Old Place have warned me that if you hold the masquerade ball on Thursday, great disaster will befall us all," she announced dramatically late Saturday night.

"More ectoplasmic herring?" I asked, looking up from the copy of the 1879 *London Times* I was reading.

"Something much worse," she said, shaking her head.

"Red snapper, do you mean?"

She did a very good impression of Ellis' pinched-nose and thinned-lip expression. "Unbelievers will be the first ones to feel the full dread of the spirits' wrath. You have been warned. If you continue forward with plans for the ball, I will not be held responsible for the outcome."

"Boy, those spirits sure are Little Mary Sunshines, aren't they? What do they do, stand around waiting for innocent people to doom and gloom to death?"

"You mock them," she gasped.

I felt like a big bully picking on her. I was supposed to be making sure everyone got along, after all. "I'm sorry, my warped sense of humor got the better of me for a moment there. Thanks for warning me, but there's nothing I can do about the date of the ball. It was arranged long before I signed on. Maybe you could talk to the spirits and tell them that."

"I have tried to explain, but they will not listen. They are not troubled by that which affects us on the mortal plane."

"Bummer. We'll just have to try to get through it without any rains of herring or whatever else the spirits have up their ghostly sleeves."

"Speaking of them so flippantly will only antagonize them," she said as she drifted toward the door, throwing one last warning look over her shoulder. "You'll see. Soon. Very soon."

I shivered despite the heat of the late summer day, looking around the darkening library a bit nervously.

"Ghosts. Bah humbug," I said bravely, trying not to feel creeped out by Mrs. Peter's prognostications. Just as I picked up the newspaper, an icy draft whizzed by the back of my neck. I jumped up and ran for the door. "I take it back, I take it back. Maaaaaaaaaax! The library is haunted!"

The next day, Mrs. Peters had more of the same to say.

"The spirits are extremely displeased with you," she said as she stood before me to go over the menu for the day. "They know you have mocked them."

"Oh, really? And how do they know that? Did someone *tell* them, I wonder?" I asked with a meaningful look at her.

She raised her chin. "They did not need to be told; their eyes can pierce the mortal veil and see what is in your heart."

"Really? So they know that there's nothing more I'd like to see than a really brawny Scottish ghost, preferably one who's naked and has a really big . . . claymore?"

"Such levity will turn back to sting you," she hissed, then, without even waiting for me to OK the menu she'd drawn up, she left. I worried about her for a bit, not just about the fact that she's spending almost all her time in the housekeeper's room, sitting in trances in an attempt to contact the spirits, but worried about her mental health. In the end, I decided there wasn't anything I could do. She'd just have to hang on for a couple more days.

Wednesday, she stopped me in the downstairs hall and held out her hand toward me. "You might scoff at what I tell you, but you cannot lightly brush away physical proof of the spirits' warning."

I looked at what she held in the palm of her hand. "It's a rock."

"Yes," she said, the sun glinting behind her, turning her frizzy hair into a halo around her head. "It is an apport. It manifested in my room as I was in my morning meditation."

"Um," I said, taking the rock when she handed it to me. It looked like a rock, nothing more.

"The windows to the room were closed," she added with great emphasis.

"Were they? Well, that does make it odd, doesn't it?"

"Apports generally are a sign of increasing poltergeist activity, an indicator of the spirits' unhappiness with those of us who tread the mortal coil. This one is a fine specimen, which demonstrates the power of the spirits is building. Such is clearly seen in the apport."

I squinted at the rock. "I'm afraid I don't see that. To be honest, Mrs. Peters, it looks just like any one of the gazillion rocks that make up the drive. Maybe one of the guys is having you on a little bit?"

She straightened up and snatched the rock from my hand. "I have been a psychic researcher for more than twenty years. I can assure you I am well versed in the tricks of the unbelievers. This rock was created outside of the realm of our understanding, and is irrefutable proof of the catastrophic events that you will unleash if you continue on with your plan to hold the ball."

"What is it about Thursday that so upsets them?" I asked, worrying again about just how stable her mental state was. "It's not Halloween or anything; it's just the last day of the month."

"It is a day of great meaning in the spirit world. It is the time when summer slips into autumn and the fabric between the world of the living and dead is thinned and easily crossed through. Beware, Tessa Riordan, for the appearance of the apports at this time shows the ghosts have marked you as one of those who will know their true power."

She turned on her heel and marched through the door to the servants' hall, leaving me to worry that she might have something planned to give her spirits a helping hand.

"What are we going to do about her?" I asked Max that night as we snuggled down together in his huge bed.

"Nothing," he answered, running his hand down the curve of my hip. "There's only one day left. She can't do anything to stop the ball."

I didn't believe that for a second. "We can't just let her run around prophesying doom and gloom, not even for one day." I sucked in my breath as his hand skimmed up my back, and flexed my fingers through the hair on his chest, teasing his darling little nipples.

"Why not?"

I stopped teasing to prop myself up on my elbow and glare down at him. "Because she's the housekeeper! She's supposed to keep house, not spend her days tipping tables and catching ectoplasmic herring. I don't care what she does in her spare time, but Alice has had to take on the bulk of Mrs. Peters' work, and that's not fair. Alice has enough to do. This party is a massive undertaking from the servants' point of view, and we're going to need every helping hand we can get. Obviously, I have to figure out some way to snap Mrs. Peters out of her preoccupation with the Worston ghosts."

"Tessa," Max said, pulling me down on top of him. I squirmed a little, the hair on his chest tickling my breasts. "I know Roger told you that you're in charge of the servants and making sure the house runs smoothly, but, sweetheart, you're taking this too much to heart. You're not responsible for anyone else, especially someone who obviously has an obsession with things of the spectral nature."

"It's my job—" I protested, squirming even more when his hands drew erotic little circles on my behind.

"No, it's not. I know you're doing everything you can to keep everyone working together, but you have to be able to let go of situations out of your control."

"Out of my control!" I reared back, irate that he thought I couldn't deal with servants who threatened to walk out at any moment, one or two of whom quite possibly were bonkers, an upcoming masquerade ball for one hundred people, and oh yes, there was the little matter of the apocalypse as enacted by a couple of moth-eaten ghosts. Out of my control? Oh, how I scoffed! "I happen to be in perfect control of the situation, buster. PERFECT CONTROL! The only reason I asked your advice is because I love you, and that's what people in love do: They share things. You might want to store that nugget of information away, not that I expect you to actually volunteer to tell me anything about yourself, you great big hairy poop, you."

"Tessa, I have the feeling you want to start a fight with me in order to relieve the stresses and frustrations you feel over the situation with the servants, but I'm not going to allow you to use perceived personal problems to do that."

"Perceived!" I yelled, and pushed myself off him. "What do you mean by that? Do you think you're so damned perfect that you don't have any faults? If so, I'm here to tell you that you are dead wrong, bucko. You're positively oozing with faults, and the inability to share your private life with me is just one of them."

I got to my feet and grabbed my peignoir, huffily jerking it on.

"Tessa?" Max said, lounging on the bed like a sleek panther, all rippling muscles and coiled strength.

"What?" I asked, ignoring his heated eyes and warm, wonderful body as I stalked to the door to the bathroom.

"I love you."

"Oh, you do *not* play fair," I said, facing the door with my hand on the knob. Part of me wanted to bolt, to run into my bedroom and manufacture a great big hissy fit over Max, but the sane part of my mind pointed out that he was right. I wasn't really mad at him; I was just taking out my frustration on the nearest warm body. There are times when I *hate* the sane part of my mind. "You can't just throw that in my face."

His voice came from right behind me. "Why not? It's the truth. I love you, madly, wildly, with every atom in my body. I worship you, I want to spend the rest of my life with you, touching you, talking to you, arguing with you."

It was the last bit that did me in. Only a man truly in love would look forward to the arguments as well as the happy times.

His arms went around me, warm and strong, his breath gently steaming on my neck as he nuzzled my hair aside. "Tessa, let it go. I know you're trying to keep everyone happy, but for tonight, at least, let me make you happy."

Now, how was I supposed to resist that? I couldn't. I melted.

I leaned back against him, turning my head so I could nibble on his jaw. "You always make me happy, when I don't want to throttle you for being pigheaded and stubborn, that is, and honestly, Max, I haven't wanted to throttle you for days now. Maybe even a whole week."

"We must take advantage of such generous feelings," he said, his lips finding my shivery spot.

"Oh, heavens yes, take advantage of them. Take advantage of me! I insist, really, I do!"

"Hmm," Max said as I turned in his arms, his eyes alight with passion and desire and something utterly wicked that set my blood on fire. "Do I hear begging? Are you pleading with me? Does someone wish to play games?"

He kissed me hard, his lips and tongue all pushy and demanding, shoving their way around my mouth like a bully in a school yard. I was just about to pin his tongue by the swings and teach it a few manners when he retrieved it, scooping me up into his arms with a very male smile.

I socked him in the shoulder. "You grunted on purpose! I've been dieting, not that I've had any choice in the matter—there's no way you can eat enough to stay alive when you're wearing a corset—but still, that's a diet of sorts. I can't possibly weigh as much as I did the first time you picked me up. You take that grunt back!"

He grinned. "I'll take it back if you beg me to take advantage of you again."

"Well, I don't know," I said as he stopped next to the bed. "Does this mean you want to play the Victorian Rake and the Shy, But Sensual if Somewhat Fleshy Albeit Delectable Duchess?"

"Yes," he said, with a rakish Victorian leer.

"OK, but this time I get to be the duchess."

He dropped me onto the bed. "Saucy wench! You dare impugn my manhood?"

I gave his manhood, which had been poking me in the thigh while he held me, a little tap.

Max's whole body stiffened for a moment, then suddenly I was flat on my back with him covering me. "You will commence begging now, duchess."

I opened my legs just enough to trap his arousal between my thighs, then closed them tightly around it. Max's eyes crossed for a second.

"Now, my dear lascivious rake, we'll see who does the begging."

Max groaned as his hips moved. I smiled with the ease of my victory, thinking to myself that men were such easy creatures to deal with. That was the last coherent thought I had, because just then Max lowered his head and started laving my breasts with heat and fire and sharp teeth that nipped very gently along my flesh. My whole body went up in flames, and I'm sorry to admit that within seconds it was me who was writhing on the bed, begging him to put me out of my sweet, delicious misery.

"Here, right here, here is where I want you, put your manhood right here," I said as I parted my legs, wrapping my fingers around him as I tried to guide him home.

"Manhood? What happened to *arousal?*" he asked, trying to brush my hand off his long, hard length.

"I thought it sounded more manly. Max, right there. Stop pulling away from me—you need to go right there. All the way in, hard and fast. No holding back, got that?"

He laughed then, an evil laugh, a laugh of a man who has been begged to plant his manly parts deep within a woman. "Oh, no, my fair little temptress. It's not going to be that easy for you. I haven't forgotten last night when you did things to me with that delicious hot mouth, things that no mortal man could survive. No, my sweet, you want to play games with a hardened rake, now you will pay that price."

"Oh, god, I love it when you role-play!"

He leaned down, scraping his teeth along one nipple. I arched my back and thrust my breasts up to his mouth, grabbing his hair and tugging on it. "No, wait, you're not letting me be shy! I'm supposed to be shy! I can't be shy if you do that to me, Max! Do it again!"

He did it again, and to the other breast, too, until I was nothing but a big old blob of quivering putty in his hands.

"Max, I want you inside me, filling me, making me feel wicked and wild and all the other things you make me feel that I can't think of now because my brain has shut down and is running on autopilot and dammit, man, take me now!"

"Oh, I will take you now," he said, then suddenly he was gone and I was flipped over onto my stomach, the bedspread cold and rough on my sensitive breasts. "I will make you feel everything you want to feel, my shy little vixen. That's it, struggle; your feeble attempts to escape my wicked rakish attentions arouse the passion in me."

"You are reading way too many smutty Victorian books," I told the pillow, then shrieked as he parted my legs, grabbed my hips, and hoisted me upward. "Max! You can't do that! Stop! Stop!"

He stopped, his fingers holding my hips. "Why can't I?"

I looked over my shoulder at him. He was positioned between my legs, my butt looming large before him. "Because it's a singularly unflattering position, that's why. You can see my butt, all of it when you're standing there, cheeks spread and all and—*STOP LOOKING AT IT!*"

He didn't, the rotter; he looked down at my butt again, then back up to me with a puzzled expression on his face. "What's unflattering about it? You have a lovely derriere."

"Derriere schmerriere. Go on, say it—it's an ass and it's big and not lovely in the least sense of the word.

Max, please, you can't possibly like the scenery. Can't we just do this face-to-face?"

"No," he said, then to crown my embarrassment, he move backward enough to press a kiss to each mortified cheek. "I do like the scenery, and you do have a lovely ass, so we'll stay like this. I find it very arousing to have you like this."

I blinked. "You do?"

He smiled then, and his fingers moved in a gentle caress on my (big, no matter what he says) behind.

"Very much so. It's not just this part of you," he said, giving me a little pat, "but other vistas beckon to me as well. I've always found the small of a woman's back a particularly erotic sight. It's the curve, I think, the lovely line and swell of her hips, the gentle sweep down to her bottom that makes my mouth water."

His hands moved as he spoke, stroking a path up my sides, down my spine, around to my hips.

"Ooooh," I shivered.

"And your back, Tessa, is the most beautiful back I've ever seen. It is the back of a goddess, meant to tempt men into giving you their soul to touch it. You have beautiful soft curves made to fit my hands, curves that make me want to . . ."

"What?" I asked, a tad desperate, so aroused was he making me just by touching my back.

His fingers bit down into my hips as he suddenly plunged into me. "Possess you!" he cried, my wordless shout of ecstasy in my ears as I clutched the blankets beneath me, Max's thrusts pushing my breasts against the cool material.

I forgot my ignominious position, forgot the nagging worry that Max would suddenly find me too fat and too old for him, forgot the fact that he thought my back was beautiful. Every thought went flying out of my mind except one—he made me complete. And when I yelled into the pillow, he was right with me, thrusting hard into my body, trembling within me as my newly discovered muscles tightened around him.

We collapsed on the bed, Max panting heavily into my shoulder, his body strong and warm behind me.

"Now," he gasped, pressing hot kisses to the back of my neck. "Tell me I didn't like the scenery."

I lay there boneless, too exhausted to even think until he rolled to his side, taking me with him. Even then I didn't say anything for a long time. There was just too much pleasure in knowing that I had given him my trust and he had returned it with love.

A long time later I gathered up enough wits to speak.

"Tomorrow's our last day to go riding," I said, lying relaxed and near sleep, Max curled up behind me, his even breath ruffling the hair next to my ear. He'd blown out the candles and we lay cuddled together under just a cool linen sheet. "I'm sure Melody is going to want to come, but maybe we can find time later in the day to go for a good long gallop, just you and me?"

"I can't go riding tomorrow," he said, the intimate sound of his sleepy voice rumbling next to my ear warming me as much as his body spooned against mine. "I meant to tell you, but your wanton demands on my poor man's body drove every thought from my mind but satisfying your carnal desires."

"You love my carnal desires." I smiled into the darkness and snuggled back into him. He bit my earlobe. "Why can't you go riding?"

"It's the last day. I have to visit the tenants one final time and accept some sort of award. 'S Roger's idea."

"Drat. Well, I guess it will be just Melody and me, then."

The soft, warm, sleepy Max turned into a hard, stiffened Max of steel.

I turned in his arms and kissed his chin. "Max, I swear to you, I won't let her get hurt."

"She doesn't need to go riding—"

"No, she doesn't, but she'll want to. You yourself admitted how good the riding lessons have been for her. She's much happier now, not just because tomorrow is the last day, but because she's enjoyed showing you that she can ride. Aw, Max, she's come so far—she hasn't had a temper tantrum in almost ten days. She calls me by my name. She *talks* to me, really talks, not just snarls and tells me she hates it here. I like that. I like her! You can't snatch this one last prize from her, not when she's worked so hard to earn it."

Max didn't say anything for a moment. I couldn't see his eyes in the darkness, but I knew they would be icy and cold, as they always were when he fell back onto his need to shelter and protect.

"Tell me you trust me, Max," I said against the pulse in his neck. It was beating fast; the muscles of his arm lying beneath my hand were tense and tight. I knew he must be going through horrible agonies of doubt and worry, but I also knew that for Max, familiarity would not breed contentment. I had to push him now, had to test his faith in me. "Tell me that you trust me with your daughter. Tell me that you know I will protect her and keep her safe, just as you would. Tell me that I'm a part of your family now."

A long time passed, probably only a handful of seconds, but to me each one was an eternity.

"I trust you," he finally said, his voice hoarse and thick with emotion. "You are a part of me, Tessa. I trust you."

"I promise you, I swear by all that's holy, I will not let her come to any harm."

"I know." He pulled me tighter, his arms hard around me, his body taut despite his words.

I smiled into his neck even through the tears that swam in my eyes, my love for him a sweet, sharp pain that filled my soul. We fell asleep like that, not in the sprawling, sated tangle of arms and legs as was usual, but holding on to each other, our hearts pressed together as if they would fail us should we be separated.

It took Max a long time before he relaxed into sleep. I lay awake, heavy with worry about the next twenty-four hours. What if something happened to Melody while we were riding? It would destroy Max's trust in me, destroy our relationship. What was Mrs. Peters planning? Was she mad enough to give her spirits a helping hand should they prove reticent to fulfill her prophesy of destruction? What about Barbara? She'd been very quiet lately, almost avoiding me, not speaking to me at meals, not even the nasty little barbs she'd been letting fly since the garden party. Was she up to something, or merely too involved with keeping tabs on Henry? His lady love, Dorie, and Charles were invited to the ball, as was Cynthia. A little spike of jealousy reared up at the thought of her, but I pushed it down as being unworthy of Max. He loves me, not her.

Right? Yes. Right. He loves me. I'm absolutely positive of that fact. He wouldn't trust Melody to me if he didn't love me. I'm being stupid. Of course he loves me.

Why does everything look so damned awful at three in the morning?

Melody. Oh, god, Melody. I hated to admit it, but I really liked the little snot. Underneath all that unhappiness was a very smart, witty girl who had her father's charm, and I truly enjoyed spending time with her. It wasn't just for Max's sake that I was worried about her hurting herself; for the first time I started thinking that maybe Max had the right idea in keeping her protected and safe from the woes life dealt.

Only the memory of my own recent rebirth to the human race kept me from running back into his bedroom and telling him he was right, that life was too short and too precious to take chances. That was no way to live, and well I knew it. It was better for Melody to fall down and pick herself up than live in limbo.

That doesn't mean I didn't make a mental note to get some rope and tie Melody onto Penny so she couldn't possibly fall off.

Just another twenty-four hours. If I can just get everyone through the next twenty-four hours, we'll be OK.

Gah! I'm going back to bed.

—m—

Thursday
September 30
3:41 P.M.
Library, hiding from Max

Oh man, oh man, oh man, oh man. Oh. Man.

I am in such deep trouble, I can't even begin to explain it. Well, OK, I guess that's a lie, because I'm going to explain it right now, I have nothing else to do with my time, nothing like lending a hand getting the house ready for the big masquerade ball that is taking place tonight—oh, no, not that.

Gah.

Melody and I went riding this morning, per my begging and pleading and pushing Max's back to the wall. Melody, of course, was delighted with the news that we were going riding, even more so when I told her that Max couldn't go.

"Dad doesn't let me have any fun riding," she told me in a confidential tone of voice as she hooked the laces on her boots. "He never lets me go fast or do any of the fun stuff."

Needless to say, I was gravely aware of my responsibility to Melody. "Yeah? Well, I have news for you, squirt. You're not going to get to go fast or do any fun stuff with me, either. Your dad is a bit touchy about you going out without him to keep an eye on you, so we have to show him that you'll be just fine without him."

Her lower lip started forming into a mutinous pout. I shook my finger at the Lip. "This benefits you, too, missy. Just think—if he sees that we can go riding without you hurting yourself, he'll be more inclined to loosen up on other things. So it behooves you to be on your best behavior."

"Oh." Her old familiar scowl was present for a minute, then she sucked the lip back in and gave me a blinding smile. "OK."

I stepped back, shaking my head. "You look just like your father when you smile like that. God help him, you're going to bring the boys to their knees. It'll drive Max mad."

She grimaced and grabbed the short coat that went with her ruffled skirt. "I don't care about *that*. I just want Dad to let me learn how to jump and do cross-country like he used to do."

I didn't tell her that I seriously doubted if Max would ever let her do that, but I sure thought it.

By the time we reached the stables, Melody was chatting merrily about what sort of a horse she wanted when she got back home. Just before we reached the horses, saddled and waiting for us, she stopped and half turned to me, giving me an odd sort of assessing glance out of the corner of her eye. "Are you coming home with us?"

"Um." Max had told me he would tell Melody about us before we left the house. Since there was just today left, I assumed that he had either forgotten to do so or, what was more likely, put it off until it couldn't be ignored any longer. Max's tendency to procrastinate over unpleasant tasks really irked me; I always face the ugly stuff right away, just to get it over with. "It's interesting you ask that, Melody. As it happens, yes, I will. I love your father a whole lot, and he feels the same about me, so we were thinking about getting married. I don't expect you're going to like that, but much as I like you, I'm not willing to give up your father for your happiness."

Her brows pulled together. I braced myself for a hissy fit. "You like me?"

Why fight it? I blinked in surprise. "Um. Yes, yes, I do."

"You called me a little snot."

"Did I?" I asked, tapping my lip as I thought. "Did I call you a little snot, or a little booger? Because if it was snot, then that's OK; it means I secretly liked you but didn't want to tell you. If it was booger, well, that's a different matter. I could never like anyone who was a little booger."

Her frown relaxed. "It was snot, I remember."

"Ah. So we're OK then, right?" A lot hinged on her answer. I wanted Max and I wasn't prepared to give him up, but it would make our lives so much easier if she would accept me.

She eyed me from my ears to my toes. "All right."

"You know, Melody," I said as we started across the stable yard to where the horses waited, "one of these days you're going to actually say something nice to me, and then where will we be? I'll probably cry."

"I don't like it when you cry," she muttered into Penny's neck as she hugged the horse.

Rats, I was right. I sniffled back a couple of tears and turned away so she wouldn't see how that grudging admission of affection hit me.

"Oh, to hell with pride," I swore, then grabbed her thin little shoulders and hugged her tight. She stood stiff as a board for a few seconds, then hugged me back. When I let go of her, we both turned away immediately and busied ourselves with getting on the horses.

"You tell anyone we did that and I'll get out my grapefruit knife," I warned a grinning Alec. He just winked at me, and it took me a couple of seconds before I was able to drag my eyes off the masculine picture of manly attributes that he made standing in the sunlight. "Right, Melody, off we go. Remember—nothing over a trot!"

It was a lovely morning, our last day at Worston. England was enjoying a warm Indian summer, the air warm and quiet, the sky hazy above, while closer to earth iridescent blue-and-black banded dragonflies zipped about gaily. It was as close to idyllic as we were going to find, and I think even Melody, who usually spent her ride focused on her riding technique, relaxed enough to appreciate the beauty of the surroundings we rode through.

It wasn't until we were headed back that I wanted to strangle the little wretch.

"Come on, Tessa, I'll race you," she cried happily, digging her heels into Penny, who promptly tossed her head, realized she was going back to the stables where a lovely breakfast awaited her, and took off at warp five.

"No, Melody! Never run a horse back to its stable," I yelled, then swore and bent low over Talisman's neck as I urged him into a full-out gallop.

Melody sawed desperately on the reins, one hand clinging to Penny's mane.

"She won't stop!" she yelled back at me, her face twisted with fear. She evidently realized that she was no longer in control of her horse, and made an attempt to pull Penny back into a slower gait, but all that did was send Penny veering off the path we'd established and straight toward a thin line of trees bordering the outbuildings near the house.

"Damn," I swore, and urged Talisman faster. It was awkward galloping in a sidesaddle, but he was closing the distance on the slower Penny. Just as we came on them, Penny swerved around a tall pine tree.

"Try to turn her," I shouted. "Keep her in a tight circle and she'll slow down."

I was so busy yelling instructions to Melody that I didn't see the branch until it was a hair's breadth in front of me.

"Oh, no—aaaaaaaarrrrrck!"

Now, here's the thing about a sidesaddle—your right leg is crooked around a curved pommel. It's not strapped down or anything but it is solidly wedged against the pommel, which is not normally a problem, unless you're about to run smack into a tree, and if your horse twists to avoid a branch while you hit another one . . . well, you run the risk of injuring your leg on the pommel.

I didn't realize I was on the ground until Alec appeared, a weeping Melody standing behind him. "Tessa? Where do you hurt?"

I blinked up at him, the sunlight creating a corona around his golden head, and slowly, bit by bit, my senses returned. First was vision. I could see Alec and Melody, and to the right of me Talisman cropped at the grass, the sidesaddle hanging drunkenly from his back. Then came the warm odor of the sun-baked earth and acid bite of the tall grass, a faint breeze bringing with it the scent of hay. . . . Then, unfortunately, feeling returned.

"Bloody effing hell!" I yelled as I sat up. "Oh, my god, I've broken my leg!"

Alec shoved up the long green skirts of my riding habit and looked at my legs. "Ow. Can you move your toes?"

I could.

Gently, he prodded the area around my right knee. "I don't think it's broken, but it looks to me like you've dislocated your kneecap. Come on, we need to get you to hospital."

"No, wait—" I started to protest, but he ignored me and with a really loud grunt, hoisted me into his arms.

"That's it, I'm never eating again," I grumbled as he told Melody to lead Talisman.

"You're not so bad, just a bit on the hefty side," he answered.

"I'm going to get you for that, Alec, just see if I don't."

He grinned, but it was a quick grin, as if he didn't have the energy to expend on maintaining it.

"Tessa, I'm sorry, I'm really sorry," Melody said, her face blotchy and red from where she had been crying. She wiped her nose on her sleeve, and I bit back the comment that her sleeve wasn't her handkerchief. "I didn't know you were going to get hurt. Dad's going to kill me."

"No, he's not," I said grimly as Alec clumped heavily into the stable yard. "Just set me down there, Alec, on the bench."

"Yes, he is. He's going to be mad at me because you got hurt instead of me," she wailed.

"Don't be melodramatic. Your father would move heaven and earth to keep you from being hurt, and he's not going to kill you because he's not going to find out this happened. Thank you, Alec. I hope I didn't strain your back too much. Would you mind fetching Roger's car? You can take me to the hospital while Max is out seeing the tenant farmers."

Alec frowned down on me, pinching his lower lip between his fingers as he eyed the knee I was examining. "I don't think that's wise, Tessa. Max will want to know—"

"Well, he's not going to, at least not until tomorrow. If he finds out what happened, he's going to come unglued. We have to get through this one last day, Alec. Everyone is hanging on by their fingernails; I'm not going to have Max going ballistic and ruining everything. Now go get Roger's car. Melody, I didn't ask—you're not hurt are you?"

"No." Her forehead was wrinkled with worry lines, her eyes still red and damp-looking. "Penny stopped at the stable and Alec helped me down."

"Good. Needless to say, you aren't to say anything about this to anyone. Go upstairs and have your morning lesson with Mademoiselle, and I'll see you at tea, OK?"

"Dad will know you're hurt," she pointed out. "He'll find out and then he'll be mad at you, too."

I sighed. "I know, but I'm hoping that doesn't happen until late tonight when we go to . . . um . . . until late tonight. I think Alec's right; nothing is broken, it's probably just sprained, like your wrist was. They'll tape it up just fine, and if I'm careful, your dad won't know anything about it. You can help me by doing what you're supposed to be doing. If he sees you wandering around when you should be at your lessons, he'll know something is up."

She frowned. "That's just an excuse to get rid of me."

I sighed again, getting up on my one leg as Alec backed Roger's steel blue car into the stable yard. "Yeah, I know, it was a pretty pathetic one, too, but it's the best I can do right now. Come on, help me hop over to the car, then you scoot."

It will come as no surprise, I'm sure, to know that I wasn't nearly as optimistic as I made out to Melody. My knee had swelled to cantaloupe proportions and hurt like the very devil. Alec lectured me all the way to the hospital about the folly of trying to hide a serious injury from Max, but I ignored him after the first couple of minutes. He wasn't telling me anything I didn't know. Once Max found out I'd lied to him—by word or deed, he wouldn't differentiate between the two—he'd be hurt and angry and I'd lose his hard-won trust in me. But it was that or the project, and everyone had worked so hard I couldn't let all their sacrifices go for nothing.

Two hours later I was back at the house, feeling pretty happy thanks to the shot of pain meds I'd been given.

"How are you expecting to hide those, then?" Alec asked as he helped me from the car, nodding toward the pair of crutches that resided in the backseat. My knee wasn't seriously hurt, just wrenched badly with some strained muscles, but the doctor thought I shouldn't stress it for a couple of days.

"Don't need 'em," I said, higher than a kite. I smiled at him and may have patted him on his cheek, I'm not quite sure; I don't exactly remember. "Have a plan. Cane. No one'll see it. Hide it in my skirt. Smart, eh?"

I hobbled forward, Alec hovering anxiously at my side as I one-footed my way up the front steps. My knee was wrapped and encased in a leg brace, and although it was weak and felt a bit bulky and unstable, I was sure no one would notice anything out of the norm.

"Thanks, Alec. 'Preciate it. Gimme a kiss."

Alec looked startled for a minute.

"C'mon, you know you wanna. Kissy-kissy-kissy!"

Alec backed away, holding his hands up to keep me from vaulting into his arms. "Er . . . Tessa, no offense intended, but I don't have a death wish, so I think I'll get back to the stables, if you don't mind."

I grinned and waved bye-bye to him as I entered the hall. Teddy, rushing through with a salver full of punch cups, paused to give me a puzzled look.

"Are you all right, Tessa?"

"Dine and fandy!" I said brightly, and moved with exquisite grace toward the library. "Tell Alice I'm back from . . . from . . ."

"Your ride?" he asked, still eyeing me strangely.

"Yessir, that's it. Ride. Tell her I'm back an' I'll be inna library if she needs me. Ever'thing OK, Teddy-pants?"

His eyes widened. "Erm . . . yes. You haven't . . . eh . . . been tasting the champagne for tonight, have you?"

"Nope." I waved to him, too, and sauntered my way into the library, plopping myself down on a long leather couch and promptly falling asleep.

Max woke me up an hour and a half later.

"Tessa, what's wrong with you?" he asked as I tried to sit up, feeling groggy and leaden. "Alice said she tried to wake you up three times. Are you all right? You're not getting sick, are you?"

It was the anxious note in his voice that penetrated the drug-hazed hallways of my mind. "Oh, god, it's Max. I can't let him know. Shhh. Be quiet, and he won't figure it out."

Max blinked his adorable little eyes. "Tessa?"

I made kissy noises. "You've got the cutest little eye-peepers, Maxikins, do you know that? I could just suck them right out of your head, they're so cute."

Max's cute eye-peepers opened really wide. He leaned forward and delicately sniffed the air around my mouth. I made kissy lips at him, just to show him how much I loved him.

"Tessa, what's wrong with you?"

"Nothing's wrong with you, you're almost perfect," I said, grabbing his head and pulling it down so my kissy lips would meet his.

He let me kiss him, then gently pried my fingers from his head. "You're not ill, are you?"

"I'm fine, except for my knee, but you don't know about that, so it doesn't count, does it?"

"Your knee?" He looked down at me. "You're still wearing your riding habit."

"We went riding," I said proudly, lying back down because it was too much of an effort to stay sitting up when I couldn't hold on to his hair. "Melody didn't get hurt, not one little itty-bitty scratch, no sir, she sure didn't. I watched over her really, really carefully, Max, cause I knew you'd stop loving me if I didn't."

"Tessa, I will never stop loving you, however, I would appreciate knowing just what happened." He leaned over me, peeling back my riding habit to expose my legs.

"Max! It's the middle of the day! You've picked a fine time to get friksy."

He sucked in his breath. "You have a brace on your leg."

I frowned, concentrating hard. Somehow my tongue got twisted up on itself. "Firsky."

"Frisky," Max said, his voice sounding as if he was gargling concrete.

"Well, if you insist," I said, and hauled him down on top of me. "Gotcha!"

He levered himself off me, despite my cry of unhappiness. "Max! Don't you wanna get frisky with me?"

"I want you to tell me what happened to your leg. Did you fall off your horse?"

"No!" I said with much dignity. "I can't tell you what happened, because then you'll just make a big scene about it and you'll ruin everything and all the servants will be mad at me and Roger will yell and Kip will glare at me and most of all, you won't love me . . . any . . . more. . . ."

The tears of pity that burned behind my eyes spilled over my lashes at the contemplation of just how mad Max was going to be at me when he found out what happened.

He bent down to kiss my damp cheeks. "I will always love you, Tessa. Did you happen to take any pills when you were at the hospital?"

"No," I said, snuggling down into the couch. My body,

particularly my eyelids, felt as if it was held down by lead weights. My eyes drifted shut. "But they gave me a really nice shot."

"Who drove you?"

"Alec, but you don't know that, OK? I don't want him to get in trouble with you."

"He won't get in trouble."

I dragged one eyelid up enough to pierce him with a steely gaze. "You promise I won't tell you?"

His puzzled frown returned.

"I mean, you promise you won't tell yourself? Oh, never mind, it's too confusing. I'm just going to take a little nap and then I'll straighten it all out."

He said something else, but the couch was too comfortable, and I was too tired to pay attention.

When I woke up again, it was just after three. I had missed lunch, but that wasn't what bothered me. With consciousness my memory had returned, and I sat with my head in my hands and groaned at the memory of Max's puzzled frown as I told him to not tell himself about Alec and my injury. "Stupid mind-muddling painkillers," I mumbled into my wrists. "Stupid blabbermouth. Now he's going to have kittens and everyone will kill me. Gah."

After a good wallow in self-pity, I got my act together and figured I'd better go find Max and see how bad it was. The ballroom was on the other end of the house, but it was still suspiciously quiet outside the library; for a house gearing up for a major party, *too* quiet.

I swung my legs off the couch and stood up, almost falling when my right leg buckled beneath me. I swore and fell back onto the couch as pain lanced up from my knee. "Oh, wonderful, the painkillers have worn off."

"I'm not surprised; you've been sleeping all afternoon."

I stiffened for a second, then relaxed when I realized that it was a woman speaking to me and not Max. "Oh, hi, Alice. Um. You have my crutches in your hand."

"Max thought you might need them when you woke up. How do you feel?"

"Worried," I said, taking the crutches. "How is he?"

Her eyebrows raised. "Max? Fine."

"No, I mean, how *is* he? Is he ranting and raving? Has he locked Melody away in her room? Has he ordered a litter to carry me upstairs?"

She laughed. "Nothing so dramatic. Oh, I won't say he's not a little angry, but he's actually been very helpful this morning. Raven was inclined to be a bit sulky about cleaning up the dishes, but he set her straight."

"So it's still on?" I asked, slumping back in relief. A little angry I could deal with. "He hasn't canceled it or anything?"

"No. Did you expect he would?"

I made a little moue. "Kind of. Where is he now?"

"In the ballroom, overseeing the decorations."

I flinched. That had been on my list of chores to see to. "Ah. Since I'm sure he's doing just fine, I believe I'll let him do that by himself. In fact, I think I'll just stay out of his way altogether. It's probably better that way, huh?"

She laughed again and started toward the door. "You're going to have to face him sometime, Tessa. You can't hide all day!"

"Says who?" I asked as the door closed with a quiet click. I ran over the mental list of things I was supposed to do, the talks I had planned for the staff, the encouragement I was to give them to keep them working together as a team one last time. "Come on, Tessa, you wanted involvement. Now you have it. Stop feeling sorry for yourself and get on with it. The sooner you face Max, the sooner it will be over with."

The words froze on my lips as I spoke them.

I just hope it won't be our relationship that is what's over.

—w—

Friday
October 1
5:14 P.M.
Max's house, sitting room, brown-and-green striped
couch (comfy)

All right, I'm going to do this properly, I'm going to write down everything the way it happened. No foreshadowing disaster, no sudden insights into the wild events that were to come . . . Oh, pooh, I guess I just did foreshadow, didn't I?

OK, starting again.

Date: yesterday. Time: afternoon.

Eventually, Max found me. I was crutching my way out to the hall when all of a sudden he appeared at the end of the hallway, heading straight for me. I did an immediate about-face and crutched like the wind in the opposite direction.

"Tessa!" he bellowed.

I swear, if there is a land-speed record for walking on crutches on one leg, I broke it.

Unfortunately, possessing the record doesn't mean much when you're up against a noncrutch competitor, especially one with long legs that eat up the ground.

"Dammit, Tessa, I want to talk to you. Stop! You're going to hurt yourself if you try to run from me."

I stopped, the palms of my hands burning with the unfamiliar treatment. "I wouldn't run if you wouldn't yell at me."

Max grabbed my arm, turning me to face him. He glowered down at me for a couple of seconds, then made that wonderful noise deep in his chest and pulled me up against his body, his arms holding me tight against him while his tongue went a-plundering. I sighed happily into his mouth and did a little plundering of my own, deliriously happy that he wasn't so angry that he never wanted to kiss me again.

Suddenly, his wonderful mouth was gone, and he was shaking me. "Don't you ever try to hide an injury from me!"

"Ow! Geez, Max . . . ow! You're taking this a lot better . . . ow . . . than I thought you would."

He stopped shaking me and hugged me. "Dammit, I don't know whether to kiss you or shake you."

I raised my hand. "Can I pick? I liked the kissing better."

He kissed me again, much gentler this time, not that I had any complaints about his previous plundering. But this kiss was a kiss of sweetness, a kiss of gentleness that made me feel almost frail and delicate.

"Did Melody tell you what happened?" I asked once I had my breath back.

"Yes." He turned and kept a hand on my back as I crutched slowly down the hallway.

I slid a quick assessing glance his way. It didn't tell me much; his face was set in hard lines, his mouth grim. "It wasn't her fault, Max. I should have warned her ahead of time that it wasn't a good idea to give Penny her head when she was hungry and wanted to get back to the stables."

"It was her fault. It was also my fault," Max said, his voice low and harsh.

I heaved a mental sigh. Here it came, Max's diatribe on how dangerous it was for Melody to ride. I'd have to start all over again to show him that although life sometimes seemed cruel, it was better to get a little banged up living than be cocooned away in unhappy isolation.

"I should have made sure she understood that she's never to run a horse to its stable. You may rest assured she will never do it again."

"What, ride?" I asked, miserable with the knowledge of everything that had been destroyed between us.

"No, run her horse back to the stable."

Well, poop, that called for a little confused blinking. I indulged. "You mean you're not going to ban her from riding again?"

"No, I'm not. Is that what you were worried about?"

I stopped, pulling his sleeve until he turned to face me. "Are you telling me that even though I was hurt because Melody lost control of her horse, a situation that could have ended up with *her* hurt, you're still not going to stop her from riding again?"

His frown deepened. "No, I'm not."

"You're going to let her get hurt?"

"I don't want her to get hurt."

"I know you don't—neither do I—but you're going to let her do something even though there's a risk of her getting hurt doing it?"

One eyebrow rose. "She could get hurt taking a bath; I can't keep her from living, now, can I?"

I looked at him, looked into his beautiful, frowning blue eyes, as pure and as blue as the sky outside the window, and I knew that once again, I had been blessed. Love swelled within me until I thought I was going to burst into a Disney song.

"Twice in one lifetime," I said as I threw my crutches down and lunged into his arms. He rocked back on his heels but didn't fall, just hugged me tight. "Three times if you count Melody, and I do count her, so that's three times I've been blessed. Who would have thought? Max Edgerton—what's your middle name?"

Max chuckled as I stopped kissing his face to answer my question. "Anthony."

"Maximillian Anthony Edgerton, are you telling me that you still love me, and you trust me, and that you've seen the light about letting Melody live like a normal kid?"

He kissed the corner of my mouth, his lips brushing mine as he spoke. "Yes, Tessa—what's your second name?"

"See."

"See?"

"See."

"Yes, Tessa See Riordan, soon to be Edgerton, I do love you and trust you, and I've realized that about Melody, you are absolutely correct."

I captured his lower lip with mine and sucked it into my mouth. "I love you, Max," I whispered into his mouth.

"Not as much as I love you," he whispered back, then turned his attention to properly kissing me.

"Hell," a voice snorted, breaking into the wonderful miasma of passion that Max wove around us.

I retrieved my tongue from Max's mouth and turned my head to see who had the rudeness to interrupt us. Tabby stood grinning, filming us with one hand, the other outstretched as Matthew counted out pound notes into it.

"Tsk," I said to him, accepting the crutches that Max handed me. "Gamblers never prosper, Matthew. I hope you remember that in the future."

An hour later we sat down to tea, supplemented with meat pasties and a couple of cold salads, intended to stave off hunger until the masquerade ball, when the tables would groan with fish, fowl, meat, salads, savories, and desserts that Cook had been working on for the last three days.

By the time I hobbled upstairs to my bedroom to change for the ball, I was exhausted, and there were still seven hours to go.

"Calgon, take me away," I sighed as I collapsed onto the fainting couch, my crutches falling to the ground next to me.

Ellis shook out my costume and made a moue of distaste as she looked over at me. "I heard you'd gone and hurt yourself. Are you in pain?"

"Oh, yes. I don't suppose you have any drugs that would make me feel better?"

"I can prepare a willow bark draught, if you like."

I wrinkled my nose and waved the thought away. "No, thanks. I assume you want me to stand up?"

"It would make it easier to remove your gown and corset."

I sighed and heaved myself to my feet, taking most of the weight onto my good leg. "Oh, I see the costume got here. Good. I'd forgotten all about it."

"So I gathered. Lady Barbara had it, hence the delay. It seems it was sent to her by mistake."

"Ah. So how does it look?"

"Very pretty. You should look quite well in it."

I turned and pointed my finger at her. "Oh, no, not you, too! I've had enough emotional scenes today, don't you dare start being nice to me! I'll just cry, and honestly, Ellis, I don't think I could take that."

I saw the corner of her mouth twitch before she bowed her head over the knot on my corset strings. She loosened the blasted thing, taking it from me when I unhooked the front. "I will endeavor not to say anything that might be construed as pleasant."

"Good. You just be as surly as you can because otherwise I'm going to . . . oh, no, now I am! Ellis!"

I took one hop toward her and hugged her, corset and all. "I'm not going to see you again after tomorrow! Thank you for putting up with me. Thank you for being my lady's maid. I couldn't have done it without you."

"I've never doubted that you would fill the role of duchess quite well," she said, giving me a quick squeeze before she stepped back and held out a pair of lacy drawers.

I gaped at her. "You did too doubt it!"

She had the grace to look a teensy bit embarrassed. "I haven't doubted it for quite some time now."

"Just last week you said that if you were in charge you'd strip me of my title and banish me to the scullery."

"You dribbled spiced plums down the bodice of your gown."

"But I apologized! You said an armless baboon could feed itself neater than I could, and that I needed to wear a bib."

"It was a white gauze gown. I believe I am allowed a

modicum of exasperation when you present me with a white gauze gown stained red and purple."

"You said I wasn't worthy of the position. You said I should be replaced with the armless baboon."

"I was wrong!" Ellis yelled, then looked utterly shocked that she'd raised her voice.

"Oh, Ellis," I said, puddling up again.

"No," she said, holding out a hand as I hopped toward her. "One hug is enough. I do not intend to indulge in useless emotional demonstrations. . . . Oh, very well, just one more."

She patted me on my back while I sniffled and gave her another hug. "I'm sorry. I'm just a huggy kind of person. I'll stop now."

It took me a few minutes to dry up the waterworks, and another few to get out of my combinations and into the chemise and drawers that were worn under my costume. She *tsk*ed over the brace on my knee.

"I'm sorry, I know it's not period, but I can't take it off."

"You shouldn't be on your feet."

She held out a smaller, evening corset. I hoisted up my boobs and let her strap me into it. "Yeah, that's what the doctor said, but I can stay off it tomorrow. Tonight I have to be gracious and charming and all that. Besides, I want to dance with Max. This is my only chance to waltz with him. I've been practicing."

"How on earth do you expect to waltz with an injured knee?"

I whisked my secret stash of ibuprofen out of the dressing table drawer. "Modern drugs. Please don't tell on me, Ellis. This is important. I want to open the ball with Max. I want to waltz with him. I want to be his duchess, if only for tonight."

Her lips thinned as she looked at the bottle in my hand, then she spun around. "I can't complain about something I don't see."

"Oh! You're right. OK. Um. Sec. Just having a little trouble with the cap . . . oh, crap. I dropped the bottle.

Ellis, could you help me down to the floor? Without looking, that is."

Poor Ellis. She helped me down to the carpet, looking the other way while I picked up all the little brown pills, assisted me back to the fainting couch, and fetched me a glass of water when one of the pills got stuck in my throat as I tried to swallow them dry. By the time she started helping me into the costume, her martyred expression was set like stone.

"What's the matter?" I asked as she went around back to hook the skirt part of the costume together.

"There's . . . I don't quite . . . I'm afraid . . ."

"What?" I asked, trying to look over my shoulder. The skirt sagged over my belly as she let go of it.

"It won't fit."

"What?" I asked, clutching the bed frame so I could turn to look at her. "What do you mean it won't fit?"

"It's too small. Much too small. It's not a matter of lacing your corset tighter; this garment was made for a much smaller person."

I stared at the material in her hands. The costume was supposed to be that of Scheherazade, with peacock gauze skirts; deep blues, greens, and purples edged in gold; a gold bodice with matching green, blue, and purple sashes. Armlets and bracelets gave a slave touch to the costume, and the gold cap had a purple veil that could be attached or left hanging down my back. It was an absolutely scrumptious costume, one that I positively salivated over when the wardrobe people described it.

Now I knew why. "This is Cynthia's costume," I said, fingering the material.

"Cynthia? Oh, the first duchess." Ellis looked thoughtful for a moment. "Yes, that could be it. Her costume must have gotten mixed up with yours."

"Mixed up my Aunt Fanny," I snarled, hopping to the door. "This is Barbara's doing. I thought she was being too nice to me lately. Now I know why."

"Your Grace," Ellis called after me as I threw open

the door, prepared to hop my way down to Barbara's room and let her have it. "Tessa!"

That stopped me. I looked back.

"You're in your underthings."

I looked down. "Oh. Yeah."

She waved me to the bed. "I will go see if Lady Barbara knows what happened and where Cynthia is staying. She might have received your costume by mistake, as well."

I didn't hold out any hope of that, so certain was I that Barbara and Cynthia had cooked up this plot to keep me from doing the duchess thing. Ha! They had underestimated how badly I wanted the evening to go well.

"Tessa?" Max popped his head in. He frowned when he saw me standing in front of the wardrobe, trying to find something from which I could make a costume. "Why are you standing up without your crutches? Where's Ellis? Why aren't you dressed?"

It took me only a fraction of a second to decide not to tell him what had happened. I'd pushed him pretty far that day, I didn't think he needed to have his newfound tolerance stressed to the limits. "She went to fetch something from Barbara. It always takes women longer to get dressed than men. Are you ready?"

He stepped into the room, forcing a gasp from me as I ate him up with my eyes. He was dressed in the Victorian's version of an English knight, with black leggings and boots, scarlet cross garters that matched the scarlet-and-gold surcoat, a black shirt that set off the light blue of his eyes, and a sword in a golden scabbard slung low on his waist.

"Holy cow, Max, you look positively drool-worthy! Oh, baby! I get to undress you when it's time to go to bed!"

He grinned and came into the room, sliding his arms low around my hips, moving so that he was pressed up against me. "Why, don't you like the costume?"

I bit his ear. "No, I just want to touch it on you, then touch it off you, then touch you."

"That sounds like an entirely workable plan."

"I thought you'd see it my way. Hey, no fair—you're not allowed to slobber on me. Ellis just got me cleaned up and ready for my costume."

Max looked up from where he was nuzzling his face in my cleavage. "All right, but I get to undress you tonight, as well."

"Deal," I said, then shooed him out of the room by telling him I had girl things to do. I didn't really want to get rid of him, but I didn't want him around when Ellis returned.

"Barbara doesn't seem to know—what are you doing with that nightgown and peignoir?"

"She doesn't know what?"

Ellis frowned at the filmy nightie in my hands. "She doesn't know what could have happened to your costume. That's what she said, however, I suspect that she might know more than she's telling."

"Uh huh. No surprise there. I just bet you she and that swivel-hipped Cynthia hatched this plan to make me look like a boob in front of everyone. We'll, it's not going to work. Here, hold the peignoir while I get into the nightie."

"What are you doing?"

"I can't go as Scheherazade, so I have to have another costume."

"Your costume is your nightgown?"

I slipped into the peignoir, buttoning the five pearl buttons, then hopped over to the dressing table, yanking hairpins out of my hair as I went.

"Come on. Max has already gone down; we have to hurry. I'm going as a ghost. I got the idea a couple of weeks ago when I saw my reflection in the window. Where's that kohl you got? You brush out my hair, and I'll give myself haunted-looking eyes. Do you think I should have blood dribbling from a fatal wound somewhere?"

Twenty minutes later I hobbled out of my bedroom, looking as wraithlike as I could in a filmy white peignoir set, with a heavily powdered face, black-ringed, hollow eyes, and my hair streaming down my back in a suitably Gothic manner. I had also managed to swallow another handful of ibuprofen without Ellis seeing, hoping that would hold me long enough so I could waltz with Max.

"Tessa, dear! I'm surprised to see you . . . and in your nightgown? I had understood from Crighton that there was some difficulty with your costume?"

I stopped at the top of the stairs, clutching the banister and willing my leg to hold up.

Barbara stopped next to me, dressed as Queen Elizabeth, complete with red wig, long ropes of pearls, and starchy ruff.

I smiled at her. "Barbara, I feel it only right that you should be among the first to hear—Max and I are going to be married."

"Married?" she gasped, all horrified-like, as if she hadn't known it was in the wind. I couldn't imagine that she didn't know; everyone else seemed to. "But surely you're in your forties! Max is just a young man, in his prime, far too young for you. He will want to have more children."

"I'm only thirty-nine, Max knows what he's doing, I'm still young enough to have children if I wish to—not that I'm going to, but I could if I wanted to—and *don't* call me Shirley."

She missed the joke entirely.

"You are—"

"Look," I said, holding up my hand to stop her. "Nothing you or Cynthia can do is going to change the fact that Max and I are getting married. He loves me. I love him. We love each other. I even love Melody, and you've got to know what a miracle *that* is. So you might just as well give in gracefully and leave Max thinking he has a loving, supportive sister rather than a shrewish bitch who tried everything within her power to destroy his life."

"Shrewish bitch!" she shrieked. "And to think I believed you would have the decency to put your own selfish desires aside for the good of Max. I can see I was wrong."

"If you're talking about him and Cynthia, you got it."

"She loves him! They were engaged!"

"Were they?" I shrugged and started down the stairs, carefully holding on to the banister, not only to support my throbbing knee but also in case Barbara got the urge to send me tumbling down the steps. "Maybe they were at some point, but Max says they broke up months ago. Given the fact that he asked *me* to marry him, it doesn't sound like he's got a whole lot of affection for her, now, does it?"

She snarled something rude and pushed past me as I hobbled slowly down the stairs, her ruff bobbing indignantly as she stomped down the hallway toward Max's office.

"How's it going out here?" I asked Teddy, who was manning the door. Bret and Palmer, who had donned his bloody head bandage in honor of the party, carried platters of food to the gold drawing room, arranged as the buffet room. "Everything OK? No problems?"

Before he could speak, Mrs. Peters burst through the green baize door, her hair frizzed out wilder than normal. She struck a dramatic pose near the metal cranes and pointed a finger at me. "They've come! The spirits of Worston Hall have come! May the good Lord have mercy on your soul, because the spirits certainly won't!"

A man's shout and a number of tinkly crashes, as if many glass objects shattered upon meeting a parquet wood floor, echoed down the side hallway. Bret ran down the hallway toward us, swerved around Mrs. Peters, and dashed through the green baize door, Palmer hot on his tail, yelling something about throttling Bret when he got his hands on him.

"Tessa, I don't feel very good," Melody said, appearing at the top of the stairs. She held her stomach and swallowed hard, a distinct green cast to her face.

Behind her, Mademoiselle swayed into sight, clutching

the banister. "Poison! I have been poisoned!" she gasped, then fell to the floor in a dead faint.

"Bloody hell, I've cut myself on my sword. I thought these things were props? I can't wear this. I'll probably end up decapitating someone before the evening is over." Max wandered out of the drawing room, holding a napkin to his hand.

Melody doubled over and vomited on the top step.

A profound, pregnant silence fell over the hall. Mrs. Peters smiled at me.

"No, no problems to speak of," Teddy said slowly, giving me a long, thoughtful look. "Nothing out of the ordinary."

———ɯ———

Friday
October 1
8:39 P.M.
Still at Max's house, still in sitting room, on the brown-and-green striped comfy couch, stuffed full of dinner (take-out Chinese)

Now, a lesser person might well have just sat down and cried at the point where everything went to hell in a hand basket, but I am made of sterner stuff.

"Max, go wash your hand and try to find something to bandage it up," I ordered as I hobbled toward the stairs. "Teddy, run and get Roger. Tell him something's wrong with Mademoiselle, then get someone to scrape the barf off the stairs. Mrs. Peters, stop gloating; ghosts aren't likely to have poisoned the governess. Do you know any first aid? Please try to bring Mademoiselle around. Melody, come with me to my room. I know you feel awful, but I'm sure Ellis will find something to make your stomach feel better. What was the last thing you and Mademoiselle ate?"

Everyone stood frozen until I clomped my way over to the stairs. "What are you all waiting for? Let's get cracking, people! We have a masquerade ball to put on!"

Max made a detour to help me up the stairs, following behind as I escorted Melody to my room. Mademoiselle was up and about before Ellis could trot off to get some barley water for Melody. By the time Max and I determined that Melody's and Mademoiselle's illness was probably due to the two of them sharing a plate of lobster salad left over from three days ago, Teddy had the stairs cleaned up, Alice had stopped Palmer from killing Bret for knocking over half the display of crystal punch glasses, and Mademoiselle was dissuaded from the idea of calling the police to report Cook for attempted murder.

Ellis tucked both Mademoiselle and Melody into bed, the latter of whom was in tears.

"I want to see the party," she sobbed. "I want to wear my costume."

She was dressed like Lewis Carroll's Alice, straight out of Wonderland with her striped stockings and little white pinafore.

"I know you do, sweetheart, but you feel a bit hot to me. It's better if you stay in bed." Max, stroking her hair off her damp brow, glanced over at me helplessly. The look wrung my heart.

I patted her leg where it was tucked under the blankets next to me. "How about if we check on you later tonight and see if you're up to making an appearance? The party is bound to go on all night. I'll pop in later and see if you feel better. Until then, you get some sleep. OK?"

Max looked like he wanted to protest my offer, but he kept his mouth shut when she murmured her agreement.

"You won't forget?" she asked as I hobbled out the door, Max behind me.

I grinned at her. "Now, how could I possibly forget a little snot of a girl?"

She grinned back.

"Snot? You called my daughter a snot?" Max asked as he closed the door, his hackles starting to rise with outrage.

I laughed and kissed his chin. "Calm down, Max. It's a term of endearment, and she knows it."

"Snot is an endearment?" He slowed his long-legged walk to my short-strided limp. "What do you intend to call me, *boogy*?"

"I was thinking more about *love bunny,* but if you prefer *boogy* instead . . ." I shrugged.

"Tessa?"

"Hmm?"

"Why are you wearing your nightgown?"

I looked down at the frothy creation. With my chemise, corset, and drawers under it, it wasn't the least bit revealing. "Um. Change of costume plans. I'm a ghost."

"I see. That would explain the ghoulish circles around your eyes."

"Wraithlike, not ghoulish. There's a difference."

"Is there? Will you be explaining to me why you're not dressed in the expensive costume the wardrobe department provided?"

"Someday," I said as we descended to the second floor (called, for some reason, the first floor in England). "But I wouldn't hold my breath waiting for it, if I were you."

"Eeeek!" Easter, the youngest of the housemaids, burst from a bedroom and raced by us, her eyes huge. "Ghosts! There's something in there! It's slimy and cold and it touched me! Eeeugggggggh!"

I stopped Max as he was about to go into the room and investigate. "That's Barbara's room."

"Ah," he said, then did an about-face. "It can wait."

I smiled after him as he went to wash off his hand, then slowly made my way downstairs.

I stopped at the bottom of the stairs and peered around suspiciously. "Any signs of ectoplasm? Anyone else vomiting up lobster salad? Have the scullery girls taken hostages?" I asked Teddy, back on door duty.

He rolled his eyes. "No, but you missed the excitement when Sam tripped over Honey as she was cleaning the stairs. He fell half a dozen steps. Almost dropped the camera. Gave Roger a bit of a fright."

"Is Sam all right?"

Teddy nodded, then cocked an ear toward the door. "Sounds like the carriage Roger hired to bring people up the drive. Tabby! Carriage! You'd best be getting into the ballroom," he said as Tabby bolted out of the small sitting room, Matthew right behind her.

I hobbled off as quickly as I could to the ballroom, stopping in wonder at the center of the room. "Holy moly, this place is . . . wow!"

Alice and Easter glanced in from where they were restacking the extra punch cups. The gold drawing room was fabulous enough—the smaller tables in it were decked out with gorgeous flowers of russets and reds and golds—but the ballroom positively took my breath away. Roger had decided on a Greek theme for the party, due primarily, I suspected, to the fact that there was a lot of Greek props lying around the U.K. Alive! studio, but regardless of the purpose, the staff had done a wonderful job creating an idyllic bower out of a late Georgian ballroom. False columns wrapped in ivy had been placed along the walls, huge man-sized urns erupting with greenery scattered among them, tall reproduction statues of Greek gods and goddesses at every corner of the room, a faux marble temple complete with scattered cushions, statue of Athena, and fallen columns resided at one end of the room, while at the other, next to where the members of the string quartet Roger hired were setting up, several low couches in green and silver had been placed. The flames from the gas jets flickered and danced in the heat of the evening, and above it all, in a massive chandelier that hung over the center of the room, candles gave off the faint odor of beeswax.

"It's pretty impressive, isn't it?" Alice asked from behind me.

I turned to spread my hands wide in a gesture of disbelief. "I can't believe you guys did this in just a few hours."

"Well . . ." she slid a glance toward Easter. "We didn't, as a matter of fact. You were sleeping off your painkiller and Mrs. Peters was busy trying to whip her ghosts up into a frenzy, so I had to go to Max. He saw that there was no way we would get everything done in time, so he made Roger bring in a couple people to help decorate."

"Oh, geez, I'm sorry I wasn't here to help," I said miserably. "I feel horrible that you got stuck with everything."

"Don't. It all turned out for the best. There's only the buffet supper to be got through, then the cleaning up tonight, and it'll all be over."

"How are things downstairs? Is there anything I should be doing there?"

"No," she said, biting her lip. "Although . . . everyone, the girls and Cook and Alec and Thom, they'd like to pop up to see the guests in their finery."

"Tell them they're welcome to come and join the party."

Her eyes opened wide. "Oh, we couldn't do that. Roger would be livid if the servants mingled with the guests."

"Screw Roger," I said blithely. "You guys have worked your respective butts off for a solid month. You all deserve a chance to enjoy the last bit of fun."

"But, Tessa—"

"I'm still in charge of you," I said with faux hauteur. "You have to do what I say until the ball's over, and I say you tell the rest of the servants that they can join the party any time they want to."

"Perhaps later on, after Roger has the footage he needs of the nobs dancing and stuffing their faces."

I giggled, then sobered up when I realized how much of a friend she had been to me. "I can't thank you enough for everything, Alice. All your support and help and . . . well, everything. It's meant a lot to me to know you were on my side. I hope we can stay in touch after all this is over."

She gave me a knowing smile. "You'll be staying in England?"

"You'd better believe I am. It's not every day a girl finds herself a real live descendant of a duke."

She laughed and gave my hand a squeeze before hurrying over to stand at the table holding the champagne and punch, taking her position next to a morosely dignified Palmer. I turned to greet the first of the guests as they came laughing and chattering into the ballroom.

The next hour was spent greeting people, most of the time with Max at my side, mingling, keeping an eye on Bret and Michael as they moved through the room passing out glasses of champagne, answering questions about my pronounced limp, and other hostess-type duties.

Cynthia showed up after an hour, wearing the most indescribably lovely fairy costume I've ever scene. It was made up of ultrathin layers of wispy silk that floated around her as she moved. Her hair was arranged in beautiful golden curls, over which she'd spritzed some glittery stuff so her hair sparkled in the light of the candles and gas jets. It was also a very low-cut, and not in the remotest sense Victorian, costume.

"Max," she positively cooed as she oozed over to him, her hips working overtime. She could have worn a sign that said WANTS TO JUMP HIS BONES and it would have been more subtle than the way she walked up to him.

"Darling, you look positively scrummy. I could just"— she paused to lick her lips and send him a look that a blind man wouldn't have mistaken—"eat you."

"Hello, Cynthia," I said, limping my way forward, trying to stop my teeth from grinding. "Max is mine. We're getting married. If there's any eating to be done—and I have to tell you, he tastes delicious, all of him, every square inch—I'll be the one doing it. Just thought you'd like to know that. Buh-bye."

She eyed Max carefully. He wrapped his arm around

my waist and hauled me up next to him. "I see. Well, I hope you'll both be happy."

I stared at her. "What? What? You hope we'll be happy? You're not going to throw a fit and claim him as your own and try to weasel your way into his good graces again? You're not going to try to steal him from me, not that you could, but you're not going to even try?"

"Certainly not," she said, a faint line forming between her brows. "I'm not so desperate for a man that I have to fight for one. Quite the reverse, I assure you."

I gave in and had a good goggle. "Would you tell me why, then, you've been wiggling your hips after Max? And why you switched your Scheherazade costume with mine? And why you've been plotting with Barbara to make me look bad in front of him?"

Her eyebrows went up as she glanced at Max. He gave her an apologetic smile. "She's a bit possessive. Oddly enough, I find I like it."

"Do you really? I can't say I enjoyed being pushed into that filthy lake."

I elbowed Max in the belly. "Don't talk about me like I'm not here. I'm not possessive. Well, maybe just a little. OK, a lot, but that still doesn't explain why Sheba here was slinking around after you."

Cynthia made an expressive little movement of her head. "Barbara said that Max had wanted to renew our relationship. I'm not seeing anyone at the moment, and as I had a little free time—and he's a very good lover— I thought we might enjoy a long weekend together. But it became quite clear the day of the garden party that he was not interested in me, and that you were prone to regrettable acts of violence in staking your claim on him, so I left."

"But, the costume . . ." I said.

"Yes, what about the costume?" Max asked, his voice rumbling deep with suspicion.

"Barbara switched the costume the wardrobe ladies made for her with mine. Hers was . . . er . . . a bit snug."

Cynthia eyed me but said nothing about the obvious. "That you will not be able to lay at my doorstep. I had nothing to do with that. I've told you; it was quite clear to me that you and Max were together. I have no intention to steal him away from you."

"Gah!" I shouted. "I just hate it when someone I'm all ready to hate turns out to be nice and decent and almost likeable."

"Almost?" Cynthia asked, one of her blond eyebrows arching in a perfect curve.

"There was that 'very good lover' comment. I had to take a few points off for that," I explained.

"Oh yes, of course," she nodded, understanding completely, and after a couple more minutes of chitchat about her studio and an upcoming show she was participating in, she moved off to mingle. She was instantly swarmed with men, a fact that made me feel particularly smug since there was one man who wasn't tempted by her dancing hips.

I saw Barbara talking with her a short while later. Barbara didn't look very happy, but although she shot me some glances that should have dropped me dead on the spot, she didn't say anything to me. I hoped the matter was settled in her mind and that she'd just let me be. It was going to be difficult enough to start a life with Max; I didn't need a sister-in-law who hated my guts.

Despite the cameras and anachronistic language around me, it was quite easy to forget that we were in the twenty-first century. When the quartet sounded the opening notes of the waltz, my heart started beating wildly as people cleared the dance floor. Max walked across the floor, his eyes lit with something that looked very much like love and pride, something so soft it had me stepping out to meet him halfway.

"Have I told you how lovely you look?" he asked, taking my outstretched hands in his.

"No, and I think you're going to have to be punished

for that later on," I answered, smiling up into his warm, deep, endlessly blue eyes. "I love you, Max."

He lifted my hands to his lips, kissing my fingers, then turning my hands to kiss my palms. "You are my life, duchess. Can you manage once around the room if we take it slow?"

"I can do anything, now that I have you," I vowed, and stepped into his arms.

All right, I'm willing to admit that we won't take any prizes for waltzing and that my movements were stilted and a bit jerky, but I will remember for the rest of my life the feeling of waltzing around that room, the flames dancing in air made turbulent by the movement of so many people, the heady scent of flowers mingling with the spicy essence of the man who smiled down at me. Faces familiar and unfamiliar flashed by us in a blur of color as we danced slowly in a circle, a spate of applause dying as others joined us in the elegant sway and dip of the waltz.

"Shall we stop?" Max asked as others whipped by us.

"No, not unless you mind dancing in the slow lane," I laughed, my heart dancing a waltz of its own as I fought back tears of happiness. I was so happy, so utterly happy, in Max's arms that I could have sworn nothing could ruin that.

You know thinking thoughts like that is tempting the fates.

A couple hours later, while most everyone was scarfing down the cold ham and turkey, cucumber salad, lobster patties, shrimp puffs, and copious other goodies—not to mention guzzling great quantities of champagne, punch, wine, and whisky (although hopefully not at the same time)—I went upstairs to take some more ibuprofen and check on Melody.

I peeked into her room and found her sitting up, reading *Alice's Adventures in Wonderland*.

"How you feeling, squirt?"

"A lot better. I haven't thrown up again, and Ellis said my fever is gone. Can I see the party? Please?"

I felt the back of her neck, then put my lips to her forehead.

"You kissed me," she said, her eyes big.

"Naw, I was just checking to see if you have a fever. Didn't your mom ever do that?"

She shook her head. "Dad kisses me there, but he uses a thermometer to see if I have a fever."

"Sometimes the old-fashioned ways are better."

She eyed me suspiciously.

"OK, maybe it was half a kiss and half a fever check. Is that better?"

She shrugged and tried not to look pleased. "I don't care."

"Come on, let's get you into your Alice outfit. How's Mademoiselle doing?"

Melody climbed out of bed, frowning at the door that connected the governess' room to hers. "She's sleeping. She *snores*."

"So does your father."

She waited until I was buttoning up her costume before addressing that comment. "Dad is happy."

"I hope so. He makes me happy. Doesn't he make you feel that way?"

Her thin little shoulders rose and dropped. "Sometimes."

I tied the bow on her pinafore while she donned the Alice headband. "There you go—good enough to eat. And speaking of that, I want you to go easy on the snacks. Stick to the bland stuff, like the turkey. I know it's no fun, but you don't want to overload your stomach while it's still touchy."

She wrinkled up her nose as we walked down the stairs.

"And nothing but punch! Your father will have both our hides if he catches you drinking anything alcoholic. OK?"

"OK," she agreed, rolling her eyes in that time-honored preteen way.

"Tessa?" she asked a minute later as we came down the last flight of stairs.

"What?"

She grinned over her shoulder at me, skipping down the last few stairs. "You sound just like a mom."

I'm telling you, I cried more that day than I have in the last three years. Melody ran down the hallway to where music and laughter drifted out of the opened doors to the ballroom while I pulled a handkerchief from between my boobs and dabbed at my eyes, getting kohl all over it in the process.

A shrill, high scream pierced the night air, followed by a roar I identified as Max's.

"I knew it was too good to last," I groaned as I hurried to the ballroom as fast as my leg would let me.

A wave of people erupted from the ballroom, racing down the hallway screaming and yelling, soaked with water and flinging small, silver-gray objects off their heads and shoulders.

I felt like a salmon swimming upstream trying to push my way through the narrow hallway to get into the ballroom, a comment made particularly apropos when I discovered (after stepping on one) that the silver-gray objects were small fish.

"Oh, my god, Mrs. Peters was right; it really is raining herring!" I pushed my way into the ballroom, only to be hit on the cheek with a cold, wet fish. The room was emptying quickly, but I could see Max fighting his way to the corner, behind the temple, where the fish seemed to be originating in a spray of water that looked like it came from a fire hose. He was having a hard time since the floor was now slippery with fish. Every time he took a few steps toward the temple, the spray of water turned on him and knocked him to the floor.

Barbara—screaming nonstop—had taken refuge behind the bass (instrument, not the fish), much to the unhappiness of the bass player, who was trying to drag it away from Barbara's clutches.

The other musicians had tipped the silver-and-green couches on their sides to form bunkers and were hiding behind them, hunched protectively over their instruments.

"It is a sign!" Mrs. Peters stood in the doorway to the gold drawing room, her arms outstretched as she raised her face to the ceiling. "It is a manifestation of the dread spirits of Worston Hall! At long last they have chosen to make their presence known to the unbelievers!!"

She dropped her arms and spun around, gesturing to someone behind her. "Quickly, all of you, we must record this outstanding example of spirit manifestation. Kendall, the video record. Edward, the spectral analyzer. Who has the infrared scope? There, the apports are manifesting in that corner; you will get the strongest readings there. Alex, quickly, you must bring the atmospheric sensor. The presence of the spirits is sure to register on it."

A swarm of serious-miened people laden with all sorts of electronic equipment rushed into the room even as the last of the guests ran out the double doors to the hall. The ghost hunters scattered, each scrambling to record the rain of herring on whatever gadget they held. Sam and Tabby, both sheltered by adjacent pillars, the sound people crouched behind them, were trying to film everywhere at once. Alice ran across the room, slipped on a herring, and went down. Sam dropped the camera and ran out to help her.

"Where did everyone go?"

Raven and Shelby trailed the last of the ghost hunters, taking their turn to stand in the doorway of the gold drawing room. I ducked, unable to keep from staring at the girls, as a stream of water and a couple of fish flew past me. They were dressed alike . . . no, wait, the word *dressed* is misleading. They were almost dressed alike, as harem girls, I was guessing (that or strippers). They wore some sort of fur nipple muffs over their nipples, a heavy chain around their necks, and a couple of chiffon scarves sewn to what looked like a leather G-string.

"What the hell is happening?" Raven shrieked, stomping her foot and swearing. "Here we go to all the trouble of getting Viking slave costumes, and there's no one here to see us!"

Ah, they were Viking slaves. . . . that would explain the furry nipple guards.

She marched over to where Tabby was filming Sam helping Alice off the slippery floor. "Here, we worked up a dance, Shel and I did. Shel! Come on, they want to see us do our dance!"

Shelby shook her head and started backing toward the door.

"Damn it all to hell! Here, you, film us! We didn't wash a million pots not to be filmed when we finally look good! Shelby, come *on*!"

Shelby turned tail and ran out of the room . . . smack-dab into Palmer.

"My leg," he screamed, and toppled to the ground. "I've broken my leg."

Then the lights went out. The gas lights, that is; there were still a dozen or so candles in the great chandelier that hadn't been doused by the rain of fish. The light they cast threw an eerie, flickering glow over everything, making elongated shadows that danced and swayed against the walls. The edges of the room were in sepia-toned shadows, dark and forbidding.

Roger appeared suddenly in the doorway, panting and dragging Kip by his collar. Evidently, Roger didn't see Palmer lying in his path until the last minute. He tried to jump the butler's prone body, but Kip jerked back just as he started his leap.

"My hand!" Palmer screamed as Roger landed on his arm, hitting a high note I hadn't thought possible. "Now my hand is broken, as well!"

"What the bloody hell is going on here?" Roger roared, ignoring Palmer to grab Kip again, dragging him forward until the two of them skidded to a halt on the guts of trampled fish. "I leave for one minute to catch this bastard, and all hell breaks loose!"

Melody ran toward me from the safety of a palm frond that spouted from one of the huge urns. "It's Uncle Henry," she said, grabbing me and using me as a shield.

"What? *Henry*?" I felt a bit dazed. Henry was responsible for the fish? Why was Roger mad at Kip?

"He's behind the big stone thing, throwing fish. Aunt Barbara *hates* fish. She got bit by one when she was little, and she's been scared of them ever since."

"She got *bit* by a fish?" I asked. "A shark, do you mean?"

"Matthew, hold him; he's our saboteur." Roger shoved Kip toward Matthew, who dropped his sound equipment to grab Kip's arms.

"I only did what should have been done," Kip snarled, jerking his arm from Matthew's hold. "Your time is over, old man. The fiasco here will just prove to the studio that they need a younger man to replace you."

Max must have finally reached Henry just then, because there was a horrible scream, followed by Max's bellow.

"It's a man," one of the ghost hunters shouted, holding up his digital ionizer to scan Henry as Max dragged him around from the back of the temple. "At least I think it's a man. The guy dressed as a knight is."

"No!" Mrs. Peters screamed, and lunged at Henry. "No, it can't be! It's the ghosts. It's the spirits of Worston Hall coming forth to lesson the unbelievers! It can't be him—he's nothing."

"Kip is the saboteur?" I asked Roger.

"Caught him turning off the gas," Roger grunted as he stormed by Melody and me. "I thought it was him all along, but didn't have any proof."

"I bet that will come as news to all the servants you interrogated for two days," I said. Roger ignored me, his eyes fixed on another target.

Max dragged Henry over to where Barbara had climbed on top of the couch bunker and was now dancing with anger, screaming what she was going to do to Henry when she had him alone.

"I told you it was Uncle Henry," Melody said, coming around to my side. I wrapped an arm around her shoulders. "I think he's gone crackers."

"I'd say that was an apt statement."

Henry, who had squirmed out of Max's grip, stood shouting and gesticulating at Barbara. Max started over to where Melody and I stood, making a sudden detour when Roger finally figured out who was to blame for ruining the ball.

"I'll kill him! I'll kill the bloody bastard! Let go of me, Max, I just want to kill him. Just a little. Not a lot, but hell, man, you see what he's done! Just let me kill him a little bit."

"Can someone ring the hospital for me?" Palmer appeared in the doorway, leaning on one of my crutches, his left hand cradled against his chest. "I believe I'm going to faint."

He staggered over to the quartet and tried to faint on them, but they pushed him back. The two women musicians stood up, now that the rain of fish was over.

"What do you mean you can't film me adequately in this light? I can see just fine! Now, look, we have this dance. It's really cool. See? I do this, and then I bend over backward. . . . Hey! You're not filming *me!*"

"It is the spirits; it has to be them. They possessed that man's mind, made him the tool of their will. I know. They spoke to me. They told me things—"

"This doesn't look too ghostly to me," Matthew the sound guy yelled over to Mrs. Peters as he dragged a tall metal drum out from behind the temple. "Looks like he rented a power washer and hooked it up to a drum full of dead herring."

Roger stopped pleading with Max at the sound of a metal drum being scraped over a polished, wet, hardwood floor. He started running toward Matthew, sliding every other step, waving his hands and shouting. "Stop, you fool, stop! I have to pay damages! You're tearing up the floor! Do you have any idea how much money that will cost me to repair?"

The violinist played a couple of notes to see if her strings got wet, then suddenly started in on a Celtic jig. Sam and Alice looked at each other, smiled, then began dancing, laughing as they twirled around in a circle. The viola picked up the tune and joined in.

"Is it safe to come in now?" Teddy asked, the male servants peering in around him.

"Sure, come and join the fun. I think there's some champagne left, if you want it."

"My back!" Palmer cried as he slipped on a fish and hit the floor.

"My floor!" Roger wailed, then sat down on a broken pillar and started sobbing into his hands.

"Oooh, look at Raven, will ya? Doesn't she look hot!" Bret asked, and ran over to where she was performing an odd sort of belly dance for Tabby's camera.

"You don't understand. I spoke with them. They *swore* they were coming," Mrs. Peters sobbed to her husband as he gently led her out of the room, murmuring soft words, keeping a protective arm around her. "It's all her fault, it's all the American's fault. They don't *like* Americans."

"*I* like Americans," Max said, smiling and holding out his arms for us. Melody ran to him, hugged him, then cuddled up against one side.

"What are you waiting for? Dad has two arms," she said.

I frowned and shook my finger at her. "No. I absolutely forbid you to do that. Don't you dare be nice to me, because then, oh, man, I'm doing it again."

"She cries a lot, doesn't she?" Melody asked Max as he wrapped his free arm around me, pulling me tight against his side while I sniffled into his neck. "Do you think she's going to always be doing that?"

"I think so. I know it's a lot to ask, but I guess we'll just have to learn to live with it," Max said.

I stepped on his toe. Hard.

He laughed and kissed Melody on the forehead. "Up to bed with you, Lady Melody. Tomorrow we go home, back to televisions and computers and all the wonders of the modern age."

"Yay!" She did a little jig, grinned at us, then ran off to her room.

"What about me, Your Grace?" I asked, turning until I was flush against him, my hands sliding up his surcoat to his shoulders, then up farther to the black silk of his hair. I teased his lips with my own. "Are you going to order me to bed, as well?"

He growled into my mouth, then scooped me up in his arms, ignoring my startled "Max!"

"Tabby, did you get that?" he asked, turning in the doorway to face the ballroom.

"I did," she answered, giving us the thumbs-up.

"Good. Proof positive, my beloved duchess, that I can lift you without grunting."

I kissed his chin, then his nose, then teased his lips open until I could taste him. "I'm not sorry to be leaving, but I have to say, I'm going to miss everyone."

We surveyed the remains of the party. The floor was awash in fish carcasses, the walls dripping where the hose had blasted them. The few pieces of furniture that had been in the room were lying around topsy-turvy. The remaining candles flickered wildly as beneath them Barbara and Henry argued at the top of their lungs, Henry punctuating his comments by throwing fish at Barbara, who promptly shrieked and took refuge behind a pillar. Kip twisted and turned to evade Matthew, dodging behind the urns in a desperate attempt to escape. Teddy sat on the fallen ruins of the temple, holding Roger while the latter sobbed into his dress suit. At the opposite end of the room, Palmer was being assisted to his feet by Shelby and the cook, Mrs. Billings, while before them Sam twirled a giggling Alice as Alec and Thom danced with Easter and Honey. Bret and Raven clutched each other the dim light of the corner, snogging for all they were worth. Michael and Sally were kicking aside fish, trying to clear the center of the room.

Max snorted and turned, walking carefully down the black hallway. The main hall and the side rooms were full of party guests, all of them talking at once, asking questions, demanding explanations, some laughing, others outraged. At the foot of the stairs Ellis and Reg stood, holding oil lamps and trying to bring order to chaos.

The voices rose when the guests saw Max. At my urging he set me onto my feet, then turned to face the crowd. He looked them over carefully, then put his hand to his chest and made a formal bow. "Roger will be happy to answer any and all of your questions. He's in the ballroom, which I assure you is no longer raining herring."

There was a stampede as party guests hurried down the hallway back to the ballroom.

Max took an oil lamp from Reg and turned to me, gesturing toward the stairs. "My duchess, shall we retire for the night?"

Behind Max, Ellis stood watching me, her eyes unfathomable for a minute, then miracle of miracles, she smiled.

I took Max's arm, looking into his warm blue eyes, marveling that I had found such a wonderful man to love. "Yes, my darling duke, we shall."

Read on for a preview of
Katie MacAlister's
contemporary romance

A Hard Day's Knight

Available from Onyx

"What the bloody hell were you thinking? You could have seriously hurt someone!"

How mortifying. My first half hour at the Faire, and I was being yelled at by a big, handsome knight. On a horse.

A really *big* horse.

"Argh!" I clutched the angry knight's arms as it suddenly struck me that I was perched a good six feet off the ground. "Look, I'm sorry, but this cat I'm babysitting ran out, and I just wanted to grab him before he ate someone's tent."

The knight glared at me for a second. "I'm not talking to you."

"You're not? Oh." It took me a minute to realize that he was narrowing his eyes at the man facing us on the murderous white horse, the one that had almost run me down. I turned to add my glare to his. "Yeah, what he said. I could have been seriously hurt, not to mention what would have happened to Moth, and if you think I want to explain to my aunt that her precious baby was stomped to death by a horse, you can just think again."

The man on the white horse unhinged his metal helmet and took it off, pulling off a soft white cloth cap before shaking out a glorious mane of shoulder-length golden hair. Even red-faced from riding in full armor under the broiling August sun, he was handsome, handsome, handsome —tanned, sun-streaked hair, vivid blue eyes, and one of those chiseled chins with the dimple in the middle. He didn't even give me a glance as he fought to control his slobbering-all-over-the-bit, almost-bucking horse. "Walker, what a completely unexpected surprise. I had heard that the motley group of misfits you call a team had registered for the competition, but I never thought you'd actually have the balls to show up. That's not really your forte, is it? Actual jousting, I mean, not just hulking around the fringes reliving the distant, vague images of your former glory."

"Farrell, I might have known it was you," Walker rumbled. A little shiver went down my back at the sound of his voice. He was English (my favorite accent!), and his vocal chords must have been wrapped in velvet because the words that emerged—when he wasn't bellowing them—had the same affect on me as if I was being stroked by the softest touch imaginable. "No one else would be so arrogant, so self-centered, so *stupid* as to gallop a green horse through the tents."

"Green, but fully under my control," the blond man named Farrell snapped. Evidently he didn't like being called stupid by the rich velvet rumble that came deep out of Walker's chest. I had the worst urge to lean back against him to listen to its source, but managed to keep myself in control. This wasn't the moment to investigate the interesting man behind me, this was the moment to request that he put me down—very slowly and carefully. Before I could ask, though, Farrell smirked and slapped Walker with a zinger. "Perhaps you've forgotten what it's like to have a prime piece of flesh between your thighs, but I assure you that I am more than capable of controlling any ride."

"Ooooh, that was a low blow," I told Walker. "You're not going to take that, are you?"

He turned his narrowed gaze to me, and I saw again just how pure his eyes were. They were like silver discs edged with black. "Do I know you?"

"I'm the damsel in distress you dashed in and rescued in the very best brave knight manner," I answered.

"In other words, I *don't* know you."

I offered him a perky smile. "No, but I *am* sitting on your lap. That's gotta count for something, don't you think?"

"No," he said, and tried to swing me off the side of

the horse. Evidently the black monster he was riding didn't care for the act, for it tossed its massive head in the air and snorted that warning snort that horses always give before they start doing things like trampling little girls, or eating their hair, or knocking them down, or any of the gazillion other things that loomed up out of my nightmares as the torments I used to suffer with my mother's horses.

"Don't drop me!" I screamed, and twisted my body around so I could cling to Walker. I got one leg wrapped around his waist as I clutched at his head, struggling to free my other leg from where it was confined in the yards and yards of cotton that made up my Wench Skirt. "Please, whatever you do, don't drop me!"

"What is wrong with you, woman?" Walker asked. His voice was a bit muffled because straddling as him as I was, his face was smooshed into my overflowing breasts. Beneath us, his horse shifted sideways.

"There's nothing wrong with me that can't be cured by being off this horse!"

"I'm *trying* to get you off, blast it!"

"You're going to drop me! I'll fall and break something!"

"Having a bit of trouble with your wench?" Farrell asked. He managed to get his hooves-of-death horse under control and rode over to my side.

"I'm not his wench, and I'm—argh!" The black horse evidently took exception to the white horse's nearness, because he snorted again and did a little sideways dance that had me shrieking and clawing at Walker's back when he tried to peel me off him.

"For God's sake, woman, I can't breathe," he gasped as he strong-armed my overflowing chest off his face. His gaze dropped for a minute to my bosom (heaving, in the proper wench fashion), and added in a much softer voice, "Not that I don't appreciate the wubby, but I'd prefer one that isn't conducted on horseback."

"What are you talking abo—oh my God, he's going to rear! Don't let me fall!"

"Marley is too well-bred to do any such thing, but he doesn't like you squirming around," Walker said as he pried me off his chest. "Sit still, will you? Marley, stand!"

"Clearly the lady wants away from you, a fact that illustrates her obvious good taste and intelligence. My lady, I am your humble servant. If you will allow me to remove you from the knave Walker's slug of a horse—" Farrell reached for my arm as he maneuvered his horse even closer. He grabbed my wrist and tugged me to the side, nearly making me fall off.

"Augh!"

"Let go of her, you damned fool," Walker snarled as he nudged the black horse in the opposite direction.

"HELP!"

"*You* let go of her! It's obvious she doesn't want to be near you." Farrell pulled me harder toward him until the front half of me was draped over his lap, while my lower half was held tight by Walker's arm around my waist.

"Someone, please, help me!"

"It is *not* obvious, she just admitted that I saved her. And she shoved my face in her breasts. Women who don't want a man near them don't shove his face in their breasts. Now, let go of her!"

Farrell jerked at my arm. "She said she wanted off—"

"*I* will put her down if you just let go of her," Walker said stiffly.

Oh, lovely, they were fighting over me. Why couldn't they do it when I wasn't strung between two horses? I stared down at the ground that seemed a long, long way down, and swallowed hard. "GARK! Guys, I feel like a really big human wishbone here, and I don't think either horse likes having me half-on, half-off him—"

"Let go of her before you hurt her," Farrell demanded, the white horse doing a nasty little up and down move that made my teeth rattle. Farrell's grip slipped a bit as the horse sidled, leaving me hanging by my wrist between the two men.

"I had her first," Walker said, tightening his hold on my waist.

"You didn't want her," Farrell said. "You tried to throw her off that slug you call a horse."

"THROW ME OFF?" I screamed to the ground.

"Whether or not I want her is not the issue. I had her first, so she's mine to put down. I realize that you don't have a shred of chivalry in your sun-bleached soul, but if you did, you'd know that the finders keepers rule applies here, and let go of her."

"Ok, I'm starting to seriously panic now," I felt it wise to inform them, trying to quell the note of rising hysteria in my voice. Whitey turned his head to give me the evil eye, then tried to bite my arm. "HE'S TRYING TO EAT ME! Let me down, let me down, let me down!"

"Screaming like that isn't going to help," Walker lectured me. "Horses like calm, confident people. Screaming and yelling and whining on about nothing just upsets them."

I lifted my head and glared back over my shoulder at him. "Do you think maybe we could save the horse etiquette until a time when I'm not doing an imitation of a badminton net?"

"I was just trying to point out—"

"I know what you were trying to point out, but dammit, look at me!"

Both men eyed me stretched out between them.

"She doesn't look very comfortable. It's ridiculous for you to keep her when she wants away from you. Release her, Walker," Farrell ordered.

"Oh, for God's sake," I muttered.

"She's safer with me than with your ill-mannered stallion. Here, you, whatever your name is, let me have your arm." The white horse snapped at my head again as I clung with one hand to Farrell's leg, the other still behind held in his iron grip. "Christ, Farrell! Can't you control that loose cannon you're riding? Will you stop screeching, woman? You're not going to fall. My horse is too well mannered to do anything to harm you."

As the words left his mouth, a white and orange streak shot from the shadows of a tent to a stack of boxes about four feet high. The premonition of what the cat was going to do left my blood turned to ice, my jaw dropped open, and my heart in my momentarily speechless mouth. "Moth, no—" I screamed just as all twenty-four pounds of massive cat hit Marley's rump, feline claws extended to give him a better grip on the glossy, well-groomed horse.

Marley, not unreasonably, I'm willing to admit, took exception to such treatment. He rose up on his back legs, let out a disgusted snort, and slammed back down to earth with a teeth-jarring buck.

"Oh, very well, have it your way," Farrell said at the exact same moment, and released my arm as the white horse tossed up his head and jerked Farrell's leg from my tenuous grip. I did a beautiful half-gainer off Marley as Walker released me in order to grab at the reins.